D0090268

# NIGHT TALK

# NIGHT TALK

## GEORGE NOORY

A TOM DOHERTY ASSOCIATES BOOK | NEW YORK

NIGHT TALK

Copyright © 2016 by George Noory

A Forge Book
Published by Tom Doherty Associates, LLC
175 Fifth Avenue
New York, NY 10010

www.tor-forge.com

Forge® is a registered trademark of Tom Doherty Associates, LLC.

The Library of Congress Cataloging-in-Publication Data is available upon request.

ISBN 978-0-7653-7878-1 (hardcover)
ISBN 978-1-4668-6430-6 (e-book)

Our books may be purchased in bulk for promotional, educational, or business use. Please contact your local bookseller or the Macmillan Corporate and Premium Sales Department at 1-800-221-7945, extension 5442, or by e-mail at MacmillanSpecialMarkets@macmillan.com.

First Edition: July 2016

Printed in the United States of America

0  9  8  7  6  5  4  3  2  1

FOR MY MOTHER, GEORGETTE,
WHO STARTED IT ALL!

# ACKNOWLEDGMENTS

My family: daughters Wendy and Kristina and son Jonathan; my mother and late father; my two sisters, Gail and the late Glinda Foster; and of course my amazing staff of Lisa, Tom, Stephanie, Lex, Shawn and Dan Galanti. And two special people in my life: Julie Talbott and Kraig Kitchin.

# NIGHT TALK

## 1

*Los Angeles*

T his is Night Talk with the Nighthawk. We're back on the phones with time for one more call before we sign off. Let's go to Josh in Grand Junction, Colorado."

Greg Nowell's late-night radio talk show ran from ten at night to three in the morning. He had been sitting in front of the microphone for five hours, still going strong but a little tired because the show required a lot of energy and staying constantly on his toes. Tonight's show had been filled with guests who had spoken about near-death experiences, a psychic who led the police to a child killer and a UFO incident over Stonehenge, followed by "Open Lines," in which callers from all over the country called in to discuss what troubled or interested them.

"Thanks for having me on, Greg. I listen to your show every night but I haven't gotten up the courage to call in. I . . . I like your show because you listen to people; you aren't out there lecturing everyone, telling people what they should have done instead of what they did. But like I said, I haven't had the courage."

It was closing in on the time for Greg to make it a short call and hang it up for the night, to go home, put his feet up and have a glass of red wine. But something in the man's tone caught his attention.

Colorado was an hour ahead of L.A., making it nearly four in the morning for Josh. Greg sensed both fatigue and tension in the man's voice. Not just the nervous tinge some callers get when they suddenly realize they're on a national radio show, but sadness, even grief. Josh obviously wanted to talk but it was hard for him. Like he said, he had to get up his courage to make the call.

"You got the courage tonight and you're among millions of

friends coast to coast and overseas. We have strength in numbers and we're here to share with you."

Greg shrugged as Vince, his broadcast engineer, gave him a grin and a shake of his head. The engineer had picked up on the stress in the caller's voice and Greg's empathetic response. His late-night talk show got all kinds of callers, some with fear and anxiety about the world they lived in, some with information or observations they wanted to share and sometimes a caller who just needed a sympathetic ear. Many sensed that they lived in a world manipulated by unknown forces that operated in secret and conspired to achieve complete control.

Greg was seated at the broadcast desk. In front of him, almost in his face, was a big microphone that hung from a flexible arm mounted on the desk. Besides the microphone, the large desk held his keyboard, computer monitor and other screens displaying information. Three other positions with computer plug-ins and mics were available for in-studio guests.

Vince was positioned at the control console across the room. To Greg's right was a large window that divided his soundproof broadcasting booth from the control room where Soledad, his producer, and her assistant were positioned.

Soledad was the show runner. She screened all incoming calls, putting the callers she approved in a queue. Their names, locations and subject matter appeared on a screen in front of Greg so he could introduce them.

The studio was located in L.A.'s historic Broadway Theater District, where twelve movie palaces, grand dames of the Golden Age of Hollywood, still stood.

"It's about what happened to my family," Josh said. "Three years ago, out near the Four Corners, where those states all bump. We were making our way home after visiting my wife's family in Albuquerque . . . me, Emma and our baby."

"Four Corners; I've been there, out to the monument and some of the small towns in the area," Greg said. "Give me a second; I want to bring up a satellite view of it on my screen."

He brought up a map and then a ground image of the quadri-point where Arizona, Utah, Colorado and New Mexico came together, the only place in the country where four states touched. A short distance off Route 160, at the exact spot where the corners of the four states met, was a monument maintained by the Navajo Nation.

The region was sparsely inhabited at best and much of it was under the auspices of Native American nations. Rocks, dirt, stunted plants and not much else populated most of the region. Even the sagebrush looked lonely.

"That's quite a desolate stretch, Josh. Some of it looks like the moon."

"It's the dark side of the moon at night. You drive for miles and miles and there isn't anything but sagebrush and rattlesnakes in every direction."

"True. But it's a hot territory for UFO sightings. All of New Mexico is—Roswell, Aztec, Dulce, the secret experiments at Los Alamos. UFOs seem to flourish out there like orchids in a hothouse."

"Yeah, that's because there are places out there where nobody is going to see what's happening."

"You see something out there, Josh?"

"Yeah, but they won't believe me."

"Who won't believe you?"

"Nobody. Not one damn person." His voice cracked. "Not the police, my wife's family . . ."

"What happened out there, Josh? What did you see?"

"It came down right in front of me with lots of lights, just like in the movies. A big disk, just hovering there over the highway."

"A spacecraft?"

"Yeah, a UFO with blinding lights. Lights that felt like they were sucking out my eyeballs. Hypnotizing me as I stared at them. I couldn't take my eyes off of them, I couldn't see the road, couldn't feel the steering wheel in my hand. I felt like I was being sucked out of the car, into the darkness, but no one believes me."

"What about your wife? What does she say?"

Soledad shot him a look with her eyebrows raised and Greg

grimaced. He realized he had asked a bad question as soon as it rolled off his tongue. The man wasn't grieving because he saw a UFO, but because of what happened after he was blinded by the light.

There was a heavy silence on the other end of the line. Greg could hear Josh breathing, choking back a sob.

"She—she . . . they . . . Emma and the baby—Oliver, that was his name, the name of our son . . ."

Greg's guts tightened. He wanted to crawl under his desk and hide but he had to help the guy out. The man had kept the story festering in his heart for too long. He needed to get it out and realize that he was not alone, that there were others who had had tragic incidents. Greg spoke softly. "They're gone, Josh?"

"They said I ran off the road. I told the cops that I was hypnotized by the lights, the blinding lights, but they said that it happens because the road is so damn long and straight and narrow that people just doze off and run off the road. We rolled—rolled over a couple of times."

Greg had heard the story before—cars drifting off long, narrow flatland roads and rolling. The highways in the Four Corners region were classic flat roads, slender black ribbons elevated a few feet off the desert floor on either side to keep them from being washed out by flash floods. Elevating the road with little shoulder room on either side meant it didn't take much to go off and roll.

With no houses or traffic for miles in any direction, it was also a perfect place for a UFO encounter—long distances with little traffic, especially at night, settlements few and far between.

"I told them but they wouldn't listen to me," Josh said. "They thought I was making excuses and there weren't any witnesses."

Greg felt the need to relieve some of the man's pain.

"Sure there was, Josh; you're an eyewitness, you were there. You saw what happened. You're just another witness that gets discredited because you saw something the powers that be don't want us to know about. That's how it's been since the beginning. The government discredits anyone who stumbles onto evidence that we have visitors from the beyond."

Josh sucked in a breath. "You're right, you're right, I saw it, I am a witness. They should have taken my word."

Greg eased Josh off the air and went through sign-off. He crumbled broadcast notes into a ball and tossed it at Vince. "Let's shut this place down."

Soledad came into the room.

Greg said, "You knew he'd be a tough one for me. You should have warned me."

She gave him a grin. "You're at your best when you suck in someone else's problems."

"The poor guy is consumed with guilt. And you know what, who knows what happened out there? It's the kind of place where you could set off a nuke and no one would notice."

"You're not off the hook yet. Your favorite hacker insists on talking to you."

She tried to hand him the phone and he waved it off.

"How does he sound?" Greg asked.

"Weird. Frightened. Scary."

# 2

A woman wearing a knee-length black cashmere hooded overcoat and boots walked quickly, purposefully, down Los Angeles's Broadway Theater District. Her boots were also black and came up to just below the knee. The overcoat she wore was more to hide her features than for the weather. She didn't want to be seen well enough to be identified.

Under the coat she was thirtyish, tall, a hair below five-ten, slender but toned from a gym membership she bullied herself into using three or four times a week.

Her feet forced her along as her mind wrestled with dilemmas. Serious-minded in ordinary times and not always approachable because she tended to become engrossed with whatever she was dealing with, she had a tendency to give a small, efficient smile even when brushing someone off. Tonight she was tense and anxious as she hurried to a rendezvous with a man she hadn't met before. They were to discuss taking part in a crime.

The night air in the City of Angels tasted like moist exhaust fumes recycled from tailpipes on the warm, dark, smoggy-foggy night.

It was late, just after three in the morning, long enough past midnight for few cars or people to be on the downtown street, but still not a safe place for a woman alone. Cops said nothing good happens on the streets after midnight.

Her right hand was in a side pocket of the overcoat gripping a can of wasp spray. The woman running a self-defense course she took had recommended it over pepper spray because it sprayed accurately up to thirty feet and would cause an attacker severe pain.

The instructor also recommended that if she sprayed anyone that she should tell the cops she had been carrying it for a wasp problem and not to ward off a human attacker since it might damage the assailant's eyesight.

She was both practical and expedient. She didn't want to blind anyone, but if someone was going to get brutalized during a criminal act, she preferred it be the criminal. And she would follow her instructor's advice and tell the police the spray was for wasps.

She knew she was being filmed as she walked. Cameras on the street operated twenty-four/seven but they were CCTV units, closed-circuit television. Most likely she was being filmed but not observed because there was little chance security people were monitoring the images.

Her destination was a movie palace on the street. The movies were born in Los Angeles and no place showed it better than Broadway. There were still twelve movie palaces in six blocks, each a glittering work of art where the stars of yesteryear, like Katharine Hepburn, Cary Grant, Clark Gable, Fred Astaire and Ginger Rogers, walked—or danced—on red carpets to attend gala premieres while powerful searchlights on the street out front of the theaters sent beams of light into the night sky that could be seen for miles.

Not all the theaters were restored and some were being used as a flea market or church, but the Los Angeles, Million Dollar, Roxie and other surviving palaces were the tattered remains of grand dames from an elegant time before the center of the city had been abandoned by everyone who could afford the move, leaving the streets first to winos and the homeless and then to the undocumented immigrants who reclaimed it as the Hispanic outpost it had once been.

She was hurrying to the "newest" of the great movie palaces on the street, the Los Angeles. The theater opened in 1931 with a premiere of Charlie Chaplin's *City Lights*, a romantic comedy in which Chaplin's Tramp falls in love with a blind girl. Albert Einstein had been in the audience opening night.

When the location had been chosen for the rendezvous, she

Googled the theater and found out it was on the National Register of Historical Places. The exterior of the building had tall Greco-
Romanesque columns; the lavish interior had a crystal fountain that
stood at the head of the grand staircase and was modeled after the
Hall of Mirrors at Versailles.

The theater hadn't been chosen because it was a historical land-
mark, however, but because it was convenient.

The *boom—boom—boom* of Latino rap rattled store windows as a
black Cadillac Escalade low rider came down Broadway.

The woman picked up her speed and got under the marquee
and back behind the box office as the low rider cruised by carrying
four gangbangers. The hood of the SUV had a painting of a saucy
senorita with bold dark eyes and incredibly large breasts riding
a bull.

"Shitty neighborhood."

She almost jumped out of her boots as someone behind her offered the observation.

A tall man, bony, with a buzz cut, an ebony complexion and
a musical Jamaican accent, asked, "Alyssa Neal?"

She nodded.

"I'm Rohan," he said.

She let out a breath she'd been holding and relaxed her finger
on the wasp spray trigger.

He wore a rimless soft cloth pull-on cap with red, yellow and
green bands, an olive-drab mesh wife beater and green running
pants. The form-fitting shirt bulged from a protrusion of beer belly.
He had facial hair that was too long and too frowzy for a fashion-
able two-day shadow.

The most significant impression he made on her was that he was
frazzled. From fatigue and nervous exhaustion. And probably too
many pills that wind you up and bring you back down, she thought.

"Ethan won't talk to me," Rohan said. "He's been smoking so
much glass his head is spinning."

Glass was crystal meth.

"I can't get him to respond, either," she said.

"He says he's going to see Greg Nowell," Rohan said. "Wait for Nowell to come out of the building after the show. That's why I asked you to meet me. We better hurry."

She gripped the wasp spray in her pocket tighter.

# 3

E than sounds pretty wired."

Soledad tried handing Greg the phone again.

"Tell Ethan I'm not available. Better yet, I've been beamed up and won't be back for a light-year."

Ethan Shaw was a computer hacker. Caught hacking, he was given the choice of working for the government to test the security of systems or going to jail. But Ethan didn't come across to Greg as an antisocial tech whiz who wanted to shut down Wall Street or the government just to see if he could do it. Greg welcomed him on the show because he brought good ideas and insider information to the discussions. Like Greg, Ethan believed that information gathering and invasions of people's privacy by government and businesses were way over the top.

In his first call Ethan had spoken about how connecting common household devices onto the Internet for access was creating an "Internet of Things" that threw private lives open to hackers—like himself.

"From anywhere in the world you can control your home alarm system," Ethan had said his first night on, "or use cameras to check on kids, baby-sitters and workers, set the temperature for the house and the fridge, turn on the sprinklers and open the garage door. Cars are getting electronic interconnections so you know how fast your kid's driving, check your tire pressure and brake fluid and even stop a car thief from getting away.

"But this Internet of Things is going to be the Internet of Everything Wrong because what you can do, a hacker can do. Someone with the fraction of the talent for hacking that I have can walk up to your house with their cell phone and turn off your alarm and open your door. Do you have a system that can turn off your engine remotely if the car's stolen? If you can, so can a hacker. The road rage incidents of the future are going to involve a hacker in the car behind you accessing your car's programming and ramping up the speed of your car while you're driving it or turning off its brakes or activating the anti-theft device that causes the car to come to a sudden stop.

"I can go on and on about what low-level hackers can do but check out this. You don't like people getting access to your computer and your money? Guess what, hacking into your house isn't that complicated. How are you going to like it when a neighbor hacks into that camera system you set up in your house to check on your kids and turns your family into reality show stars? And puts it online with you wandering around in your underwear."

"You heard it from a hacker's mouth," Greg told his audience.

Unfortunately, besides having tech knowledge the young hacker also had a recreational drug habit that cranked him up. He had behaved himself on the radio until a week ago when he suddenly started dropping f-bombs. The show had an FCC-mandated seven-second delay that permitted the host or producer to keep broadcasting sins off the air and Greg used it to erase the profanity. If the show hadn't taken action, the FCC would have levied a fine.

Ethan was permanently barred from the show, but that didn't keep him from calling and at first begging for another chance, and when it was refused, leaving messages for Greg that he was on to something big and needed Greg's help. Not just big, but world shattering.

Like Greg and so many of the show's listeners, Ethan questioned the necessity and objective of government putting its own citizens under microscopes, invading every aspect of their lives. What was the necessity of the government gathering so much information about its citizens? To be able to identify everyone by their facial features or know and store everything a person has said or written on their phone, e-mail or social networking?

Along with the government's unnecessary intrusions into the

lives of its people were corporations whose microscopes on people were even more powerful than the government's. Businesses know what food we eat, books we read, movies we watch, clothes we wear, who we admire and who we hate—even the sex toys we buy and who we use them with.

Everyone has been split apart, Ethan said, dissected in a thousand different ways so businesses can pinpoint exactly what our needs and desires are and dangle them before us. And all that information is available to the government.

Despite his own computer expertise, Ethan was concerned by the dilemma and plight faced by living in a world that had become so high-tech and complex electronically that few could deal with it. He was wildly idealistic about how the world should be and darkly pessimistic about how he saw it. For Ethan, the glass wasn't half full or half empty but filled with nitroglycerin.

"Better talk to him, Greg. He's not rational. He wants you to come to a window. He says he wants to show you something across the street."

"Show me what? That he can fly? We're ten stories up. What's to be gained by playing his game?"

She hesitated. "I don't have a good feeling about it. He's even weirder than before. It scares me. He might be the type who would drop in with a gun to settle his grievances."

"The world is out of control when we have to worry that we're going to be killed by some suicidal narcissistic bastard who thinks mass murder is his way to fifteen minutes of fame."

"Good line. Use it on the show sometime. In the meantime, let's pacify the guy so he doesn't go postal."

"I don't think Ethan's the gun type. He'd be more likely to attack an enemy by infesting their computer with a terminal virus. He probably got a bad dose of something he cooked up himself. Tell him I'm not talking to him and not to call again. He's been eighty-sixed permanently."

"Greg . . . could you please talk to him? Just for a minute. He sounds really depressed. All we need is an angry hacker with a grudge to direct our broadcasts to Mars."

"Oh my God—so now we're being held hostage to drugged-out crazies with computer skills? This guy can hold a computer program to our head and demand our money or our lives?"

Soledad threw up her hands. "Welcome to the world you talk about five nights a week."

"If this is where technology has gotten us, I want to get off at the next digital exit. C'mon, I surrender; let's get to a window. It's showtime."

There were no exterior windows in the broadcasting room and he followed Soledad to the front office, where a large window provided a view of the building across the way and the street below. The glass was coated with dew. Greg slid the window open.

There was nothing to see directly across the street except a building being renovated. It was two stories higher than the building they were in.

Soledad spoke into the phone. "Ethan? I'm putting Greg on. Listen, we're all tired around here. You have thirty seconds and then I'm cutting you off."

Greg took the phone and leaned out the window, peering down, trying to spot Ethan on the street ten stories below. The street was dark and deserted, as was most of the business area of downtown at this time of night.

"All right, I'm here," Greg said. "What do you want?"

"You did this, you did it!" Ethan shouted. His voice was hoarse, panicked.

"Did what?"

*"You killed me!"*

"What—"

*"Look at me!"*

Greg heard breaking glass and looked up. It came from a twelfth-story window of the building across the street. Glass exploded out, propelled by a body that came out behind it.

In a rain of glass Ethan Shaw flew down a dozen stories to a concrete sidewalk.

## YOU ARE A SUSPECT

Every purchase you make with a credit card, every magazine subscription you buy and medical prescription you fill, every Web site you visit and e-mail you send or receive, every academic grade you receive, every bank deposit you make, every trip you book and every event you attend—all these transactions and communications will go into what the Defense Department describes as a virtual, centralized grand database. To this computerized dossier on your private life from commercial sources, add every piece of information that government has about you—passport application, driver's license and toll records, judicial and divorce records, complaints from nosy neighbors to the FBI, your lifetime paper trail plus the latest hidden camera surveillance—and you have the supersnoop's dream: a Total Information Awareness about every U.S. citizen.

This is not some far-out Orwellian scenario . . .

William Safire, *The New York Times* (2002)

The "Total Information Awareness" program capturing literally *every movement of every US citizen* was in fact put into effect by Congress as the Information Awareness Office (IAO) in 2002 and later defunded after objections were made. However, the 2013 NSA revelations revealed that major parts of this "mass surveillance" system of US citizens was kept funded and still operates in secret by changing the names of the programs.

# 4

*You killed me.*

The words, a wild, crazy accusation, had no meaning to Greg as he burst out of the building and ran out onto the street where death had happened. Soledad and the rest of the staff rushed out behind him.

Ethan's body was crumpled facedown on the Broadway sidewalk, his head in a pool of blood. There was no movement. The drop had been over a hundred feet onto concrete.

Greg stopped short of the body. Gawking would dishonor the dead. Soledad and the others went by him. He said, "Don't—" intending to tell them not to touch the body but stopped because someone should at least make sure the young man was dead.

He was petrified and shivered, not from the cold, but from the tragedy. A life had ended. Suddenly. Violently. He had been in a serious car accident once as thousands of pounds of metal suddenly banged and crunched into each other. For moments afterward the accident had felt unreal to him, as if he were in a mental twilight coming out of a dream. That was how he felt now. The body and blood didn't seem real. The horror did.

Sudden death was a strange business. Nothing fit in place. It was all the more perplexing because he didn't know Ethan well enough to understand what drove the young man to kill himself.

*You killed me.*

What the hell had he been talking about? Why would he say something so crazy? He tried to remember what else Ethan had said but his brain froze and wouldn't back up.

He looked up at the building that the hacker had burst out of. It was too dark to make out the broken window. But it was unbelievable. Incomprehensible. Ethan had spoken to him on the phone and then flung himself through the window. A dozen stories down. Propelled by what? Meth? Coke? Some new street compound that fried brains?

Soledad got on her cell phone as she walked back toward Greg. A good show runner, she was the one who called the police. There may have been other calls to 911 but it was after three in the morning and only a couple cars had passed. Greg didn't see any pedestrians when he stepped out of the broadcast building. The only people at the body were staff members.

A police car pulled up and officers shooed everyone back from the body and took a quick look. EMT arrived with a blaring siren and examined the body for life as officers taped off the area.

Greg sent the staff home except for Soledad before the coroner and evidence teams arrived and went to work. The others had witnessed nothing. Soledad had seen the falling body but had not heard the accusation Ethan made over the phone to Greg.

Plainclothes officers were the last on the scene. Greg gave his statement to a female sergeant while Soledad was taken aside and gave hers to the sergeant's male partner.

Ethan was identified by the contents of his wallet. None of the radio program's staff had ever seen him.

Greg had no explanation for Ethan's wild accusation and had little to offer about the young man, period. "I never met him in person," he told the officer. He cringed when he related what Ethan had said. "I have no clue as to what he was talking about. I never met him," he said again. Ditto for having no clue as to whether Ethan had a spouse or family the police could contact.

The sergeant had an explanation for Ethan's dying words. "The guy was high on drugs, upset because he couldn't get on a radio show. He wasn't a virgin when it came to a needle. People with fried brains don't need a rational basis to blame others for their problems or even to kill them or themselves—the dope provides all the hallucinations they need."

Soledad and Greg stayed and watched the coroner's people and crime investigators prepare the body for transport and take pictures. The sergeant told him entry had been made through a back door that had been kicked in. Then up the service elevator to the top floor, which was vacant and gutted like the rest of the building.

"That twelfth-floor suite had floor-to-ceiling windows," she said. "They scare me just standing by them even when they're not broken. I think the guy just took a run and crashed right into the window. Probably thought he could fly and went out flapping his arms."

The image shook Greg. He'd heard about a high-rise-building manager showing an office with big floor-to-ceiling windows that didn't look like anything was holding them in place. When asked by the prospective tenant how safe the windows were, the manager showed off by hitting a window with his shoulder. The window gave and he fell through. When Greg heard the story, he wondered what the guy was thinking on his way down.

Greg's own high-rise apartment had floor-to-ceiling windows but ones that looked more anchored than those in the building Ethan crashed through.

Soledad stayed closer to the body so she could hear what was being said by the crime scene techs. Greg hung back, leaning against the wall next to the door to the building that housed his broadcasting studio, watching the parade of officialdom come and go.

He spotted someone in the entryway of a closed store across and half a block up the street. A woman wearing a dark, hooded overcoat. She was too far away for him to see her facial features or even tell her age. From her body language he was sure she realized that he was looking in her direction.

She left the doorway and walked quickly in the direction opposite of the police activity and disappeared around a corner.

When the police and other agencies wrapped up and the body was gone, the night was quiet, the street deserted again except for him and Soledad.

Greg felt empty.

Death was a lonely business even for the living.

# 5

I'll walk you to your car," Greg told Soledad.

Her car was in a secured lot down the street and they headed for it, walking slowly down Broadway. The only sign of life on the street this late except for an occasional passing car was the glow of a liquor store sign.

South Broadway had three or four traffic lanes, depending on where you were standing, and a faded 1950s look: shopworn low-rise buildings selling shoes, clothing, booze, hamburgers, tacos; jewelry stores; bridal shops; and both pharmacies and *farmacias*.

The street looked ready for urban revitalization or a wrecking ball. Greg was on a committee trying to keep wrecking balls off the street.

"You have to call Liz," Soledad said.

He had already thought of that. Liz Tucker was the in-house attorney the network assigned to the show. She would have to be told that Ethan had called to announce he was going to kill himself and about the strange accusation.

"Liz is in Aspen for her son's wedding," Greg said. "I'll call her later."

Soledad wore her hair pulled back in a severe bun. In her fifties, she had dark hair with creeping gray she didn't attempt to hide. She didn't have the wrinkles at the corners of her eyes ironed away, either. She accepted and welcomed her age rather than trying to airbrush the years away.

She ruled the studio staff with the stern but benevolent efficiency of a drill sergeant, leaving him free to focus on dealing with millions of listeners.

"Why would he do such a thing?" she asked as they walked.

The question of the day. "The cop had a good explanation. She said Ethan had an altered perception of reality from using too many drugs too often. Crystal meth was the likely candidate. Cheap and easy to get. Or to cook up yourself if you did an Internet search for a recipe and could get your hands on some cough syrup or cold pills with pseudoephedrine in them."

Feelings of panic and paranoia were common side effects and Ethan sounded on the phone as if he was experiencing both altered states. *You killed me.* Greg wondered what the hell he'd meant.

With the pulsating lights and uniformed techs gone, the area had shut back down. Downtown L.A. in the wee hours was even more deserted than the center of many other great metro areas because the city-center streets were ones of faded glory—the city's pulse had moved closer to the ocean to something called the West Side, with Beverly Hills, Santa Monica and West Hollywood thrown in, none of which was actually part of L.A. but rose like concrete islands as the city swept west to the coast.

He chose downtown for his broadcasting studio over beach towns and the Valley because he liked the moody, darkly atmospheric, almost film noir atmosphere of the area, which had been too long forgotten but was haunted by the ghosts of movie palaces from the Golden Age of Hollywood and visions of grand days long gone.

Tonight the street no longer felt like a fit for Greg. Ethan's body would always be there, not on the ground but in his head each time he came and went into the building. It would take a while to get the studio moved, but he'd start thinking about a new location from which to broadcast.

They walked under the marquee of the Million Dollar Theater on Broadway. The theater was nearly a hundred years old and was one of the first great movie palaces. He loved movies, and old classics were his favorites.

"I wonder what he meant," Soledad said.

He knew what she was referring to. The last words from Ethan. A bizarre accusation.

"I don't know. Some thought generated by whatever chemical cocktail cooked his brain."

"He'd called earlier."

"Earlier this evening?"

She shook her head. "No, the last couple of days. I didn't pass on the calls because he was only a little crazy. Not threatening. He said they were trying to play God."

"Who's 'they'?"

"He never said and I didn't ask, but if you remember his hot point over the air to you was the overwhelming intrusion into our lives by the government and business. Not that I blame him. People used to worry whether having a social security number would permit the government to keep track of them. Today we can't watch a movie, buy a loaf of bread, make a phone call or send a text message without some governmental or business entity storing the information."

"Worse than that," Greg said. He nodded at the bank across the street. "We're being filmed right now not only by cameras at the ATM but by most of the businesses on this street. Getting to work in the morning in any big city means getting filmed dozens of times; I've heard as much as a couple hundred times when you add in all the traffic cams. A lot of people are bothered by it, but Ethan was particularly agitated."

"Angry," Soledad said.

"Maybe he was just more aware of it than the rest of us because he was aware of how intrusive electronics can be. Did he ever tell you which government agency he worked for?"

She shook her head. "When I interviewed him for airtime he said he wasn't allowed to disclose where he worked, but hinted it was secret stuff. I took it to be something to do with terrorism because everything secret today seems to head that way. He said he got caught hacking into someplace and got one of those get-out-of-jail-free cards by testing security systems for the good guys."

"He had a dark view of the future, like many of us. He talked about how mass surveillance created by the electronic tracking that is recording everything we do has paved our way to being controlled from birth to death, that we're already there and just don't know it. He mentioned *1984* the first night he was on. He said it was the only novel he read in school that stuck with him."

In Orwell's *1984*, a totalitarian regime ruled through mass surveillance. People in the dystopian book were constantly reminded that "Big Brother" was watching.

"Ethan's not the only one," she said. "I can't surf the Internet without ads targeting me because my buying history has been recorded and sold to businesses. I can't get away from it no-how. When I go through a thirty-day supply of pills I get a message from my pharmacy. Remember the condoms?"

He remembered. A caller to the show claimed that just before taking a business trip out of town, a friend of his bought condoms at the local drugstore. To get a discount, he unwittingly scanned his family's drugstore card that registered purchases. Not long afterward his wife got an email from the drugstore offering a discount on more condoms. It wasn't hard for Greg to anticipate the punch line—naturally, the husband and wife didn't use condoms.

True or not, it illustrated the fact that people were stripped naked mentally and physically by what they purchased.

"The invasion of our privacy by our every move being watched on the Internet and our being filmed when we step outside is like the weather," Greg said. "We bitch but still put up with it. Not just because we're told it's for the war on terrorism but because the information on us is being collected in so many different ways from thousands of entities—from government to businesses—that we have no control over. Worse, most of the time we don't even realize what we're revealing when we send an e-mail or swipe a credit card. They know our loves and hates, wants and desires and needs, even our sins—what we read, what we watch, what we buy, who we do it with and who we don't."

"You've been hammering that fact on the air for years."

"And we still elect the same do-nothings to Congress. I doubt if they ever can stop the ball rolling. The onslaught on our personal lives has become a world-class steamroller with the war on terror as its mantra. Remember the caller who theorized that it wouldn't be long before movies we stream are programmed for an ending the system knows we would prefer and with computer-generated images of the actors we preferred in the role?"

"Sounds good to me," Soledad said.

"Sounds like *Brave New World* and *1984* are no longer dark visions of the future but the society we are coalescing into."

They stopped at the entrance to the parking facility.

She squeezed his arm. "You look pretty devastated. I shouldn't have insisted you take the call."

"It's nobody's fault, not even Ethan's. For some people suicide is the only way they can see to avoid the pain they're experiencing."

He felt bad for the guy. He didn't get close enough to the body to pick up any of Ethan's physical details other than he had dark hair, but he had a mental image of the hacker from the call-ins. Probably late twenties, early thirties, a techie with his head stuck up a C drive, a computer geek who was better able to communicate in a computer language than table talk.

Like most young people today, he probably was more comfortable communicating with people through an LCD screen on a computer or cell phone than face-to-face. But from the calls into the program it was obvious Ethan was also bright, inquisitive—an idealist who opposed Big Brother spying down on everyone from the electronic cloud.

Greg said, "There had been a noticeable difference in Ethan's calls during the past few weeks, as he became more angry and paranoid about what he claimed was not just the government's efforts to invade our privacy by tracking everything we do, from social media to shopping at the supermarket and what we order at the drive-through window, but to use that information against us."

As he parted with Soledad and headed for his apartment it occurred to Greg that the turning point for Ethan had been about a week ago when he'd started ranting about dark forces out to get him. He cussed during a call and that was when Soledad had done a profanity block and barred him from the show.

How it got from there to a nosedive from the twelfth floor was a puzzle.

Deep in thought, he didn't notice the white van behind him.

# 6

*I'm going to kill you."*

The man in the white van behind Greg was alone, but he spoke the words aloud—a whispered thought. He had been pacing the man on the street, keeping the van far enough back so as not to appear obvious, the rage in him building. God had told him to follow Greg.

His name was Leon and he killed people. He used to kill because he was criminally insane. He was still crazy but brain surgery, cutting-edge "biohacking" in which his brain's programming was altered, had harnessed his killer rages so the lethal impulses could be controlled. Like a rabid pit bull on a choke chain, now he only killed on command.

Leon believed that a "Voice" in his head was giving him commands from God.

Voices, those of his father's, teachers and strangers, had always been significant in his life. The voices would send him into rages that got him convicted of murders and institutionalized in a high-security mental facility as criminally insane. But those voices no longer spoke to him.

He first heard the Voice of God's messenger when he awoke in a hospital after having brain surgery. He was told that the surgery was necessary because he had a brain tumor and had been transferred from the institute for the criminally insane to a surgical facility for the operation.

The Voice was louder and clearer in his head than the voices he had heard before the operation.

The Voice told him he was to obey its commands. When he asked if it was God speaking, the Voice said it was God's messenger.

He couldn't tell whether the Voice was male or female. It was just there, neutral, though it was soothing when Leon obeyed and abusive when he didn't. It was generous both about the privileges and rewards Leon got when he did well and with the pain that was inflicted on him when he disobeyed or failed.

After the operation he had not returned to the high-security psychiatric hospital where he had been imprisoned and subjected to around-the-clock lockup in a prison cell. Instead when he recovered from the surgery, he obeyed the Voice's instructions to walk out of the surgery facility. Walk, not escape.

He seemed to be the only person surprised when he put on street clothes that had been provided, walked down hospital corridors and out a side door to a parking area where a van similar to the one he was driving tonight was waiting for him with the motor running and the key in the ignition.

He wasn't aware of it, but all records of his existence had been erased. Birth, school, orphanage, prison, police, court, hospitalization, driving, DNA, fingerprints and all other documentation that he ever existed were destroyed.

He was a nonperson. But he hadn't had much of a footprint on the world anyway, except in the criminal justice system for the trail of violence and rage he had paved. He had never owned a home or even a car that was properly registered; never married or even had a relationship with a woman. He had no friends, no family, no acquaintances and no permanent home since he left the orphanage.

In between jail time he had lived out of a van that had a camp burner, a small mattress, blankets, a few supplies and a lot of used fast food containers—all the comforts of home for a person who kept continuously on the move.

His personal routine had not changed too radically since in his own mind he had become a warrior angel. Most of his meals came from fast food drive-throughs and were eaten in his van or motel room, but that suited him. He was not comfortable going into restaurants because he believed people stared at him and could hear the Voice talking to him. He spent nights in cheap motel rooms that had been rented for him and left unlocked so he didn't have to go into an office and register. When it was time, the Voice directed him to a motel and gave him the room number.

Even laundry was simple for him—every few days he found fresh clothes in the van after he returned from doing errands he'd been instructed to do. The clothes were always the same type, saving him from having to make a decision about what to wear—underwear and a uniform shirt and pants similar to what a deliveryman would wear.

The company name on the uniform was the same as on the van and changed each time he was told to leave a van and get into another.

He had no credit cards. He used cash to buy food and gas. Money was left in the van when clothes were delivered. He never had contact with anyone working for the Voice. Before deliveries were made to the van, he was instructed to leave the van and take a walk. He found the clothes and money when he returned.

The name on his driver's license, the name the van was registered under and the company name on the side of the van were periodically changed. He didn't bother remembering the name on anything, not even the driver's license. The van and names were always changed after he completed an assignment the Voice gave him.

He never questioned why one day he woke up with a clear, authoritative voice in his head that gave him commands and provided for his needs. It was there, it took care of what he required to live day by day, it had the power to gratify his need and inflict pain when he disobeyed.

The Voice hadn't told him the name of the man on the street and he had no curiosity to ask the name or why he was following the man. He had been told to hang back and get a good look at the man. He had his look and now waited for the Voice to tell him if he was to run the man down. His foot on the gas felt antsy. He wanted to run him down, feel the thump as the wheels went over the man. The anticipation fueled the rage building in him.

Even though he hadn't heard the man's voice, he was sure it would remind him of that bastard father who had abused him.

Researchers at the penal psychiatric hospital had investigated his childhood as part of a study to see whether serial killers typically had been abused as children. They discovered many serial killers had been abused, but Leon, who attributed his abuse to his father, had been raised until the age of eight by a single mother with a heavy drug problem and a short life that didn't include a male in the household.

He didn't lie when he told police and doctors that he couldn't control his impulse to kill when he heard the sound of his "father'"s voice, although he admitted he heard other voices in his head besides that of his father. The fact the abuse from his father never happened revealed to the researchers why his rage could be triggered by both men and women. They concluded that when he focused on a person he wanted to kill, he interpreted the person's voice as that of his father, regardless of the sex or age of the victim.

He spent most of his childhood and early adolescence in an orphanage because attempts to get him into foster care all ended with terrified foster parents returning him. By the time he was sixteen he was spending more time in a juvenile detention facility than anywhere else.

His killing state was a great surge of pent-up rage against his target and the world in general, which he released on his victim. Afterward he felt no remorse, empathy or sympathy. Peace and relief, a feeling of well-being, came immediately after he released the fury but lasted only a short time.

He hung back with the van, not approaching the man, because he had not been told to make the kill yet.

He had little patience. Few things captured his attention for long and he was growing impatient waiting for the Voice in his head to give the kill command. As he waited in the van behind the man walking, the rage kept building. There would come a time when he would not be able to control the fury.

## WE KNOW YOUR FACE

The U.S. government is in the process of building the world's largest cache of face recognition data, with the goal of identifying every person in the country. The creation of such a database would mean that anyone could be tracked wherever his or her face appears, whether it's on a city street or in a mall. Today's laws don't protect Americans from having their webcams scanned for facial data.

Kyle Chayka, "Biometric Surveillance
Means Someone Is Always Watching"
*Newsweek*, April 17, 2014

# 7

Greg's apartment was on Bunker Hill overlooking Broadway. His walk home took him from the broadcasting studio on Broadway in the Theater District to a strange little railroad that lifted him up to Bunker Hill. It was only a few city blocks from the studio to the railhead. He got out of the show after three in the morning and he usually enjoyed the walk's solitude of closed stores and little traffic after being on his toes for hours but tonight the streets felt gloomy and abandoned.

He had turned off onto a side street that was even more deserted than Broadway when he noticed headlights behind him.

A white van had stopped about a hundred feet behind him. It was the only vehicle in sight. A plumber on an emergency call looking for an address?

The van's brights came on and he turned back to walking as the headlights dimmed.

He usually walked with a lighter step. He stopped and stared at his reflection in the display window of a closed clothing store. He saw a man in his forties who looked grim and severe, scowling and worn at the edges after a rough night. But not as rough as Ethan's had been.

He was tired. No, beyond that. Weary. And ill at ease, as if he expected the next shoe to drop. He scoffed at his own sense of dread, but couldn't shake off the fact that someone in his life, peripheral for sure, had killed himself.

His own beliefs were shaped by what he considered to be fundamental laws of the universe: People have free will. Stupid people act stupidly. Evil people act evilly. Good people try to survive without harming others. Do unto others as they do unto you. Never start a fight, but don't back down from bad people doing bad things. An eye for an eye is a good yardstick by which to measure the administration of justice.

He did not believe that all things could be seen with the eye of science, that science was infallible or that you could find God in a test tube.

He believed that humankind was not alone in the universe, that not all the intelligent life on the planet was human, that visitors from the beyond had come to Earth in ancient and modern times and that the visible world was not the only world that existed.

Most of all he believed in the truth, demanding it and inquiring until the real facts were on the table.

Staring at a mannequin in the window display, he wondered if he was being filmed by a camera in the eye of the dummy. If someone had told him when he was a kid that someday store mannequins would have camera eyes equipped with a facial identification program that told the store salespeople whether he was a returning customer and what his previous purchases were, he'd have thought it was science fiction.

He considered facial recognition as one of the most serious electronic dangers to society and was certain what Ethan's reaction would have been to its uses. The young hacker would have supported his aversion to it and would have sided with him during a heated discussion about the program last week when Greg was a panelist at a Harvard conference in Boston on computers and the future of technology.

On the panel with him were a computer scientist, a programmer and a social network executive. Greg was invited as the sole voice of dissent about the incredible attack on personal privacy the computer age had created.

"It bothers me that I have a Big Brother that's always looking over my shoulder," Greg told the audience. "As a matter of fact, he's a brother to all of us. One of his nasty little gadgets he's come up with is computer software that identifies a person by viewing their features. Once the person's identity is known, another app gives access to everything available on the Internet about the person in the blink of an eye.

"Facial identification cameras will soon be common wherever I go. Even if it is my first visit to a store, the salespeople will be able to access my history of purchases not only for that store but anywhere I slide a bank card. It irks the hell out of me that a person in a back room at a store watching a computer screen will know what I eat and drink, read and watch, my preference for clothes and cars. It won't be hard to find out how much I earn and who I make love with.

"If I go into a restaurant, I don't want the waiter to know how I like my steak or what kind of tipper I am or who I was dining with last night."

He went on to tell the audience that the NSA was aiding and abetting the process by capturing millions of facial images from e-mails and other social media posting of pictures. Throw in passport, school and military records, and driver's license pictures and it was pretty much a wrap.

"The agency is not bound by constitutional rules because privacy laws have no express protections for facial recognition data. But it isn't just faces that are being cataloged. Keep in mind that identifying our faces links to an incredible amount of information about each of us—*information that is exposed to strangers.*

"It gets more shocking and dangerous for us because anyone with a smartphone, including a sex offender or thief, can identify each of us and instantly find out an incredible array of personal information as they pass us on the street.

"What kinds of information will the curious and criminals be able to access? We're moving toward a society in which so much information is gathered about us electronically that it will be easy to check out our employment, credit rating, address, marital status and much more.

"Sounds like fun—unless you're the one being targeted. I leave it to your imagination what the dangers are if the target is a child in a park and the person with the cell phone app is a sex offender."

He didn't get cheers and a standing ovation. And he didn't

expect them. What he got was a long, uneasy silence from the audience. He wasn't just attacking their livelihood, but their worldview and passion. What he saw as dehumanizing and dangerous, they saw as a marvelous new technology that advanced electronics ever further.

The computer programmer pointed out that facial identification programs were used in the war on terror not only to identify terrorists, but that by interpreting the movement of facial muscles around the mouth, forehead and eyebrows, even a person's emotional state could be determined. "It could recognize if someone was nervous, as a terrorist with a bomb strapped to the chest might be," she said.

"I'm not a terrorist," Greg said, "nor are more than three hundred million other Americans whose every movement is already being observed, recorded and sucked into vast storage facilities in electronic clouds."

Greg's phone rang, taking him out of Harvard and putting him back on a dark L.A. street. He pulled the phone out of his pocket and looked at the caller's name.

*Ethan Shaw.*

# 8

Leon leaned forward in the seat, hunched over the steering wheel as he watched the man in front of him. The man on the street had stopped walking to answer a phone call. He still had his back to Leon.

"What's the matter with you?" Leon asked aloud. "Don't you know where you're going?"

As if he had heard the questions, the man started walking again.

Leon was told by the Voice to follow the man, but not to approach or harm him until he received a command to do so. He was to hang back, but close enough so that the man would feel intimidated by the van's presence.

Leon accepted the Voice as part of his being and had no suspicion that the commands came through a microdevice that had been implanted in his head during the surgery he was told was needed to remove a tumor. Doctors at the psychiatric hospital were told that the operation was done to install an experimental control device that would automatically feed Leon a dose of an antipsychotic medicine when triggered by Leon's emotions.

That was partly true. He could feel a small device on the inside of his right thigh, but didn't know that the mechanism was used to feed a calming drug through an artery whenever he became difficult to control—and another drug that spiked his manic state when his controllers wanted to increase his rage. He had tried to take the device off once and suffered excruciating pain.

But in addition, an internal receptor was placed in his head that carried sound and mechanical vibrations along the acoustic nerve to the temporal lobe, permitting the Voice to speak to Leon. A similar system transmitted Leon's spoken words back to the other end.

He was "punished" by the Voice frequently in the beginning when he failed to instantly obey commands. The mildest form of punishment began with loud, harsh, grating noises in his head followed by the triumphant sound of his nonexistent father beating and humiliating him. The greater the sin, the more severe the pain. When he obeyed, he was rewarded with praise and allowed to watch his favorite movies and play violent games. As time went on he disobeyed less frequently.

Installation of the communication mechanisms and drug dispensers that gave control over Leon's actions had been predicated upon two scientific facts about the human race:

The brain operates like a computer and can be biohacked to change the programming.

Second, the behavior of humans can be modified and controlled by punishment and rewards. Pavlov proved it with dogs and Skinner with lab rats.

Long before computers, Pavlov, a Russian scientist, discovered that dogs produced saliva not only when they were shown food but when they saw the white jackets of the lab attendants who brought the food to them.

He put holes through the side of the dogs' mouths to have salvia drain. He took the experiments further with children—paying the parents of poor children to permit him to drill holes in the side of the faces of the children so he could put tubes through to collect salvia as he showed them food.

He also discovered that if he gave dogs a series of painful shocks of electricity while a metronome ticked, the dogs would cry out as if they were shocked when the metronome was played but no shock was administered.

Pavlov received the Nobel Prize in Medicine for his work.

Decades later B. F. Skinner came along with the Skinner box, which used rats that got food for good responses and electric shock for the wrong ones. Considered the most influential psychologist of the twentieth century, Skinner once noted that the primary issue concerning mankind was not how to free people but how to improve control over them.

Like the dogs and rats, Leon usually avoided punishment by giving the right responses. But he had been conditioned not to salivate but to direct on command his mad dog urge to kill.

Leon had never heard of Pavlov or Skinner but he would have enjoyed drilling holes in children's faces.

# 9

*E*<sup>*than Shaw.*</sup>
     Greg stood rooted and stared at the caller ID. It took his breath away. He pressed a button to take the call and snapped, "Who is this?"

No answer. Nothing from the other end. "Hello—hello?" No sound. The phone line was so empty of sound it was an electronic vacuum.

He stared at the LCD screen. The caller ID was gone. For a flash he wondered if he had imagined it but he knew he hadn't. The name had been there. Ethan Shaw. A dead man. At least there was a body on the street that he assumed was Ethan's. He never saw the face and told the police he couldn't identify the body because he had never seen Ethan.

He hit "call return" to dial back the last call received and stopped when the number to his broadcast studio popped up. He had gotten a call from the studio earlier in the evening prior to arriving for the show.

He checked his "received calls" bin and recognized the number of the last received call—his producer Soledad returning his earlier one. The phone's voicemail was empty.

He realized there was a reasonable explanation for the call. It could have come from the police, from Ethan's cell phone, in an attempt to locate Ethan's family or friends to identify his body.

He thought about that for a moment and found a flaw. Ethan wouldn't have his private number in his phone contacts. Greg's sole contact with the hacker had been by way of his radio show phone lines. However, a person's whole life is open to hackers. It would have been a piece of cake for Ethan to have gotten his private number. But if he obtained Greg's number by hacking, he would have been calling it rather than getting blocked when he called the radio show.

A sick joke played by one of Ethan's hacker friends?

Ethan's death didn't mean someone besides the authorities couldn't have used his name. Greg knew that you could buy a phone app that lets you disguise the number and caller. But Ethan's body was still warm. Few people outside the first responders would even know about his death.

An eerie thought struck him—he had had callers on the show who claimed to have received calls from the dead.

That was a pleasant thought on a dark and lonely street after witnessing a violent death. *Keep it up,* he told himself.

He tried to shake it off but the phone call spooked him. The most probable answer was that Ethan had his private number but didn't use it, and someone at the police department had made calls from the contact list in the phone to find next of kin and had hung up or got disconnected before Greg answered the call.

The conclusion about the call didn't make much sense to him but neither did the bizarre accusation or Ethan free-falling over a hundred feet.

*Give it up,* he told himself. He needed some rest and sleep before he drove himself nuts trying to unravel a mystery wrapped in a conundrum.

Headlights from the rear were on him again. He turned around and the lights went high beam and he spun back around. He was sure it was the van and this time it disturbed him. It had moved up the street with him and stopped about the same distance behind him. Stopped and didn't move. It hadn't pulled over and stopped in front of a store or a business building. Nothing was open. And no one got out of the van. The driver just sat there, silently, unmoving, hitting him with the brights when he turned to look. That really bothered him. Bright lights from out of the dark erupted deep fears from out of the past. As for Josh the caller, blinding lights had special meaning to Greg. They threatened him.

Fears hidden deep in Greg's subconscious gripped him. *Stop it!* he told himself. He was overreacting. He pushed through his fears. The guy was a plumber or an electrician looking for an address. That's all it was. Had it not been the wee hours there would have been more traffic on the street and he wouldn't even have noticed the van.

He walked on, his back to the lights, and got his thinking straight. There was no ghost in the phone. Ethan had his private number and just hadn't gotten around to using it. Someone trying to find the next of kin had been hitting the buttons on the young hacker's phone.

It wasn't a ghost call, but he chuckled as he admitted to himself he wouldn't have been averse to a call from the beyond. Having been a seeker most of his life he had analyzed and investigated the claims of paranormal encounters with everything from ghosts to poltergeists, ancient aliens to yesterday's UFO sightings, as well as ESP, telekinesis, life after death, reincarnation, faith healing and human auras, along with a host of cryptids—creatures whose existence was controversial, such as Bigfoot, the Loch Ness Monster, the New Jersey Devil, werewolves, Yeti and Mothman.

It had been over only the past few years that another creature of the night, Big Brother, had raised its ugly head by dehumanizing people with the dark side of technology.

His investigations had not convinced him that every claim of paranormal activity was genuine, but it had convinced him that most claims deserved to be investigated, that too many were ignored for no good reason and that there was enough evidence supporting some claims that a pattern of proof had been established.

The callers and listeners to his show were also seekers, reaching out, looking for answers and sometimes coming up with ones that others found bizarre. He wasn't judgmental about callers whose claims or ideas might seem outlandish to others because his own experiences had not been conventional. Sometimes at night he lay in bed, not sure if he was awake or dreaming as he sensed a presence around him—paralyzed by the sensation that whatever was in the dark was studying him as if he was a matter of curiosity . . . as if he was being looked over to see how the dissection should go.

The weather was still aping the strange events of the night, staying dark and dreary and sullen as he moved on, trying to shrug off the sense of dread he felt as he walked toward the funicular that would lift him from the flatland of Broadway to Bunker Hill where his apartment was located.

He was mulling over Ethan's strange death and dying words when he realized the van was still behind him. As he had moved down the street, it had moved. Two or three times now.

He didn't turn because he knew the high beams would go on. He looked at the van's hazy reflection in a store window but saw only that the van was white and had something written on the side panel.

He was being paced on the dark street.

Unfortunately, he remembered one of those unusual things he had learned as a late night talk show host:

Vans were the vehicle of choice for serial killers.

# 10

The street was deserted except for Greg and the van. Like most big-city business districts, the downtown Los Angeles business corridors were a no-man's-land after the offices and after-work watering holes had closed—creating a perfect storm if you wanted to rob or murder someone.

*My imagination is working overtime,* he told himself. *Keep moving, keep thinking good thoughts, get to your apartment, put up your feet and have a glass of wine. I'm not being stalked, it's just a coincidence.*

But his body didn't agree with what his rational mind was telling him. He was tense, his adrenaline pumping, getting ready for flight or fight.

He deliberately stopped at a window and stared at the lighted display of a clothing store. The van stopped. He didn't need to turn and look. He could tell from the headlights shining in his direction. It kept about a hundred feet behind. Not much space between them if the driver wanted to suddenly run him down.

Now that was a pleasant thought.

It wasn't easy to follow someone on foot from a motor vehicle and be subtle about it. And there was nothing subtle about the way the van shadowed him. It kept pausing and creeping forward, making it obvious the van was following him.

He thought about walking back and confronting the driver, but decided getting to the funicular that would lift him above the deserted street to Bunker Hill and his apartment was a more clever idea. In his own mind there was only one person in the van. A man.

He knew for sure that it wasn't gangbangers because they would have gotten right to business and not played any games.

He usually enjoyed the sudden quiet and calm of the dark, empty streets after being on the air. With the van behind him pacing him like a demon-possessed car in a Stephen King horror story, tonight they were long, lonely blocks. Worse, there were streets to cross. Picking him off on a crosswalk would be easier than jumping the curb to nail him.

Greg thought about it some more, took some steps forward and then said, "What the hell." He spun around to face the van and headed toward it.

L eon slammed back against the driver's seat, letting out a startled yell. What the hell was that bastard doing? He was coming at him, to attack him.

He popped the clutch and hit the gas pedal, burning rubber as the van shot forward.

"You're dead!" he screamed.

G reg froze as the van jumped the curb with the passenger-side wheels and came at him, half on the sidewalk. He couldn't move or think as the van surged forward like a rocket. Some primeval instinct kicked in and he threw himself to the left, slamming up against a shoe store display window.

The van's side-view mirror brushed his right arm and wind whipped him as the vehicle flew by in a flash. It hit a city trash can on the corner and sent it flying into the intersection.

The van made a sharp right turn, rear end swaying, tires screeching, and disappeared around the corner.

Greg leaned against the store window. He was breathless. The crazy bastard had nearly killed him. He was lucky he hadn't broken the window.

He hurried to the corner and looked for the van. It wasn't in sight. Someone with a malicious sense of humor, he thought, and then corrected himself. If he hadn't moved fast, it would have hit him. This was no joke. Yet had the intent been to harm him, the van could have done so earlier when he had his back to it. The attempt to hit him was an impulse. But isn't that how many killers operated? They suddenly saw an opportunity and went for it?

He still thought it might have been a company van, someone on a call or returning from one. As it flashed by he again saw the wording on the side, probably a company name, but didn't catch what it said. And white vans were as common in the city as smog alerts.

Even if he had gotten a look at the company's name and reported it to the police, the driver would probably tell them he'd been moving slow, looking for an address, when some crazy guy on the street suddenly charged at him. He hadn't gotten a look at the driver.

He stared at his own reflection in a store window. He looked even worse than before. Now he looked like a man who had lost a battle but still didn't know who the enemy was.

It had been a hell of a night. Ethan killing himself. Getting stalked and nearly killed by a crazy in a van. A call from the dead.

Maybe Chicken Little was right.

In the van Leon's sense of glee had immediately deflated as soon as his rage dissipated.

He knew he was in trouble with the Voice. He had been told to follow the man, but stay in the background and intimidate him with the van's ominous presence. He would be punished for his disobedience and it would be painful because while logic and reason had little impact on his behavior, severe pain did.

When it started he pulled the van quickly over to the curb.

The feeling began in his testicles, a feeling that something had grabbed them. And squeezed. He cried out but the pressure got worse. Squeezed until his balls felt like they were being crunched in a vise.

He shouted promises, swearing that he would never disobey an order again.

Then he screamed.

# 11

The iconic little funicular called Angels Flight was the shortest railroad in the world, about the length of a football field. The cable cars connected Hill Street up a steep incline to Bunker Hill.

Greg had a laundry list of things like insufferable traffic and dirty air that he hated about L.A. What he loved was the city's surprises. Like a good movie, the City of Angels had constant plot twists to keep you on your toes as you made your way around its vast basin, which extended from the desert, being chewed up by four-by-fours, to beaches lined with surfboards.

Only a block or more from some of the greatest movie palaces ever built on the planet, in an area that had been going through a Latino renaissance but was bordered by Skid Row, where the homeless lined the sidewalks with tents, trash bags, boxes and shopping carts, he was about to step aboard the smallest and strangest railroad in the world. The cable car would lift him a few hundred feet to Bunker Hill, an elegant water garden and billion-dollar high-rises.

Bunker Hill overlooks Broadway and the rest of downtown. It was once the bastion of L.A.'s wealthy, who looked down their noses from elegant Victorian mansions at the common folk in the flat streets below. Stately mansions slowly evolved into slum housing as the rich moved away from the smells and traffic of downtown, the old buildings eventually got torn down, the terrain got lowered a bit and glassy skyscraping office and residential high-rises and art and museum venues went up.

Despite all the changes to Bunker Hill over the years, one thing hadn't changed from Victorian times—you could still see the common folk and Skid Row on the flatlands from its heights.

A cable car was waiting and he hurried to board before it started up. The tiny railroad had two counterbalanced cable cars—Sinai and Olivet. One car went up the short, steep incline as the other slid down. Operating in opposite directions on overlapping tracks, the railcars appeared destined to collide at the halfway point but swerved at the last moment to pass. At least that was the theory. In 2001 there was a fatality and injuries when Sinai, nearing the top, suddenly reversed direction and went down, hitting the other car.

The two cable cars had an unusual layout inside: the interiors were just as steep as the tracks because the tracks were on a steep grade from start to finish. After entering the steep interior of the bottom car, passengers climbed a series of steps and platforms to exit at the other end once the car reached the top.

No staff were in the cars—the operator stayed in the small station house at the Bunker Hill end. The ride cost fifty cents and you paid exiting at the top.

Two of the greatest names in film noir and detective stories, hard-boiled Philip Marlowe and hard-hitting Mike Hammer, rode the little railroad while investigating the city's dirty underbelly.

He didn't realize a woman had entered behind him until he made his way up the sharp incline to a seat at the top platform of the car. The woman was the only other person in the railcar. She took a seat at the bottom soon after entering instead of making her way up the ascent to the top to be close to the exit, as most people did.

He did a double take and quickly looked away, not wanting to appear obvious. Was it the same woman he saw in an entryway when the police and EMTs were tending to Ethan's body? He hadn't gotten a good look at the woman earlier but two different women in similar dark hooded coats was too much of a long shot. But he didn't know what her presence now and earlier added up to. And he didn't feel comfortable approaching a woman with a question about what she was doing alone on the streets at night. It was the sort of situation that could go to hell fast.

Not wanting to get caught staring, he snuck a look at her out of the corner of his eye. Around thirty or a little more, he guessed, tall, slender. Her hooded coat was black. The coat looked expensive, probably cashmere. Some untamed chestnut hair stuck out from the hood. Her features were partially covered by the hood but he could see that her complexion was pale. He wasn't sure, but guessed her eyes were light, maybe green or gray.

He knew why he was out on the street in the wee hours, but wondered about her. Too early to be on her way to work at an insurance company or law office in a Bunker Hill tower. Had she been on her way home from a night on the town or with a lover?

Something about her didn't jibe with being a businesswoman. She didn't seem artsy, either. It was something else. She was self-absorbed. Introspective. More than just being cautious about making eye contact with a strange man. Her body language was guarded and tense.

He left the railcar when it stopped at the top. The ticket booth was just outside the exit gate. Beyond the ticket booth was California Plaza's water court, a granite oasis with a dancing water fountain, open-air eating areas and greenery set in the shadows of two skyscrapers.

He dropped his ticket in the drop box and was walking away from the cable car, deliberately going slow in the hope that she might give him an opening to talk to her. A polite smile or a nod would do it.

He heard her say something and he swung around.

She was still in the cable car, standing at the railing in the car's exit cage. The railing was closed because the car was about to descend.

"I'm sorry, were you speaking to me?" he asked.

"It's just begun."

"What do you mean?"

The car started its descent and she turned and went into the interior as he stood rooted for a long moment.

*What the hell?*

He slowly let go of the urge to take the next car down and chase after her on the street below. He wasn't sure he'd heard her right.

No, that wasn't true. He'd heard what she said, he just didn't know what she meant. She might be a crazy and start screaming for the cops the moment he approached her. He shook his head. All he needed to wrap up a strange night was to tangle with a woman on the street who accused him of harassing her.

He turned in the direction of his apartment and got his feet to move, but the impulse to run after her stayed with him. So did her cryptic remark.

*It's just begun.*

What bothered him most was the dead accuracy of her remark. The sky sure seemed like it had started falling.

# 12

A feeling of morbid anxiety, gloom and doom followed him from the water garden to his penthouse apartment. It wasn't one thing but everything, as if he had accidentally kicked the lid off Pandora's box and unleashed some of his own demons to taunt him.

Entering the apartment didn't bring a sense of relief. The place felt empty even though it was well furnished—expensively, at least. It had modern white sectional couches with straight lines set before a large-screen TV and entertainment center he rarely turned on except for music; large smoked-glass coffee and end table; a well-stocked Italian gray marble wet bar, and more marble on the hearth of a fireplace that rarely got turned on because it was in L.A.; those floor-to-ceiling windows that now were reminders of a tragedy; and a balcony beyond. There was no artwork on the walls, just some Mesoamerican art pieces scattered around on tabletops.

He had left the furnishings to an interior designer because he had little interest in the apartment. It was hollow to him because it was just a place to sleep, to camp out in between shows and for entertaining. There was little of him in it.

He felt more at home where he could walk barefoot in the sand than on the plush carpeting of a martini penthouse. A little north of Malibu he had a weathered beach house that had been pounded by wind and surf and roosted on by gulls long before he walked the earth. He had felt at home there the moment he walked in and bought it as a place to think and recharge on the weekends as guest hosts ran the show.

He was on the road so often with speaking engagements he

didn't get a lot of time at either place he hang his hat. When he was in town, he enjoyed having a date and interesting guests to his beach house. He moved freely around people, that's what made him a good talk show host, but he also would hang back at a party with a glass of wine and study people rather than be in the limelight. He was so used to extraordinary people and ideas that pushed the envelope swirling around him that he found small talk a bore.

He turned on his cell phone after he entered. He didn't remember turning it off on the street, but he must have after getting the strange call. A voicemail signal popped up and his guts clenched. Another phantom call from the dead? Someone asking about Ethan? He was too beat, too raw and empty inside to hear from someone calling out of curiosity because they'd heard about the suicide on the news.

The moment he heard a Jamaican accent he knew it was Rohan, a best-selling author who, like a rock star, went by one name. Rohan was a media personality in the area of alien abduction. He claimed he had been abducted and examined by aliens during a university sleep and dream experiment. The experience involved a strange encounter with what appeared to be a woman on the surface but that Rohan realized was an alien taking the form of *women*—Rohan observing changes in the age, look, color and shape of his partner as they had sex.

Writing about it turned out to be a money machine for him. He'd been on the show a number of times to talk about his experience, always emotional about being violated. Rohan was angry that he had been used as a guinea pig. "The teachers running the program sold my soul to aliens," he said in the opening to his book. "To the professors it was no different than parting out the organs of someone close to death so they can get rich."

Accusing the university of selling people to aliens sold a lot of books.

"It's started," Rohan said on the voicemail. "They killed Ethan because he got too close to their secret objective. Now they'll come after the rest of us who can expose them. Any one of us can be next but agitators like you and me will be first on their list to eliminate.

We have to stick together or they'll pick us off like Ethan, one by one. Don't call me—I made this call from a neighbor's phone because they'll be listening in on my calls. We need to talk, to figure out what to do before Murad's creatures get us. Get over here so we can talk."

The words came out at the speed of bullets in a tone frantic with fear and paranoia. There was enough slurring to make Greg wonder what he had been drinking or smoking before he made the call.

Rohan's allegations about aliens were nothing new—he was constantly on the run from things from the dark side sent by Carl Murad, the psychology professor who oversaw the sleep experiment and who Rohan claimed was in league with a secret entity that was seeking world domination.

There were two strange things about the timing of the call. Rohan had made it twenty minutes after Ethan jumped, fell, threw himself out the window or however it would be described. The ambulance had hardly arrived by the time Rohan called. Far too early for Rohan to have heard a news report.

Second, Greg had looked at his phone earlier when he got the phantom call—and there had been no voicemail icon.

He ignored Rohan's request not to call his number and tried it anyway. He got a recording that said the line was not in service. The message gave him pause. He could understand if Rohan turned off his phone or refused to answer and let it go to voicemail, but "not in service" meant the line had been disconnected.

He tried Rohan's neighbor's line. Not in service.

Greg checked the time. Unless he was in some sort of time warp, it hardly seemed possible for Rohan to know about Ethan's death and to have disconnected his line with the phone company and have a "not in service" message up and running in the middle of the night while Ethan's body was literally still warm.

Another curious thing about the call struck him. Ethan had appeared on the show under his user name, RainbowHat, but Rohan had used Ethan's real name in a familiar way, as if he knew the hacker. It wasn't impossible that the two knew each other, but while they were both into conspiracy theories, from what he knew about them Greg couldn't see much common ground between them. So what were they up to that had Rohan panicking?

Stealing government secrets and using Greg as their fall guy was the answer that came to mind.

He stood on his balcony while thoughts roiled in his head—Ethan, a call from the dead, intimidated by a van, a mysterious woman, now Rohan jumping in and generating more questions.

The woman at Angels Flight had ripped open and exposed wounds he already had. Her enigmatic comment implied that worse things were coming and at the moment he wasn't ready to rebut that take on his life.

The root of his connection to callers troubled by strange forces went back to a time when he faced the unexplainable and incomprehensible. He had been the sole witness to his own strange encounter, but as with so many reported encounters, there was a void in his memory. It happened when he was in his teens, but he still felt the trauma and even the fear. He was sure everything he experienced was still registered in his brain, but it had a lock on it. He was certain he had the key to unlock the memory, but the door refused to open, remaining just out of reach.

For a time he was relentlessly and even foolishly drawn to probe the dark matter lying just out of reach in his subconscious, and those urges still erupted some nights when he awoke in the middle of the night. With sleep eluding him, as oblivious to the danger as a moth batting its wings on the edge of a fiery volcano, he tried to probe his memory, to reconstruct what had happened when he encountered the terrifying and the mystifying.

His whole life—his relationships, his career, his fears and triumphs—had been affected by that knowledge wrapped in fog and shadows in his mind, which he couldn't access.

Greg hadn't spoken to another person about the experience in nearly three decades, but it was still there, in a dark place in his mind.

When he was a kid and spoke about his traumatic experience, his parents warned him not to tell others because people would make fun of him—even think he was lying or imagined it. When he did tell friends, he got howls of laughter and ridicule rather than understanding.

He got the last laugh because as an adult he took on a challenging career that brought him into contact almost on a daily basis with people who had experienced strange encounters.

But the early experience left him not just with empathy for people who'd had their lives twisted by events that defied acceptable explanation—it taught him that paranoia can be heightened awareness of the strange and unimaginable because he often sensed things about people and places that were out of reach to the five senses.

He gave his callers the freedom to tell the world their innermost thoughts, but kept his own deepest beliefs a secret—along with his fears.

His experience made him a seeker on a quest that he couldn't define. Rather than backing away from the unknown, he had been drawn to it in a large way, driven to become a national nighttime host of a radio show with a paranormal theme because he sought answers to the unexplainable.

The show wasn't just a job for him, but part of his quest to find answers. He had told Josh and many others that they were not alone, that he had had an encounter with the preternatural, as had many callers on his show. Millions more looked up at the stars and the utter darkness of the infinite universe beyond and realized that we are not alone in the universe. Even the pope in Rome had established a committee to investigate the existence of extraterrestrials.

He left the balcony and collapsed in bed weighed down by death and conspiracy, a warning from a strange woman and a threatening set of headlights that tried to run over him.

He was awakened hours later by a call from his producer.

"There's a homicide cop here who wants to talk to you about Ethan."

# 13

Two plainclothes officers were waiting in the reception area of the broadcast studio. Greg invited them into his office. He hated talking to people over a desk and had them sit with him in the conference area in the corner of his office, four chairs around a table.

Lieutenant Batista was with the LAPD and introduced his companion, Mond, as being with Interagency. Greg had never heard of Mond's department. The name of the agency was so vague it sounded like one of those units that had sprouted between the cracks of bureaucracy. He assumed it dealt with suicides.

Batista looked like a man who had seen and heard everything and didn't believe much of it. He had shiny black hair combed straight back, tired eyes framed by wrinkles and a mouth shaped by cynicism.

Mond was short, stocky and bald. His thick face, broad nose and large eyes reminded Greg of a big frog. A poisonous one. Mond's dark eyes were recessed behind puffy pouches and all Greg could make of them was that they never altered from looking at him, as if the man was seeing something behind Greg's facial mask.

Mond's quiet menace made Greg more uneasy than the homicide cop's blunt approach. The expression "lock and load," about getting ready to fire, came to mind as the big frog stared at him. He hoped Mond wasn't the person whose duty it was to pass news of Ethan's death on to loved ones.

Batista started hammering him with rapid-fire questions about his relationship with Ethan the moment the two police officials sat down. How long had he known Ethan? What was their relationship on and off the radio? When did they first meet? When was the last time he saw Ethan?

Greg didn't like the machine-gun approach but figured cops only expected other people to pass an attitude test. And his responses were simple—Ethan had been a caller for a couple of months. They had never met in person. The only thing about Ethan's work he knew was that Ethan was a reformed hacker working for a government agency. Which agency, he didn't know.

Only Batista hit him with questions. Mond sat quietly and stared, like a frog ready to pounce. Or lash out with its tongue.

The questions appeared to be fishing for a connection between him and Ethan. There was none. "I know zero about Ethan's personal or professional life other than what I've told you. He's one of hundreds of callers to the show who shared his concerns about the state of the world."

"But you had enough problems between the two of you to ban him from the show," Batista said.

"We had no problems between us. He wasn't allowed on the air recently because he sounded like he was high and used profanity. The FCC prohibits it. Look, I don't mind telling you what I know about Ethan, but if he committed suicide, why do I have a homicide cop asking me questions?"

"Just routine, violent death, we need to fill in the blanks. So you say you never met in person."

"Never met in person. What little I know about him was what he revealed over the air. Said he'd got busted for hacking and ended up working for the government testing security systems. I don't know how old he was—"

"Twenty-seven."

"Or much else about him. He was concerned about what he considered hidden forces attempting to control our society but that's a fear many of my callers have, including me."

Batista leaned forward with a smirk. "Mine's aliens that look like big snakes. I saw the movie." He chuckled and turned to Mond for support but the agent didn't crack a smile or divert his stare from Greg.

Batista put back on his serious face and puckered his lips. "So you say this guy was just another conspiracy theory nut who called in, period, full stop."

"I said he was concerned about the state of the world as he and many others see it. About the only thing that set Ethan Shaw apart from other callers I've gotten over the years was that he started losing it during calls. Using foul language and sounding high. Ranting about how the time had come, that the world was coming under control of secret forces."

"Your producer confirmed that you banned him. But you took a call from him last night anyway."

"Not on the air. We took the call to pacify him."

"And he said you killed him."

"And he said I killed him. And you focus on that despite the fact that I was here with witnesses when he threw himself out of the building across the street. Are you finished with your questions?"

"Close. He said you killed him. What did he mean by that?"

"I don't know. Crazy talk. I told you he sounded high."

"Your producer said he sounded panicked."

"That, too. Why do we keep going back to what Ethan said? He was obviously high and I didn't kill him. I'm getting the feeling that you're trying to make something out of nothing."

Batista waived off the accusation with his hands. "Hey, he said you killed him, I have to ask. Maybe he was using the accusation metaphorically. You know what I mean?"

"No. Killing by metaphor is a little too far-fetched for me."

"Maybe he got himself deep into something with someone and killing himself was the only way out."

"Because of something I did? Is that what you're saying?"

"I'm not making accusations, I'm asking questions. For all we know, someone might have bullied him into killing himself. When I was a kid bullying was bad behavior—now it's a crime."

"He was just a listener calling in."

"Your producer says you had trouble with him."

"You keep going back to that but it's not that kind of trouble.

Every word I've ever spoken to him has been on the air and none of it was personal. And I told the cops last night what he said."

"All he said was you killed him? Not how or why?"

"I'm going to start grinding my teeth and run up a dental bill if you keep asking me that."

"Do you keep copies of the calls?"

"We keep everything on a cloud server. He talked about technology out of control, about global conspiracies. He was out of control."

"He had enough meth in him to kill an elephant."

"From the way he sounded, I imagine he did."

"The medical examiner says he took some really rich stuff, so pure that it's hard to imagine it out on the street. What he would have considered to be his usual dose blew his brains out."

Greg tried to hold back his exasperation. He learned the hard way as a kid that arguing with a cop was a no-win proposition but he had had it with being treated as a suspect. "Okay—he's a drug addict who overdosed. Why are you asking me about it as if I was his meth supplier?"

"I'm just—"

"Doing your job. Can we get this over with so I can do *my* job?" That wasn't exactly true; it was the weekend and guest hosts handled the show.

Batista glanced at Mond. "We want a copy of all of Ethan Shaw's calls."

"Easily done. The calls are indexed by date and name of caller."

Greg left the room and told Soledad to download a copy of the calls.

"How are you doing in there?"

"Cops two, me, zero. The homicide cop has a laundry list of my sins, all imaginary. The other guy hasn't said a word but he stares at me as if he'd like to stick my head in a toilet and call it waterboarding."

He left Soledad to do the download and returned to Batista and Mond, holding up his hand to block a question from Batista as he walked in.

"I understand that this is a tragedy," Greg said. "I don't know Ethan's personal circumstances but there's probably family out there grieving. It's too bad he couldn't get the help he needed, but there was nothing I could do about that; I didn't really know Ethan. I've given you everything I can. You've held me upside down by my ankles and shook all I know about Ethan out of me."

"What about the money?" Batista asked.

"What money?"

"The money you were paying him."

"For the top-secret information he passed you."

That from Mond.

# 14

Greg stared at Batista with openmouthed surprise. "That's crazy. I've never paid him anything. If someone told you that, they're a liar."

"Actually, it was Ethan who told us," Batista said.

"If he did, he was hallucinating."

"You might say it's a voice from the grave." Batista took a piece of paper he had tucked between the pages of his file and threw it on Greg's desk. "This was found on him."

Greg picked up the paper to read it. The two officers stood up.

An electronic deposit had been made to an Ethan Shaw's bank account for $25,000 yesterday. Hours before he died. As he read the details of the transfer, Greg gripped the paper tighter. He didn't know his bank account numbers by heart but the transfer came from the bank he used.

"What's this supposed to mean? I never gave him anything."

"Actually, you did. The bank transfer tracks back to you. Your account."

"That's impossible. I didn't transfer any money to him."

"Well, Mr. Nowell, you say you didn't, but the transfer came from your account, at your bank. So from my point of view, it was either you or the ghost in the machine who did it." Batista snorted.

"This is insane." Greg stared at the silent Mond. Batista hadn't told him Mond was a federal agent but that tag fit, with the accusation of a secret information exchange. "You think I gave him money for secrets. That's bullshit."

Mond said, "Shaw hacked into a top-secret file and downloaded it. We know he did it for you because he told people he did. The money trail proves that. We want that file."

"That's nonsense—all of it. I don't have a file, I didn't pay him anything. What kind of crap is this?"

Mond said, "The kind of trouble that gets violators life sentences. The kind smart people start plea bargaining on right away."

"We're finished," Greg said. "You people ambushed me with this bullshit. You can do your talking to my lawyer."

Soledad stuck her head in. "Greg, there's a problem."

"What?"

"The cloud files. They're all gone."

"What do you mean?"

"Erased."

"All of our caller files are gone—erased?"

"Just Ethan Shaw's calls."

Mond pulled a small transmitter from his side pocket and said, "Geronimo." He tossed papers on Greg's desk.

"Search warrant," Batista said.

From the entry and outer offices came the sound of doors flying open, a stampede of footsteps, voices yelling, "Federal agents!"

Batista grinned. "You can save your place from being torn apart by giving us what Shaw gave you."

# 15

"Have Mr. Nowell and his staff wait in the reception area," Mond told Batista.

"I'm calling my attorney," Greg said.

"From the reception area," Batista said.

Soledad, Vince, their assistants and the clerical staff were already gathered in the reception area. An officer whose blue jacket said INTERAGENCY was standing between them and the elevator.

"They think Ethan gave me something secret he was working on for the government," Greg told them. "He didn't give me anything or even offer to give me anything."

"How could the calls have been erased?" Soledad asked.

"Not just erased, but it was done with a surgical knife deleting only Ethan Shaw's. Hang on," he said, "I have to make a call."

He went to a corner to get what privacy he could and dialed attorney Liz Tucker. He gripped the phone tight and clenched his teeth as it rang ten times and took him to voicemail. Keeping his tone neutral, he quickly explained what had come down. "Call me as soon as you get this message. I need help."

Liz was the network lawyer for the show. She was smart and re-sourceful, the kind of lawyer that rolled with the punches but then hit back hard. She was also the only attorney he knew, except his tax attorney, who was out of his league with any issue beyond the tax code.

"Ethan Shaw's calls getting erased. How could that happen?" Greg asked Vince, the broadcast engineer.

"Wouldn't take much," Vince said. "It's just a cloud account with a simple password. Every caller is a separate file. Hell, we didn't sct it up to hide it from anyone, just as a convenient place to store the calls in case questions arose later. We only keep them for ninety days anyway, before they are automatically erased. We didn't think a backup was necessary."

Greg was listening but his mind was spinning in the background about the accusation that he had paid Ethan for secrets. Anyone could have erased the calls but transferring money took effort because he was the only one on the account who could have done it. He would check his bank accounts when the feds cleared out but he didn't think they were lying about the money transfer. A lie that easy to check would be stupid.

His paying off Ethan also fit nicely with everything else that had come down—the strange accusation from Ethan, the missing calls, the fact that his show with its known theme of suspicion of overreaching governmental authority would be a perfect place to broadcast evidence of wrongdoing by the government.

If someone wanted to implicate him—frame him—in a stolen-secrets incident, a money transfer to a hacker with a criminal record would quickly put the noose around his neck and kick the chair out from under him.

He had no enemies. No, that wasn't true. No one had actually been threatening him though it had happened in the past. It was hard to be well known and deal with controversial issues and not tick off someone. Even a bunch of someones, but stolen government secrets and clandestine money transfers were way over the top.

Equipment was being carried out and Greg passed a message to Mond through an agent that they had better leave equipment necessary to go on the air or they would have the network going after them.

Batista came out of an inner office. "They're removing computer equipment that has stored information to examine at their offices. They'll let you continue to broadcast until they make a decision about your future."

"That's big of them. While they're making decisions about my future, I'll ask my lawyers to start looking into *their* futures. As far as I know there's still a constitution in this country."

Batista grinned and threw up his hands. "Hey—I'm just the messenger. This is a federal thing. They just wanted me along for window treatment."

"What agency did you say Mond's with?"

"It's on the papers. I never dealt with them before, but feds are all the same when it comes to us local cops. They want us to do their dirty work so they can keep their hands clean."

Batista did another disappearing act. Greg looked at the search warrant. It was issued by a federal judge. The request for the warrant came from Agent Mond, Interagency. Which told Greg nothing.

Soledad said, "This is insane."

"Tell me about it."

# 16

Walking to his apartment building Greg felt as if he had been wrung out, hung up and left out to dry. And paranoid. He called Liz Tucker again and left another voicemail message. It was too early for her to be at her son's wedding and she was good at answering calls, but he was sure she would call the network's general counsel before getting back to him.

He left the studio after the homicide cop, the federal agent and the searchers faded away. The place looked pretty much the same as it did before the search, but it wasn't the same. Things had been lifted up, inspected and put back in a slightly different way. Drawer contents that had been orderly were now a mess and some that were a mess looked more orderly. They had taken everything that could be used to store data on but left the studio able to broadcast.

Greg was relieved that he wouldn't be hosting the show for the next two nights. More than anything else he was angry. And puzzled. Questions swirled in his head like ghosts in an attic.

Money got paid to Ethan from one of his accounts—he had called and got his account balance before leaving the office. There had been a $25,000 electronic transfer to Ethan's account using Greg's account number and password. As simple as that—someone entered his account and transferred money. And Ethan removed top-secret documents from the government. That had to be a given, if for no other reason than the feds were tearing apart his life to find them.

Mond had refused to answer Greg's questions about what evidence they had other than repeating that a receipt for the money transfer was found on Ethan. Mond wouldn't tell him even the subject matter of the materials he claimed Ethan hacked into and gave to Greg. Or the name of the government agency Ethan worked for or hacked into to steal secrets.

Ethan was a hacker who had been in trouble before for illegally accessing forbidden territory. That he'd done it before elevated the odds he'd done it again. Greg didn't know who or what Ethan hacked, but the fact he went to work for the government and had access to top-secret material after being arrested made it a good bet that a federal security agency was Ethan's employer. That Ethan was on the West Coast and most federal agencies were headquartered near D.C. didn't matter. Computer work often was done from regional offices and even from home.

The bottom line was that money got transferred from him to Ethan, Ethan stole secrets, the feds thought Greg paid him to do it and, most important of all, Greg couldn't give them a good reason for the money transfer to refute their suspicion that he paid Ethan for secrets.

Mond said Ethan "told people" he gave secrets to Greg. Who would Ethan tell about stealing secrets? That he committed high crimes and misdemeanors? Was that something hackers bragged about to each other over a beer? Something like, "Hey, guys, wanna know what the CIA is up to this week?"

Another possible twist to Ethan's strange accusation occurred to Greg as he neared the apartment building.

What if Ethan wasn't the one who hacked into his account and transferred the money? What if someone else had led Ethan into believing that he was doing something for Greg? And then someone had hacked into Greg's account and transferred the money to Ethan so Ethan would buy the story. Then Ethan killed himself when he found out the feds were after him.

That theory made as little sense to Greg as the other notion that Ethan thought he killed him and got money from his account.

The "what if's" were still swirling around his head as he entered his apartment building and stopped at the reception desk, where Jose was manning the day shift.

"A woman left a note for you a few minutes ago," Jose said.

"Did she give her name?"

"Nope."

"What did she look like?" Greg asked as he took the note.

"I was on the phone and didn't get a good look. She just dropped the note and left. Not too old, too young."

Greg stared at the message. *Get out—they're coming*

He kept his features blank. "About thirty? Wearing a coat with a hood?"

"Yeah, that's her. Not bad-looking, now that I think of it. And a guy came by to see you earlier."

"Who?"

"Didn't leave his name. Said he was a friend and asked to be let in to your apartment to wait. I told him no way and asked him if he wanted to leave a message and he took off like a bat out of hell."

"What did he look like?"

"Tall, bald; it was that guy with the Jamaican accent that's on your show sometimes. I've seen him on TV. The writer who says aliens abducted and raped him. Know who I mean?"

He was describing Rohan. "I know who you mean."

"He was kind of frazzled, jumpy. I started to ask if he was that writer guy but he shot out of here too fast."

"How long ago?"

"Two hours."

Greg tried Rohan again when he got to his apartment and got the "no longer in service" recording.

What put Rohan into such a panic? What was his relationship to Ethan? Hacking? Rohan had been in a battle with the university for years over his claimed abduction. Had he hired Ethan to hack in?

None of the scenarios between Rohan and Ethan explained how money from his account got to the hacker and why Greg was being accused of having paid for the theft of government secrets.

He heard a knock on his door and peered through the peephole at Mond's face. Greg opened the door and was pushed back by Mond as agents poured in behind him.

Mond shoved papers at him. "Search warrant. Secure him."

Two agents grabbed him and started cuffing him.

"What are you doing? Are you arresting me?"

"Securing you for your own safety and that of the officers." Mond nodded at the agents and they pulled Greg out into the hallway.

A neighbor poked her head out of her apartment, saw Greg cuffed and stared wide-eyed. Jose would be watching on the security monitors. And telling every tenant who came in about it.

Intimidation? Embarrassment? Mond had him cuffed not for control but as a power play because he could.

They hauled out his possessions with a single hand truck. His computer, disks and every piece of paper he had.

Mond had him uncuffed after the hand truck left. He flashed Greg's passport in his face.

"Don't bother trying to leave the country."

"That passport was at my beach house. You went there first." They must have searched it before they even sat down in his office to talk.

"The beach house is also in the papers you just got. Call me if you want to help yourself out by coming clean." He offered a business card.

Greg ignored the card. "My attorney will be doing the call."

"Ask your attorney if he'll do the time, too."

"While you're hounding me, somebody is getting away with whatever Ethan took. That seems to be the plan and you're falling for it."

"Funny thing about that. So far you're the only 'somebody' whose name pops up everywhere we turn, not to mention your pal the hacker fingered you as the guy who drove him to it."

Mond paused on his way out. "You may think you have some news-gathering protection, but you're wrong. Stealing government secrets is punishable by life in prison. Smart people make deals."

# 17

Greg stood in the middle of his apartment feeling violated, even more so than after the search at the studio when they took his business records. This was personal. His home life was in that computer. His financial history. His love affairs. Prides and prejudices. They took everything electronic except his phone. But it wasn't an oversight. Like Rohan said, phones leak. Every call made or received was registered by the phone company and it was easy enough for the feds to capture every communication.

He called Liz Tucker again and got her this time. "I was just going to call you," she said.

"They searched my apartment, been to my beach house, holding my passport; I feel like I'm swirling in some kind of crazy vortex. I woke up in the Twilight Zone."

"More like Dante's *Inferno*. What a horrible mess. Unbelievable," she said.

Liz was blond, anorexic and, unlike Soledad, was airbrushed to blow away the years. She sometimes had the finesse of an ax murderer when dealing with issues she didn't like.

"You should never have spoken to the police. You should have called me."

"They ambushed me. I thought I was just a witness to a suicide. I didn't know I was suspected of stealing secrets until they suddenly dropped the accusation on me. But all they got from me was my jaw dropping because I don't know anything. Liz, they never told me my rights, the Miranda stuff. And they handcuffed me when they searched my apartment."

"They didn't have to give Miranda rights. You get rights before

being questioned if you're arrested. They didn't take you into custody. But they can handcuff someone during a search for officer
safety or just for failing to pass their attitude test. Knowing you,
you probably let the cop know he was a dirt bag."

"Do I have any rights?"

"You have the right to keep your mouth shut. So do it. Don't
answer any questions from anyone, don't talk to anyone but a lawyer
about the case. Cops, newspeople, your bartender or whoever you're
sleeping with, all you give them is a 'no comment.' Better yet, don't
even say that."

"How do we handle this? What's my next move?"

"I don't do criminal cases, so I can't give you any advice about
the allegations. You need a criminal defense lawyer."

"Criminal defense." He hadn't thought of it that way despite the
seriousness of the allegations. He wasn't a criminal.

"You realize, of course, that the network can't be involved in any
form or manner."

He got the message. He was on his own. What kind of crazy
turn had his life taken that he was ending up facing criminal charges?

"Okay, how about some nonadvice."

"I called a classmate who's a prosecutor in the U.S. Attorney's
office in L.A. This is definitely a federal matter; the locals will be
out of it. She hadn't heard anything about the case yet but it sounds
to her that you are in a world of trouble."

"I caught that much myself from the cowboys with badges who
questioned me and tossed my studio and apartment. Is anyone interested in hearing my side of it or should we just start seeing how
many years they'll give me if I save them the money of doing justice and simply plead guilty?"

"Greg, I'm sorry, but I have to tell you that I've already heard
enough of your side of it to know you're in quicksand up to your
neck. Your message said that the dead guy told people he stole secret
files for you, he got a large sum of money from your bank account,
that evidence of your dealings with him has been destroyed."

"It's all bullshit. The only contact I had with the guy was some
calls that were broadcast nationally. And that crazy call last night."

"All of which are missing along with any other possible phone or e-mail contact with him."

"Liz—"

"Please, I'm not accusing you, I'm just stating the obvious. This is one of those cases where there's so much evidence on the table you're going to have to prove yourself innocent rather than hope the prosecution can't prove its case. Even who you are is a strike against you. My friend says you're felony ugly."

"What the fuck is that?"

"Sorry. I didn't mean to drop that on you. It's a prosecutor's expression for people whose appearance fits the crime. If you look like a guy who would rob a liquor store and you're charged with robbing a liquor store, the jury will assume you rob liquor stores. You're an antiestablishment—"

"Talk show host who would plot with a whacked-out hacker to steal secret files from the government and expose them to the world. Did your U.S. Attorney friend also tell you what the penalty is for stealing top-secret stuff?"

She hesitated. "You need to talk to a criminal defense attorney."

"What did she tell you?"

"Treason is punishable by death but can be plea bargained down to as little as five years in prison."

"Hey, that's great. I could broadcast from death row."

"You can't do that."

He took a deep breath and tried pushing his pounding heart back down his throat. "I was joking, Liz, joking. This is insane."

"I'm sorry, Greg. You've always been terrific to deal with. Some celebrities are a pain in the ass but you never talk down to anyone. Your staff loves you, they're all for you at the network."

"But—it's business."

"Yes, it's business. The network has to, uh, stay neutral until the matter is decided in the courts."

"Neutral. Meaning stay the hell away from me. I don't blame them. I feel like I'm trapped in a Kafkaesque story. I woke up this morning felony ugly. I'm in a nightmare."

She hesitated again. "There's one more thing. You're, uh, suspended until things clear up. I'm sorry."

"I'm sorry, too. I need an attorney who handles this type of thing. Know anyone?"

"I don't know him personally, but I've heard Carl Nevers speak at state bar events. He handled the Tom and Maddie case."

Tom and Maddie were a shock-jock team who relied on outrageous stunts to keep an audience. They were busted for paying a hospital employee for information about celebrity medical records with an emphasis on treatment that had anything to do with sex.

Greg said, "They each got three years in jail. Barred from broadcasting for life. Bankrupt. Probably suicidal."

"Probably a win-win for them. The prosecution had a strong case."

"The testimony of a hospital clerk with a heroin habit on fire is a strong case?"

"Sound familiar? Only in your case you won't even be able to get the addict on the witness stand to cross-examine him because he jumped out of a window. Ask yourself this. How do you rebut the word of a dead man who had a receipt for money from you in his pocket?"

He didn't have an answer.

"Nevers is probably at the state bar event this weekend in Santa Barbara. Give him a call first thing Monday morning. The arrest warrant will probably be issued soon. Nevers can arrange for you to surrender and work at getting you bail."

They signed off politely and he hung up. He felt again as if he had been beat on. The worst thing about the call wasn't just her opinion that he was in deep shit but something he picked up from her voice. Liz thought he was guilty. And he couldn't blame her. No question—he was felony ugly when it came to exposing sins of the government. The crime fit him like a glove.

He also remembered something he'd heard about Tom and Maddie and their attorney, Nevers. When they asked the attorney what his fee would be, the attorney's reply had been, "Everything you have."

# 18

He had been set up. Stolen secrets, money transfer, destroyed evidence. A dying declaration that was an accusation. But he was sure Ethan had been used rather than doing the manipulation. The hacker had been too terrified, pressured to the point of breaking on the phone. Greg didn't see Ethan as diabolical enough to commit treason and blame it on him. To the contrary, whistle-blowers who expose secrets want their own fifteen minutes of fame. The frame-up was all too well engineered, too ruthlessly efficient to be the work of a young hacker with a drug problem.

Greg's role was the fall guy, to take the heat when the government found out secret files had been stolen. Who, why and how were out of his reach, but he grabbed at pieces and tried putting them together.

The van had a role. It had been stalking him. Could have killed him but only made an attempt when he turned and started walking toward it, challenging it. What the purpose was of the stalking, he didn't know. To spook him? Get him worried and scared and wondering what was going to happen next because rattled people make mistakes?

The woman was part of it, too. Cryptic messages. A tease. Who was she? Why was she playing games with him? What had she been doing on the street after Ethan took the plunge? How did she know that the fallout from Ethan's death wouldn't end with blood splattered on the street?

He had only one solid piece of information about her other than a general idea of her appearance: She had an inside track about

Mond's plan to search his apartment. And even before that she had warned him that it had just begun.

The "it" was his life being caught up in a maelstrom.

There was something else, too. Something that made his skin crawl.

He slid open the balcony doors and stepped outside to get some air and shake the sense of dread he felt.

Like the sword hanging over Damocles, his encounter as a youth with the unexplainable had left him with both a looming fear and a certainty that someday he would be revisited by the nightmare.

He couldn't explain even to himself why he identified the bad dream he was in with what happened to him decades before, but he sensed a connection with the past. But what was it? How could top secrets and money transferred to a hacker have any connection with a paranormal incident he suffered years earlier?

He had to put his fears from the past aside and concentrate on what he knew was on the table. There was a connection among Rohan, the woman, the van, the money, missing documents, a whirlwind of people and strange events swirling around Ethan.

What had Ethan been involved in? The hacker's hot spot had been the invasion of privacy that electronics interconnecting the world had created. As an electronics geek, Ethan understood better than most people the power and scope of the intrusion.

Greg also feared and fought the control that the electronic invasions had brought to people's lives. A great number of his callers shared apprehension about the electronic invasion. And there had been nothing new and radical about Ethan's conspiracy views, that everyone was being tracked by the Web sites they visited, the movies they saw, the books they read, even the food they ate. Those invasions were common sense, not the stuff of conspiracy theories.

But Rohan had said Ethan had gotten too close. Too close to what? Ethan wasn't just a man on the street talking about how electronics expose individual prides, prejudices, finances and souls. From what Ethan had revealed about his past over the air, he was actively involved in some phase of invasive electronics—obviously with his forced employment at an intelligence agency like the FBI, CIA or one of the other agencies identified by their initials.

Ethan hadn't identified which agency he worked for and was probably barred from doing so by the agency's rules. How Mond's Interagency fit in was a puzzle that Greg hadn't had an opportunity to check out yet. But Mond had left him with a way to do it. His smartphone.

Getting on the Internet, he immediately realized he had been stupid to refuse to take Mond's card. He didn't know if Mond was the man's first or last name or if "Interagency" was the full name of the organization Mond worked for or an abbreviation.

A search of Web sites brought up many types of interagencies but nothing that signaled there was a separate governmental intelligence organization with that name. The most common use of the word was a unit set up among agencies to deal with a specific issue.

Was Mond's Interagency not an actual independent agency, but an organization set up by intelligence agencies to deal with leaks since the Manning and Snowden exposures? Even if that were the case, Greg was surprised that nothing popped up about it on the Internet.

Something was obvious to him.

Everyone knew more than he did. Even the dead.

It was time he got some answers. Time for the worm to turn. He'd start with cold-calling Rohan in Marina del Rey. On his way out of the building he'd ask Jose if he had told Mond about the note from the woman on the funicular.

# 19

A woman he hadn't seen before was manning the front desk when Greg came through on his way to retrieve his car from the parking garage.

"Is Jose around?" he asked as he grabbed his newspaper off the counter.

"Jose's mother is sick. He went to Guadalajara to see her."

"He was here earlier."

"He's gone now."

She looked too well dressed to be manning an apartment house front desk and not laid back enough to sit quietly for eight hours.

"I'm new." She handed him his mail.

He almost asked her how long she'd worked with Mond but shoved the mail into his pocket without looking at it. All he received at the apartment was junk mail. He turned to go to the elevator but spun back around. "You know my place was searched by the police?"

She gave him a blank face and veiled eyes.

"I put some trash in the chute," he said. "Don't let the police look at it unless they have a warrant. I'll be removing it later."

He stepped into the elevator biting his lip to keep from grinning. He hadn't dumped any trash and he knew from a criminal defense lawyer that had appeared on his program years ago that the cops didn't need a warrant to search trash that's been dumped in a public place. He just thought it would be fun if Mond's crew spent hours poring through the whole building's trash to see if they could find something incriminating on him.

"Childish," he muttered as he stepped out of the elevator. He was acting stupid. His gut was tight and he'd just played a dumb joke on the guy who could kick him some more. Liz Tucker was right. He would never pass a police attitude test.

As for the absence of Jose, mothers get sick. Having one in Guadalajara was more a norm in L.A. than having one in St. Louis or Cleveland. But he could think of a good reason for the feds to get rid of Jose and replace him with one of their own people. It made it easier to keep track of Greg if the person behind the security desk had access to the building's security camera monitors.

He got into his car and paused behind the wheel, going through the newspaper for a story about Ethan. He expected to see it on the front page, but didn't find it anywhere. The paper had probably been put to bed before the news broke.

He checked news on the Internet with his phone. No mention of Ethan's death, not even with local news. Ethan might not have been important enough to make national headlines, but a suicidal dive off a downtown high-rise would have been big local news. Had the feds put a blackout on news because Ethan had tapped into something critical? That sounded like a real possibility.

No news about a national talk show host having his office and apartment tossed by federal agents, either. But that had to break soon.

Coming out of the garage, he immediately started looking in his rearview mirror to see if he was being followed and quickly gave up the ghost on that issue. This was Los Angeles, a city that had more cars than people and where freeway traffic was bumper to bumper and door to door. Besides, it wouldn't be hard for the feds to keep track of him in a forest green '73 Jaguar XKE roadster. They were as common as wildebeests on the freeway.

Rohan lived in Marina Del Ray, forty-five minutes from downtown. Forty-five minutes or more from downtown to almost everywhere else in the L.A. basin was his yardstick. Sometimes it took a few minutes less, other times twice as long.

He checked news stations on the way. Not a word about Ethan, himself or stolen secrets. Someone jumping out of a high window while literally on the phone to a national radio host should have been the type of news that got repeated all day, especially when there was no hot item crowding it out. The news blackout was getting eerie. Getting a reporter to hold a story sounded feasible. Getting the whole news media to hold it didn't sound doable. The feds would have had to stop the story by gagging the EMTs, cops and coroner people who showed up at the scene.

He entered "Ethan Shaw" in a news search engine again on his phone, doing it as discreetly as he could. It was illegal to use a phone while driving in California and he wasn't in a mood to deal with another cop.

Nothing. *Nada.* Not only was there no news about Ethan Shaw killing himself, nothing popped up about hacker Ethan Shaw. Zero. Ethan was well known in the hacking culture, had a criminal record, and being a computer guy probably left a lot of footprints on the Internet. Nothing popping up was another surprise when every step Greg took brought more of the unexpected.

He remembered Ethan talking about his Web site, where he had laid out his personal beliefs about the state of the world. But that was also a no-show with a search.

He searched his own name and was relieved to find that he still existed on the planet. But there wasn't a word about one of his callers taking a dive off a tall building after phoning him. Or that he was a "person of interest" in the theft of government secrets.

"Incredible," he said. What could Ethan have gotten into that would make the government put a lid on sensational news in an era where newsflashes flew around the world in seconds and got discussed by millions of people?

He thought about sending out a message to close friends and family that if he suddenly became a "nonperson" to look for him in a CIA-type secret prison, but decided he didn't want to push anyone he cared for into the arms of Mond and Company.

# 20

Greg retrieved the phone off the seat and did a search on Rohan. He got thousands of hits—the abducted author still had his feet on terra firma. The location of his head, though, was questionable. Rohan was always high-strung and accusatory when it came to his abduction. On the earlier telephone recording he sounded like he was being propelled by rocket fuel—or maybe meth from that same batch that the medical examiner said fried Ethan's brain.

The only time Greg had been to Rohan's apartment had been for a gathering of people who shared abduction stories. Rohan had been a little drunk and a lot arrogant, even contemptuous of the others, challenging their claims that they had been abducted, implying that he was the only one who ever had the experience.

Greg found himself stepping in to run interference for those whom Rohan lashed out at. Greg believed nobody had a lock on the truth about strange encounters. He knew that from his own experience. He also believed that listening to others was an art form that many people didn't possess. Rohan was too full of himself to patiently listen to someone else's experiences or opinions.

Tall, skinny, and full of himself, if Rohan hadn't experienced a strange encounter that turned into a money machine for him, he struck Greg as a guy who would have ended up in a corporate cubicle answering customer questions about phone service problems and telling coworkers at break time how they should lead their lives.

On the flip side of the coin, Greg read Rohan's best-selling book and had him on his show for hours talking about his strange encounter and was convinced that the man was telling the truth about having been abducted.

The encounter occurred when Rohan had been a student at UCLA five years earlier. He volunteered for a sleep-dream study experiment for course credit and some cash. The study sounded like something from the acid sixties—an injection of designer drugs to test how they affected dreams.

Rohan claimed that he came out of the overnight sleep-dream experiment with weird flashes of shadowy events and terrible headaches, but nothing he could put a finger on—until nature played a hand and he was struck by lightning while caddying on a golf course.

Nearly getting crispy-fried opened a memory door of what Rohan had experienced that night he took part in the university sleep-dream study—he remembered he had been taken by aliens to a laboratory where his reproductive function was examined. The entities that examined him wore formless masks, gloves and clothes so he couldn't see their precise shape or features, but saw enough to be convinced that they were reptilian.

Rohan then wrote his best-selling book about his experiences, claiming that the professor who oversaw the study, Carl Murad, was a lapdog and procurer for aliens, who controlled the world.

Made well heeled by the success of the book, he brought a lawsuit to force the university to let him examine the sleep study's computer system and records, but lost the case.

With Rohan having no legal way to get the files, Greg wondered if the man had persuaded Ethan to hack into the university's computer system or that of Professor Murad. Rohan was pretty wild about his accusations and even kept challenging Murad and the university to sue him for libel if they were innocent.

Murad, a psychology professor, was also a noted skeptic about abduction claims and had appeared on Greg's show several times to debunk them. Greg invited both believers and skeptics onto the show to state their positions in order to get a complete picture of an issue.

The professor said he had studied hundreds of abduction

scenarios and maintained that most encounters were described as almost exactly the same, what he called a monkey-see, monkey-do syndrome based upon what the abductees had heard others say. He also claimed that abductees mimicked scenes and physical objects they had seen in movies.

Murad's position was that none of the UFO sightings or alien abductions reported had an extraterrestrial basis. The UFO sightings from witnesses whose credibility could not be doubted he simply brushed away as weather phenomena, terrestrial aircraft or other terrestrial occurrences, quoting air force "investigations" for his conclusions.

He debunked most abductee claims with accusations of fraud, lies, hallucinations, psychopathic desires for publicity and every other embarrassing and humiliating explanation he could come up with. Trashing the claims as strongly as he could was his meat and potatoes for selling books and gaining a reputation as an "expert."

On the show Greg asked Murad why he and the university never responded to Rohan by getting a court-issued restraining order. Murad's reply was there was no way anything good would come from suing a student who'd had an unfortunate reaction to a scientific experiment. Rohan would make wild accusations that would turn any proceeding into a media circus. "What would come out of an attempt at a reasonable dialogue would be another best-selling book castigating the university and me," Murad said.

Murad claimed he regretted Rohan had a "pathological reaction" to the medication that was used but that Rohan had not been capable of sitting down and discussing the situation rationally even before he had been medicated.

To Greg, Murad was a cold bastard, but smart and analytical, with a pit bull grab-at-the-throat approach to arguments. There was no question that some abduction claims and UFO and other strange-encounter sightings were faked or even the product of delusion. Murad used the obviously faked claims to attack the credibility of all encounters, no matter how credible the person making the claim was.

It was pretty much the tactic the government had used when

dealing with the unknown or unexplainable—deny and pull the covers over it.

Murad had reproached Greg for what the professor called giving the lunatic fringe a place to express their experiences and opinions.

Greg's reply to him had been that as Hamlet told Horatio after seeing the ghost of his murdered father, there are more things in heaven and earth than Murad realized—including the paranormal.

Ethan. Rohan. Murad. Greg realized something about the triad. He was a connecting link among them.

# 21

Leon waited in a white van parked near Rohan's apartment building. His instructions were to wait in the van until the man he had followed previously on Broadway downtown arrived and went into the building. Once the man entered, he would be given more commands.

He usually didn't focus on potential victims for long even before he began getting instructions from the Voice—when he saw someone he would like to harm but the opportunity didn't arise, he would move on, forgetting about the person.

His blood boiled now as he waited for the man he had tried to run down on the street. The pain that had been inflicted on him for disobeying had not lasted long in his groin, but was so severe he'd screamed aloud as his testicles felt like they were being twisted in a vise.

This time he had no intention of disobeying. But he had a special place in his heart for the man who had caused him the pain and would settle the score in ways that the man could not even imagine in his worst nightmare.

While he waited he booted up his computer tablet, which provided a steady stream of words of praise for him, horror movies, S-and-M porn and the most violent and sadistic action games ever devised. Being denied use of the tablet by the Voice as punishment for indiscretions was as stressful as physical pain.

As he sat in the van playing a computer game that was banned in every civilized country he was not aware that everything he said or did was being captured by cameras. Nor that when he left the van, audio devices and cameras hidden in his clothes and tools kept him under constant surveillance.

He put aside his tablet as his prey arrived. Soon after the man got out of his car and went into the apartment building, Leon got instructions to go into the same building. He got out of the van, carrying a gunmetal gray, tubular device two inches in diameter and a foot long. It had a handle and an on-off button at one end. He wore overalls with the name of a heating and air conditioning company on a small tag on the front and spread out on the back. The business name on the overalls matched the name on the van, but Leon didn't pay attention to the names. The name, overalls and van were all changed frequently by his providers. He paid little attention to detail and did no planning more than a few hours in advance, and those plans usually related to eating, sleeping or being rewarded.

Right now his attention was directed toward the man who had caused him so much pain the night before. The thought of cutting open the man's chest and ripping out his heart while it was still beating made Leon's mouth water.

# 22

Rohan jerked the door of his apartment open as soon as he saw Greg through the peephole.

"Get in here." He pulled Greg in and took a step out to peer down the hallway before closing the door and locking it.

Red-eyed and haggard, Rohan and his clothes needed a pit stop. His dark green A-shirt and running pants were wrinkled and stained, his beard scruffy. He was frenzied and looked ready to launch from whatever upper he had taken to get himself out of a downer.

"You okay?" Greg asked.

"Were you followed? Did you check—watch? They can do it without you knowing. Cameras are everywhere, peeping down from the sky; they don't need choppers."

"Calm down," Greg said. "I wasn't followed, but it doesn't matter. It's not difficult for the government to keep any of us under surveillance."

Rohan hurried to his balcony's glass doors, pushed them open and stepped outside. He took a quick look up and down the street before rushing back inside, sliding the doors closed behind him.

"You shouldn't have come here," he told Greg.

"You called me."

"Yes—yes—you're right, I called you."

"You mentioned Ethan Shaw."

"Yes, Ethan, they got him."

"Who got him?"

A car alarm went off out on the street.

"What's that?" Rohan rushed back to the balcony, pushing the doors open.

"Rohan! It's a car alarm, that's all. It's stopped."

Rohan stared at Greg for a long moment and seemed to deflate. He came back into the room, looking defeated.

"No sleep, I need sleep. I'm confused. Too much shit coming down." Rohan waved at the mess in the apartment. "Too much of everything. I didn't use to have much more than the clothes on my back and a car that didn't run half the time. Now I got money and nothing's right."

The apartment was as confused and cluttered as Rohan's mind—Chinese take-out boxes, dried-out pizza, beer cans and an almost empty bottle of vodka. The room had a chemical, sweet smell. A small burner on the coffee table had whitish chunks next to it.

Rohan looked as if he had spent the night fighting an attack from flesh-eating zombies. Maybe he had. Real ones or those created by inhaling crack cocaine.

"You have to leave," Rohan said. "I got a call. The police are coming; they want to talk to me about you and Ethan. I don't want them to catch you here, they'll try and pin something on me. They're after me, they—"

"How'd you get a call? Your phone's been disconnected."

"My phone's been disconnected?" Rohan stared around, puzzled. "My phone's been disconnected. You're right. How'd I get a call?"

To accommodate the police, the phone company could turn a phone line off so calls couldn't come in and then turn the line back on to allow a call through, but Greg didn't share the observation.

"I need to talk to you about Ethan," Greg said.

"Ethan's dead."

"I know, I saw him commit suicide."

"Suicide—hell no, they killed him." He stared at Greg, wild-eyed. "If you saw them kill him, you must be one of them."

"Rohan—"

Rohan backed off. "Keep away from me!"

"Listen," Greg said softly, "I came because you called me. Ethan called me last night then jumped out of a window of the building across the street. I saw him fall, so did—"

"He was pushed, they killed him."

"Who killed him?"

"They did, the ones that Murad works for, the ones that control everything we do."

He was excited, manic, moving around as if he expected threats to suddenly materialize in the room.

"Were you using Ethan to hack into the university to get evidence of your abduction?"

"That bastard Murad is hiding the names of people he fed to aliens in that sleep program he uses to supply them. The judge wouldn't let me subpoena the list—he's one of them. They've got the cops and the judges in their pocket."

"What did you mean when you said Ethan got too close to them? What's the secret file that Ethan was after?"

Rohan was too wired to stand still. He paced a few steps one way and then back. "They're going to get us, we don't stand a chance. We have to go undercover, figure out—"

"Stop. No one's going to do anything to us if we keep our senses and fight back. We can go to the news media—"

"All controlled by them."

"Who are 'them'? We need—"

"You know who they are," Rohan shouted, "the controllers, the ones in charge, the ones that Murad works for."

"Calm down and listen to me, Rohan, you're talking in circles. We need facts we can back up, not unsupported accusations. Ethan got into a secret file and he or someone else did a money transfer from my bank that I didn't authorize and the feds think I did. How did he—"

The doorbell rang. It sounded like a shot in the room. The two men froze and both looked to the front door.

Rohan said, "The police. They said they were coming."

"Did someone say I was coming? You know of a fed named Mond? Something called the Interagency?"

"You have to get out of here. If they find us both here they'll think we're in it together."

"In what?"

"The back, out the back."

"Tell me what's going on, what you and Ethan were doing."

The doorbell rang again.

Rohan pushed him. "Out the back, the back."

Greg went slowly, trying to get Rohan to focus. "Did Ethan give you a file? Do you know how he got the money from my account?"

"They can't find us together."

It was useless. The man was wasted—mindless and panicked.

Greg followed Rohan through the kitchen to the back door but he hesitated at the door as Rohan fumbled with the deadbolt. His instincts told him not to run but face whatever was coming at him from the police, but Rohan was vibrating and ready to unravel, so he stepped out.

Rohan slammed the door behind him and hurried to the front door as the doorbell rang for a third time. His mind was swirling. It hadn't been on track since he started on alcohol and cocaine to get it into whack.

He jerked the door open to a man in a utility worker's uniform.

# 23

Greg wavered on the landing, trying to decide whether to go down the steps and leave or barge back into the apartment. Getting caught sneaking out the back as if he had something to hide would not just be humiliating but be interpreted by Mond and the police that he was involved in whatever Rohan and Ethan had going.

It was now a given that Rohan had some hacking deal going with Ethan but he hadn't pinned Rohan down about the secret file that Ethan was supposed to have passed to Greg. He was sure Rohan was involved in the scheme.

He heard something—an exclamation from Rohan? He reached for the door handle and gripped it but froze without turning it, not sure what he was hearing. Rohan was so high he could be shouting at the cops or even being cuffed so he wouldn't interfere as they ripped apart the apartment as they had done his.

Greg struggled with whether to leave and fight another day or confront Mond with Rohan there in the hopes of getting Rohan to blurt out the truth. He decided the hell with it—if the police ask Rohan questions about him and Ethan, he wanted to hear the answers.

He opened the door and paused to listen. No sound was coming from the living room. He moved through the kitchen to find the living room empty, the front door closed. Had they arrested him? In and out that fast? Without a wrecking crew searching the place? Not likely. He called Rohan's name and checked the bedroom and bathroom.

Excited voices came through the doors to the balcony that

Rohan had left open. The voices came from the street two stories below. It didn't sound like cops but a crowd.

Greg ran out onto the balcony and looked down. Rohan was lying on the sidewalk, with people gathered around. It looked like neighbors, not police. He was facedown, his head at an unnatural angle to his body, as if his neck had snapped. He wasn't moving; blood was on the concrete next to his head.

A woman kneeling beside him stood up. "There's no pulse."

A teenage boy with his foot on a skateboard pointed up at Greg. "That's him—I saw him throw the man over."

Greg shouted down, "No, you didn't! Not me."

"I saw it!"

"You didn't see me!"

"Call the police," someone yelled and someone else said they'd been called.

Greg backed away from the edge of the balcony and went back inside, half stumbling. Mindlessly, in shock over seeing Rohan's lifeless body and the kid's crazy accusation, he went through the kitchen, out the back door and down the stairs to the parking lot in the rear of the building.

He made his way past the side of another apartment building and to the street beyond. His car was on the street that had the crowd and he wasn't ready to face accusations again.

He wasn't going anywhere, just walking, trying to get his head on right, trying to comprehend what had happened. The kid was right about one thing—Rohan had been thrown off the balcony. The kid was a typical eyewitness who didn't get a good look at the person he saw push Rohan, but now had an image of Greg burned into his head because he'd connected up the two in his mind. An image he would convey to the police as an impartial eyewitness.

Rohan had expected the police to arrive and ask questions about Greg, had opened the door to someone, and now he was dead. Like Ethan. High on drugs and dead from what appeared to be suicide but wasn't, because the skateboarder had seen someone put Rohan over the edge.

Greg realized that besides the kid's testimony, his own finger-prints were in the apartment; his car was nearby on the street. Some-one in the crowd might have recognized him or would when there came an explosion of publicity about him: two deaths and stolen secrets.

He was going to be arrested. That was now a certainty. Going from being the host of a nationally broadcasted radio show to be-ing arrested for murder. In a matter of hours. It made no sense. He was being framed but by who? Why? Why was the sky suddenly fall-ing? The sands were shifting under his feet so fast he was being kept off balance. Had a strange encounter over twenty years ago come alive to haunt him? *Were they back?*

*Crazy crazy crazy.* He was up to his neck with murder and trea-son and who the hell knew what else. He felt as if his feet were in quicksand and he was being sucked in—not slowly but in big gulps.

Ethan. Rohan. What did they get into? What the hell did they unleash? Why did they get him involved with a money transfer? Questions pounded in his head. None of it made sense. Not the lack of publicity about Ethan's death. Not the clamp-down on what should have been sensational reports about a bizarre death in one of the biggest cities in the country; not Ethan's being turned into a nonperson by wiping him off the Internet.

He dialed Liz Tucker and got her voicemail. She was either dodg-ing the call or was at her son's wedding with her phone turned off.

"Liz—things are getting worse. Something else has happened. I need to contact that lawyer you mentioned." He hung up, his mind swirling. She told him that the lawyer was at a bar meeting. What was the lawyer going to do? Tell him to turn himself in? Arrange for him to surrender? Try to get bail? Do they even give bail in mur-der cases? Rohan claimed Ethan was murdered. Was he going to face two murder charges? Murder for hire, in Ethan's case?

Forget proof. Liz already told him there was enough to hang him. Forget bail for sure if he faced two murder charges. He would rot in jail for the years it took a sensational case to get to trial. Help-less while he lost everything he worked for. Everything. His repu-tation. His freedom.

He had walked two blocks from the apartment building when he heard sirens. A police car with flashing lights was coming toward him and he stiffened and stopped walking, not daring to invite a bullet in his back by turning and running.

The cop car made a left turn and disappeared from sight in a direction that could take it to Rohan's apartment building.

The next siren he heard would be one coming for him.

A car pulled up beside him. A red Mini Cooper convertible with the top down and a woman behind the wheel.

She said, "The first thing you have to do is get rid of your cell phone. They let you keep it because there's a leash attached to it."

The woman who had been in the doorway when Ethan's body was on the sidewalk.

The woman passing cryptic messages to him.

# 24

S he was about thirty, slender, and had short chestnut hair with caramel and gold highlights. Green-framed sunglasses and a pink cap with a peace icon on it complemented her smooth rosy complexion and seemed to even go with the snazzy little red convertible.

She wore a white lacy pullover and black linen pants. Her clothes were snappy casual, not what one would wear to a formal office atmosphere like that of a lawyer or doctor or even to lunch at a Melrose restaurant, but wrinkled casual, just a little dressier than those of the Silicon Valley young Turks who ruled the computer world while dressed in T-shirts and jeans.

She struck him as a professional but in a nonconventional business, maybe even a teacher, a no-nonsense one, businesslike with confidence but reserved—even a bit on the grave side.

Her long slender fingers had no nail polish and were neatly trimmed to make sure they didn't get in the way of working with a computer keyboard. And because Ethan was a computer guy, he took her to be part of the computer world, too.

There was an edge to her, tension, as though she was holding back from hitting the gas and leaving him in her car's dust, but that may have been because more sirens were blaring. The sirens were electrifying. He had to fight the urge to run.

"Who are you?" he asked.

"A friend of Ethan's. He got me into trouble, too."

"What kind of trouble?"

"Your kind. What you've been battered with since Ethan's death. The fallout from cracking a secret program."

A helicopter was in the distance, closing in on the area.

She said, "That's probably a police chopper. I saw people crowding around a person on the sidewalk. Unconscious, I think. Maybe it's a medevac."

"Rohan. He's dead."

"Rohan?"

"The guy on the street. He got thrown off of his balcony."

"Someone killed him?"

"A kid on the street saw me come onto the balcony and thinks I did it."

She gave him a look.

"I didn't. Rohan pushed me out the back door when he thought the police had arrived to question him. I came back in when I heard something and stupidly walked out onto the balcony."

"Who killed him?"

"I don't know, the place was empty when I came back in. I stepped out on the balcony and a kid on the street started yelling. He thought I was the one who threw Rohan off. Right now I'm puzzled as to why you don't know Rohan but you have been driving around his place."

"I'm following you."

"Why are you following me?"

"I told you, Ethan got me into trouble. He hacked into something that has started a firestorm."

More sirens.

She said, "I'm leaving. Get in or stick around and talk to the police. It's your call."

He climbed in.

# 25

He looked her over after they pulled away from the curb and he checked the traffic to the rear. No police cars. She had a serious cast to her features. Maybe it was a permanent demeanor. She struck him as a person who didn't laugh very often, but then again there hadn't been anything to laugh about lately.

She hadn't said much, but Greg was already sure that she wasn't being completely open to him. So far she had told him just enough to place herself in the same predicament as he was in and for the same reason—Ethan Shaw. That explained almost nothing and made him certain she was playing him for sympathy and comradeship. He didn't know if she was instinctively cautious or if she had something to hide. Or thought he had something to hide. Probably all of the above.

She took her eyes off the road to shoot him a quick look. "I'm Ali, for Alyssa Neal."

"How did you get my name?" he asked.

"Ethan. I told you, he is—was a friend."

Greg said, "You may know Ethan, but you're not a friend of his. His friends spend their nights cracking open cybersecurity and their days sleeping off whatever they smoked while they were hacking. Besides, your car is spotless. Their cars look slept in—because they often were."

"The car's borrowed and you're right, I wasn't really a friend of Ethan's, not in a social sense."

"What were you doing on the street last night, hiding in a doorway while Ethan was on the sidewalk?"

"Same thing you were doing, I suppose. Gawking. Ethan was planning on talking to you. He was going to wait for you to come out of your building. I went there to talk to him about the mess he got me into. We worked together."

"Where?"

"NRO. Familiar with it?"

"National Reconnaissance Office. The agency that controls sur-veillance satellites for all our intelligence agencies. Spies in the sky watching what the North Koreans and Iranians are cooking. What's going on? What was Ethan doing? What are you up to? What did you people steal? Why's it been dumped on me?"

She met his eye for a moment before looking back at the road. Hers were green and inquisitive. Intelligent eyes. Grave. The worldly eyes of someone who played it close to the chest, like a poker player hiding a hand. She put Greg in mind of a cat—sleek, stealthy, not housebroken. Cats were smarter than dogs—or maybe just slyer—more of a mystery and more dangerous.

She nodded at a patrol car coming in the opposite direction. "While we're deciding whether to trust each other, we need to get rid of your phone. And find somewhere to talk where we don't pass one of them every few minutes."

"If this were a movie, I'd leave the phone in a taxi and let the police chase after it all day."

"Getting a taxi driver to cooperate would take some effort." She pulled up next to a curbside trash bin. "Will this do?"

He took the chip out of his phone and ground it under his heel on the curb, picked it back up again. He kept the chip and threw the phone into the can.

He got back into the car. "Stop at the next can."

He checked the chip to see if it looked damaged enough not to be reused. It looked reasonably battered.

"You're really paranoid," she said.

He gave her a harsh laugh. "Like hell I am. I used to be paranoid, now I'm just running from reality."

He spotted a city water drain along a curb and told her to pull over. He tossed the chip down the drain and got back in the car. "Turn left here."

"Where are we going?"

"A different direction than where we were when I got rid of the phone." Her phone was in the center divider. "What about your phone?"

"I bought it an hour ago with cash. And bought the chip at a different store. With cash. Where do you want to go to talk?"

"My car is back near Rohan's."

She shrugged. "If that's what you want, I can drop you off near it."

"No, I'm just thinking out loud. There might be video surveillance in front of Rohan's building. It would show me coming in and whoever killed him coming in behind me."

"I doubt it would show him getting pushed off a balcony, but there might be a camera at the building across the street."

"No building across the street, just a small park. Even if there was a video, it might get erased. They—whoever *they* are—managed to erase the recordings of my broadcasted conversations with Ethan. I wouldn't bet a surveillance video being back there unless it's been edited to exclude the killer. Leaving me on it, of course."

"This is getting complicated."

He scoffed. "Getting complicated? Two people I know are dead, I've been framed for treason and murder, a strange woman is leaving me cryptic messages and hiding me from the police. Hell, this isn't complicated. It's a living nightmare. And I still haven't heard your story. It'll top things off nicely if you tell me you're a serial killer."

"A serial idiot is more like it."

He said, "Turn right."

"To?"

"Venice Beach."

She did a double take, gawking at him. "Are you joking? You want to go to Venice Beach? The place is a zoo on the weekends. There'll be a million people there. And police up the yin-yang."

"Good. It's better than an isolated spot where killers or cops and us are the only ones around."

He noticed a spray can next to her purse on the center divider. He thought it was hair spray at first glance but realized it was wasp spray.

"For pests," she said.

# 26

Ali tried to keep from glancing at Greg as she drove although she didn't think he'd notice because he appeared to be concentrating on whether they were being followed. Without making it obvious, he casually glanced at the traffic behind them and coming in from the sides. She was certain he was also concentrating on figuring her out.

She wore her hair in a chin-length straight bob that was easy to care for and that suited her because she was too busy and impatient to spend time dealing with it. She was fortunate that she had a fair skin tone with natural color in her cheeks that permitted her to get away with little makeup because she also had no patience for cosmetics.

She had thick, naturally groomed brown eyebrows over her light green eyes, which gave a frank stare and didn't break their hold quickly to wander, a look that made her appear blunt and intelligent but not socially outgoing; not cold but a little distant, even a little cautious and conservative in her personal dealings. She wouldn't be very approachable if she was sitting alone in a lounge because she'd most likely have her head buried in her tablet or phone, working on some problem she'd dealt with that day at work.

Her father was a civil engineer who designed and built environmentally friendly waste plants, her mother a high school computer science teacher. Between them her heritage was high-tech from the get-go but she tried to keep her head out of computers enough to see the world around her, though wasn't always successful and came across as preoccupied or even aloof.

She had a marriage straight out of college that lasted only a year and had ended a three-year relationship recently as she and the man grew apart.

Part of the problem with her terminated relationship was that she had been a little aloof even to her lover because she didn't easily share herself. She blamed that characteristic on being an only child—she'd heard that an only child often had difficulty sharing with others because he or she hadn't experienced the give-and-take of having to share with siblings.

Observing Greg out of the corner of her eye, she thought he was a nice-looking man but not easy-going, not at the moment, at least. Like her, he was grim and tense for good reasons, though she thought she didn't show that she was wound as tight. He reminded her of a crouching tiger facing an enemy that was trying to back him into a corner.

She guessed his age as a bit older than her, maybe forty. He appeared trim and fit, a person who frequented a gym and watched what he ate and drank.

Although she didn't know how he usually dealt with people, she'd listened to his show and her impression was that he was calm and relaxed, thoughtful and even supportive toward his callers, at least on the air. He seemed to have a real concern for their problems. She believed that empathy was most common in people who had suffered hurts and losses themselves and wondered what his loss had been.

She saw none of the ego or superiority she believed would come from a man who was a national personality. But at the moment she felt as if he was analyzing her as a lawyer would a hostile witness. He wasn't concealing very well that he didn't trust her, but she couldn't blame him for that.

If he had his suspicions about her, she also had them about him. Her world today was not the same as it was yesterday and she was sure it would be even more different tomorrow. Shadows were everywhere; what was real and true could be illusions.

# A HIDDEN WORLD, GROWING
## BEYOND CONTROL

The top-secret world the government created in response to the terrorist attacks of September 11, 2001, has become so large, so unwieldy and so secretive that no one knows how much money it costs, how many people it employs, how many programs exist within it or exactly how many agencies do the same work.

These are some of the findings of a two-year investigation by *The Washington Post,* which discovered what amounts to an alternative geography of the United States, a Top-Secret America hidden from public view and lacking in thorough oversight.

The investigation's other findings include:

- Some 1,271 government organizations and 1,931 private companies work on programs related to counterterrorism, homeland security and intelligence in about 10,000 locations across the United States.
- An estimated 854,000 people, nearly 1.5 times as many people as live in Washington, D.C., hold top-secret security clearances.
- In Washington and the surrounding area, 33 building complexes for top-secret intelligence work are under construction or have been built since September 2001. Together they occupy the equivalent of almost 3 Pentagons or 22 U.S. capitol buildings—about 17 million square feet of space.
- Many security and intelligence agencies do the same work, creating redundancy and waste.

- Analysts who make sense of documents and conversations obtained by foreign and domestic spying share their judgment by publishing 50,000 intelligence reports each year—a volume so large that many are routinely ignored.

# 27

The Interagency's Los Angeles facility was an inconspicuous suite of offices at the back of a dead-end corridor in a subterranean level, a vast concrete catacomb under the cluster of federal buildings that stood between North Spring Street and North Alameda. The Metropolitan Detention Center, a high-security federal lockup, was conveniently located nearby.

A simple sign at the entrance to the corridor in the network of tunnels that led to the Interagency office's entrance said, Authorized Personnel Only. The sign gave no clue as to who was authorized and no indication as to which of the thousands of federal agencies was housed there. The door at the end of the corridor had a simple sign that said, Interagency, with lettering so small it was difficult to read from a distance.

Nor did the Interagency's off-the-beaten-path location give a clue that the agency was in fact one of the most powerful, and secretive, organizations in the government. The other federal resources in that area of the underground complex were not the offices of high-profile federal agencies like the FBI, U.S. Marshall or department of this or that, but the worker-ant variety—the building and maintenance units that did everything from providing lights, water and heat to the offices, to sweeping the floors.

The choice of location in Los Angeles was not unlike that of the headquarters of the opaque agency in the Pentagon. The Interagency there was also located in a subterranean corridor with no outlet, but the odds of bumping into it by accident were much more remote than bumping into one of its branch offices: there were eighteen miles of corridors in the vast Pentagon structure.

Like its branches, the only close neighbors of the Pentagon headquarters facility were supply and utility rooms, with the foot traffic that passed by the dead-end corridor being composed almost entirely of office maintenance workers, none of whom went down the hallway because the agency took care of its own janitorial needs.

An AUTHORIZED PERSONNEL ONLY sign similar to the L.A. version was posted conspicuously at the front of the Pentagon corridor. Again, there was a simple INTERAGENCY sign at the office entrance. The offices had even more stringent security than that required to get into the inner chamber of the Secretary of Defense.

With over three thousand federal and privately hired agencies in ten thousand locations nationwide dealing with national security, it wasn't difficult for the Interagency to stay below the radar.

Megan Novak, an Interagency analyst, hurried down the corridor leading into the Los Angeles facility. She stopped in front of a door where a camera permitted a security officer inside to identify her with a facial recognition program despite the fact he had had coffee with her in the break room dozens of times.

She next looked into the retinal-scanner eyepiece, where a beam of infrared light so low she didn't detect it shined into her eye to verify the pattern of blood vessels with that stored on the scanner's database. Barring accident or eye disease, capillaries in the eye are unique like fingerprints and stay pretty much the same over a person's lifetime, making an eye scan a highly effective identification tool.

The facial and eye scan, both of which had been compromised by clever intruders at other facilities in the past, only got her into a windowless vestibule, where she placed her palm on a DNA scanner to verify her identity a third time. Her DNA got her past the entrance and into the inner sanctuary, a long, straight corridor with offices on each side and the office of the regional director at the end.

Novak was the best surveillance specialist in the region and had gotten a call to get to the office ASAP. Like most Interagency analysts, she had a military intelligence background, having joined the army and becoming an MP before transferring to Army Intelligence.

She came to the agency after years of establishing that she was the type who did a good job, was comfortable doing the assignments she was given without being overly inquisitive and didn't question orders. The mission statement for the agency was simple and allowed as little light to radiate through as the agency itself did—protect and defend the nation's security, but do it covertly to protect the agency's mission.

There was a vague understanding that the agency operated under the auspices of the National Security Council, an organization that itself is rather ambiguous because the council is chaired by the president and members include the vice president, secretary of defense, chairman of the Joint Chiefs, and the like, all of whom had in common no time or interest individually or as a team to administer a small, rather autonomous, even anonymous, agency located in subterranean offices down shadowy corridors.

The ambiguous, undefined connection to the White House was inferred mostly by the security clearance the agency personnel held.

There are three security clearances: confidential, secret and top secret. The highest security clearance is top secret—and it's not a very exclusive club, as close to a million Americans have that clearance based upon a supposed need for access. Edward Snowden, who unleashed the contents of a Pandora's box of spying, had a top-secret clearance. Considering how lax the government can be, he just might still possess it.

But top secret is not the greatest access to secrets. Two more levels increase access to the most sensitive documents. One is top secret/sensitive compartmented information, or TS/SCI. TS/SCI provides clearance to especially sensitive information, but it is not a blanket clearance for all extremely sensitive information; rather, it is access only to a designated range of information, which is why it is called "compartmented."

Yellow white is the second category, providing greater access to secret documents. Designated civilian and military personnel who work closely with the president must pass a background check even more stringent than that required for a top-secret clearance because they may be in a position to hear or overhear the most sensitive military and national security information.

Interagency operatives had to qualify both on top secret/sensitive compartmented and yellow white criteria and even a step beyond: They carried a clearance of top secret/sensitive uncompartmented. That designation permitted them access to about anything they wanted to see anywhere in the country.

If the president could see it, so can Interagency operatives.

Because of the stringent requirements, psychological and lie detector tests, emphasis on prior intelligence agency or military experience, any observant person around Interagency operators would wonder if everyone working for the agency was stamped out of the same mold. And of course they essentially were. Novak had pretty much the same attitudes about life and service to her country that every other Interagency analyst possessed.

As a surveillance specialist, her job was to use the vast spy apparatus of the United States intelligence agencies, the NSA, CIA, DIA, NRO and others, to track people the agency wanted located.

The stated focus of the agency was terrorism—domestic and foreign. That gave the agency a long reach into the lives of just about everyone on the planet because "terrorism" involved people.

As the NRO brags about its satellites that nothing is beyond their reach, the Interagency's private boast was that there was nowhere to hide from them.

As Novak entered the outer office of the regional director, the director's assistant raised his eyebrows and told her to go on into the executive office.

"Mond is waiting."

She knew why the eyebrows were up. It was a gesture between sympathy and wonder. Mond was a well-known name in the agency even though she had never met him and didn't know if he had ever been in the Los Angeles office before. Or even if Mond was a first or last name, though she assumed it was his family name.

He was known in the agency for handling only the most critical security breaches, ruptures with national and international consequences. The sympathetic lift of eyebrows came from the fact that Mond was legendary for being utterly ruthless and for having zero tolerance for mistakes or the inability of subordinates to keep up with his fast pace.

What she had heard about him from people she'd met during training sessions in Washington whirled in her head as she headed for the door. The word was that his office was totally barren: no pictures on the wall, no paperwork, no personal items, not even a laptop or a pencil in the room—or even a landline phone. There was a desk, but no one knew if the drawers had anything in them.

All of which said something about him but no one was quite sure what that was. Not even people in human resources or the payroll department could provide information for the rumor mill because neither had a file on him.

No one knew if he was married or divorced, had a girlfriend, boyfriend, BFF, any friend at all, or even a dog, cat or parakeet or had sex with anyone. The questions were rhetorical because everyone assumed that like his office, his personal life was completely barren.

He had machine-like efficiency that was almost robotic because he lacked any patent sign of aggression or passion. An early supervisor described him as an artillery round—a faceless projectile that went directly toward a target without ever deviating. No one had ever seen him smile.

Novak paused and took a breath before opening the door. The old tale about the lady and the tiger and the consequences of opening the wrong door flashed but she told herself she had nothing to fear. She was good at her job. And America's spy agencies were outstanding at collecting every teeny-weeny piece of metadata from its citizens.

# 28

Venice Beach's boardwalk had walkers, joggers, jugglers, roller skaters, skateboarders, break dancers, fortune-tellers, pumped muscles, waxed bodies, body hair and more tattoos, nose rings and tongue diamonds per square foot than anywhere else on the planet. It had art for every taste, great, bad and some inspired while the artist was under the influence of any number of hallucinatory substances, intoxicating ice cream, legal and street bud, trashy sex stuff and tourists with money for buying all that crap. It was a circus with two-legged animals. A freak show. Counterculture. The boardwalk had everything but boards.

Greg and Ali drove in silence and parked the car in a lot. They got away from the car quickly, as if it had been infected with something contagious by being filmed by street cameras along the way. And there surely was a camera in the parking lot, Ali said.

They walked on a wide concrete path with sand and ocean on one side and stores on the other.

Greg kept his mouth shut until they hit the boardwalk. Now he had urgent questions that needed quick and honest answers before a black helicopter with men in battle gear from an unidentifiable military unit swept down and grabbed him and he disappeared into that Area 51 hotel where there's no checkout.

He needed to know the real reasons she had been stalking him and was now hiding him from the police—along with herself—but decided to start with the big picture rather than jump on her about what she and Ethan had been up to.

He also had instant distrust for anyone connected to Ethan or

Rohan. He needed to avoid showing it until he got what he could out of her. That meant using finesse and diplomacy in dealing with her.

"What were you and Ethan up to that got the feds and every other cop in L.A. on my ass?" he asked.

So much for diplomacy.

She gave him a look. "That's a nice friendly start."

"Sorry. I guess I should start by saying that I don't know you, and from what little you've told me, you're in league with the devil and I should ask why the hell you and your pal got me into this mess. Like I said, what were you and Ethan up to that has the sky coming down on my head?"

She gave him an aggrieved smile and took his arm above the elbow. "Why don't we start with you wiping that anger off your face? You look like an angry husband about to hit his wife. People are staring."

He smiled. "That okay?"

"Like a shark grinning at a swimmer. But in regard to your question, you need to know a little about what Ethan and I did at the agency. The agency's mission is to look into places which our country has been barred from. We need to look because the reason a facility is being camouflaged is almost always that it's being used for a purpose that's averse to our interests and averse to the peaceful interests of the rest of the world, too.

"We point our cameras and equipment from satellites down at terrorist camps, Iranian nuclear bomb projects, North Korean missile sites or anywhere else we've been denied access. Most targets know we're looking for them, so they try to hide their activities. That's where I come in. I examine photos of the targets and of things that might be connected.

"Let's say you were trying to find where a secret military or nuclear facility in North Korea or Iran was located. Using satellite cameras, you could easily follow the flow of trucks carrying equipment and parts down freeways from the factory to the facility, but the people we're spying on know that. So the rogue nation will disguise the movements. It's a game. They know we're spying on them, we know that they know and it all comes down to who's the cleverest."

"Sounds like how drug runners and the cops operate."

"I suppose so. My job as an analyst is to find the facility by figuring out how the flow of equipment and supplies has been disguised and then follow the materials to the facility. Thousands of photos would be shot from satellites flying over the region each day. A computer quickly goes through the photos, tagging ones that need further examination by human analysts."

"So you look for something suspicious."

"Exactly. Let's say there are photos of a large truck going down a narrow road off the beaten track. Because it's not an ordinary event, the computer tags them. The photos then come to us to do further checks. It might turn out the truck is carrying hay bales, but on closer inspection something might not jibe.

"A clue may be the brand of truck, which could turn out to be one used by the military rather than farmers or merchants. Sometimes even the tires on a truck are a clue. Trucks that carry hay don't need tires capable of carrying super-heavy objects, but those transporting materials to a nuke or missile silo would."

"The balance of world power comes down to tire size."

"Maybe even tire pressure."

He shook his head. "Even tire pressure." Electronics had opened up a mindboggling array of super-spy apparatus that could be and was used on everyone, even the citizens paying the bill for the equipment. The NRO kept track of tire pressure and everyone on the planet not only by peering down from eye-in-the-sky satellites, but by checking communications that came through its satellites; like the NSA, it monitored phone calls, tweets, e-mails or Internet sites visited.

The CIA, FBI and dozens of other intelligence agencies have boots on the ground everywhere, gathering information, sucking it in, filling vast electronic storage vats with information about everything everyone does every day, but no agency except the NRO is capable of doing so much spying so completely and so clandestinely because no one can monitor its satellites.

"What did Ethan and you get into at the NRO that can get us thrown into prison for treason?"

"Ethan, not me. The only time I ever saw him was at briefings in Virginia. Ethan was a cracker that got caught and went to work for the government testing how secure their systems are."

A cracker was hacker-speak for a person who breaks into computer systems illegally. Some called them black hat hackers. Greg had had all colors of hacker-crackers on his show.

"I worked on the same project as Ethan but in a separate department. I did analysis of pictures while he was involved with testing the system to make sure it was secure. That project is only classified secret, not top secret. Whatever he hacked into wasn't just top secret in terms of its contents, the existence of the program itself wasn't even supposed to be known outside of those directly working on it."

"What's the program—the one he hacked?"

"I don't know." She gave him a look. "The feds think you do."

"They need to get their thinking straight. You must know something about it if the authorities think you were involved with him."

"Everything that goes on at the NRO is kept on a need-to-know basis even within projects, so unless you're working on the same, exact thing, you don't know what anyone else is doing. That's especially true for Ethan and me because we work from home and, like I said, only saw each other at meetings. The NRO is headquartered in Virginia. We went there once a month for a briefing."

"You work on top-secret materials from home?"

"Secret only. We can access files designated secret and work them at home but alarm bells go off if you try to download them. That way there's no danger if your computer gets stolen. For top-secret projects we have to go into the L.A. field office and use their computers."

It occurred to him that as a hacker it might not matter where Ethan worked—he could hack from anywhere he could get his hands on a computer.

"I need to know what went on at the NRO with Ethan."

"Like I said, we worked on the same program, but not doing

the same job. I'm an analyst who studies results; Ethan was a hands-on cracker who tested and designed security shields. He was also a program writer, which made him even better at it than most hackers. I can tell you this about what we worked on—it's a project creating a superfast, quantum Internet that can be accessed by all the country's security agencies, the CIA, FBI, NSA, Defense, army, the whole nine yards."

"That program is public knowledge. A guy from MIT has talked about it on my show."

"I know, but what we're doing to make it secure is secret, which is why I can't say more about it. Besides, that's not where the leak is. This thing with Ethan started when I was back at NRO headquarters in Chantilly for a briefing. I had drinks after the meeting with a guy who thought he could come on to me by telling me about the ultra-secret program he was working on." She hesitated and looked around.

A chopper overhead was going out to sea.

"Coast Guard," he said. "What's the program he bragged about?"

"The most I can tell you is that what he talked about is beyond my comprehension. It was so weird. I thought it was BS, bar talk he made up to impress women. He called it the God Project."

"The God Project. What's its purpose?"

"I don't know. I really don't. But Ethan did. The moment I told him about it he got excited. He said he'd heard rumors about it from other hackers. It intrigued him because it was the most secret project in a place where secrets swirl around as you walk down an office corridor."

"That would be the Holy Grail to hackers," Greg said. "So you know nothing about it? Not even the subject matter?"

"The guy told me that they were creating a program that was the closest thing to playing God that had ever been done. He said that the security shield was so far advanced it was impenetrable, like nothing that had ever been conceived before. And, like you just said, to a hacker a security shield that no one had ever pierced is a Holy Grail. It's like a mountain climber getting a shot at the highest unclimbed mountain. Ethan was an addict, you know."

"I know. I barred him from the show because he came on high."

"I meant an addiction to hacking. All the good ones I've met are hopeless addicts. They're driven insane when they can't get access to a site. They have to break in and then beat their chests by letting the world know they did it."

"He broke into the God Project?"

"I'm sure that's what all the excitement is about. I got tangled into it because I sent Ethan an e-mail asking him not to tell anyone I'd mentioned the existence of the project to him. Shame on me. Incrimination by e-mail like all those dumb politicians who shoot themselves in the foot."

"What was Ethan going to talk to me about last night?"

"I couldn't get anything rational from him but I gathered that he wanted to talk to you about what he'd cracked into. Getting the information out to the world, I guess. He was going to wait for you to leave the building after the show. I went there to confront him. I wanted him to give the file back before we got arrested."

"How do you know the government found out about the file?"

"That's easy. Even if you succeed in hacking into a super-secure site, you have to get in and out fast because the entry will send off alarm bells. It may take a while for them to find out who made the entry, but they would have quickly found out the site had been accessed."

She wasn't telling the truth. Not all the truth, he was sure of that. He believed what she said about Ethan, but not that she was the innocent bystander she claimed to be. She struck him as too sharp, too perceptive to fall from grace so easily. But so was he and they were both on the run.

It was also a sure thing that she didn't completely believe or trust him, either. The money transfer and Ethan's accusation over the phone were pretty strong evidence to others that he was more involved than he'd let on.

"Why did Ethan implicate me in this thing?" he asked.

She faced Greg. "I assume because you and he made a deal to get out to the world revelations about the NRO treading on our civil liberties."

"He told you that?"

"No, but in a way your friend Mond did." She shrugged. "The NRO, NSA, even the CIA have hackers working out their sins by using their talents for the government. When Ethan suddenly dropped from sight a couple of days ago and rumors started swirling that he had gotten into something big, I got a hacker to show me how to access the NRO's internal security site. Strange as it sounds, it's one of the least protected areas on the agency's computer system because it's administrative, not a working project. But everything concerning internal security goes through there, including Mond's reports to his boss. That's how I knew they were on to you, that your apartment was going to be searched."

"You give me tight jaws every time you connect me with Ethan and stealing secrets. If you can't believe I wasn't involved in anything with Ethan we might as well part company right now. The first time I heard about the God Project or that he worked at the NRO is from you."

"You got no information from Ethan?"

"I got nothing from Ethan except the quagmire I'm drowning in."

"Why do they believe you did?"

"Because twenty-five thousand dollars was transferred from my bank account to Ethan."

"All right. How do you explain that?"

"I don't know who did it but how it was done is easier to guess. It wouldn't take much for a good hacker to transfer money between accounts. And whoever did that could have also accessed my broadcast archives and erased Ethan's calls to my program. We had zero security except a password. And it wouldn't be hard for someone who claims she's not a hacker but seems to be able to crack even the internal security site at one of the world's most secretive spy agencies."

She grinned. "Touché. But I didn't do it."

He stopped and faced her. "You're lying. You knew about the bank transfer; it would have been in Mond's reports."

# 29

Novak sat in the operation room at a control position that faced a wall-size electronic map of the greater Los Angeles region. The geographical area covered by the map was about fifty miles long by twenty-five miles wide. Hemmed by ocean, mountains and desert, the region was larger in physical area than Rhode Island and had a population of over fifteen million people.

The purpose of the display was to give a bird's-eye view of people, places and events. Calling the big screen the war board was Novak's idea, an exaggeration but it worked well with her rigid military mind-set.

From her position she could zoom in at any place on the display and convert from map to satellite not unlike Google Maps, but with many more options and much more precision. With the press of a button she could bring up live feeds from all around the world.

Satellite imaging was important, particularly when it could be directed to a particular area by planning ahead. However, when tracking a subject on the move, cameras on the ground and overhead carried by planes and drones were usually more effective.

The average American had little idea of how frequently they were filmed by a camera during the course of a day. A person living, working or going to school in a metro area was filmed an average of two hundred times a day as they left their homes and went by cameras at buildings and parking lots; out onto the street, past gas stations and convenience stores, ready tellers, strip malls and big malls; getting tracked by traffic control and traffic violation cameras and so on, ad infinitum. But they were lucky they don't live in the UK—in London, the average person is viewed over three hundred times a day.

Despite the vast array of filming being done by satellites soaring around the planet and the millions of cameras on the ground, not everything was being filmed everywhere all of the time. Most cameras on the ground were closed circuit TV. There was an increasing effort by the government to have the capacity to bring CCTVs online wherever they were. Any of those brought online could end up on the war board.

Which ones to bring online was guesswork for Novak because she didn't know the exact route the suspects were taking. The requests to bring the CCTVs online to view the screen took time to process because the cameras could belong to a variety of different government agencies or security businesses, from traffic cams to ATM machines.

Once Novak had an idea of where to search, she had the ability to bring online CCTVs, drones, planes and satellites and display them on the war board, making it hard for even a mouse to avoid surveillance.

If the purpose was to take the subject into custody, a press of a button showed the location of every federal, state and local law enforcement agency in range for a takedown, though in almost every case the Interagency used only its resources for dealing with the apprehension and interrogation of suspects.

Mond had ordered a satellite surveillance of the street in front of Rohan's apartment when they realized from Greg's route and attempt to contact Rohan that he was on his way there. But the tracking of Greg Nowell had begun much earlier, as soon as Mond and his search team walked out of the broadcasting studio. Left behind in every room were miniature film and sound devices. The building's elevators and hallways were also bugged with sound because the security cameras used by the building did not have audio.

The same procedure was followed when Mond had Greg removed from his apartment. Cameras were placed so his movements were tracked in every room—even bathrooms, which were a favorite place for criminals and spies to hide evidence and run the water in the sink like they'd seen characters do in movies because they thought it would prevent them from being heard. Every toss and turn during the night was recorded.

Following Greg to Marina Del Rey had not taken surveillance skills. With bumper-to-bumper traffic and frequent jams, the agency didn't bother having Greg followed closely by agency vehicles. Instead a GPS tracking device had been placed on the undercarriage of Greg's car. Several flybys by drones with cameras confirmed Greg had not discovered the tracking device and put it on another vehicle.

"Bring up the satellite images of the street in front of the apartment," Mond said. "Take it back to Nowell arriving."

"Do you want our personnel to monitor high-interest areas while we use the big screen in here?" The standard procedure was for a team of analysts to be checking high-interest areas for Nowell—airports, rail stations, bus depots and key freeway cams, along with his credit cards and ATM uses.

"No. All monitoring is to be in here. And you are not to mention what goes on in this room to anyone, not even your supervisor. Is that clear?"

It wasn't clear to Novak, it sounded like a surprising waste of time and resources, but she merely said, "Yes, sir."

When the video appeared on the war board, Novak said, "That's Greg Nowell's car."

The Jaguar pulled into a parking space and Greg got out. Mond zoomed the image to get a closer look as Greg left the car and disappeared into the apartment building.

"Are there cameras inside and outside the building?" Mond asked.

"There are, but the system was down at the time Nowell arrived and the man he was visiting, Rohan, was killed. Contact was made with the building manager and he said the circuit breaker had been thrown, possibly from an electrical surge."

The video froze as soon as Greg went into the building.

"What's happened?" Mond asked. "Why has it stopped?"

Novak checked and looked up from her console. "That's all there is of satellite images."

"What? That can't be. I ordered a four-hour surveillance. That wasn't forty seconds."

"There's been an override on your order."

"Does it say who overrode the order?"

"No, sir, but I can—"

"Leave it. The satellite was probably needed for something more urgent." He stared at the war board for a moment. "Back it up to where Nowell gets out of his car."

When the image of Greg appeared, Mond said, "Use emotion detecting on the subject."

Novak zoomed onto Greg. As she ran the video of him walking from his car to the apartment building, she began the program that analyzed a subject's mood from his body language, looking for extremes. Emotion detecting was designed to detect nervousness, anger and other strong feelings of people going through high-security checkpoints, the theory being that someone about to blow up himself and others is not going to be calm despite the attempt to hide his emotions.

Emotion detection was another example where use of a program to fight terrorism had been expanded to spying on the general public. Programs had been developed by merchandise marketers to reveal the likes and dislikes of people as they looked at merchandise, watched commercials or saw pictures or videos of politicians. Employers were using them to get an idea of how comfortable and honest applicants were during job interviews.

The programs scanned facial expressions, the slightest smile or frown, a minute lifting of an eyebrow or tightening of the lips, changes in expression that might go unnoticed by a person but were easily picked up by the electronic scan.

Mond wondered if the emotion scans would start being used by matchmaking sites to provide an electronic profile of the perfect mate. But emotion detecting wasn't new. He had been told that Middle Eastern rug sellers could tell what carpet a person was interested in and gauge the desire by observing his eyes—the pupils widened a tiny bit when a buyer saw what he liked and would most likely buy.

"Sir, it, uh, appears Nowell is tense, very tense, determined. Coiled and ready to release and maybe that's what he did when he got upstairs and confronted that man Rohan."

"Does it show anger, rage?"

"No emotions off the norm, except a great deal of tension."

"All right. Where's Nowell's car now?"

"Still parked on the street," Novak said. "Our people never saw him come out of the building. After Rohan's body was found on the street below the balcony, as soon as they could without being seen, our people made a discreet entry into the man's apartment. Nowell was gone. They took a look out back but he wasn't in sight. When the police arrived, they avoided contact with them. And we don't have satellite footage of the man's fall. We would have it if the satellite imaging had not been cancelled. It's rather unusual for our agency to have its satellite surveillance order cancelled. Are you sure you don't want me to—"

"We don't question orders. Are there any images of the apartment building from drones?"

Novak checked. "Just up to the point of Nowell parking. We didn't think it was necessary—"

"Obviously you were wrong. That's the problem with having the finest equipment and programs on the planet. The people using them are not as capable as the equipment. You should have had the drones as a backup. Roll it back to the beginning when Nowell arrived and parked."

As Nowell parked, a white van parked up the street from where Greg parked and then a red convertible Mini Cooper passed by as Greg was walking to the apartment building.

The small convertible was driven by a woman.

Mond said, "The brake lights in that red car went on as it neared Nowell walking into the apartment building."

"What, uh, do you make of that, sir?"

"A Freudian slip."

"Come again, sir?"

"The car's not really slowing down as it passes Nowell's car and the front of the building, but the driver's unconsciously revealing her interest by touching the brake pedal. The woman also looked over, interested in his movements. But she barely moved her head, obviously not wanting to expose her interest even though Nowell had his back to her. She probably was hiding her interest in case she was filmed by the building's camera. Fast-forward so we can see if we still had satellite coverage when she came around again."

The car came around again. This time the brakes lights only went on in front of the building.

"Check the car's registration," he said. "Back up the street there has to be an ATM, business or apartment building with a camera that showed the plates."

Novak ordered cameras in the area to be brought online and found one in a supermarket's parking lot that picked up the Mini Cooper's license plate well enough to read.

She ran the license plate through the California Department of Motor Vehicles and it came back as belonging to an Alyssa Neal.

Mond told her to bring up Neal's driver's license.

"There's just one thing wrong," Mond said, looking at the driver's license picture. "The woman driving the car is not Alyssa Neal."

# 30

Alyssa looked at a loss for words and gave Greg a nervous laugh. "You're right, I did. You caught me."

"So why are you pretending to be so innocent?"

"I am innocent, at least when it comes to the God Project. Whatever Ethan got out of it, he never shared it with me. Maybe he was trying to protect me. He knew that cracking open a top-secret file would mean real jail time, the life sentence variety."

Greg kicked it around for a moment. "Maybe he intended to give it to me. What's the good of hacking into secrets if you can't send shockwaves around the world with what you find? Besides, he was very idealistic when it came to spying on our own people. Ethan might have thought of me as the way to get the dirt out, if that's what he found. But that doesn't explain why he made a bizarre accusation, saying I had killed him. Or how and why money from my bank account got transferred to him. That took a good hacker and he's the only one I know—other than you."

"Rest assured that I know more about the theory of hacking than actually doing it. Like succeeding at most anything, the fine art of hacking is serious work done by people who make it their life. I know enough to call people who know how to crack a site and have them tell me how to do it."

"Including the God Project."

"No way, that's out of the class of anyone I know except Ethan."

"Since you have access to Mond's reports, let's get into them and find out what's going on."

"Can't do it. When I entered, alarms went off in the system. I got in, downloaded his most recent report and got out before the system slammed the door. Now that vulnerability is closed permanently and I don't know how to open another. Even if I called someone who could help, it would take a couple days to get back in and they will have set a trap, tracking intruders."

They continued walking as Greg digested what she told him. His gut told him to trust her—but not completely. He asked, "Are you sure Ethan actually hacked into a secret program as opposed to just bragging about it?"

"I haven't seen the actual files he got into, but I know he did it. He contacted me after he succeeded in cracking the program. He was high and pretty weird, rambling about how they really were trying to play God, something about remaking people in their image. He believed that some sort of entity, alien or some life force different than the rest of us, was trying to dominate the world. Did he tell you that?"

"He talked about it on the air briefly, but he was so wasted on whatever his drug of choice was that we had to cut him off."

"I know people talk about that sort of thing all the time on your show. Is that what you believe? That E.T. has landed and wants to take control?"

"You make a joke out of it because you've been brainwashed to believe that UFO sightings all stem from people photographing Frisbees as a joke. But catch this, Ali Neal. From the earliest advent of people on this planet, there has been a general belief that we are controlled by extraterrestrials."

She did a double take. "Wow. I have a niece who would call that statement epic because it's so astonishing. I know there's some drawings scratched on cave walls that look like flying men or chariots, but I don't recall reading in any history books they gave me at school that most people have always believed we're controlled by aliens."

"Sure you have, you just never made the connection. It's in a very old book your parents and my parents had at home and that we learned from every Sunday. It's called the Bible. God and angels are classic extraterrestrials. They live in outer space, are invisible, have super powers and pretty much control our lives. They can strike us dead for disobeying them. And that's been the case since prehistoric people scratched their beliefs on cave walls.

"In ancient times it was the gods of Olympus or the Nile manipulating mankind, and then the Eastern and Western religions came along and now are almost universal. But gods East and West either start out or end up as extraterrestrials. When you call people paranoid because they believe extraterrestrials or some terrestrial entity is out to control their lives, they are simply reflecting what humans have always thought."

"So they believe aliens in flying saucers are controlling us rather than the God of the Bible."

"I didn't say that. There is no contradiction between a biblical entity and aliens crash landing at Roswell or hovering over a lonely highway in the desert. We are an infinitesimal part of a vast universe that we are constantly probing deeper into and learning more about. We know that there are planets that can support intelligent life, so many of them that it's inevitable that someday intelligent life will be found—or will find us. There is no reason God isn't the deity of extraterrestrials as He is with the life on Earth.

"You think it's a joke to believe in intelligent life other than what you've personally experienced. But you have to have your head stuck in the sand if you don't look up and ask yourself what else is out there."

"Is that what you do—look up to see what else is up there? What do you believe in?"

He instantly tensed. It was too much, too deep into him to explain to this woman what he believed and what happened to him to shape his beliefs, but felt she deserved an answer. As much as he would reveal.

"There are some questions that have perplexed mankind since time immemorial. I think in some sense most women and men have asked the questions in one form or another."

"You mean, who are we, where did we come from, where are we going?"

"Yes, those are eternal questions, but the world we experience is many times the size of the one that our ancestors did. We are bombarded with global events every time we go on the Internet, turn on the TV or radio or pick up a newspaper. At the same time our space telescopes look back billions of years, back to the beginning of time and the universe. We're now sure that we are not alone in the universe, so I've added some more questions to those that people have asked over the ages: Who are *they*? What do *they* want? What will *they* do with us?"

"You're absolutely certain there is a *they*?"

"Of course I am. I think most people also realize that there is life beyond our own planet. And we believers have a strange bedfellow: the Vatican is already developing doctrine that includes extraterrestrials as part of God's creation. The Church is hedging its bets because it's pretty much a given there is something out there and it is either already here or is coming."

"I hear true belief in your voice, not just preaching about it, or an intellectual analysis of the existence of extraterrestrials. It sounds like you're angry about the notion we could have had visitors from another planet."

"Perhaps what you heard in my voice was fear about what type makes first contact."

"Gets there first? Like a contest?"

"Like a contest. It's a sure bet that if extraterrestrials find us before we do them, they will have vastly superior technology. And that translates into superior weapons."

"Muskets against arrows like we did with the Indians?"

"The history of progress has been the conquest of civilizations that were technologically inferior to the conquerors. Iron ruled stone, steel cut iron, city destroying atomic bombs beat bunker-busting bombs. We're now to the point where we can fry the entire planet with the rotting, decaying, leftover nukes from the Cold War but our weapons may be child's play compared to those of an entity that has traveled light-years to get to us."

"Why do you think they will come as conquerors? Maybe they'll be enlightened, far advanced culturally and will help us barbarians who are polluting our planet with our human and manufacturing excretion."

"That's a possibility. But why are they hiding if that's the case? Why do they keep their presence a secret and treat humans like guinea pigs? If they are so far advanced morally and intellectually, why don't they come into the light and help us share the wonders of the universe? You hear about people coming to the aid of other people, even dolphins coming to the aid of people. Have you ever heard about aliens saving a falling plane or sinking ship?"

"Maybe in a movie. Sorry, not trying to be facetious."

Greg said, "Some people believe that we have been visited by both good and evil aliens and that the war in heaven related in the Revelation will be an apocalyptic battle between them."

She gave him a quizzical look. "Do you lay awake nights thinking about this stuff?"

# 31

oesn't everybody?" He gave her a smile. "Just kidding, but it's a part of my life."

"Is that why you host a paranormal show? It's in your blood? Part of your soul to find answers for those eternal questions?"

Bull's-eye. She had struck a chord. He was a seeker, searching for answers. The quest had consumed him and affected every aspect of his being—including his personal life.

"Right now the answer I'm looking for is who framed me."

"One last question. Do you believe in God?"

"One last answer. I believe everyone is entitled to hold their own beliefs and keep them private if they want. And that's what I do. But I will share this with you—the world and its occupants are too wondrously incredible to have come about by accident in some soupy primal sea."

They walked without talking. Trying to get his head around everything that had come down, he tuned out the action of Muscle Beach. He realized there was a more serious danger than getting arrested. People were getting murdered.

Greg said, "Rohan was murdered in a way that would have made it look like suicide if me and a kid on a skateboard hadn't been around. It's a sure thing that Ethan was murdered in a similar way. The suicide dive from high up would be too much of a coincidence. Mond and your NRO are looking for the wrong people. I didn't kill them and neither of us is capable of throwing men out windows."

"Thanks. I appreciate the confidence. So we have to avoid getting murdered while we hunt for the file."

"You make it sound like a joke."

She shook her head. "It's no joke, I just don't know how to handle it or what to do about it. I can't go to the police for protection because I'll be locked up for the rest of my life. The only option is to find the file Ethan stole, copied, whatever he did with it."

"Why do you think we have to find the file?"

"It's the only negotiating wedge we have to get the feds off of our backs and to take care of whoever is killing the people involved. Aren't you thinking the same thing?" she asked.

He was. He didn't have what Ethan stole and whoever did was covering their tracks and leaving Greg as the fall guy. Or were so intent upon getting back the file that they were leaving a trail of murder behind them.

He saw something in the sky and thought it was an airplane. She followed his look and said, "A drone."

"We need to get undercover."

They went into a store that sold T-shirts and caps with Venice style. Inside, they separated and looked around. After a couple of minutes he stepped outside. The drone was not in sight.

He stepped back in and came up behind Ali while she was looking at a rack of T-shirts.

"Ali."

She didn't react.

"Ali?"

She spun around. "Sorry. I was, uh, thinking."

"I thought for a moment you didn't know your own name. It's gone."

They walked outside, checking the sky again before they went on.

"We should start with Ethan," Greg said. "Mond has probably already put Ethan's entire life history under a microscope but there's always hope when the government is involved that bureaucratic morass will stifle whatever they're trying to accomplish. And that people won't tell things to cops that they might tell to Ethan's friends. Ethan has a mother somewhere. He mentioned her during a show. Claims she listens to my broadcast. We can start with a cold call on her. If we let her know we're coming, Mond would probably be waiting for us."

"Good idea. Ethan told me she lives in El Segundo, down by the airport, and works at LAX. His father's out of the picture, divorced. I think Ethan lived with her off and on. She wasn't tolerant of his drug habit."

"But there are a couple things we need to do first. Your little red car is too easy to spot, your phone might be tracked already. I know someone who might help us out, up in Topanga Canyon. He dropped under the radar a long time ago."

"Topanga Canyon. That's out in the Valley?"

"The road goes from Woodland Hills in the Valley to the coast between Pacific Palisades and Malibu. Usually forty-five minutes from here, but light-years away when you figure the odds of us making it in an unusual red convertible without getting spotted."

"How are we going to do it?"

"We're going to make it up as we go."

# 32

R un the woman driving the car through HumanID," Mond said.

Human Identification at a Distance, HumanID, was used to identify people through their facial features and/or gait even at a considerable distance. It was the most highly sophisticated facial recognition program available, an advanced form of identification using biometrics.

Biometrics using a person's unique physical or behavioral characteristics had been used by police to identify criminals for more than a century. Fingerprints and voice patterns were examples. A widely used method of biometrics to identify criminals prior to universal use of fingerprints was Bertillonage, a form of anthropometry, the measurement of individual physical characteristics of people—size of their nose, distance between eyes, length of fingers, fingernails and dozens of other possibilities. Precise measurements of a standard list of body parts were taken of criminals and the information stored. When a person was arrested and their true identity was in question, measurements taken of the arrestee were compared to those in the database.

HumanID was infinitely quicker and more thorough than nineteenth-century anthropometry, but it was essentially the same thing with exceptions: the modern method had incredible speed and accuracy and most important, was not restricted to criminals who had already been arrested. Instead a vast database of the facial features of Americans was being compiled, with a goal of having the features of every single person in the country in it so anyone, anywhere, at any time could be identified.

The government had already gathered a large percentage of Americans in the database by scanning in driver's license pictures, passports, mug shots, military IDs and every other conceivable source.

The system was more sophisticated over that being used by local police, not only analyzing visible features, but using multispectral infrared technology to identify people even by their body language.

It was Mond's favorite program. Being able to identify most people most of the time by just running their pictures through the HumanID database gave him a sense of power over them.

He wasn't moved by criticism that the program was an invasion of privacy nor that private companies would soon offer facial recognition programs by pulling tens of millions of pictures off the Web. Buy an app and you could take a shot of the good-looking woman or man sitting across the room in a restaurant or bar. Not just getting their name, but incredible amounts of information exposed via the Internet, from where they lived and worked to where they played and banked.

The concept would create a handy weapon for criminals and perverts, not to mention how much a person's credit score might fit into whether they would be asked out for a date or avoided like the plague.

Novak leaned back from her console. "Sir, she's wearing a cap and the vertical angle of the satellite image doesn't show enough of the side of the woman's face to make an identification."

Mond pursed his brow. "Nowell went out the back. She might have joined him there. We don't have a satellite or drone image, but check the cameras on the street. There may be an apartment building or business with a camera."

"Got it." Novak displayed a video of Greg Nowell and the woman driving the red Mini Cooper convertible. Nowell leaned over to talk to her for a moment and then got into the car and they left.

"I ran HumanID on the woman," Novak said. "No results."

# 33

As they walked with the ocean on their left, Ali asked, "Should we be figuring out how to get to Topanga Canyon?"

"I already have. With a bit of luck, there will be a guy on Santa Monica's Third Street Promenade who can provide transportation."

"Instead of getting the car, you think we should get a bus to Santa Monica?"

"That's the Santa Monica Pier just ahead. We have to get to the Third Street Promenade. It's not far from the pier."

They had been closing in on Santa Monica since they started walking on the boardwalk.

Greg said, "We would have been on street and bus cameras if that's the way we came." He gestured at the businesses along the walkway. "Probably cameras here, too, right?"

"Right. CCTV, but most of them transmitting to a security firm who in turn can be tuned into by government agencies in case of emergency. But there are lots of people around. Until they find the car parked and empty, I think they would focus on locating the car on a freeway getting out of town." She nodded ahead. "Don't smile, you're on candid camera."

A camera was posted on a light post ahead.

"They can't check everyone who comes through here," Greg said.

"Actually, they can. It just takes a while. And like I said, they're probably focusing on the car. I borrowed the car so it should take them a while to identify it and me as the driver."

He felt as if he were being watched like an ant in the glass-plated ant farm an uncle gave him for Christmas when he was a child.

A sense of familiarity about the events shattering his life stayed with him. Not déjà vu, which would be a feeling that he had experienced being on the run from the authorities before or that there was something familiar about the woman. Rather it was a feeling that what he was going through now was expected—and with it an electrified, almost breathless tension; a feeling of walls closing in on him like a torture chamber in a slasher movie, of running from demons that had haunted him for decades.

He wasn't as shocked or surprised or completely devastated as he should be and would be if he had found himself entangled in a criminal enterprise. Like so many of his callers who saw the world through different eyes than most people, seeing layers of deceit and hidden agendas, the events that had exploded his world were not unexpected. Like an evangelical practitioner who would see the sudden appearance of heavenly fire and brimstone as prophetic, the fires raging in his own life were not unexpected.

They left the beach-side path and walked to the Third Street Promenade. He wondered how many cameras from ATM machines, traffic cams and store security were pointed at him along the way. He had heard from callers that the federal authorities were roping in the images from the hundreds of thousands of cameras picking up street images across the entire country.

How long would it take them to use facial recognition hardware to find his location? It took seconds on television shows.

They turned onto the promenade, a pedestrian street with shops, cafés, bars, movies, street entertainment and some panhandling homeless. It was his favorite Westside night spot in good weather because he and a date could just mosey along, catching the street acts and window shopping, picking up dinner at a sidewalk café followed by a movie.

Greg liked the funky, casual atmospheres of the Promenade, Westwood, West Hollywood and Old Pasadena, having been-there, done-that with the restaurants and lounges to "be seen" on Sunset and Melrose. Those in places usually only lasted less than a year before the people to be seen moved on to another place where the prices were outrageous, the food presentations were works of art and the taste was mediocre.

He led Ali to a cowboy plucking out a tune on a guitar and wailing "The Streets of Laredo."

*As I walked out in the streets of Laredo*
*As I walked out in Laredo one day*
*I spied a poor cowboy wrapped in white linen*
*Wrapped up in white linen as cold as the clay*

*"I can see by your outfit that you are a cowboy"*
*These words he did say as I boldly walked by*
*"Come sit down beside me and hear my sad story*
*I'm shot in the breast and I know I must die"*

His handwritten sign on the ground leaning against his guitar case said he was homeless and would play for food, fire or shelter. But his expensive faded blue jeans, snakeskin belt with a silver buckle of a cowboy on a bucking bronco, polished handmade pointed-toe brown cowboy boots with wiggly patterns up the sides and red silk cowboy shirt with pearl buttons and white embroidered floral on the front and cuffs made him look like a successful accountant who just wasn't into looking like what he advertised.

"Hank used to be a water resources administrator," Greg said. "He lost his job when he turned whistleblower on my show, exposing the fact that the high level of drugs making their way into our water supply was not being revealed. There are even hormones that can affect a person's sexuality. He claims it's making men grow larger breasts."

"Some women wouldn't complain about that. How does the stuff get into the water?"

"Flushed down toilets and recycled or leeched. Most waste water is reprocessed to be used keeping the sewer system flowing, but as potable water gets outstripped by water demands, especially during droughts, some of it ends up diverted to our taps."

"Good reason to drink bottled water."

"Plastic water containers aren't biodegradable. Better to drink wine and beer. I helped him get a lawyer after he was fired. He settled for more money than Midas. He picked up the cowboy garb and drawl after he got the money."

"Why does he play for peanuts?"

"Fulfilling a dream of being an entertainer? Celebrity status is an epidemic mind-set in L.A."

As soon as the dying cowboy in the song was dead and buried, Hank greeted Greg, who in turn introduced him to Ali.

"I need a big favor," Greg said. "I need to borrow a car. I can't tell you why and you don't want to know why."

"You're right about that. I learned a long time ago that curiosity is what gets me into so damn much trouble." Hank eyed them. "You both look pretty grim. Some of that talk you do at night got the kettle boiling over?"

"The kettle is full of nitroglycerin."

"You know, I've got a few dollars in the bank, besides these kindly donations which I give to the real homeless on the street." He gestured at the donated money in his guitar case. "If it's a matter of that . . ."

"Much more complicated. If you're asked by anyone why I needed to borrow your car, say I told you that we're trying to have some privacy and Ali's jealous husband is having her followed."

"Partner, that's a story that would get a cowboy to even loan you his horse. Take the keys. Leave it where you like and just let me know. I got more cars than you can shake a stick at."

The car was parked on a lot off Second Street.

"Oh my God," came from Ali at first sight.

It was an understatement. The car was a sleek 1959 radiant candy apple green Cadillac Deville. The paint job glowed bright enough to have been manufactured in Fukushima during the meltdown of the atomic power plant. It had long, swept-back, razor's-edge tailfins and duel bullet taillights. It looked ready to blast off.

"That paint job can probably be seen from a space station," Ali said. "I bet it glows in the dark."

"Just be grateful it doesn't have a set of steer horns on the hood and cowhide seat covers."

Ali couldn't kill a laugh. "The best thing is that no one would suspect us of running from the police in a car that shouts, 'Look at me!' In a strange way it reminds me of my little red Cooper."

# 34

Novak sat at her console and watched Mond out of the corner of her eye. He had been quiet for two minutes, an eternity when searching for a suspect. Getting stumped trying to identify the woman in the red convertible annoyed him.

No, she thought, not just annoyed him. He seemed to be angry that he couldn't identify her, as if he took it personally.

They had managed to follow the car for blocks but lost it after it made a turn onto a street with no cameras. He ordered drones into the search but the car hadn't been spotted yet.

He had Novak do a quick trace on Alyssa Neal, tracking her through telephone and credit card use to New York City, where she had gone to attend a wedding. She had left her Mini Cooper at LAX parking, had the keys with her and had not given anyone permission to use the car. Cameras at the airport showed the real Ms. Neal leaving the car, but were not working the day the car was stolen.

That meant the thieves had more talents than stealing cars. At the very least they were highly sophisticated hackers who invaded the airport's surveillance system.

Mond had a picture of the woman driving the convertible in front of the apartment building sent to the real Ms. Neal and she reported back that she had no idea who the woman was or how she got the car.

"Why steal a car that stood out like a red flag?" Novak asked. "You would think that the woman would have stolen a car that blended in rather than attracting attention if she was involved in a crime."

"The little red convertible was clever," Mond said. "And deliberate. People will remember the car, not the driver, especially because she blends in well. She looks like she would own that kind of car."

"Women aren't usually car thieves," Novak said.

"In today's world, it's no longer possible to categorize any activity as solo male or female except childbirth and peeing in the shower. There has to be a connection between the woman driving the car and someone involved in our investigation. Let's see if Hops can identify her. Specifically try Ethan Shaw, Greg Nowell and Rohan, the writer. Include the real Neal woman. She might be lying about knowing the woman driving her car."

Hops was a data-mining program used to find people through their interconnections—e-mails, telephone calls, blogs, chat rooms, addresses and any other connection that went over communications lines that carried phones and the Internet.

The system was originally launched to spy on U.S. citizens in 2002 through the Information Awareness Office (IAO). Called Total Information Awareness, the program was a mass surveillance tool that collected literally every electronic movement of every U.S. citizen—via land phones, cell phones, faxes, e-mails, chat rooms, social networking, tweets, blogs, Internet searches, credit card charges, the whole nine yards of personal and business communications.

In 2003 the IAO was disbanded due to public outcries against domestic spying. However, the Snowden NSA revelations in 2013 revealed that the mass surveillance programs had not been eliminated; their names were simply changed and they had been operating for the past ten years.

Mond thought of it as similar to the theory of six degrees of separation—that by way of introduction, each of us is only six people away from anyone else on the planet. That any one of us, even one of the great unwashed masses, could be introduced to someone who in turn refers us to someone else, and by the time the sixth introduction is reached, you could be in contact with anyone else in the world, even the queen in London, the pope in Rome or whoever it was that you were seeking to meet.

With Hops, the search started with one name, usually the name of a suspected terrorist. A three-hop query meant that the government could look at data not only from a suspected terrorist, but from everyone that the suspect communicated with, and then from everyone those people communicated with, and then from everyone all of those people communicated with, until from the thousands of results it could end up with a few interconnected people who are part of a terrorist organization.

The process was called "hops" because the search hopped from one person to another. By going from Ethan to Greg to Rohan and the car owner, the objective was to find not just a connection among them but a link to someone else—in this case the car driver.

After the search was done, Novak said, "There are many connections between the three main subjects, Ethan Shaw, Greg Nowell and Rohan, but none between any of them and the car owner. And nothing pops up with any of them that provided a clue as to the driver's identity."

"There are connections, but they've been erased. Shaw was a master hacker, capable of erasing the tracks. But there's one track here that Greg Nowell and the woman aren't going to be able to erase. They're in an easy-to-spot car."

She started to point out that they hadn't tracked the car yet because it had left a main street and gone into a residential area where there were no cameras they could bring online, but she shut her mouth, knowing she would just get put down.

Mond said, "Put out a stop-and-detain order to all police agencies. The two suspects are to be apprehended but under no circumstances are they to be questioned. Instead, they're to be held and transferred to our agents."

"No questioning? What if there are federal agents, the FBI—"

"I just told you, no questioning."

"Yes, sir."

"Keep a drone in the air. Just one. There will be questions about it but if we have more up it will attract attention and cause a social media buzz, not to mention news stories that would forewarn the subjects. Start searching freeway and street cameras for the red car in all directions they could have taken." Mond scowled at Megan Novak. "I want those two found. Include in the directive to police agencies not to ask questions, that their contact with the subjects other than detaining them is limited to verifying their identities."

"Should I keep trying to identify the driver?"

"Yes, but there's little chance we'll succeed, though we found out two things about her."

"Sir?"

Mond looked up at the war board as he spoke. "She's not working alone. I agree with you about the car thief. She didn't look like someone who would steal a car, which means she had help. And someone covered her tracks. A very clever hacker. Probably Ethan Shaw. So keep working on a Shaw connection. If we dig deep enough, we will find her. No one can go completely undercover."

He swiveled in his chair to face her.

"No one can drop under the radar today. You can't exist without leaving electronic tracks. Even if you pay cash for gas, the cameras at the station record images of you, your car and the vehicle's license number. The same thing happens if you walk into a store to pay cash for a cell phone. Not only are you and your vehicle captured on video outside and you inside, but every call you make goes through the government's surveillance network.

"We'll identify and find the woman."

# 35

W e found a connection between Nowell and the woman driving the red convertible," Novak said.

"What is it?" Mond asked.

"A woman left a note for Nowell at his apartment building's security desk."

"We got her on camera?"

"No—"

"Wait. It was out of order."

"Exactly. Someone knows how to tap into security firms and shut off CCTV cameras. But the security man at the desk read the note." She grinned at Mond. "Jose Ramirez, the security officer, denied to our investigators that he had read the note before giving it to Nowell but a review of the building's CCTV showed he read it after she left. Naturally the cameras started working as soon as she was gone."

Mond waved away the man's lie. "What did the note say?"

" 'Get out—they're coming.' "

" 'Get out, they're coming,' " Mond repeated.

"She was telling Nowell that we were coming to search."

"I understand that. The question is, how did she know it? I didn't even let the Los Angeles police know my plans. What else did this security man, Jose, tell us about Nowell and the note?"

"He's under the impression that Nowell wasn't expecting a message, didn't know the woman and didn't understand the message."

"Play the building's video."

Mond watched the interaction between Jose and Greg Nowell.

He observed Nowell's body language for clues because the video didn't have sound.

"No question," Mond nodded, "Nowell is surprised by the note. But that doesn't establish that he didn't know the woman before she left the note."

"There's another tape. Two, actually. One shows Nowell and a woman entering the Angels Flight rail car separately and sitting apart. Not enough of the woman's face is shown for facial recognition, but she has been identified by her body language as the woman posing as Alyssa Neal."

"No interaction between them in the train car?"

"None. But after he exits at the top she says something to him that causes him to pause. Again we have no sound."

"Show me both tapes."

Watching Nowell and Neal seated apart in the train car, Mond said, "He's curious about her. He moves his eyes, not his head, trying to get a look at her without making it obvious. Show me the second film."

Mond watched Nowell's reaction to something the Neal woman said when Nowell was walking away.

"Not enough of her features are shown to permit us to have her lips read," Novak said. "But you can see he's surprised."

Mond shook his head. "He's not just surprised, he's puzzled. I think she dropped another cryptic remark on him, as she did with the note. Notice his body language—he's ready to go after her but stops and backs off."

He got up and paced. "We can imply from what we've seen that Nowell didn't know the woman before he saw her in the railcar. Probably got his first introduction to her when she became his getaway driver leaving Rohan's. But she knew things she shouldn't have known."

What really got under Mond's skin was that the woman knew things about his own investigation, right down to what his next move was when she tipped off Nowell that his place was about to be searched. But she contacted Nowell in strange ways—a comment made at the funicular, a cryptic note left at his building, not really telling him much, just that she knew something—and giving him warnings that turned out to be true.

*She was setting Nowell up to be receptive when she finally made face-to-face contact with him.*

That was it. She was softening him so when she made her move, he would be approachable because he realized she had information that he needed. Fat chance of him getting into that car after he left Rohan's if he didn't have some reason to believe she was on his side.

What did she have to offer Nowell to get him to team up with her—beyond getting a set of wheels under him when he was walking away from a suspicious death? That was enough.

For what purpose had she entered the game? That was an easy question for Mond. She had the same motive Nowell had. She was in the game for the hacked NRO file. He had it. She wanted it.

Who was she? Where did she get her information? Who did she work for? Was there another intelligence agency involved? FBI? CIA? DIA? Maybe even an agent for one of the civilian contractors that got billions in NRO contracts that would be jeopardized if their secret activities were exposed?

Mond was sure that she wasn't with any of the major agencies. The HumanID, Hops and other identification systems used by Interagency were the most sophisticated in the world and would have even picked up on members of other secret agencies. But she didn't have to be with a major agency. There were hundreds, hell, thousands of agencies and subagencies floating in the big bureaucratic pond that made up the U.S. intelligence service.

The fact that she had insider information about his movements was outrageous. Mond considered it an invasion of his privacy even if it turned out to come from another governmental agency.

Novak interrupted his thoughts. "Sir, the red convertible was spotted by a drone in a Venice Beach parking lot. The drone also picked up two people on the boardwalk who appeared to take cover when the drone approached. They were too far away to identify but it was a man and woman who had on the right color clothes." She paused and read a message on her screen. "We also brought a CCTV store camera online through the security company that provides it and confirmed that was Nowell and the woman in Alyssa Neal's red car."

"How much time are they ahead of us?" Mond asked.

"They left the boardwalk store eleven minutes ago. The red convertible was still in the parking lot three minutes ago."

"They were heading away from the car as they progressed along the beach. They can't get far on foot. By now they have made up their minds to get another car and are heading for it."

"Rent a car? Steal a car?"

"Or borrow a car. We'll know soon enough. Get all the boardwalk security cameras online that can be brought on. Add another drone in the area and get our field agents in position to move in."

As Novak went back to her control panel, he interrupted her.

"I want to know who this woman is. Dig deep into all government intelligence agencies. She may work for one."

# 36

Leaving the parking lot, Greg turned back in the direction of Venice Beach.

"Isn't Topanga the other way?" she asked.

"They'll check bus, street, ATM and other cameras in every direction from Rohan's. It's inevitable we'll be spotted sooner or later, but let's give them a run for their money and make it as later as possible. I'm going back toward where we started in the hopes they would think that's the last direction we would take."

He turned onto a side street and went up a ways and turned again, repeating the maneuver to get the car headed in the direction of Topanga Canyon but staying on side streets.

"If we keep to the straight and narrow it's going to be easy for them to track us." He grinned. "A woman from Philly calls in regularly. She's sure that she's under surveillance and has worked out this tactic just to make it harder to keep track of her."

Ali shook her head. "Amazing. There's a whole world on talk radio I didn't know existed."

"That's because you've been one of the people looking down the microscope lens at the rest of us. But now you're not just another bug under the scope, but one that the authorities want to dissect."

"Thanks. I needed that to keep from panicking. Now that you've completely destroyed my confidence, why don't you let me out so I can stand in front of the car and let you run over me? I'd rather be roadkill than dissected."

"'I'd rather be roadkill than dissected,'" Greg repeated. "It's a good thing you didn't say that to Cowboy Hank. He would have made a song out of it."

As they drove along the Pacific Coast Highway, which would take them through Santa Monica and almost to Malibu to reach Topanga Canyon Boulevard, he continued the evasive movements before suddenly pulling over at a strip mall.

"I want to get a look at the people in the car behind us."

After an ordinary gray car with two ordinary-looking men in it went by, he put the glowing Cadillac back on the road.

"Just checking. There's a CIA field rule that if you see the same person or vehicle twice, assume you're being followed." He answered her questioning look. "Another one of the things I learned on talk radio. I also know you're supposed to ditch your phone but I was slow on the draw about that. Still in shock."

"Rohan was a good friend?"

"Rohan was an arrogant bastard, but way short of deserving to be thrown off his balcony. And putting the blame on me. How did you know I was going to Rohan's? Tapping into Mond? Did he know I was going there?"

"I tailed you. Apparently you don't always follow the CIA's instructions about being followed."

"Too many cars on one of the world's busiest freeways. Besides, I'd never guess anyone would follow me in a little red convertible. Did you see anyone go into the apartment building besides me?"

"I never saw you or anyone else go in or out of the building. I drove by as you pulled over to park. I went around the corner and came back again a couple of times. Last time I went by the building a crowd had gathered."

"It came down quickly. I wasn't inside long before the doorbell rang and Rohan shuffled me out the back. Whoever killed Rohan got in and out fast. How did you know I went out the back?"

"I spotted you walking on the street by accident. I was just trying to get out of the area. Do you think Rohan was killed by the NRO because he had a connection to Ethan?"

"I don't know. I hate to think one of our most important government agencies has gone rogue."

"Agencies don't go bad," she said, "but people in them sometimes do. The worst offenders are the ones who believe they can protect us better by cutting back on our freedoms. History shows that the intrusions they create today in the name of security often turn out to be used to oppress people in the future."

"Intrusions by the government are a common theme by callers to my show. Invasions of our privacy in the name of security have become epidemic. Have you ever heard my show?"

"I started listening to your show after Ethan talked about it. It's obvious that many of your callers have unorthodox views. Some sound paranoid."

"We just abandoned your friend's convertible, we're driving with evasive actions to avoid police and killers, we've tossed my phone chip in a sewer and your phone is operating off a cash-and-carry chip bought at a different store than where you purchased the phone. Sound a little paranoid?"

"No, I'm running from reality like you, but not because I think that little green men from Mars are following me."

"Grays, not green. Aliens are most often described as gray by people who have encountered them, though they've been observed in many different shapes and colors. Dead Roswell aliens in forty-seven were described as gray and so were the live ones the Hills later saw."

"The Hills?"

"Betty and Barney, back in 1961. They're not the first people to have an encounter with aliens, but they rate high in credibility. Both had good jobs, were active in their community and had no history of strange behavior. Betty was a social worker; Barney worked for the postal service. They were an unusual couple at the time only for one reason: they had an interracial marriage when it was not common—Betty was white, Barney was black. Both were active in civil rights causes as members of the NAACP and Barney was on a U.S. Civil Rights Commission board.

"They lived in New Hampshire on the coast and were on their way back from vacation through the isolated White Mountains region when they spotted a huge object descending toward them from the sky with bright lights. It hovered over them before landing.

Barney used binoculars to spot entities that resembled humans but were short, grayish in color and had large heads.

"The Hills fled in their car but lost consciousness for what they thought was a brief moment but later realized they had covered thirty-five miles on the rural road. Neither of them could recall what happened during the lost time. Eventually, they went through hypnosis sessions in which they related being examined by the aliens in their ship. Samples of blood, hair, tissue, and nails, items we would describe today as DNA specimens, were taken from her by the aliens."

"Any sex?"

"You'll be disappointed to learn there was no alien rape or freaky-looking babies. That only happens to Iowa farm girls in tabloid stories."

"Sorry, I've seen too many movies and read way too many tabloids. So aliens are usually gray?"

"Most but not all. People have described contact and alien abduction incidents with humanoid creatures that are very tall, with light hair and pale skin, that are commonly called Nordics—"

"Like Scandinavians?"

"That's the analogy. Rohan wrote that the aliens who examined him were mostly covered by medical-type uniforms but he observed reptilian-like skin in small areas that were exposed."

"These things came across the universe and they couldn't cover themselves well enough to keep captives from seeing their skin?"

"Rohan raised the same question. He said he was abducted during a university sleep-study program. He believed that a bit of fake reptilian skin was deliberately exposed, that the extraterrestrials weren't reptilian but wanted to leave the impression they were when they examined him."

"Why?"

"To create confusion and a lack of credibility. So many different types of alien forms have been reported—grays, Nordics, reptilian, insectoid—that it creates confusion and doubt that people were really seeing them."

"Do you believe Rohan? That he was abducted and examined during the university sleep study?"

"I don't disbelieve him. He said it happened. He was the only witness. The story he told was no stranger than many other tales of abduction. He had no reason to lie."

"He made money writing about it."

"That came later. First he made the accusation and suffered through the laugher and ridicule abduction claims always generate. I'm not judgmental about callers whose claims or ideas may seem outlandish to others—there are too many unexplained and unexplainable things happening. Many of my callers are seekers, reaching out, looking for answers and sometimes coming up with ones that others find bizarre."

Ali said, "There are conspiracy theories about this and that, whether it's 9/11 or the JFK assassination or global warming. Even about the water we drink or the air we breathe. Why do you think there are so many theories? So much paranoia about what's happening in the world?"

"What you call paranoia, I call genuine concerns. Our government is not perfect; it spies on us and oftentimes it acts stupid. No business is perfect. Some feed us poisonous food, defective products and get together to jack up the price of gas and everything else they can manage to do. All of these things are done in secret. There may be many different situations that people see hidden meaning in, but there is a common denominator for most of it and that's suspicion of and distrust of the people who control us, those in our government and transnational business entities that have the economic clout of small nations and no aim except making money. To many of us it seems as if the strings are being pulled at a deeper level than what appears."

"What do you believe in?"

"Keeping an open mind. Seeking the truth. Too often the truth is ignored. You usually have to dig deep and ask a lot of questions before you find it. Sometimes you just dig yourself deeper into the inexplicable. I have seen and heard so many things that were rejected because there was no quick and easy explanations for them that I don't automatically cast doubt on what happened."

"Some people think aliens are in control of our government?"

"It's part of the general feeling of distrust I mentioned. And the fact that it seems obvious to many of us that the government is hiding alien contact that we believe has occurred. It raises questions that don't have easy answers. Is there something out there, something from that illimitable universe that has come here? There seems to be plenty of evidence that they've been around for a long time. So what are their motives? Enslave us and eat us like farm animals?"

"Did you have to say that?"

"Blame the movies. But the possibilities are endless and many not very pleasant. Maybe they'll destroy us so we can't infect the rest of the universe with whatever primitive instinct drives us to gruesome wars and unimaginable cruelty to each other. Or would they raise our level of understanding so we can communicate and interact with them?"

"I'll go for peaceful coexistence."

"We don't know who they are, where they came from or what they really look like. We know they are operating in secret and have given no clue as to their intentions. We can surmise that they are far superior in terms of technology simply because they found us before we found them. The question of who's in control arises because it's pretty much a certainty that our government knows they are here but aren't revealing it. At this stage there are no easy answers, just a lot of unanswered questions."

She asked, "If Ethan found something, why would he come to you?"

Greg thought for a moment. "He could have come to me for the exposure he needed to get the secrets publicized. But he never mentioned it and I wonder what his relationship with Rohan was. Obviously it got Rohan killed. I think Rohan was the person who Ethan passed the information to."

She gave him a grave look. "Ethan told me he gave it to you."

# THE VALENTICH DISAPPEARANCE

Many mysterious disappearances have been investigated and ended up with conclusions that there was no known cause outside of the preternatural.

The disappearance of pilot Frederic Valentich in Australia in 1978 after he reported a large, otherworldly flying object hovering over his airplane with a green light is one that is mystifying.

Valentich flew out of Melbourne on a clear day to pick up friends at another location. En route he was recorded describing an encounter with a strange aircraft to Melbourne's air traffic control (FSU).

The following is taken from the official investigation report prepared by the Australian government investigators. The only changes made to the official report are those to make it easier to read. "PILOT" and "MELBOURNE" have been substituted for the initials used in the report. Grammatical errors have not been corrected.

PILOT    *Melbourne* this is *Delta Sierra Juliet* is there any known traffic below five thousand
MELBOURNE    No known traffic
PILOT    I am seems (to) be a large aircraft below five thousand
MELBOURNE    What type of aircraft is it
PILOT    I cannot confirm it is four bright it seems to me like landing lights
MELBOURNE    *Delta Sierra Juliet*
PILOT    *Melbourne* this (is) *Delta Sierra Juliet* the aircraft has just passed over me at least a thousand feet above
MELBOURNE    Roger and it is a large aircraft confirm

PILOT    Er unknown due to the speed it's traveling is there any air force aircraft in the vicinity

MELBOURNE    No known aircraft in the vicinity

PILOT    *Melbourne* it's approaching now from due east toward me

MELBOURNE    *Delta Sierra Juliet //* open microphone for two seconds //

PILOT    It seems to me that he's playing some sort of game he's flying over me two three times at a time at speeds I could not identify

MELBOURNE    *Delta Sierra Juliet* roger what is your actual level

PILOT    My level is four and a half thousand four five zero

MELBOURNE    *Delta Sierra Juliet* and confirm you cannot identify the aircraft

PILOT    Affirmative

MELBOURNE    *Delta Sierra Juliet* roger standby

PILOT    *Melbourne Delta Sierra Juliet* it's not an aircraft it is // open microphone for two seconds//

MELBOURNE    *Delta Sierra Juliet Melbourne* can you describe the er aircraft

PILOT    *Delta Sierra Juliet* as it's flying past it's a long shape // open microphone for three seconds// (cannot) identify more than (that has such speed) //open microphone for three seconds// before me right now *Melbourne*

MELBOURNE    *Delta Sierra Juliet* roger and how large would the er object be

PILOT    *Delta Sierra Juliet Melbourne* it seems like it's stationary what I'm doing right now is orbiting and the thing is orbiting on top of me also it's got a green light and sort of metallic (like) it's all shiny (on) the outside

MELBOURNE    *Delta Sierra Juliet*

PILOT    *Delta Sierra Juliet //*open microphone for five seconds*//* it's just vanished

MELBOURNE    *Delta Sierra Juliet*

PILOT    *Melbourne* would you know what kind of aircraft I've got is it (a type) military aircraft

MELBOURNE   *Delta Sierra Juliet* confirm the er aircraft just
   vanished

PILOT   Say again

MELBOURNE   *Delta Sierra Juliet* is the aircraft still with you

PILOT   *Delta Sierra Juliet* (it's ah nor) //open microphone two
   seconds// (now) approaching from the southwest

MELBOURNE   *Delta Sierra Juliet*

PILOT   *Delta Sierra Juliet* the engine is rough idling I've got it
   set at twenty-three twenty-four and the thing is (coughing)

MELBOURNE   *Delta Sierra Juliet* roger what are your intentions

PILOT   My intentions are ah to go to King Island ah Melbourne
   that strange aircraft is hovering on top of me again //two
   seconds open microphone// it is hovering and it's not an aircraft

MELBOURNE   *Delta Sierra Juliet*

PILOT   *Delta Sierra Juliet Melbourne* //17 seconds open micro-
   phone//

MELBOURNE   *Delta Sierra Juliet Melbourne*


   There is no record of any further transmission from the
aircraft.

   The weather in the Cape Otway area was clear with a trace
of stratocumulus cloud at 5000 to 7000 feet, scattered cirrus
clouds at 30,000 feet, excellent visibility and light wind. The
end of daylight at Cape Otway was at 1915 hours . . .


NOTE: The report states that no trace of the aircraft was
found after an "intensive air, sea and land search" and the
investigators were silent as to the cause of the disappearance.

   The report was released nearly four years after the incident.

# 37

*He gave it to you.*

Greg let the words hang as they drove but they roiled in his head. Despite his denials, she was certain he had the stolen files. So was the government and whoever was on a killing spree. Why?

"'You killed me,'" he said.

"What?"

"That's what Ethan said to me on the phone just before he went out the window. He told me I had killed him. He told you he gave me the files he stole. He died with a receipt for the money transfer from my account in his pocket."

"You can see why Mond and the NRO think you have them. They may have found something on his computer showing a transfer. He may have jumped because he knew they were on to him."

"He didn't jump."

"Because of the way Rohan was killed? You might be right."

"Might be right? Oh, I forgot, there's a witness who saw me throw Rohan off his balcony. If you believe I have the file and I'm running around killing people, you should get out of this car and call Mond."

"I'm sorry, really, I'm sorry. I just—it's so—"

"Insane?"

"Yes, absolutely insane. I even wonder if Rohan couldn't have gone off that balcony in blind panic."

"What?"

"You said he was all drugged up, he was expecting the police, maybe he went wild and ran."

He felt like banging his head against the steering wheel.

She let out a nervous laugh. "Doesn't work?"

"It works great if I hadn't been there and I hadn't been escorted to the back door by Rohan because someone had rang the doorbell. He left me to go open the front door to what he thought were the police, not take a dive off his balcony. There's also the kid with the skateboard." He was tired of defending himself. "In case it slipped your mind, this whole thing started when you and Ethan decided to crack some super-secret government file."

"I never—"

"Yeah, you're innocent, all you did was pass on to a hacking fanatic the fact that what has to be the Holy Grail of hacking was just sitting there ready for him to crack open and let the world know he'd done it. At some police agencies, like the FBI, they call that treason."

"You're right. It sounds bad, doesn't it?"

"It sounds like we better find what Ethan did with the file."

"Okay, I accept the fact you never got anything from Ethan. But why did he tell me he sent it to you? Why—"

"Did he say I killed him, got money from my account, got thrown out a window, got Rohan killed, got me and you on the run? I guess we'll know the answers when we find the file and see what's in it that's so important that maybe even people in our government would kill to get their hands on it. In the meantime, disabuse yourself of the notion that I am sitting on the battle plans of the republic. If we can't get past that I am clueless about everything that has come down, we might as well part company right now."

"You're right. I'm convinced you're clueless."

"Thanks. I needed that. While we're floundering in waters over our heads, do you have anyone you need to get in touch with? Or keep in touch with? Mother? Lover? Someone taking care of your cat?"

"No cat. My mother's on a cruise with my father and my relationship went down in flames when my fiancé chose a fabulous job in Manhattan over staying with me on the Left Coast. How about you? I take it you're thinking finding that file might take days rather than hours. Assuming we can keep on the run and stay out of Mond's clutches that long."

"I'm fine. No sensible, intelligent woman would put up with a workaholic who spends his nights talking on the radio and much of the rest of the time preparing or giving speeches."

"Divorced?"

He shrugged. "Rightfully so, at least from her point of view. Without hard feelings. I sure as hell wouldn't want to live with someone like me, who deals with aliens and worldwide conspiracies like other people do with the price of pig bellies. I don't blame anyone but myself for failed relationships. Frankly, I don't like me much myself."

"Sounds like you're not clueless on all levels."

# 38

Topanga Canyon Boulevard wound and crawled over the Santa Monica Mountains like a long, narrow black snake from beaches near Malibu to the hot, dry San Fernando Valley. Some of the more rugged parts of it have appeared in car chase films even though there isn't much to see except curves and steep, hilly terrain covered with manzanita, scrub oak and pine.

There isn't much to see in terms of civilization, either, until you get near the top, but besides the heavy vegetation where mountain lions, coyotes, kangaroo rats and rattlesnakes still prowl about twenty-five miles from downtown Los Angeles, there exists a particular type of unconventional lifestyle that the area has become famous for: bohemian.

Artists, actors, writers, musicians and hippies are attracted to the area because of cheap living, a laid-back lifestyle and the privacy to party as they want—and smoke what they want. Bohemian isn't a good description for a society that has gone digital on all fronts, but despite the fact that some of the area is actually within the boundaries of the City of Los Angeles, there is still room for a counterculture lifestyle on the back roads. Many of the roads are no more than dirt paths.

It is also a good place to stay below the radar.

Ali asked about Franklin, the man they were going to ask for help.

"Is Franklin his first name or last?"

"I don't think it's either. He called himself simply Franklin when he came on the show. Some people don't like to use their real names. If she thinks they'll be interesting and don't sound like they're going to be trouble, my producer lets them stay anonymous. I met Franklin in person because he has a large stock of used nautical artifacts at his place—anchors, portholes, that sort of thing. I bought something for my beach house from him."

"What did you mean when you said he dropped below the radar? Dodging creditors, that sort of thing?"

"More like being left alone to live his life without the government, businesses and neighbors constantly watching him. We leave a public footprint when we get a phone, a job, a house, a computer, credit card, passport, see a doctor, surf the Internet, whatever. Hell, we do it not just going to an ATM but driving down the street. Franklin's one of those people who has set out to erase his tracks. He says it's like being an outlaw on the run rubbing out the hoof prints of his horse to trick a posse."

"He's been abducted by aliens?"

"Not that I know of. This may come as a surprise to you, but not many of the millions of people who listen to my show say they've been abducted. However, like me, he has a heightened sense of awareness of the intrusions of privacy that governments at all levels practice."

"He's paranoid."

"Most realists are. Like you and me."

She ignored the jab. "What's our story with him? The jealous husband you used with the cowboy?"

"Wouldn't work. He'll need the truth—paranoid people see through BS. The truth or as much of it as we can give him without compromising him or us. It wouldn't be fair to ask for help and not tell him the last person I spoke to is dead."

The road off Topanga Canyon Boulevard to Franklin's house was on the ocean side of the mountains. It was paved with dirt and deep ruts, not the kind of road anyone would tackle for just for the hell of it. Which was one reason Franklin had his place at the end of it and made sure the road was never smoothed out.

The house and barn were hidden in a pine forest hundreds of feet from the boulevard. So was the clutter that surrounded the house and barn like a lake of castoffs from the sea—the anchors and portholes Greg mentioned, rusty old cannons removed from Davy Jones's locker, the helm to steer an ocean liner or a day fisher, propellers to drive a ship, winches to raise the sails on a ten-meter sloop, lifeboats and dinghies, oars, lines, masts, booms, buoys, engines, figureheads from the bows of sailing ships, bowsprits, galley stoves on gimbals to rock with the sea and a host of other salty artifacts, nautical treasures or junk, depending on your perspective.

Greg found the collection both peculiar and special, like a nautical museum of shipwrecks. "You don't get much of a chance to see the guts and bottoms of boats."

"He sells this stuff?" Ali asked.

"Mostly he collects and hoards it. He wouldn't take the money I offered for a porthole."

"Probably professional courtesy. You're both paranoid. Kindred spirits."

"You keep walking into it—tossed any phone cards lately because you're afraid the government is spying on you?"

"I'm beginning to think paranoia is a virus."

Franklin came out of the barn to greet them. Fiftyish, wearing work clothes and a big leather apron, with gray-streaked black hair and a beard that was white at the chin, he was carrying a hammer he'd been using at a blacksmith's forge that was smoldering in the barn.

He gave the glowing car a good look-over. "Lucky you came in something no federal agent would have had the guts or imagination to drive. I turned off the IED before you triggered it by running over it."

"Roadside bomb," Greg told Ali. "He's telling us he's annoyed we didn't call ahead. But he doesn't have a phone that anyone knows the number to."

Nodding his head as if he understood their situation, Franklin gave Ali and Greg the same thorough look he had given the car. "Radio personality, attractive professional woman, should be out together on business or pleasure, but you both look grim. What's the matter? Husband or wife trouble?"

Greg shook his head. "That was the line we used on the poor bastard who loaned us this Cad that looks like it's ready to blast off on a mission to Mars. The truth is that we're in trouble, big-time. With the government—the one we all know operates in secret. We didn't want to leave tracks coming here even if we'd had your phone number."

"What kind of government trouble?"

"Two people are dead," Greg said. "We're on the run. Some really crazy stuff is going on with the NRO. A secret file is missing. They think I have it. I don't have it and the two men involved in stealing it are both dead."

Franklin nodded repeatedly. "The NRO, yeah, that makes sense. Know what their motto is? 'Vigilance from above.' It's really con-trol from above. The NSA can't get to you unless you go on the Internet, use a phone or do something to get into their purview, but the NRO has satellites up there every second of every day ready to spy down anywhere in the world.

"Those bastards have been after me for years. You would think people would have gotten wise to the NRO when they pulled off 9/11 but most of the people on the planet are cattle for slaughter."

Ali looked from Franklin to Greg. "Pulled off 9/11? The NRO?"

"Conspiracy theory," Greg said.

Franklin scoffed. "Conspiracy, hell, the damn truth and noth-ing but."

Greg told her, "The NRO had scheduled for the morning of September 11, 2001, what they called a safety exercise for their head-quarters building. An alarm was to go off and the employees would be told a plane was about to hit it and to abandon the building."

"You have to be kidding me," Ali said.

"It gets worse," Greg said. "The NRO exercise was planned to go off at about the same time that 9/11 actually came off, both the NRO and the Pentagon are in Virginia, the Pentagon did get hit by one of the planes and there was a second plane that went down in a battle with passengers—"

"That would have hit the NRO," Franklin said. "We know that was the actual target for the second plane because the building drill was for a real attack, not the excuse they gave. And the plane that hit the Pentagon took off from Dulles airport, which was what the NRO plan called for."

"Why would they warn people about the attack?" Ali asked Franklin.

"They didn't want their whole operation shut down because vital people got killed."

"How did the NRO explain this?" she asked.

"They call it a bizarre coincidence," Greg said.

"Called it that because they had to come up with some excuse after the shit hit the fan," Franklin said.

Ali shook her head. "Wow. When it comes to conspiracy theories, I feel like I've led a sheltered life."

As they followed Franklin inside, Ali nudged Greg and gestured at her own head, signaling that Franklin had aluminum foil sticking out from under his cap.

Greg nodded up at the roof of the house. It was metal. So was the roof of the barn.

"Metal's the only thing that blocks the satellites," Franklin said. He glanced back at them. "And yes, I do have eyes in the back of my head."

# 39

The front door of Franklin's house was solid enough to keep out a SWAT team with a battering ram doing a drug raid.

Posters created by the IOA, NSA and NRO boasting of their spy-in-the-sky prowess lined the wall of the mudroom. The NSA eagle-and-flag emblem between the agency's proclamation of DEFENDING OUR NATION, SECURING THE FUTURE had a picture of Hitler pasted over it.

The NRO boast of WE OWN THE NIGHT, depicting a masked entity, was next to the infamous poster of an octopus with long arms wrapped around the world with the proclamation NOTHING IS BEYOND OUR REACH.

There was no need for Franklin to explain why the NRO posters were menacing. The images and statements spoke for themselves.

Franklin gestured at the posters. "Not too clever of the NRO to be boasting about how they can spy on all of us from the sky, is it? You'd think they'd be more subtle since the NSA revelations would have shown how much Big Brother is looking over our shoulders."

"Nobody ever accused a government agency of being real clever," Greg said. "A caller recently pointed out that the infamous Bay of Pigs invasion during Kennedy's administration went to hell because the CIA identified pictures of coral reefs as beds of seaweed."

"The reefs keep boats offshore," Franklin said. "Ancient history, but the mistakes made in Iraq and Afghanistan make that fiasco look like child's play. Look how they let bin Laden get away at Tora Bora."

Ali chimed in, "Someone told me once we bombed the Chinese

embassy in Serbia because a CIA analyst thought it was a munitions plant."

Through another solid door was a living room crowded with computers and electronic equipment. Greg assumed that much of the equipment had to do with Franklin's countersurveillance against the entities he believed were spying on him. Along with the electronics were nautical artifacts that looked like they had drifted in from outside with the tide to settle among the futuristic hardware.

The room looked unmanageable and chaotic to him, but so did the acre of nautical artifacts outside. He was sure Franklin had a handle on it all. No doubt Franklin's equipment in the room could track an astronaut sent to the moon—or an NRO satellite that was spying on him.

Greg told him, "The NRO believes I conspired with a hacker to steal a top secret file. I didn't. There have been two deaths—Ethan Shaw, the hacker who worked at the NRO, and Rohan, a noted writer on the paranormal. Have you heard of them?"

"Neither. How did they die?"

"Supposedly suicide, but I'm sure it was murder."

"Suicide, accidental deaths, missing and presumed dead, it's all nothing but murder when it comes back to their doorstep."

Greg had omitted Ethan's dying words and the money transfer, figuring that was too much even for Franklin.

"What's in the NRO file that's important enough to bring in black ops with a license to kill?"

"I don't know. I don't have the file even though the government thinks I do. I know zero about it. Ali worked with the hacker at the NRO and got entangled in the mess. She doesn't know what's in the file, either. She thinks it's called the God Project. Ever heard of it?"

"No, but it's the kind of boast those bastards make. So where's the file this hacker stole?"

"We don't know that, either. But we need to find it before we end up with the others on the obituary page."

"With two others already down, it sounds like the obituary page is a likely place for your next press release. They want to get rid of you, they know you're dangerous because you seek answers and millions of people listen to your show. They brag that they own the night, meaning that they're keeping us all in the dark, but you shined a light in too many times. Nothing works better than a frame-up followed by what appears to be a guilt-ridden suicide. They said I took secret documents when I blew the whistle on a billion-dollar program where most of the money was going down the drain to contractors who put in padded bills."

"Can you help us?"

"What do you want me to do?"

"I need to first look up an address. Ethan Shaw's mother lives in El Segundo. We want to pay her a visit."

"You can use that computer you're standing next to, Ali."

"And we need to go under the radar so we can try to find a way out of the mess. We got rid of our phones. We ditched our car and borrowed the green rocketship outside from a friend who is enjoying a second childhood."

"Borrowing a car doesn't keep them off your back. They will cross-reference you to everyone you have even breathed close to and get out a list of possible cars you'd be in. They use a program called Hops to do it. Computers can process millions of pieces of information in milliseconds so it's not going to be a long process. On top of that they know you aren't renting a car or flying away because they will automatically check all flights and know instantly the second you use a credit card. You use cash for a plane ticket and the DEA will do a body-cavity search before you step on board. Guess what they'd find? Heroin they planted on you.

"Friends won't be able to hide you at their place because once the cross-checking has revealed them, the searchers can tell if you're still in a building with probes that measure the chemical composition and DNA of the occupants. You can assume they will know about that car soon. Find the address you need on the computer and I'll put you in wheels that not even Jesus H. Christ knows about."

They followed him out the way they came in and around the

corner to the back of the house. A hundred feet to the rear, near where the lake of nautical artifacts ended, was a large shed that wasn't visible from the front of the house.

They waited outside while Franklin went into the shed.

"He's quite a character," Ali said. "Self-taught at science?"

"MIT followed by years at NASA and the Jet Propulsion Laboratory. A bona fide rocket scientist, not a wannabe."

Franklin came out of the shed behind the wheel of a silver Honda Civic. It looked in good condition, but struck Greg as probably a 1990s version. Ali shot Greg a look when she saw the car. She wasn't impressed. Greg was. No one would give the car a second look.

Greg said, "I'm sure he chose it because it was the most popular car in the country for a long time and will blend in anywhere."

Franklin got out of the car. "It's never been licensed or registered anywhere." Rather than a license plate on the right side of the windshield was the standard card evidencing that the car had been recently purchased used and was waiting for its license plate to arrive.

"No traceable vehicle ID number, either," Franklin said.

"Bought outside the country?" Greg asked. "Mexico? Cuba?"

"I'll never tell. Once you drive it off the property, as far as I'm concerned it never existed. And officially, it never did. Same goes for the phone inside."

Greg opened the door of the car and checked out the phone. It looked like a typical cordless landline handset and was the same size. But it had a cord that disappeared under the dash.

"Car phone," Greg said. "My dad had one like it in the eighties before they came out with cell phones."

Franklin said, "A dinosaur in the march of electronics, but that's a big plus in screwing up surveillance. Low-tech is much harder for the agencies keeping track of us to follow."

"It must have a wireless number that can be traced," Ali said.

Franklin grinned like a shark. "Like hunting for a needle in a haystack. There are thousands, hell, there's tens of thousands of wireless phone lines used in building alarm systems in L.A. alone. Those phone lines just sit there and are rarely used because they only go online to send an alarm when there's been a break-in or fire. The phone is piggybacked onto one of them."

An untraceable car that would fade into the woodwork once it was on the highway, equipped with a phone impossible to trace.

"This is your escape car?" Greg said.

"You got it. It's been sitting in the barn ready to be used for a good cause. The gas tank's bigger than the one it came with, the trunk's loaded with emergency food supplies so I'd be ready to head out when the time came. Better than a survivalist's big SUV that would stand out like a sore thumb. Like that green thing." He indicated the Cadillac. "On your way out of here drop that thing off at one of the big parking lots at Pepperdine. The kids will think it dropped down from a starship."

Franklin gave him a phone number and told Greg to call if he needed more help. "Don't worry about security. The NRO, NSA, CIA, FBI, DIA and the rest of those three-lettered assholes would play hell trying to tap into my obsolete equipment." He grinned. "Those bastards with their cutting-edge tech just don't know how to deal with stuff that was manufactured years ago."

Greg led the way out of the nautical jungle in the green Cad. Before pulling away in the Honda, Ali asked Franklin, "Do you really have a bomb on the road?"

"Do chickens have lips?"

She didn't know.

*NRO's octopus boasting that nothing is beyond its reach*

*NRO boasting that it owns the night*

*IAO boasting in Latin that the government's "knowledge is power" in regard to the massive surveillance of US citizens with the Total Information Awareness program*

# 40

Greg deposited the glowing Cad in a parking space at Pepperdine University down the Pacific Coast Highway, getting a "Great wheels, dude" from an admiring student.

He joined Ali in the getaway Honda and said, "Let's go back up the highway and take Sunset to the 405 to El Segundo. I don't want to go through Santa Monica or Venice again."

"Freeway cameras are easy to monitor because they go into a central terminal that police agencies connect to. We'd be better off taking city streets. Sawtelle goes much of the way and we can move on and off of it."

Ali drove and neither said much as they took streets that moved them along in the same direction as the freeway.

He tried to visualize how to approach Ethan's mother, wondering what emotional state they were going to find her. She would still be reeling from the loss of her son. The fact she would have been told Ethan committed suicide might aggravate her grief—or create anger toward Greg if she was told by Mond that Greg was connected to Ethan's death.

Ali broke the silence with a question. "Do chickens have lips?"

He thought for a moment. "I don't know. Why?"

"Just wondering."

"I'm wondering about Ethan's mother. For sure she's already been questioned by Mond or his pals. By now they've probably strip-searched her and her place. We don't know anything about her. She might call Mond. Let me correct that—she'll most likely call the cops the minute we give our names."

"I'm not sure. We know a couple things. Her son was antigovernment. And Ethan said she listens to your show. That's at least encouraging. Who knows—she may have had her own strange encounter."

It wasn't sarcasm this time. Maybe the fact that Ali was on the run in an anonymous car from murderous mysterious forces had altered her perception of the world she lived in.

Mrs. Shaw's house was on a quiet street lined with small but nicely kept houses. Hers was a single story, Southern California Spanish—beige stucco walls, orange clay roof tiles, arched windows, dark wood front door. Variations of the faux-Spanish style were widespread in L.A. No rack of iron bars on the windows of her house or any of the others on the street was a good sign in a metro area where addicts sometimes fed their urges with smash-and-grab break-ins.

They parked on the street around the corner from her house so the woman wouldn't get a look at Franklin's car.

Mrs. Shaw answered the door. And stared at Greg.

"I'm Greg Nowell."

"Yes, I can see that."

She was in her late fifties and didn't try to look younger. She wore a flowered smock over green slacks and a pink blouse. They had heard a vacuum cleaner going when they rang the doorbell. Her eyes were a little red.

"I'm sorry about Ethan," Greg said. "Unfortunately, I didn't drop by to tell you that. I came because the authorities believe that I received secret information Ethan had hacked. I didn't."

"I'm Ali Neal. I worked with Ethan."

She looked both of them over for a moment, then said to Ali, "Ethan mentioned you once when I called him. He said he was having a drink with a beautiful woman in a West Hollywood bar."

"I'm afraid I'm implicated, too," Ali said, "if for no other reason than Ethan and I worked at the same place."

"I know this is a bad time," Greg said.

"It's not the greatest time but then, I don't think it will be any better tomorrow. I guess you two had better come in."

They entered a living room that had, like the outside of the house, a pleasant, comfortable and solid, familiar feel—dark blue lush carpeting, brown, stuffed couch and chairs, widescreen TV on the wall, to the right of the TV a bookcase with a leather-bound set of *Encyclopedia Britannica* dated before the Internet.

She directed them to the couch and sat in a chair facing them. The vacuum cleaner was nearby.

"We're sorry to intrude upon you," he said.

"It's all right. Having a son addicted to street drugs didn't make the loss any less but made it less surprising. The uncertainty of loving someone who has been a ticking bomb for a decade is almost as bad as losing them. I thought I'd lost him years ago when he overdosed. It's really sad because he had such great talent. Did you know he was a child prodigy?"

They shook their heads.

"He wasn't even in his teens when he learned computer programming and started writing programs. An early hacker, too. He just couldn't stand someone not letting him open a door and look in." She sighed. "What is it that they think Ethan gave you?"

"I wish I knew. I first heard about it when the authorities barged into my office with a search warrant. They believe Ethan hacked into a secret program being run by the government. I imagine it was something that would be embarrassing to the government if exposed to the light of day. He worked for the NRO so the obvious conclusion is that it has something to do with their spying. Did he say anything to you about what he'd found?"

"Not a word. But he wouldn't have. He knew I was set against his hacking. He had such great talent to build programs but he wasted it figuring out ways to penetrate them. Mr. Mond also asked if Ethan had given me anything."

"You were also searched?"

"Thoroughly. They came in like gangbusters and swept through the house first with just their eyes. Then they went high-tech. I think they used a device that not only looked in the walls of the house, but even the containers of flour, sugar, cereal and whatever else I had in the kitchen and around the house. Some sort of handheld X-ray machine. I'm sure my neighbors thought it was a raid on a crack house."

"Did they find anything?" Greg asked.

"I don't know what they found. They took everything out of here electronic and everything that belonged to Ethan. And I mean *everything*. Not just an old computer he hadn't used in years, but shoes, socks, toothpaste, underwear, you name it. They said they'd give me an inventory but I haven't seen it yet."

"Did they mention us?" Ali asked.

"No, not really. They wanted to know about his girlfriend Jaime. She wasn't on my list of favorite people for Ethan to associate with because it's bad for an addict to be around another addict, but I gave them her address. Ethan and she were always arguing, maybe because they weren't on the same chemical mix, I don't know, but I know she's another hacker and that was another reason it was bad for him to be around her."

Greg asked, "Did Ethan ever mention something called the God Project?"

She shook her head. "No. Is that what he hacked into?"

"Maybe. Right now we don't know what he did, but the name has popped up. Do you by chance have a picture of Ethan? I spoke to him a number of times but never met him in person."

The picture she retrieved from the bedroom showed Ethan as reedy, even a bit gaunt, lanky and bony; he had a narrow face with thin lips and an intensity about him. He could pass for a computer nerd though Greg wasn't sure there was a prototype.

"That was taken two years ago after he'd completed six months of rehab. I took the picture because he looked better than he had in years. But he was never able to stay away from drugs. I guess there was a hole inside him that didn't get filled when he was born."

"The girlfriend, Jaime," Greg said, "it's possible Ethan said something to her about what he was hacking into. Would you mind giving us her address?"

She copied the address for them from a well-worn address book.

They thanked the woman and Greg told her they would be in touch if they made any world-shattering discoveries.

They were both quiet and introspective as they went to the car, even down. Greg knew they shouldn't have had high expectations from Ethan's mother, but they did anyway. The only thing of real value they got from the meeting was the full name and address of the girlfriend.

"Do you think we can really risk seeing her? She doesn't sound like she's going to be as stable as his mother. She might turn us in, pronto."

"Do we have a choice? She's the only lead we have. If we can't get something from her, I don't know where we'd go next." Pulling away from the curb, Greg said, "It's probably an exercise in futility, but I think we have to talk to the girlfriend even if Mond's wrecking crew has already been there. Let's just be ready to run like hell if she starts screaming for the cops."

"Do you think Mrs. Shaw called Mond?" Ali asked.

"We'll know for sure if the police are waiting for us at the girlfriend's place."

# 41

J aime Balzar lived in Culver City, back up the 405 freeway from El Segundo, and they again took city streets to avoid steady surveillance.

The apartment was above a Chinese restaurant that looked like all the Chinese restaurants Greg had ever seen but it stood out because the street was lined with otherwise faceless buildings, all three stories with flat roofs, no shutters, balconies or personality. The only architectural distinction in the neighborhood besides basic stucco walls and square aluminum-framed sliding glass windows were the wrought-iron bars on the bottom-floor windows and gang graffiti.

The only police presence visible when they drove down the street was a parked car with a police wheel chock to keep the car from being moved until outstanding fines were paid. Fat chance of the fines ever being paid—the car looked abandoned and stripped.

The street wasn't Crack Heaven, but the buildings needed patching, paint and more occupants who weren't cooking batches of meth in their kitchens.

Ethan's girlfriend lived on the second floor, up a dim stairway that hadn't been swept for a while. The stairs had a sharp, sour smell.

"Ammonia?" Ali asked.

"I've heard meth cooking described as smelling like ammonia. And cat urine." He gave her a grin as they went up. "Something else I learned as a talk show host. Better than reading encyclopedias."

"What else did you learn?"

"Last night, before Ethan turned my world upside down, I had on a fingerprint expert who said now they not only can ID people from the swirls, they can tell the sex of the person, what he ate and if he dealt drugs or took them."

"Fascinating. You must be a real hit at parties."

When they reached the top of the steps, he said, "Now that I'm getting to know you better, Ali, you know what I like about you?"

"What?"

"Nothing. Not one damn thing."

Jaime Balzar answered the door after they knocked three times and were turning away because they assumed she wasn't home.

Skinny, wearing a jogging outfit that looked like she had died and been buried in it, angry and stressed, Jaime didn't appear ready for company. She was twentyish going on a bad eighty. She had tired eyes and bitter lips. Life had been an uphill battle that wore rough edges on her.

"We were friends of Ethan's," Greg said.

"Ethan's dead. No friends." She slammed the door.

Greg knocked. "We need to talk to you."

"Fuck off," came through the door.

Greg glanced at Ali and said, "Five minutes, fifty dollars."

The door opened as if Ali Baba had spoken magic words. And he had. If there was one thing addicts understood it was that money bought moments of elation in their lives.

She gave them a once-over, then stood aside to let them in.

The room had a small couch that looked like Jaime had found it with a "free" sign on it outside on a curb. Two blankets were on the couch. That was about it for furnishings. The rest had probably gone to feed her habit. No computer was in sight, either. As a hacker, she must be pretty far gone to have let that go, though Greg thought it was more likely that she had been paid a visit by Mond.

"Give me the money."

He gave her twenty dollars. "The rest after you answer our questions." He hoped that it didn't occur to her that she might get more money by turning them over to Mond.

Getting a better look at her, he realized she had meth syndrome symptoms: dry skin, scratches on arms and face, "meth mouth" blackened teeth and a state of agitation.

"The feds have been here? Searched the place? Questioned you?"

"Yes—yes—yes." She scratched her head.

"What did you tell them about the file Ethan hacked into?"

"I don't know anything about what Ethan was doing. He did his thing, I did mine. I wasn't his keeper. Why don't you ask that bitch who led Ethan around by his dick?"

"What's her name?"

"I don't know, some bitch that got her hooks into him. He was always talking about her, said he'd dump my ass for her, but it was just talk. She got whatever she wanted but didn't want him."

Greg asked, "Did he say anything about her?"

"I don't know, I don't remember. I didn't give a shit about her. I don't give a shit about anything."

"What'd he tell you about the God Project?"

"The what shit?"

"Did Ethan tell you about what he hacked into at work or give you anything to keep for him?"

"Hell no. And if he did, the cops have it. He didn't have much here, but they took what he had. Mostly a bunch of dirty clothes."

Greg and Ali exchanged looks. She had to have been aware of what Ethan was up to at least in general terms. If nothing else Ethan would have bragged about what he was doing, but it was useless. If she knew anything it was probably stuck in a burned-out part of her brain.

He gave her the money and made a last try because he was desperate. "If you have real information you'll get more."

They were to the door when she dropped a bomb.

"What would you pay for Ethan's flash drive?"

Greg asked, "You have his flash drive?"

"I have it."

"Here?"

"Here."

He exchanged looks with Ali and then asked the woman the obvious. "Your place was searched. How did they miss it?"

"They're not as smart as they think they are. Ethan's the one who told me where to hide it. He's hidden stuff from narcs there."

"What's on the flash drive?"

She shrugged. "I don't know. My computer's broken. But Ethan told me to hide it because it was important."

Something was wrong with the story. But he was too desperate to walk out. "When did he tell you that?"

"I don't know, I don't remember, yesterday, a couple days ago. He told me to give it to you if anything happened."

"To me?" Greg asked. "Do you know who I am?"

"Ethan's friend."

"How do you know I'm Ethan's friend?"

"Fuck you—you said so."

She was right about that. "Did he give you my name? Tell you the name of the person who would be—"

"Stop it!" she shouted. "You want the fuckin' thing or not? Give me the money." She scratched her head and then her arms, drawing blood.

"Where's the flash drive?"

"Where's the money?"

He took a hundred out of his wallet.

"More."

He shook his head. "We don't know what's on it. It might be blank. Take it or leave it."

She went into the kitchen and they followed. Pots and pans and dishes filled the sink and poured over onto the countertop. Food was encrusted but that didn't matter to the flies.

She knelt down beside a cat litter box that looked cleaner than the kitchen counter. The cat litter smell had not come from the litter box or even from her apartment but from somewhere else in the building.

She ran her hand through the litter and came out with a sandwich bag. She stood up and threw it at him. It bounced off his arm and hit the floor and he picked it up.

"Give me the money," she said.

He gave her the money and they left in a hurry to get out of the depressing place. He took out the flash drive and tossed the bag.

Greg walked so fast for the car Ali told him to slow down.

"I can't keep up. You look like an angry husband running from your wife."

"Sorry. She's probably on the phone right now calling Mond to see if there's a bounty on our heads."

"More likely she hocked the phone for a fix. I didn't see one lying around. Greg, that scratching?"

"Meth syndrome. It's called crystal meth lice. They feel things crawling on their skin."

"Terrible. What harm people do to their bodies for brief moments of feeling good. More information supplied by your callers?"

"It's an eclectic education, for sure." He started the car. "We need something that can read the flash drive."

"A mall, take me to a mall. I'll run in and buy a small tablet. You might be recognized."

"Risky. What if it's traced?"

"It won't have a tracking device in it because they don't know we're buying it. I'll pay cash."

He started to pull away and braked.

"What's the matter?"

He shook his head. "Nothing. Just thinking about what the girl said about giving the flash drive to a friend."

"It's possible."

"Yeah, anything's possible at the moment."

He had learned something else during the talk with the girl, but he wasn't ready to share it with Ali.

# 42

He sat in the mall parking lot while she went inside to buy the tablet and thought about what Jaime Balzar had said about "the bitch" who led Ethan around. Was she talking about Ethan being led around romantically? Or getting him to steal secrets?

One thing for certain—Ali had lied to him.

Ali said that she and Ethan both worked for the NRO, but separately, from their residences, and only saw each other periodically back east during meetings. But that wasn't true—she had been in a bar with Ethan in West Hollywood when his mother called.

Why were they out together? Business chat? Not likely. She said they had separate functions at the NRO. On a date? A real long shot unless Ali had been leading him on, getting his testosterone levels to spike in order to get him to do her bidding. Greg wouldn't find that hard to believe—she got his own levels soaring.

A romantic relationship between the two of them just didn't work for him, not, at least, one that was honest. Ali was too mature, too sophisticated to be involved with an awkward geek who had a drug problem. He couldn't see them as romantically involved though he could imagine Ethan being attracted to her. Yet they had more of a connection than she pretended.

They had connected enough for her to tell Ethan about the God Project, which fed his hacking addiction. As she said, the fact it was the holy of holies in the world of hackers spying on spies would be irresistible for him.

Connected enough for the authorities to suspect her of conspiring with Ethan to hack into the project. Enough to meet in a bar and Ethan to brag to his mother that he was out with a beautiful woman. To stir the jealousy of Ethan's girlfriend. Enough for her to lie to me about their relationship, Greg thought.

Ali came back to the car with the tablet in a box. As she unwrapped it, she told him that they were in a wireless hotspot for the Internet.

"Ethan may not have the actual files on the flash drive. NRO national security files will be huge. He probably hid them somewhere in a cloud. In that case, I'd expect him to have a link to wherever he hid the files on the flash drive. It may take hours to find the file and access. Maybe days. Maybe the rest of our lives."

"Why?" Greg asked.

"Ethan had the ability to crack complex programs and protect them. God only knows how many levels of encryption we will hit."

"God only knows how much time we'll have to try and access the file before Mond finds us and sticks garden hoses in our mouths."

"Does what?"

"Waterboarding."

Nervous energy drove Greg out of the car while she inserted the drive into the tablet to check on its content. He walked around feeling uneasy, even antsy, ready to boil over and confront her.

The story she fed him about innocently passing on the name of a secret project to Ethan had never set right. She said she wasn't a hacker—yet she could hack into the internal security files at the NRO, one of the world's largest and most secure spy agencies.

He didn't have a problem giving her a motive for leading Ethan on. If she was a hacker, she probably had the same insatiable urge to crack into the project as Ethan had, but didn't have Ethan's talent for doing it. Even if Ethan did the actually cracking, if she was in on it with Ethan, why didn't she have the file or at least have some notion as to where it was?

He did believe the reason she gave for contacting him. If she had been connected to the theft of a secret file and didn't have it and was frightened that she would get arrested at any moment, getting it back to the government or at least finding out what was in it would be high priority.

Greg also didn't think that she was faking her concern about being arrested. She was scared for sure. And his gut was telling him that she was more heavily involved in whatever Ethan had been up to than she claimed—but not involved enough to have the file. Could she be working for Mond or some other federal agency? What do the cops call it when they get a suspect to work for them? Turning them? Hooking her onto him to get him to lead her to the file? If that was the case, they—whoever they were—would be unpleasantly surprised to find out that he actually didn't have the file.

He thought about making up an excuse to get her out of the car and leave her standing on the street, but couldn't go through with it. He didn't completely believe her so he didn't totally trust her, but he also wasn't ready to dump her when it might mean throwing her to the wolves—not to mention that if he abandoned her to Mond's tender mercies, she would reveal the car he was in and that Franklin had supplied the car and phone.

He had to consider whether he was misjudging her, too. He recognized that she was reserved and was not being completely open with him but he didn't know if that was because she was instinctively cautious with others or if she had something to hide. Probably both, was his call.

A frown and puzzlement on her face brought him back in.

"What's the matter?"

"I got by a layer of encryption and I'm into one that will maybe take me an hour to crack, but I'm sure I'll be able to do it. I've seen the type of encoding before."

"We need to find somewhere to hide out while you work on it."

She shook her head. "Something's wrong."

"What?"

She stared at him, the wheels in her head turning. She looked away for a moment before she came back with an answer. "It's too easy."

"You said it could take an hour."

"That's the point. No security program Ethan would use could be broken in an hour. But the program on the flash drive let me break into step one in minutes and I'm not near as good as Ethan and most crackers. And I recognize the encryption class used for the next step and I'm sure I'll be able to crack it."

She shook her head again. "This isn't how Ethan would do it. If he did something you thought was easy, you would soon find that you were in a digital maze and play hell trying to find a way out. This just doesn't read like Ethan. It's like looking at a signature to see if it's genuine, and it's not his.

"You have to consider something else. Why would Ethan encode a file he prepared for you? He knows you're not into computers, knows you couldn't break even the simplest encryption. So why would he bother putting any encoding on access to the file when he knows you wouldn't be able to break it but that any mid-level hacker could easily crack?"

"It's a setup," Greg said. "That's the feeling I've been having in my gut while you were working on it. Everything has been too easy. Ethan's mother welcomed us in without blinking an eye despite the fact she had already been visited by Mond."

"As if she was expecting us."

"Right, as if she was expecting us. And directs us to the girlfriend who conveniently has a flash drive in her cat litter. Remember what his mom told us—they even X-rayed the walls and cereal boxes? Think they would have left cat litter untouched?"

"I don't know."

"They're not stupid. I've heard of searchers taking toilets off the floor to see if something is hidden in the pipe underneath. They would have checked the cat box." He banged his head with his palm. "I should have thought about it. The cat litter was clean. Hell, it was cleaner than the kitchen counter. And we didn't see a cat. I'll bet she doesn't even have a cat."

"But why would Mond set us up with a flash drive containing false information if they believe we already have Ethan's stuff?"

"It may not be Mond. It may be someone who knows we don't have whatever Ethan stole."

"The black ops Franklin mentioned? But what good would it do to give us a useless flash drive?"

"To track us."

"My God, you're right. Let's get rid of this damn thing." She rolled down the window to toss the flash drive and he stopped her.

"No, that makes it too easy for them to figure out that we ditched it. Let's find another way."

He spotted a bus approaching a stop on the street next to the mall parking lot not far from where they were parked.

He jerked the flash drive out of the tablet and slipped out of the car. "I'll be back."

He was waiting at the stop when the bus arrived. He went aboard and immediately flopped into an empty seat.

"Fare," the driver said.

"Oops." Greg slipped the flash drive in the crack where the bottom seat met the back. "Wrong bus."

# 43

He got out of the bus and hurried back to the car.

"What now?" Ali asked.

"There's someone else that factors into both Ethan and Rohan. A UCLA professor, Carl Murad."

"How does he fit in?"

"He's the one who supervised the sleep study which Rohan said he'd been abducted during. He's also a skeptic and debunker of anything paranormal, from Bigfoot to E.T. He claims stories of abduction come out of movie watching. I've had him on my show several times to give another view and we always end up butting heads. He simply rejects all incidences of paranormal encounters without bothering to deal with facts. Some experiences are contrived, but others need to be investigated and some need to be thoroughly investigated when no cause was discovered other than the contention that it was a paranormal event."

"What's his connection to Ethan?"

"Rohan. He had something going with Ethan. I think Rohan was using him to hack into Murad's computer system."

"You think Rohan was behind the NRO hacking?"

"I don't know, but I'm sure he and Ethan had something going. Rohan had an obsession about Murad. He believed that the professor ran the sleep study to provide drugged people to aliens so they can be examined. He called Murad a whore master for aliens. He made that accusation in his books and talks over and over, so it's no surprise if he hired Ethan to get into Murad's system for evidence."

"With Rohan running around accusing Murad of conspiring

with aliens, it sounds like fertile ground for a defamation of character lawsuit."

"Murad claims suing him would have just given Rohan free publicity and another platform from which to hurl accusations. Rohan once told me he'd make a deal with the devil for a peek inside Murad's computer."

"Ah, you think Ethan did it."

"I'm leaning that way, plus it's a little more in line with what we're dealing with. Lately Rohan had kicked his attack on Murad up a notch, claiming he was getting proof from an unimpeachable source showing that Murad was working for an entity that sought world control."

"That unimpeachable source being the file Ethan was cracking?"

"It seems to fit. There's something else, too. Rohan knew Ethan had died shortly after it happened."

"How did he find out? Could he have been there? Saw it?"

"I had a phone message from him shortly after Ethan died. He lives in Marina Del Rey, said he used a neighbor's phone because he was worried that his was tapped. I think he was telling the truth. That means someone told him, someone who was at the scene."

"The killer?"

"I don't know. He got the word somehow. But I'd like to find out what Murad knows about Ethan. I'm only going to find out if I talk to him."

"You're going to risk calling him?"

"I was thinking more in terms of a cold call."

He started to pull out and she said, "Wait."

A black SUV came by with a white van following behind it.

"It's used," Greg said, referring to the SUV. "Not something the government or rogue ops would use."

The vehicles continued in the direction of the bus.

He pulled out of the parking lot and drove the other way.

## THE McMINNVILLE UFO PHOTOS

Paul and Evelyn Trent lived on a farm about nine miles outside of the town of McMinnville, Oregon. On May 11, 1950, at about 7:30 p.m., Mrs. Trent was feeding her animals when she saw a large, metallic-appearing, disk-like object in the sky. It was heading in her direction and moving slow.

Mr. Trent was in the house and she yelled for him. He came out and also saw the flying object before going back inside the house and getting a camera. He snapped two pictures of the UFO before the object left the area.

Like other pictures portraying UFOs, the Trents' pictures are not without their controversy, but unlike others, their pictures and they, themselves, have passed considerable scrutiny by skeptics, and their photographs are generally accepted as among the most telling shots of a UFO ever taken.

Their pictures are viewable at Wikipedia and the McMenamins UFO Festival site (ufofest.com).

# 44

As Greg drove toward UCLA, Ali asked, "How are we going to waylay Murad? Wait for him outside a classroom?"

They had already confirmed with a call to his home that Murad was on campus supervising a Saturday research project.

"Not a good idea. It would put us in the campus a long way from a getaway car we'll need in case Murad starts shouting 'Murderer!' and yelling for the campus police. Considering the way violence is happening at schools, half a dozen people would pull out guns and start shooting. Even if we got away alive, it would cause a lockdown and we'd have every police agency for a hundred miles gunning for us. Not that they're not already."

"Thanks for reminding me how weird the world has become. Getting shot at a mall or school doesn't sound paranoid at all to me."

"I'm paranoid enough to have you keep the motor running as I get out of the car to lie in wait for Murad."

"Then we need to lure him into the parking lot."

"I think I have it. He drives a classic Mercedes. On his author's book cover picture he's sitting in it wearing sunglasses and a beret. Something about the picture made me dislike him even more."

They drove around the faculty parking lot nearest to his office until they found a classic Mercedes. Being the only one in the parking lot, it had to be Murad's car by default. Decades old, it looked like it just came off the showroom floor.

"Murad treats his car better than he treats people," Greg said.

Ali called the psychology department secretary to report that her car had made physical contact with the professor's car in the parking lot.

"It's just a small scratch," she told the woman who answered, "on the door. I'm sure he won't even notice it."

She hung up and told Greg, "You're right about the car. She said when she tells him I'll be able to hear his scream from the parking lot."

Ali was parked on the street out of sight as an obviously agitated Murad hurried to the faculty parking lot. He found Greg waiting for him.

"It's okay," Greg said, "it's a false alarm."

"I see. You're being clever." Murad's hand went to his side pocket.

"If you pull out that phone, we won't be able to talk."

"Sorry, but my wife is waiting for me. I was just going to let her know I'll be a little late."

A lie, of course. "You can call her afterwards."

Murad shrugged. "Fine. From your tense body language, I suspect this won't take long. What did you want to talk to me about that's important enough to put up such pretense and an ambush?"

Murad had broad, heavy features, a flat nose and cheeks, thick lips, a boxer's cauliflower ears and a bad complexion. He combed his unruly hair with his fingers only because he believed wild hair added to his intellectual persona. Short, stumpy, like a doctor who knew he saved lives, he radiated impatience and arrogance without even having to open his mouth to tell you that he was too intelligent to have time for mere mortals.

"Rohan is dead," Greg said. "So is Ethan Shaw."

He raised his brows. "I understand Mr. Shaw left a provocative dying declaration about you. It would seem that people associated with your show have an unusually high mortality rate. Should I be worried?"

"I'm the worried one. Rohan said he spoke to you. Those were just about his dying words."

"He was a crazy bastard. Excuse me for speaking ill of the dead, but the fact that Rohan has died doesn't wipe away the harm he's done in his lifetime. That he was besmirching me with his dying breath comes as no surprise."

"How much does being murdered redeem him?"

"He can burn in hell for all I care." Murad smirked. "How he got headfirst from a balcony to a street below apparently is something that the authorities want to discuss with you."

"You must have an inside track on their sudden deaths. Neither Rohan's nor Ethan's deaths are being reported on the news."

"One of my former students keeps me informed. He's with the police. But now that you've waylaid me, is there something I can assist you with? Frankly, I'm very busy."

Murad pulled the phone out of his pocket and pretended to check the time.

Greg said, "Rohan called you."

"Oh, yes, one of his usual rants. I change my number periodically but he has someone hack into phone company records to get the new one. And the call came through identified as my wife. Childish. Ditto for hacking into my computer." He tapped his forehead. "Anything I have to hide is all up here."

"You might try aluminum foil to keep out probes from satellites. What was he ranting about?"

"The usual, of course. He wanted me to talk to him about controllers, the grays, snakes, cockroaches from the beyond, whatever the kooks who claim to see them to get their fifteen minutes of fame are calling the things they imagine are controlling the world. He said he finally has the proof that I'm the procurer, whoremonger, quisling, whatever label he was pinning on me at the moment, for alien entities taking over the world. He said that that crazy old woman from the UFO program is going to help rat me out."

He raised his eyebrows and smirked again. "I have to confess, if I had a choice between aliens light-years ahead of us and the miserable human beings of this polluted planet, I'd sell out."

It was the sort of over-the-top assertion Murad liked to make during his speech circuit.

"He had Ethan Shaw hack you?"

"The hacker could have been Satan herself for all I know. I don't really care. There was nothing to get from my computer except poorly reasoned student papers and the well-reasoned bad grades they received. You know, you haven't done the world a favor by providing an outlet for weirdos."

"I let you on the show. As for my callers who have seen, heard or want to talk about the strange and unusual, things that seem preposterous at one point of time in history often end up as the gospel later. People like you who deny solid evidence that we have had visitors remind me of the cardinals who refused to look into Galileo's telescope for fear they wouldn't see heaven."

"That's not historically correct."

"That's okay, it perfectly describes the attitude of self-serving ignorance that was used then and is still used to batter down anyone who dares ask questions that others find sacrilegious. There are unimpeachable sightings and encounters that get swept under the carpet because someone doesn't want the facts known. Anyone who has the courage to speak out gets ridiculed."

"Ignorance cuts both ways. Rohan tainted an important scientific study of how sleep and dreams shape the mind and body because he had polluted his own mind with one recreational drug too many. I worked hard on that project and he made it a joke and got rich and famous doing it."

Murad hadn't done badly himself, running around demeaning and ridiculing people.

Murad glanced at the time again. "I'm afraid that's all the time I have in which to enlighten you. Besides, the way things are going in your life, standing next to you I might get hit by a meteorite."

"Did Rohan tell you what the proof was that he'd gotten his hands on?"

"That's what you're wondering about, isn't it? How much Rohan let out of the bag, whether he ratted you out? Well, there's no more honor among conspiracy theorists as there is with thieves. He told me that you had the secret file and were going to broadcast it to the world."

Murad whipped around as he was walking away and tapped his head. "I just got a message from my pals from Planet X. You can save yourself by giving them what they want."

He howled with laughter as he climbed into his Mercedes.

# 45

Ali was getting as paranoid as Greg—she was double parked and had the motor running when he got back. She got the car moving as he was still closing the door.

"Any luck?" she asked.

"Yeah. He says Rohan told him I had the stuff to blow the lid off of Big Brother. But it's okay, because Murad can broker a deal with the aliens if I just give them the evidence."

"He said that?"

"Claimed he was joking, at least about brokering a deal. The only thing I really got out of it was that Murad knows more than he should. But he claims he has a friend in the police department. Also, he says he's been hacked by Rohan. I'm sure that Ethan did it for Rohan. One interesting thing. He said Rohan had teamed up with a crazy old woman to rat him out. I didn't dare show any interest because the woman might end up flying out a window if Murad is in league with the devil. Old woman, crazy or not, ring any bells with you? Something to do with Ethan?"

"Maybe. Ethan talked about a woman who was part of the government's UFO investigations a long time ago. I guess that would mean she was old, at least to someone his age. And crazy to Murad probably simply means she's allied with his enemies." She thought for a moment. "Kaufman, Inez Kaufman. I'm sure that's her name. He was going to visit the woman after we talked, so she must be in the L.A. area."

"Did Ethan say what he was going to talk to Kaufman about? Is she linked to an NRO program?"

Ali shook her head. "He said she was a UFO expert. A long time ago."

"Nothing about her having a connection to what he'd discovered hacking into the NRO system?"

"No."

"And he never told you what he'd found?"

"I already told you he didn't."

"I don't understand why you weren't curious since you'd got him going on the God Project in the first place."

"I didn't get him going—okay, maybe I did, inadvertently, by telling him about the conversation I had over drinks with that guy. And yes, I was curious. And worried he'd hack into something that would come back and bite me. But when I called Ethan and asked what he'd discovered at the NRO he wouldn't talk over the phone. Said he'd tell me later in person, but we never met up."

"When was that supposed to happen?"

"The night he died."

There had been a hesitation in her voice.

"What did he tell you about the Kaufman woman?"

"Nothing, really, just said she knew something about UFO investigations. Like I said, it got to the point where he was talking crazy more frequently, the kind of sound bites that came from whatever he'd been smoking. And he sounded exhausted. Said he'd been riding dirty."

"Riding dirty is having illegal drugs in the car when you're driving."

"He was talking about the illegal hacking."

"Probably meant he was hacking while on drugs. Do you remember at least what the subject matter of the gibberish was? Some clue to what Ethan had found at the NRO? It seems incredible that Ethan would have told so many people that he was getting information for me without disclosing what it was—even to me. Ethan doesn't sound like he played things that close to the chest, especially when he was self-medicating."

"What he said to me was all over the place. He said we'd been visited by aliens for thousands of years and that E.T. didn't have to call home long distance anymore. I know it sounds like a joke, but when he said it he was really worried, even panicked. Then he said he couldn't talk, they hear everything, and he hung up." She threw up her hands. "It was so frustrating. It seemed like the deeper he got into the hacking, the more he got into bending his head with drugs, always going up or coming down, but never stable enough to get any real information from."

To Greg it sounded like Ethan didn't completely trust Ali. But drugs could have played a role in that. The drugs warped his thinking about him, too. Greg couldn't think of any other explanation for the accusation that he had killed him.

"Ethan wasn't on anything when he first started calling into my show, at least nothing that showed up in what he said or how he sounded, but the last couple of weeks he was, as he put it to you, riding dirty when he called in. And he focused on the presence of visitors, just as he did with you. But that we had or have visitors doesn't ring any alarm bells for anyone who listens to my show. It's pretty much a given."

"Did Rohan mention Ethan's UFO fixation?" she asked.

"No, but we spoke only for a few seconds before the doorbell rang." He thought for a moment. "Sounds like we need to find out more about Inez Kaufman. Let's see if we can track down an address for her with Franklin. And hope he's right about this phone being untraceable."

"Greg, you look bummed out. Like a man who has been running from demons all day."

"My mind is too fried to sort it all out." He rubbed his temples. "So far everyone I've run into knows more about this than I do and all of you believe I am much cleverer than I really am."

He didn't care if she heard the suspicion and irritation in his voice that included her. She gave him a look but didn't say anything and he let the comment hang until she spoke as she pulled up to Sunset Boulevard.

"We need to talk."

"Talk."

"You're reeking with suspicion of me."

"Really? I can't imagine why. You just dropped into my life from somewhere with a confession that you aided and abetted Ethan into breaking into a secret program, igniting a killing spree that's left me running from the police and murderers."

"I didn't cause it—I'm as innocent as you." She glared at him. "If you are innocent."

The car behind them honked its horn. The light was green. She got the car moving down Sunset.

She said, "Ethan told me he gave you the file. You told me he got money from your account. I think I have a right to wonder about you."

It was futile and he knew it. They would rehash the facts and accusations and end up at a dead end again. He made a peace offer.

"Whatever has come down, we're both in jeopardy, so beating on each other isn't going to help. I apologize for being suspicious of you."

"That apology sounded as sincere as a car salesman when he apologized for selling me a lemon. But I accept your offer of not beating on each other until we have more proof."

More proof of what? His guilt? Is that what she meant? He clamped his mouth shut to suppress a retort.

"Where to, Sherlock?" she asked. "At the moment I'm not clever enough to think of anywhere to hide out short of a five-star hotel with great room service. Think they'd be a bit suspicious if we paid cash? Not that I have enough on me. A little too late to hit a ready teller. I have less than a hundred."

He took out his wallet and counted the money. "A hundred and eighty-six. Goes to show you what an amateur outlaw I am. If I had more practice being on the run I would have hit an ATM first."

Taking out cash now would put helicopters into action scanning the area. Hell, what was he thinking—helicopters were for show—they would send nasty little drones that can come down and tap you on the shoulder when they see you and satellites that can spot ants on the ground.

"We need somewhere to stay, short of using a credit card. And think. Sort things out. We can't go to Franklin's under the theory of never going back to the same place."

"More knowledge from your show?"

"Hard-earned experience gained from being a fugitive at the moment." He grabbed the car phone. "Franklin says this can't be tracked. Let's ask him where he'd hide out."

"Bob's place," Franklin said after they were connected.

"Who's Bob?"

"A guy hiding in plain sight but so far under the radar that his mother doesn't know he was born."

"Bob have a last name?"

"Call him Bob."

"Is that his name?"

"Call him Bob."

"What's Bob hiding from?"

"He keeps that under the hat, too."

"One more favor. The home address to an Inez Kaufman. All I know is the name and she probably lives in the L.A. area."

Franklin put the phone down as he surfed the Internet. He came back on and said, "An Inez Kaufman pops up. Clinical psychologist. Retired."

Greg got the addresses for Bob and Kaufman and hung up.

"Bob or whatever his name is lives in the foothills, off the 210 near a place called Azusa. At the moment. Sounds like he moves around a lot, looking over his shoulder. Kaufman lives on Wilshire back near Westwood. She's a retired psychologist."

"What would a psychologist have to do with UFOs?"

"Maybe E.T. needs a shrink."

# 46

Leon didn't like the Topanga Canyon area. He got on the winding road from the Pacific Coast Highway a couple of miles back and hadn't seen a town or even houses yet. He was used to city streets, traffic lights, buildings, fast food joints, cars and people.

He knew how to deal with a city, but he felt exposed, naked, with trees and bushes on each side of the road. It made him nervous but he didn't let the Voice know. He maintained a pretense that he had endless courage when in fact he had the mentality of a bully, puffing up with courage and fortitude when the opponent was smaller and weaker, running away when it looked like the tables were going to turn on him.

Even though he hadn't been there before, he wasn't concerned about finding the dirt road he was to turn onto. He didn't have GPS and never had a need for it because the Voice always gave him precise directions.

He had also been told that even though the sensors giving notice of intruders onto the property had been turned off, he was to make as little noise as possible, to park the car as soon as he saw the buildings on the property and go the rest of the way on foot.

Franklin was in his barn working on a replacement getaway vehicle for the one he gave Greg and Ali. The barn was as deceptive as the house: it looked rustic but was space age inside. From the outside the barn looked abandoned to mice, dry rot and the relentless Southern California sun, but on the inside it was as clean and modern as a high-tech surgical ward—except the tools, equipment and testing devices were for cars, security devices and Franklin's other "toys."

He was making revisions to a Jeep Cherokee he chose because it had been first sold in Mexico and was never officially licensed in the States. What he really liked about the car were the secret hiding places underneath and in the passenger areas, which once were used to transport cocaine but he would use as storage areas for his survival gear.

He used a two-post electric hoist to lift the car two feet off the concrete floor and then slid under it with a mechanic's creeper, lying on his back to install a gas tank larger than the one that came with the car.

He didn't know someone had entered the compound without triggering his state-of-the-art security system until he saw a pair of shoes and pants legs standing by the car.

"Who the—"

Leon leaned down and grinned at him. "Don't look now, but the sky's falling." He pressed the button labeled "LOWER" on the hoist.

Franklin tried to push out from under the hoist in the opposite direction from the killer but the creeper stopped as its wheels hit tools in the way. He heard the whine of the hoist motor and screamed as the hoist descended and touched his body.

Leon stopped the car just as it pinned Franklin to the floor. He bent down to see Franklin's face.

"God has some questions for you," Leon said. "By the way, did I tell you your voice reminds me of my father's?"

# 47

If there was a "main street" in Los Angeles, it would be Wilshire. The boulevard ran all the way from the heart of the city to the ocean in Santa Monica, slicing through Beverly Hills, Westwood, Brentwood and West L.A. on the way. It was a business district pretty much of the way, with scattered residential areas.

Inez Kaufman's apartment on Wilshire near Westwood satisfied the real estate mantra of "location, location, location."

The building where Kaufman lived was down the street and around the corner from Westwood Village, a small café and shopping area made interesting by the fact it was almost the front campus of UCLA. Bel Air and Beverly Hills weren't far. Neither was the busy 405, the San Diego Freeway, one of those concrete and asphalt arteries that connected to everywhere else if you had the time and patience for traffic that often crawled.

They did a drive-by of the apartment building. It had white-washed stucco walls and a red tile roof, giving it that faux-Spanish look that Ethan's mother's house and so many others in Southern California had. Not seeing any vehicles parked nearby that screamed "police" at them, they made a second drive-by and then used underground parking down the street and walked back to the building.

Coming up to the intercom at the front entrance, Greg suggested Ali identify them.

"Hearing a woman's voice might put her more at ease."

A sign above the communications panel told them they were on camera.

Ali pushed the button labeled KAUFMAN.

"Yes," answered an older woman's voice over the intercom.

"Ms. Kaufman, my name is Alyssa Neal. I'm here with Greg Nowell, the radio talk show host. We'd like to talk to you."

During a long pause they could hear the woman breathing.

"Come up."

The door buzzed and they pushed their way through to a small lobby and elevator. There was no security station.

Inez Kaufman was waiting for them by the elevator when it opened on her floor.

"Please hurry. I don't have much time."

She fluttered, a nervous bird, leading them into her apartment, looking up and down the hallway as if she expected her neighbors to be peeking out their doors. Greg wondered if Mond had been there already. Or whether she called Mond as soon as she got off the intercom.

The apartment's bold colors created an Art Deco feel—a print of Wassily Kandinsky's *Composition X* with its medley of bold colors was on the wall above an orange velvet couch that had blond wood trim. The large coffee table was round and mirrored with a bright brass frame. The place had a 1940s feel, reminding Greg of apartments in movies made during the Golden Age of Hollywood.

"Please . . . sit." She gestured at the couch and took a seat in a brown leather club chair anchored by oversize arms on each side.

She folded her hands in her lap as if she was waiting to hear a lecture—or a confession.

"You're not surprised to see us," Greg said. "You never asked why two strangers were at your door."

"No." It was a nervous chirp. She appeared edgy, even harried. In her seventies, she had tightly drawn skin, a narrow nose, thin lips and dark eyes. Skinny, almost skeletal, she looked brittle.

"You expected us."

"In a way. I recognized your name. Rohan told me that you want me on your show."

Her statement implied that Mond had not paid her a visit and told her Greg was on the run.

"I understand Ethan Shaw had also been in contact with you."

"Ethan? Yes, the young hacker. He asked me about the UFO invasion. Among other matters."

"What's the UFO invasion?" Ali asked.

"When they came here to stay. Or I should say, when we first got proof of their visits in modern times regardless of the fact they had been visiting us for thousands of years. There got to be so many sightings it became apparent that they stopped being visitors and had started colonizing the planet."

"Can you tell us about it?" Greg asked. "I know a bit because of my show, but Ali is new to the concept that we made contact with extraterrestrials long ago. And some of them have hung around. I, uh, understand you have been dealing with the situation for a long time." A shot in the dark, he thought. He wanted her to talk, to get comfortable with them.

"It is coming back to haunt me now, but there was a time when investigating extraterrestrial sightings was my job. I'm a clinical psychologist. I worked for the government in its UFO investigation program."

"Project Blue Book?" Greg asked.

"No, the one without a name, but I'll get to that. To understand the invasion," she said to Ali, "you should start with what Mr. Nowell said . . . we have had visitors for thousands of years. Some of the visitations were recorded by early civilizations, Egyptian, Mesopotamian and Peruvian, but even earlier than that Stone Age people left images carved on the walls of caves."

"Flaming chariots flying across the sky, that sort of thing?" Ali asked.

"Flying machines, yes, but also many other images ranging from creations that appear to be elaborate landing sites that can only be seen from the air to technology that was too far advanced for its time. There are also specific historical records of sightings of airships going back to medieval times. Of course, you don't have to go back hundreds of years to find records of UFO sightings. They happen frequently in our own time though it is interesting that even centuries ago the sightings often came in clusters, appearing in different parts of the world over a period of years. Then there would be no more reports for decades, even centuries. Suddenly the sightings would pop up again."

Ali asked, "As a psychologist does that strike you as people wanting attention saying they saw UFOs because other people got attention from having seen them?"

"Not at all. I would expect many sightings to be seen by a number of people. Also before modern times information often took years to travel great distances and sightings were often continents apart, so sightings wouldn't have been part of a mass hysteria event. Beginning in the 1940s and pretty much ever since there have been so many sightings in so many different places that it's obvious that something besides visits was happening."

"The invasion," Ali said.

"Yes, and it's okay to be skeptical; I detect that in your voice. Most people are doubtful or even cynical on the subject of extraterrestrials. I certainly was until I became enmeshed in the process. But when I took a good look at the evidence, so many of the encounters are difficult to debunk, and that left me with a reasonable presumption that we are not alone in the universe. At this point, it's hard for me to understand why there isn't a universal consensus that we have been visited over the millennia and that they have now set up camp here, so to speak."

"Even the Vatican is hedging its bets," Greg said. "Because of the advances of astrobiology and clear scientific evidence that there are other planets that can support life, they've brought together astronomers, biologists and physicists to study the existence of extraterrestrial life and the implications for the Church when the presence of aliens is no longer a secret."

"What occurred in the forties?" Ali asked.

"Many things, too many to talk about, but I can give you some of the high points. In August of 1944 during World War II the crew of a Royal Air Force reconnaissance plane returning over the English Channel from a mission reported they had been intercepted by a metallic object that hovered silently by them, pacing them before it flew off at a high rate of speed. According to the report, U.S. and British intelligence chiefs, along with Churchill and Eisenhower, discussed the incident and Churchill ordered that the incident be declared top secret because it could cause panic among war-weary people."

"What sort of corroboration is there of the sighting?" Ali asked.

"The incident was revealed sixty-six years later in 2010 by the BBC after the United Kingdom's National Archives released the information. While pilots in general are in a good position to judge other flying objects, it's interesting that it was the crew of a military reconnaissance plane that made the report. We have to assume that these wartime airmen were highly trained observers whose job it was to report accurately what they saw."

Greg said, "Sounds like their jobs were similar to that of analysts who interpret the pictures from our spy satellites."

Ali gave him a stone face.

"There were many other wartime reports of similar high-speed UFOs pacing our planes," Greg said. "Fighter pilots called them Foo Fighters and thought they were some new type of enemy aircraft. After the war there were also significant civilian observations."

"Yes, Arnold and Chiles would top my list from that era," Inez said. "In 1947 Kenneth Arnold was a successful Idaho businessman and pilot active in search-and-rescue missions. He was flying near Mount Rainier, Washington, looking for a Marine Corps transport plane that had crashed in the area when he saw UFOs flying in formation. Because he had a technical background, he was able to calculate both the supersonic speed and size of the UFOs.

"The Arnold incident was very important not only for what was reported by a pilot, but demonstrates the peculiar way reports of UFOs were handled from the very beginning. The military intelligence investigators who investigated Arnold's report labeled the UFOs a mirage, an optical illusion, despite the fact he was an experienced pilot and the founder of a successful business.

"The investigators also ignored the fact that a man prospecting in the area reported that on the same day Arnold saw UFOs he saw the same type of flying objects through a small telescope. The prospector's report was labeled as the first 'unexplained' UFO report to the air force and Arnold's was rejected outright—yet both men were describing the same objects."

"Was there any further confirmation other than the prospector with a telescope?" Ali asked.

"There were sixteen sightings in the region during that time period, but the hardest to rebut came ten days later on July 4th from the crew of a United Airlines flight. The airliner was over Idaho, en route to Seattle, when the pilot and co-pilot observed a UFO similar to what Arnold had described. They said it paced their plane for ten to fifteen minutes. The fact the report came from an airline crew should have had serious import with the investigators but it didn't. But it comes as no surprise to those who have come to believe in UFOs that reports were being discredited without consideration of the evidence and regardless of the credentials of the observers."

"Chiles and Whitted were also airline pilots," Greg said.

"Yes, they certainly were. That encounter occurred the following July. Chiles was the pilot, Whitted the co-pilot of an Eastern Airlines passenger plane over Alabama; about three in the morning they observed a rocket-shaped UFO with windows sweep by at high speed. What really intrigued the air force investigators was that a report from the Netherlands gave the same description of a UFO."

Ali shook her head to clear it. "Are you telling me that there were all these reports and the government did nothing?"

"Of course they did something—they began a cover-up that has lasted right up until the present. Remember now, I am only giving you the high points. There were many other reports, a number of them from air force pilots and military ground personnel with technical and scientific backgrounds. The reports were coming in so frequently and so many questions being asked that the government finally conceded it had to examine the phenomena.

"Under pressure, the air force established Project Sign in 1947 to investigate reports of UFOs. They staffed it with investigators that included aeronautical and missile engineers. However, when the air force investigators created a report that there were sightings most likely of extraterrestrial aircraft, the project was quickly shut down."

"No," Ali said. "There would be a stink."

"There was a stink. So the air force formed another project to investigate the sightings, this one called Grudge. However, Project Grudge from the start earned a reputation as being out to debunk all UFOs sightings even though I've been told that some personnel tried to be fair. It served its purpose by soon issuing a report denying UFOs had an extraterrestrial origin. The report was issued in 1949 and the project was then closed down for all intents and purposes even though a skeleton crew was left for a time. Because Grudge so lacked credibility, under pressure again the air force came up with Project Blue Book in 1951."

"Three different projects in four years," Greg said, "all formed because the government was compelled to do something. That speaks loudly about the state of our investigations of extraterrestrial activities."

"Wasn't there also a famous sighting in Roswell around this time?" Ali asked.

"The most famous sighting of all." Inez nodded. "But Roswell has been tainted by so many wild claims and intentional governmental misinformation that many ufologists not only avoid studying it, they won't even talk about it. It began by air force officers who examined the wreckage calling it a space vehicle and the government lying by giving out a false report that it was a weather balloon. Then came reports of strange sightings at the airbase, some of which were obviously false."

"Roswell suffers from what Carl Sagan called self-deception when it comes to extraterrestrial visitation," Greg said. "Some people eagerly accept UFO incidents as real even in the face of meager evidence and others reject the notion of aliens out of hand because they don't want it to be true. Both attitudes get in the way of serious study of a phenomenon reported by thousands of people around the world."

The telephone rang and Inez got up and excused herself. She left the room and went to her bedroom to answer the call.

Greg leaned over and whispered to Ali, "Let's hope that's not Mond."

"Maybe it's E.T."

# 48

S orry. Where was I?" Inez asked as she returned to the chair with the oversize arms.

"I suspect you were about to describe Project Blue Book to Ali."

"Yes, well, it's pretty much the same story as the other two, isn't it? There were thousands of reports to be examined, most of which could easily be explained as weather or some other natural phenomenon. Then there was an occasional hoax by someone who had a saucer-shaped pie pan, some fishing line and a camera and thought they were funny.

"When it was all over, Project Blue Book was closed down in the late sixties, but it had served its purpose by ensuring no sighting, no matter who made it or how credible it was, was ever classified as extraterrestrial."

"Everything was classified as terrestrial?" Ali asked.

"No, that wouldn't work because of the shape and speed of the objects seen. What the investigators first did was discredit the observations like they did in the past by saying they were caused by weather, optical illusions, that sort of thing. By the late sixties the project had debunked so many sightings that had credible witnesses, including one involving police officers from several jurisdictions chasing a low-flying UFO, that the project simply lost credibility. Like Grudge, it left with a report that debunked an extraterrestrial connection to UFOs, but its specific conclusions were doozies.

"Even though it couldn't give terrestrial explanations to a large number of the sightings it examined, the project came out with a final report that said UFO sightings were the result of misinterpretation of conventional objects, mass hysteria, hoaxes and psycho-paths."

"No," Ali said.

"Oh, yes. Can you imagine how respectable airline and military pilots felt? To be labeled with having a mental disorder because they reported seeing a UFO? It isn't hard to imagine that most people would keep their mouths shut rather than face ridicule and ruin of their careers. And that's exactly what happened. As soon as the crazy and ridiculous labels were attached to sightings, most people refused to report what they saw."

Ali waved her hands in frustration. "Is this still going on? Strange sightings being shoved under the table?"

"Constantly, consistently and vengefully until it takes an act of bravery to report a close encounter because of the stigma the government has associated with seeing something that they say doesn't exist. The stigma is especially directed against airline pilots, who risk loss of their careers for reporting UFO sightings."

"How do Betty and Barney Hill fit into all this?" Ali asked, giving Greg a glance.

"I'm guilty of telling her about how two intelligent, educated people with good jobs and strong community ties reported an encounter with a UFO and extraterrestrials and that their sighting was not seriously investigated."

"Did you also tell her about the JFK connection?"

He shook his head. "Be my guest."

"There is a theory that the assassination of JFK was related to the Hill and other encounters. In the sixties there was another rash of UFO sightings, some of the most credible ones that Project Blue Book dealt with and was unable to come up with explanations for. So many, in fact, that it was like a repeat of the forties invasion all over again. In New Mexico and New Hampshire the sightings were by respected police officers; in Australia two hundred students and teachers outside saw a UFO descend and land briefly before taking off again.

"The Hill incident in 1961 was among the most sensational but even though they reported it to the authorities soon after the incident, they didn't go public with their ordeal until 1963. After their sensational story hit the presses, President Kennedy demanded the files on UFOs that the air force was concealing. He knew that President Truman had issued a secret order during the 1947 invasion creating a clandestine group to deal with UFOs."

"Majestic 12," Greg said.

"Yes, code name Majestic 12. As the reports of UFO incidents poured in, Kennedy realized that we had been invaded and that key elements of our military had been subjugated by the invaders. He was killed shortly after making a demand for the secret files. Some believe that Robert Kennedy was assassinated because he also took up a sword against the invasion. Project Blue Book was phased out in 1969 following Robert Kennedy's death."

"You haven't told us your role, Inez," Greg said.

"As you might imagine, publicly shutting down Project Blue Book didn't stop the actual investigation of UFOs. The reports kept coming in and had to be investigated even though Blue Book was sucked into the same black hole as Sign and Grudge and for the same reasons—it had lost all credibility as an impartial investigator of encounters of any kind. But the government still had to have people dealing with UFO reports, even if it was done covertly, if for no other reason than we were in the middle of the Cold War and the next unidentified flying object streaking across our skies just might be a Soviet intercontinental missile carrying a nuke."

"How did they manage to do it covertly?" Ali asked.

"By not giving it a name; that's all it took. They referred to it internally as the interagency. And we were instructed never to capitalize the *I* because that would imply it was an actual government agency."

"That's certainly vague enough," Greg murmured. "Interagency" was how Detective Batista had described Mond's position and what the search warrant had said. Which meant Mond's day job might be investigating—or deliberately not investigating—UFO incidents. Or more likely Mond was an enforcer—taking care of business when the sightings were reported with more accuracy and enthusiasm than the "interagency" wanted.

"I went to work for the interagency, the project, whatever you want to call it, in the late seventies right after getting my PhD. I had no problem with the mission statement given to me when I was hired—I was to evaluate the mental faculties of people who claimed to have seen UFOs, aliens, or had been abducted. I assumed I would be doing a thorough, professional psychological workup of the people.

"But that's not how it came down. Most of the reports that came in turned out to be easy for the investigators with aeronautical skills to provide mundane explanations—weird cloud formations, freak atmospheric phenomena, weather balloons, meteors, Venus glowing, even flares dropped from planes and Chinese lanterns. And we got the occasional person with a psychopathic disorder that caused them to see things that weren't there for the rest of us. There's no question that most UFO sightings were reported by well-intentioned people who saw something strange that turned out to be something explainable besides the spacecraft of extraterrestrials.

"However, we wouldn't be here having this discussion if all UFO sightings could be explained by things we earthlings are comfortable with. Occasionally something is seen that simply defies any explanation other than it is not of earthly origin. When that happened, the true mission of the nonagency called interagency was to summarily debunk it. No one realizes how easily these things are simply swept under the rug without an investigation by handpicked personnel who are only looking for ways to discredit the sightings.

"Take the incredible sighting at Chicago's O'Hare airport in 2006 when twelve airport employees and several people outside the airport witnessed a hovering disk-shaped UFO before it shot up and disappeared into clouds. It was during daylight, about four in the afternoon. Here again, the most bizarre thing is not that the event occurred but that no investigation was done. The FAA first denied that anyone had reported the incident until the *Chicago Tribune* uncovered the fact that a supervisor had called in a report. Confronted with their lie, the FAA stated that the sighting they say they had no record of and had not investigated was a weather phenomenon."

"Unbelievable," Ali said.

"Routine," Greg said.

"I'm surprised you never went on Greg's show," Ali said.

"I haven't gone public with what I know because I'm ashamed. I was able to do my job honestly a lot of the time because most sightings can be explained. It usually wasn't difficult to do a psychological analysis of a person who claimed to have seen aliens or had been abducted by them and disprove their claim because they had a history of seeing things that weren't there. By the time I got to reasonable people describing credible sightings, they were angry, defensive and humiliated by the ridicule they received from everyone around them. Even with credible people, it wasn't hard to label their sighting as a misinterpretation or an overworked imagination.

"But of course, it was inevitable that someday I would start hating myself as I swept people's lives into the black hole. It was a sighting by a police officer that did me in, one of those close encounters out in the desert where he was the only witness and the officer's dash cam was found to have malfunctioned; at least, that's what our investigators said. For sure it wasn't working after they got through with it. But he was a brave man who refused to back down and it ended his career, his marriage and finally his life when he overdosed because of shame and frustration.

"It was because of him that I had to face my demons and admit to myself that I had not been hired to fairly evaluate people, but to discredit them. Oh, I had a good excuse. I was a single mother of a child with special needs and I had to stay on the job for the benefits. Lacking the courage to go public, I stuck around until I was able to get a university teaching position."

She threw up her hands. "So there you have it. I have been wallowing in self-pity, angry with myself for my lack of courage, afraid to go on Greg's show and expose the fraud to the world. My mother was a survivor of the Holocaust, a woman of substance with an iron rod for a backbone. If she were still alive she would be ashamed of me. I'm ashamed of myself."

Greg asked, "What were you working on with Rohan?"

"Yes, Rohan. He arrived at my door with his story of having been labeled delusional because he experienced being abducted during a university sleep study. I spent several weeks going over his story and emotional state before I reached a conclusion that he had in fact been abducted. He wanted me to go public with my support of him and reveal how many other people had been labeled as psychotic. I have been wrestling with my conscience and my courage about going public with my diagnosis of him."

"Rohan is dead," Greg said.

She sighed. "Yes, I know; so little, so late on my part. Ethan has also crossed the great divide. I only met Ethan briefly. Rohan had referred him because Ethan was very curious about the onslaught of extraterrestrial activity starting in the forties. Also, Rohan thought I might be able to help the young man with his addiction. I'm afraid I was of little help to him. He saw me only once, asked me many questions about extraterrestrial sightings and didn't come back when I asked if he wanted to consult me about his addiction. He wasn't ready to deal with his personal demons."

"Has Mond been here?"

"No. He's very much aware that it would be futile because I won't speak to him. I haven't gone public and he'll leave me alone as long as he thinks I will keep my mouth shut. He worked for the interagency when I was there. I knew of him but never quite understood his function except that mention of his name would bring an uneasy silence with people having coffee in the break room. A prototype man in black, pitch black with not a hint of light, working among those of us who were only in shadows."

"Will you continue to keep your mouth shut?" Ali asked.

"I think I'm ready to go public. I worry about it, but I'm getting old and I would hate to be on my deathbed agonizing over the fact I hadn't shown even a smidgen of the courage my mother had."

"My show is temporarily off-hook," Greg said, "but when I get back to it, I'd like to have you on. Assuming that there will be a show after Mond gets through with me. He's a fascinating creature—like looking at a snake under glass in a zoo."

"Just don't stick your hand in the cage," Inez said. "We can talk about how to get my message over to the public if you two manage to stay alive or not get shut away in some black-op prison."

She smiled at the look on their faces. "But I may be able to help a little in that regard. You need friends, allies in a better position than an old woman with dry bones. The opportunity to do this is with Aaron."

"Who's Aaron?" Ali asked.

"Aaron isn't a who but a what. It's a group of people interested in making sure that the Internet and Web are kept free of control by governments out to enslave people and ideas."

"Hackers," Greg said, "a secret organization of them."

"Hackers? I don't know, I've never asked about their methods. You've heard of them?"

"No, but I suspect they've chosen a name in honor of a young man who was accused of hacking into MIT and killed himself when the government charged him with serious crimes."

"I admit I don't know anything about them except for their goal. I was contacted by them after I met with Ethan. I got a call from a woman who asked if it was all right if someone from the organization dropped by to talk. A few days later a young man about Ethan's age came by."

"What did he want?"

"The same as you. He asked about the UFO invasion and how the government dealt with reports of extraterrestrial encounters. Particularly as to whether we had reports of electronics such as computers or programs that were far beyond human capability."

"Were there reports?"

"Yes, I heard about one now and again, usually someone claiming their computer had been taken over by some unknown entity. Unfortunately, in this world, where most of us are linked through our computers and smartphones, there are so many Trojans, back doors, rootkits and other malware that aliens would have to get in line behind the local invaders."

"Was Ethan an Aaron?"

"He said they were helping him with a project. I didn't get the impression that he was an Aaron, especially since he used his real name with me."

"Can you arrange a meeting with these people?" Ali asked.

"It's already been done. The phone call a few minutes ago was confirmation. An Aaron will meet you at Universal CityWalk in an hour."

"You called them after you buzzed us in," Greg said.

"I actually returned their call. They called earlier and asked me to let them know when you showed up."

Greg exchanged looks with Ali. How did the hackers know they would end up at the woman's place?

"Did they mention both of us?" he asked.

"Only you. You're wondering why only your name. I can't help you with that. Perhaps because you're so well known."

"The person meeting us—no name but Aaron?" Greg asked.

She nodded.

"How do we make contact? CityWalk's big and usually crowded."

"The Aaron will find you. I'm not sure what they meant but I'm to tell you to stand by the big guitar but don't make it obvious. The Aaron knows what you look like and that you will be with Ali."

"You don't know if it's a man or a woman?"

She shook her head. "I've spoken to both."

Greg asked a question that had been bothering him. "I wondered how you knew both that Rohan and Ethan were dead. Was it the Aarons who told you?"

She slowly nodded. "If you want to know if that scares me, the answer is yes. But I am determined to just close my eyes and keep taking steps forward."

# 49

They were back on the street, on their way to the car, trying to spot anything out of the ordinary and not look too obvious, before they spoke.

"Do you believe Kennedy was assassinated because he was going to expose a UFO cover-up?" Ali asked.

He let the question hang for a moment as he wondered if Inez had been honest about her dealings with Mond. It didn't seem likely that Mond would back off from harassing her as easily as she indicated. But it was possible he didn't push her because she knew so much.

"The interesting thing about the Kennedy assassination is that there are a large number of reasonable conspiracy theories about why he was killed and each of the theories has identified a perpetrator having a motive. The most bizarre thing is that Lee Harvey Oswald, acting on his own, didn't appear to have a motive. Jack Ruby silenced Oswald so quickly that we'll never know the truth about Oswald or Ruby. Mafia, CIA, Cubans, Russians, J. Edgar Hoover, Vietnamese are just a few of the dozens of alleged conspiracies that have identified over two hundred people as potential conspirators. A UFO cover-up fits as well as the rest of them.

"A while back, a British tabloid put out a purported letter from Kennedy to the director of the CIA demanding information about UFOs shortly before he was assassinated, but the word 'defense' was spelled in the British manner, with a *c* rather than an *s*, raising questions about whether a White House secretary would use it that way."

"So the letter was a hoax?"

He shrugged. "I don't know what it was. Bad spelling by a secretary? A hoax prepared with an obvious flaw to make it appear that the notion of Kennedy being killed because he sought information about aliens was ridiculous?"

After they got into the car she said, "You know how your head is telling you that everyone else seems to know more than you? Well, that's what mine is telling me. I just don't know how much of it is true."

# 50

CityWalk was several blocks of tightly packed cafés, night spots, shops, entertainment and dining venues for tourists to throw money at before entering the Universal Studios Hollywood tour. There were enough bright, flashing, garish lights to entertain astronauts on the International Space Station.

Greg and Ali parked as close as they could get to the big guitar but the complex was large enough so that even what was called "front gate parking" made a quick getaway impossible.

The brassy big guitar Inez told them to hang around was in front of the Hard Rock Café. The restaurant stood like a neon-trimmed Rock of Gibraltar at an intersection where the Walk split into two lanes.

It was a good spot to hide in plain sight because of the colorful eye candy for tourists, who could take pictures of each other and buy things that would be shown to friends when they returned home and eventually end up at a yard sale.

Greg and Ali shied away from the big guitar itself because a group of Japanese tourists were using it as a backdrop for pictures. They wandered in the area, trying to fade into the crowds while looking for someone that they hoped would stand out like a sore thumb. If an interagency tech was watching on the cameras that kept the Walk under constant surveillance, she would have easily spotted Ali and Greg because their attempt to act like carefree tourists was belied by their tense body language and the fact they looked at people and not things.

There hadn't been much discussion between Greg and Ali about the Aarons on the way over. That there was a secret organization involved in tackling the nation's electronic spy apparatus didn't surprise him. Snowden wasn't the first to attempt it, and after his revelations, more people certainly would try it. The fact Ethan had dealt with them gave Greg hope that the group could provide information about what the hacker had done and maybe even offer him and Ali safe haven.

He didn't know how long they could duck being discovered while running around in Franklin's car and hoping someone would give them a bed for the night. It wouldn't be long before they had to attempt to get money from an ATM for gas, food and a roof over their heads. Both were certain that a cash withdrawal would result in their capture.

He realized Inez's narration about the history of UFO sightings wasn't just to inform Ali, but to make him comfortable with the fact that there had been genuine encounters with visitors from the beyond. That wasn't necessary when it came to him. He knew that the encounters that had begun in the forties and were still going on today involved too many people who were hard to discount. Hoaxes, natural phenomena of one sort or another and earthly aircraft explained most sightings, but it was a stretch to discount those that happened when weather was reasonably clear and the reports came from people who had credibility.

The phrase that came to Greg's mind was that where there's smoke, there's fire. But how Ethan and the NRO fit into the sightings was something he hoped the shadowy Aarons would answer.

A child, a girl about ten, ran up to them.

"Hi, Mr. Nowell." She handed him an envelope and dashed away.

Inside were two VIP passes to the studio tour.

"Close to eight hundred dollars for two," Greg said, showing Ali the passes. "I treated important guests with VIP passes. The Aarons must have somebody with money behind them."

"What are we supposed to do with them?" she asked.

"Do what comes natural: take the tour. Let's find the VIP entrance."

In the VIP section they were directed to a trolley driven by a woman and took a seat in the back row. They were the only passengers and the trolley didn't move. Aaron apparently hadn't arrived. Greg wondered if Aaron, he or she, was watching to see if the coast was clear.

"Interesting," Greg told Ali. "If we are being watched, it won't be easy for Mond's people to commandeer a trolley and chase after us. They'd look like the Keystone Kops."

"I wonder where we're going. Getting the whole tour?"

The answer to that question climbed aboard and took a seat in front of them.

"Welcome aboard. I'm Aaron."

Aaron was big, a couple inches over six feet, with a large head and broad features; thin, rimless glasses straddled a wide nose. He carried a lot of body weight, most of it soft, probably from too many years spent hunched in front of a computer. His food choices didn't appear to help, either—he had a sausage dog overflowing with mustard and beans in one hand and a giant soda in the other.

As the trolley got started Greg said, "VIP, nice touch. I hope you didn't have to go out of pocket for the tickets."

"Not a problem. We have their computers trained to ask how high when we tell them to jump. Unfortunately, the only thing we will be using the trolley for is a quick ride. It would take too much time to hit the attractions." He grinned. "Besides, I think you have your own house of horrors to deal with."

Greg took an instant dislike to the guy. He reminded him of another Murad, a smirker who thought he was superior. He was superior, of course, when it came to understanding computer programs but that was the limit of it. From the looks of him, Greg decided a more fundamental problem for the arrogant jerk was to know when to come in out of the rain.

"You asked for this meeting," Greg said. "What do you want?"

The trolley veered off the path and went behind a building, where it stopped in a dark area off the tour path.

"What did Inez Kaufman tell you about us?" Aaron asked.

"Not much," Greg said.

"We're techs who track down and expose the outright spying and invasions of privacy that the computer age has permitted governments and corporations to engage in against the common person. You know what's happened to the country, to the whole world. People used to worry that J. Edgar Hoover had them under surveillance or their social security number was like 666, the number of the Beast that would arise to control their lives.

"Today's surveillance is all-seeing. What's crazy is that Snowden sat in Hawaii with his computer and showed how easy it is to access all that information, and there are thousands of Snowdens out there who have access to our information. Every phone call we make, e-mail we send, everything we buy from carrots to beer, our financial deals, all are tracked electronically. Government surveillance by electronics has to be curtailed and the only way it's going to happen is if people like us Aarons who have the tech knowledge fight back."

"Sounds like a full-time job for an army of computer experts."

"It is, but there aren't that many of us because most people are too scared of the consequences of being caught. We operate undercover and keep our identities secret as much as possible, even from each other, so that if one of us is busted, he or she won't be able to name all the others."

Not knowing the names of other conspirators was a standard tactic of secret cells of dissenters dating back to the days when interrogation automatically started with a torturer and a bone-breaking rack.

Greg said, "What you do can't be that illegal. Unless you're hacking into secret sites to check them out. Are you?"

Aaron shrugged with a little grin that boasted that he was indeed hacking. He took a bite of his sausage dog, then talked while chewing with his mouth open, letting some bean juice dribble down the corner of his mouth.

"We need anonymity to keep down reprisals. Some of us work for the very business or governmental entities we expose. We're all called Aarons, but we have a second handle so we can tell each other apart. I am Aaron one-one-one-oh-one."

Ones and zeroes were computer-speak. It made the guy sound like an android. A little over the top to someone like Greg, whose heart didn't beat to the same rhythm of positive and negative binary bits, but maybe 11101 and the other geeks really were flesh-covered motherboards. It was an era of game playing in which individuals and vast military complexes jockeyed to decide the fate of nations. From the sound of it, the Aarons were into game playing, too.

Greg didn't like the way the guy ate, talked and failed to hide his contempt for mere mortals who didn't care what 11101 spelled. The mission the man described was admirable—the government needed oversight by citizens to keep it in line with its security needs and the Constitution. Saving the world from invasions of privacy, however, was more likely an ego trip than an idealistic venture for this Aaron. Even his sausage dog and giant soda annoyed Greg. Worse than the man's food intake, Greg had decided that the guy was not going to be any real help. But he needed to learn as much as he could about Ethan before everything went to hell with 11101.

"Was Ethan Shaw an Aaron?" Greg asked.

"Shaw contacted a programmer who worked at the NSA, asking for information. The person is one of us."

"What did Ethan want?"

"Access to a quantum computer system the NSA had developed to break computer encryptions. He wanted to crack an NRO program that was locked tighter than anything he'd seen before. And he needed to do it on a zero-day basis."

"Which is?"

"He had to crack it on the first try by finding a vulnerability no one else had ever attempted because he would only have one chance. Once they became aware of an attempt to enter by an intruder, the file would be moved and buried somewhere else."

It was all going too easy. He was asking questions and the man was answering. There had to be a catch.

"What was he looking for at the NRO?" Greg asked.

"He had a theory that the visitors you discussed with Inez Kaufman can hide from radar because of their stealth designs, because even we unwashed earthlings can do that. And when conditions are right for people to get an actual glimpse of them, the sightings can be explained away by the weather phenomena or be ridiculed. But there's one thing that can't be explained."

"Pictures," Greg said, "hard evidence. A picture would be worth a thousand eyewitnesses."

"Exactly."

" 'Vigilance from above,' 'nothing is beyond our reach,' " Ali said. "Not even flying saucers would be invisible to cameras pointing down from satellites."

Aaron 11101 said, "A ring of satellites whipping around the world, filming twenty-four/seven, has to be the worst scenario for the visitors. We expected Ethan to find those pictures in the program he cracked."

"And he didn't," Greg said. The conclusion was evident from Aaron's tone and Greg immediately saw a flaw in the reasoning behind the picture theory. "The images would have been erased as soon as they were recorded."

"Yes, that's what we ultimately decided. They are too smart to leave the evidence stored in a file that could be hacked into."

"The greatest danger to the visitors is the NRO," Greg said. "There's more chance of exposures from satellites than any other sources. That makes controlling the NRO a necessity."

The NRO had in constant motion reconnaissance satellites ringing the entire planet, snapping thousands of pictures every day. The cameras wouldn't be directed toward UFOs but it was inevitable that pictures would be taken of them. The visitors would also have to deal with any other satellites capable of detecting them, but the NRO would be the main risk of exposure.

Greg asked, "What did Ethan actually find?"

Aaron gave him a look over a sip of soda. "That's what we need to know from you."

*Here we go again.*

"What if I told you Ethan never gave me anything?"

"I would say you're a liar. Ethan told us he had gotten the information for you to expose on your show. And he showed us proof because we wanted to know what he planned to do with the information he found."

"What proof?"

"Receipt for a money transfer from you to him. He said you had given him the money so that he could get out of the country and go into hiding when you released the information over the air. He was going to share the information with us at the same time, but he didn't. He got so cranked up on meth that we couldn't get anything from him except gibberish. Another Aaron told me he thought Ethan had taken a dose that fried his brains."

Perhaps provided by someone who wanted Ethan's brains to be scrambled, Greg thought.

"I can't explain why money got transferred out of my account to Ethan's, but I guarantee you it got there without me knowing anything about it."

"Is that what you told the police?"

"They didn't believe it."

"Neither do I."

"It should be obvious that if I had the information you believe Ethan got from cracking an NRO program, I wouldn't be running around trying to find it. Like Ethan told you, I'd be on the air with it, not on the run from the police, hiding out in a trolley at an amusement park."

"We don't believe you. And we're willing to make a deal. Give us the file Ethan downloaded and we'll help you disappear."

"Disappear? I don't want to disappear. I want to clear my name."

"You don't have another choice. Unless you turn over the file to us, you'll be met by the police before you can exit the tour. One of our people is hanging out by the police substation in CityWalk. If I give a signal, you'll be grabbed before you make it back to your car. We know where you parked, of course." He smirked again. "We have access to the cameras."

The smirk really pissed Greg off. It gave him tight jaws. "That's a good, public-spirited attitude," he said. "Blackmail me rather than help me out." As he spoke he slipped his hand into Ali's handbag. "I don't think I like you, one-one-whatever your number is. I think you're an arrogant asshole."

Greg brought his hand out of the handbag with Ali's phone and leaped forward and grabbed 11101 around the neck, jerking him close with the side of his face against the Aaron's. He snapped a selfie of himself and the jerk.

The Aaron pulled free. "What the hell are you doing?"

"Get us back to CityWalk, you prick, before I send your ugly mug to my Web site and it goes viral. When that happens you can explain why you helped me steal secrets—if you can talk between gulps of toilet water they'll waterboard you with."

Walking to the car, Ali said, "That was quick thinking on your part. I can't even imagine how you thought of it or how you pulled it off."

"An act of desperation and frustration arising from being an innocent man caught up in a web of intrigue. I'm not only tired of everyone knowing more than me, but of everyone thinking I know more than I do. And being called a liar."

# 51

Leon followed the silver Honda Civic carrying Greg and Ali from the CityWalk parking lot down the hill to a right on Lankershim, up to Cahuenga and then the Ventura Freeway heading toward Pasadena. At Pasadena the Honda merged onto the 210 East, with the white van behind it.

Leon already knew the destination of the people he was following. It was the Azusa safe house that Franklin had arranged for them.

He proudly repeated every turn he made, speaking aloud to continuously update the Voice on his progress, all of which was unnecessary since the van was being tracked by his controllers. He tried to keep the Honda in sight but it wasn't necessary since it was also being tracked.

The Honda got off at the Azusa exit and pulled into the drive-through of a fast food place.

Leon pulled over to the curb and stopped at a spot that kept the Honda in sight.

"Is it time to punish these people?" he asked the Voice.

*There will be a time to punish the man, but the time is not right. But it will be soon.*

The Honda pulled over to a parking space in the fast food lot after receiving the food.

"They're gonna eat it there," Leon said.

He hated the waiting. He worked best and was most manageable if he had simple goals with quick results. Anything that required patience, planning or introspection was pushing the envelope with him.

He had thoughts, but they didn't stay around and build into anything. Thoughts about childhood, of his nonexistent brutal father and absentee mother, dark days at schools and the orphanage where he beat on children he could hurt and took beatings from ones who could hurt him, flashed like cars speeding by on a dark road, but little of it stuck to be mulled over.

Everything that went through his mind was real to him despite the fact some of it never happened and much of it came down far different than he remembered.

He had no abiding interest in people. He was an emotional desert with occasional volcanic eruptions of rage, a person who had no need for friendship or companionship, and had never been in love with or even infatuated with a woman or even had an intimate, down-and-dirty, personal, let-it-all-hang-out conversation with anyone.

The lengthiest conversations he had were with psychiatrists, during which he lied about anything important and said what he thought the doctors wanted to hear. He fooled no one, but he believed he was being clever and manipulative and it gave him a satisfying sense of power.

He never had much schooling and knew little about the world other than the range of things that affected him. He didn't possess the commonsense skills needed to survive daily life at the most basic level—working for a wage, paying rent and utilities and buying food.

Early on he found it easier to commit crimes to get the necessities of life because he couldn't hold down a job. Getting locked up in a prison or mental hospital was a relief—it meant he was in a controlled environment in which he didn't have to survive on his own. Confinement worked well only temporarily because he was unable to control his impulse to do violence. He would soon become fixated on how he could murder someone in the facility.

Being captive to the Voice was comfortable, almost like being back at the hospital, because it didn't require that he keep a job and pay bills. It was even better than prison or a psych ward because it gave him an outlet for his rage.

He had been chosen for murder assignments because he had few needs beyond eating, excreting and sleeping. What he enjoyed most beyond eating and sleeping was playing violent video games and watching action films.

He also had a fascination for virtual Internet gambling, but only for the slot machines. He played them on the Internet at every opportunity, even if it was just pausing for a few minutes in his van. The simplicity and mindlessness of the slots with their colorful displays, sound effects and loud payoffs held his attention.

He didn't question the reasons behind the commands he was given because the Voice satisfied all his needs without raising his ire. He got rewards when he did well, extra time playing computer games, slot machines and watching action movies. There had been a time when violent porn had been on his cravings list, but no more because he no longer had sexual urges.

Years earlier he would have had sexual cravings for both sexes that were violent and impossible for him to control. Those uncontrollable urges were dulled after he was chemically castrated in the mental hospital. He had agreed to the process because it got him out of his cell and a look at his surroundings and thoughts about ways to escape.

He was still being chemically castrated as part of his management by the Voice. The drug was part of the cocktail of antipsychotic drugs that kept his violent sexual urges under control. It wasn't a once-and-then-done treatment, but had to be periodically administered to keep the drive from returning.

The castration drug reduced Leon's sex drive, the compulsive, violent sexual fantasies he used to suffer and his capacity to achieve arousal and erection. The rest of the cocktail kept his other murderous impulses in check, at least until they were needed to complete missions.

The purpose was not to protect society from a violent, sexually deviant psychopath, but for his controllers to keep him on a choke chain and direct his aggressions for their own use.

A side effect of the castration drug would be apparent to anyone who saw Leon's naked chest before he had been given the drug—his breasts were larger now. Gynecomastia, the development of larger than normal breasts in men, was a side effect of the drug. So was an increase in body fat. The physical side effects were similar to what eunuchs suffered.

The Honda left the fast food parking lot and he followed behind it as it headed in the direction of the foothills that began just a few miles from the freeway.

The car made a left turn into a residential development but he didn't follow behind it because he was concerned he would be spotted. Instead, he drove farther up the road and made a U-turn, coming back and turning into the development. He already knew the address.

The Voice said, *Park at least a block away from the house, Leon. And wait until I tell you it is time to go.*

"What will I be doing?"

*God's work, Leon, as you always do, as Saint Leon did before you.*

"I'm hungry."

*Later, after your work is done. You haven't heard the man you are following speak, have you, Leon?*

"No. Not yet."

*When you hear the man's voice, it will be familiar to you. He sounds like your father.*

# 52

Novak hated telling Mond things he didn't like hearing.

"The woman using the name Alyssa Neal has not been identified as a member of any governmental or private intelligence agency. Or anywhere else, for that matter. Ditto for any other documentation about her."

"She's been erased," Mond said. "It's difficult but not impossible to do. We've done it many times."

She started to ask why the agency had erased people but a look from him stopped her: she was certain he regretted making the statement. A signal coming through on her control panel saved her from getting snapped at for his mistake.

Novak said, "Sir—Nowell and the woman have been spotted."

"Put it on the screen."

The scene that came up on the war board was of Greg Nowell and the woman calling herself Alyssa Neal standing by a garishly lit store selling tourist items.

"Where are they?"

"CityWalk. The outdoor mall at the Universal Studios tour."

"When was this shot?"

"Twenty-nine minutes ago. It's the mall's CCTV put online."

"Twenty-nine minutes. We might be able to catch up with them. First let's see if they're still there. Go directly to the parking exits, starting with the one closest to where they're standing."

Novak entered a search command on all the mall's cameras for images of the two suspects and brought up images of them in the parking lot getting into a silver Honda Civic to leave CityWalk.

They followed the car out of the parking lot and down the steep incline to a right turn on Lankershim.

"You familiar with the area?" Mond asked her.

"Yes, sir. I live in North Hollywood."

"Where would you guess they're heading?"

"They could be going anywhere, but if they stay headed in the same direction they would be able to get onto the Ventura Freeway."

"Which goes to?"

"It goes east and west and connects to other freeways that also go north and south. I'll pull up the east and west freeway on-ramps to see which one they take."

Mond got up and paced. She had not seen him so excited till now, but they had a chance to close in on the suspects.

"East, sir, they're heading in the direction of Pasadena, but the freeway connects to the 10 that goes all the way to Florida."

"Scan the exit cameras for the car starting with the closest one to where they got on the freeway."

The agency's superfast computers flew through each exit camera in seconds. Novak jumped in her seat when she got a hit.

"Got 'em, sir. They got off the freeway just a moment ago. A place called Azusa. It's not a heavily populated area."

"Get our field people headed there in copters, direct drones for immediate aerial surveillance, get satellite coverage and notify the local police to immediately detain them but they're not to question—"

"Wait!"

"What? Don't interrupt me."

"Sir, there's a priority-five message for your eyes only."

Novak passed the link to the message to Mond's cell phone. She tried not to look but it was obvious that the message did not sit well with Mond. At first he seemed surprised, a slap-in-the-face surprised. And puzzled. Now he appeared petrified. She cringed, wondering if she had done something to generate the message of the highest priority.

When he spoke, he didn't look at her. "We have been ordered off the surveillance. Shut down all programs being used. Get the word out to our field agents to return to—"

"That can't be!" Novak gasped. "We've found them in real time. We just need to get the local police to grab them."

Mond's face had turned pale when he read the message. Now it went red. "Don't ever question an order. I should have you reprimanded."

"I—I'm sorry, sir, I just—"

"You don't understand, you're not seeing the big picture."

Mond got up and paced, getting control of his anger. He waved up at the image of the car on a street in Azusa.

"The decision's made. They will deal with Nowell and the woman in another manner."

# 53

W hat's the matter?" Ali asked.
Greg had been peering in the side and rearview mirrors since they got off the freeway in Azusa and ate fast food. They had stopped at an In-N-Out Burger before heading out of the business district, going north, toward the foothills.

He kept checking the car's mirrors as they headed for the neighborhood of Bob, Franklin's under-the-radar friend. It was dark and all Greg saw in the mirrors were headlights.

"I don't know. Paranoia. I noticed a van behind us as we got off the freeway. I can't tell if it's still back there."

"What kind of van?"

"I'm not sure, a company van, white, maybe a plumber or something."

"You really are paranoid if you think we're being followed by plumbers."

"Yeah, but a van almost turned me into roadkill on my way to the funicular the night you passed me that cryptic message. Don't forget Rohan was paranoid, too, but he might have opened the door to a guy in a work uniform. I'm trying to remember if I saw a company van on Rohan's street when I got there, but nothing pops up."

Azusa was one of the hundreds of unmemorable bedroom towns and districts for the nearly 20 million people of the L.A. combined area that spread out from the coast to the desert for about fifty miles in every direction. The main part of the town hugged the area between the 210 Freeway and the foothills of the San Gabriel Mountains.

Not far from the freeway the foothills began, rising to nearly nine thousand feet, not particularly high peaks when compared to the Sierras. Narrow roads, not all paved, led up the foothills from the flatlands, with most of the roads ending in dead ends, often at lakes or reservoirs.

The trees and bushes were the typically moisture-stunted variety found in Southern California. The farther east one went, greenery stopped and the sparse, sandy Mojave and Sonoran deserts unfolded. The basin turned into an oasis only where water stolen from the north of the state and other western states was used.

"I'm wondering what comes after Bob," Ali said.

He knew she was not happy about the way things had gone with the Aaron. She thought Greg hadn't been tolerant enough with the jerk.

"We need them," she told him earlier as they headed for Azusa. "How else are we going to get help?"

He didn't see the secret organization of hackers as rescuers. They had their own agenda and he doubted it amounted to much more than what the CityWalk Aaron had said—*give me the secret file or we'll turn you in to the cops.* Once they had the file and their fifteen minutes of fame, Greg and Ali could rot in prison.

No one was going to protect them from the authorities. No one could for long, anyway. Once he ran out of friendly, safe places to stay, and Bob might be the last one, and ran out of places to search for the file, which he already had, he wondered what else was left except to wave down the nearest cop and tell him he'd made his day by helping him capture a desperate criminal.

He sensed the darkness closing in on him, smothering, as if he had disturbed some primeval, preternatural underworld that dark things escaped from. He felt claustrophobic. He needed to get out of the car and walk but that wasn't in the cards at night in a strange town. He would just attract the attention of the police.

He gripped the wheel tighter and told himself to deal with it, to walk away from where his fear and imagination were taking him. He needed to focus on the next step, the one beyond Bob.

Going to a newspaper or TV news station sounded plausible but that would work only if he had something to prove his innocence with or could provide evidence of wrongdoing by the government. Even at that it wouldn't keep the two of them from being arrested, although it might keep them from being buried alive in some remote place, a "black hotel" where you check in but never check out because it's a secret prison of a U.S. intelligence agency.

He relayed his thoughts to her.

"Black hotel?" she said. "That's an interesting take on vacations. Enjoy waterboarding, taking freezing-cold baths, losing weight on a bread and water diet, getting a massage on an inquisitor's rack. Frankly, I'd rather get into bed with the Aarons."

"I don't trust one-one-one or any other number."

"The number thing sounds kind of dumb, but what do you expect from computer geeks? Boys and girls with their toys. How does any port in a storm sound?"

"Like a shipwreck."

"We can't go to the news media without proof and we don't have the proof. Shipwreck, train wreck, plane crash, going down for the third time—no matter how you cut it, we need help finding the file."

"Why do you think one-one-one and his pals will help us? You know that I have to give them something I don't have or they'll turn us in."

She glanced at him and looked away, hesitating.

"Spit it out," he said, "tell me something you and everyone else knows but that I'm completely in the dark about."

"They'll help us out because they believe you still have it."

"I don't—"

"Wait, I know, you say you don't have it and I believe you. But remember, Ethan told them he gave it to you."

"He didn't."

"Not that you're aware of."

"This thing keeps going around in circles with you, Mond, Aaron and everyone else who knew Ethan. Get it straight for the umpteenth time—*I don't have it*. And I checked my e-mails and text messages after Ethan was killed. The only other way he could have gotten it to me was from the spirit world after he hit the sidewalk. But that's a possibility. He did call me postmortem."

"What do you mean?"

"My phone rang when I was walking home. The caller ID said Ethan Shaw."

"Maybe that's it."

"Ethan was on his way to the morgue when the call came through."

"He might have sent you a message with a built-in delay."

"There was no message, period. I thought it was someone with the police trying to track down Ethan's family through Ethan's phone's contact list. But if it was a secret message it is now floating in the L.A. sewer system. So that's my story. You and everyone else can go hunting for the file in sewers."

She put her hand on his arm. "I can't explain the phone call; you might be right, someone might have been looking for Ethan's next of kin. I know you don't believe you have the file, but I also know that as crazy as Ethan was, he was also a mad genius. We're talking about a twenty-something kid who managed to crack what is probably the holy of holies of the secret world of spy organizations."

"You think I have the file and just don't know it."

"Yes. Ethan loved hiding his trail. He was super-inventive about it. I'm sure Mond has by now connected me with you, but I don't think he's found a direct link between me and Ethan, despite our phone calls and text messages. Ethan would have covered our tracks."

"Okay, so your plan is to hand me over to the Aarons and what? Will they hypnotize me to find the file in my subconscious? Get me on a psychoanalysis couch so Inez Kaufman can unleash my repressed memories?"

"Stop it! Please. I know what you're going through, I'm here with you. My point is that we don't have any other choices. I'm pretty sure Ethan got into the file or he'd still be alive. He said he gave it to you. The Aarons can tackle every possible way that Ethan could have done it. Even that phone call. The file might be sitting right now in your e-mail account, an invisible file that you would never find. But Mond's people will ultimately find it if we can't get the Aarons to jump in and help."

He was getting tight jaws but her argument made sense. Even he was now convinced Ethan had given him the file. And getting it to Greg so the file would be invisible to prying eyes was how Ethan most likely would have done it.

Ali said, "You haven't told me yet what your plan is when we wake up tomorrow morning and Bob shows us the door—if he even lets us in tonight. We can't keep shuffling around to whoever your friend Franklin can find. We've made zero progress towards finding the file. What are we going to do if we can't find it? I think we're in a holding pattern, waiting to run out of fuel and crash. Going to jail or your black-ops hotel isn't something I want to experience. At least the Aarons might get us to a country where we wouldn't be extradited because they hate Americans."

"Sure, and they'll probably support us for the rest of our lives in the style we've grown accustomed to. One look at Big Soda Cup Aaron didn't give me confidence in turning my life over to him."

"Don't let the wrapping one-one-one-oh-one came in fool you. If he and the other Aarons were capable of giving Ethan a hand, they're major-league hackers."

Greg shook his head, trying to get all the pieces to work. "Look, I don't disagree with you. Finding the file is the only way out. And the best bet would be with the Aarons because they have the know-how. But I'm not ready for that yet. You keep reminding me that Ethan said he gave the file to me. So maybe you're right, maybe I'll get a sudden revelation and the answer to where Ethan hid it will explode in my brain. Besides, we don't know how to contact the Aarons."

"Inez Kaufman can put us into contact with them," Ali said.

"Let me think about it," he said. "Sleep on it."

More likely he would lie awake, staring up at the ceiling, wondering why the boogie man had come back into his life.

# 54

They did a drive-by of Bob's house. It was the last house on a quiet street at the back end of a residential area. The backyard ended at arid, rocky terrain with stunted trees and bushes—the beginning of the San Gabriel foothills. There was no house directly across the street; the closest one was to the right on the same side as Bob's. Bare windows and an overgrown front yard gave the neighboring house an abandoned appearance.

"Good place to drop under the radar," Greg said. "If nothing else, it doesn't look like a neighborhood where there would be many surveillance cameras."

Ali pointed up to the heavens with her forefinger. "Nothing's beyond their reach."

A white Ford F350 pickup with a camper shell was parked on Bob's concrete driveway. Dents, scrapes and faded paint showed the truck and camper were well traveled.

"The camper makes him independent," Greg said. "He can stock it with basics, maybe beans and flour and peanut butter, and head into the wilderness for months without having to venture back into civilization. Franklin probably has an emergency food supply ready to grab and go."

She gave him a look. "Wilderness survival something else you learned on talk radio? Do you have a grab-and-go, too?"

"I'll take the Fifth on that question because I won't win with you no matter how I answer it."

They parked the car two blocks away and walked back, not meeting anyone on the street or seeing a passing car. From what they saw through windows as they walked, most people were bellied up to the dinner table.

The house was a one-story, weathered ranch with vinyl siding, a composition roof and gabled louvers at each end. The other houses in the neighborhood were chips off the same block, comprising a low-end housing development built several decades earlier on what was cheap land. They were now fighting off dry rot after being toasted by Southern California sunshine and scorching Santa Ana winds. As with the camper, the shine was gone from the homes.

Bob's house had iron bars on the windows, as did a couple other houses they passed on the street, a feature probably motivated by the fact there was a middle school down the street.

The windows were dark but a little glow around the edge of a drape at the front window hinted there was a light on in the living room.

"Call me Bob," he told them when he answered the door. Greg wondered if that was really his name.

Raw-boned, tall, broad-shouldered, with a beer belly folded over his belt, he had brown hair streaked with gray down to his shoulders, a full beard that was white at the tip, coffee-colored, thick-rimmed old-fashioned glasses, tan wash pants that had been used while painting, a wrinkled, faded, dark green long-sleeve shirt, black running shoes and a purple and gold Lakers' cap. The hat, shoes and other clothes, like the truck, were well traveled.

Greg didn't know if the beard helped keep Bob under the radar. While beards tended to stand out because they were not as common as clean-shaven, the beard could be reduced to a mustache or to no facial hair to quickly change looks. The same for the long hair, which could go to a buzz cut in seconds.

He wondered if the thick-framed glasses were also for a quick change.

"I know who you are, listen to your show," he told Greg. "Even been on. More than once, but I never talk about the same thing twice. That way I don't leave tracks."

"What name did you use on the show?"

"Used different names."

"Right now I could use a different one," Greg said.

"Franklin said you needed shelter. Didn't tell me why, I don't want to know. Loose lips sink ships."

A man of few words and tight lips.

The living room was furnished basic—stuffed couch, dark colored to hide the wear and tear, stuffed recliner, coffee table, lamps on tables on each end of the couch. The only personal touches were a portable TV that looked like a boom box and a laptop that sat on the coffee table along with a bottle of beer, a tall Styrofoam soda pop cup, a crunched KFC box, a jar of peanut butter and saltine crackers.

It struck Greg that the house was a furnished rental and that Bob had moved in with just a few items, ready to leave on a moment's notice. Even the camper truck had been backed into the driveway, ready to head out.

Bob noticed Ali eyeing the living room décor. The couch had a sleeping bag thrown on it. Greg took that to be Bob's bedding, period.

"I'm a floater," Bob said, "carried by the current and the wind wherever it takes me. Whenever I want to go. Tried settling down, but I realized that they always have a camera on you even on the street and on the job. I finally packed up and started drifting when I realized that I was being filmed and recorded by feds through light fixtures and wall plugs."

"Do you believe they're watching everyone?" Ali asked.

"Not yet, just the ones who have let it be known that they're on to their game. But it will come to that. That's where it's headed for sure. When I was a kid, no one was keeping twenty-four/seven tabs on you, but as electronic surveillance gadgets got as tiny as pinpoints and able to pick up sounds through walls, it became obvious to some of us that somebody"—he eyed them—"or something was picking up information about us."

"How did you discover it? What tipped you off that you were being kept under scrutiny?" Ali asked.

To Greg she sounded like a prosecutor cross-examining a witness—curious, but doubtful.

"Small things at first. At work personal stuff about me was being discussed that had never left my house. At first I took it to be coincidences. Thought I was just being overly paranoid. But I moved on to another job and pretty soon it became obvious that things that happened behind closed doors were deliberately being revealed to harass me and keep me off balance. And it all started after asking questions about what was going on around me."

He gestured at the sleeping bag and portable TV.

"It isn't a life for everyone. If you're lonely, you sure as hell will be a lot lonelier if you keep on trucking from one place to another, but it's my way of keeping them off balance. You have to be a minimalist to live like I do, but I pack a lot of baggage compared to the true minimalists."

"Who are the true minimalists?" Ali asked.

"The homeless and the dead."

They followed him down a short hallway that had a bedroom on each side and a bathroom at the end. He led them into the bedroom on the left. The bed had a bare double mattress covered by a sleeping bag that was unzipped and spread out.

"Not much I can offer you in terms of creature comfort, but it shouldn't be too cool tonight."

"Are we taking your bed?" Ali asked.

"Nah, I sleep out in the camper most of the time. If I'm not here in the morning, it's because I got carried away by the current. You won't find anything to eat in the kitchen, but there are fast food joints down toward the freeway."

He left them alone, closing the door behind him.

Ali shook her head and whispered, "Very strange."

Greg said, "There have always been people like him, totally divorced from society. Living in remote areas, mountains and deserts with no one else for miles, few amenities, no TV or Internet or social media. Probably no family or friends. He just has a set of wheels under him and keeps on rolling."

"Floating, he's swept along with the current. Franklin didn't give any clue as to why Bob's on the run?"

"He may just be fleeing the thing that many of us fear—authority. The overwhelming amount and abuse of it by our government. And a feeling of the inevitable, that someday what he fears is going to come pounding at his door in the middle of the night."

Greg had just described his own fears. "Feeling like a stranger in a strange land?" he asked.

"I feel like I'm in an America that I didn't even know existed. I knew about the domestic spying, that Big Brother is always looking over your shoulder and we have to fight it, but I didn't realize so many people were so totally alienated from our society. You read about survivalists whose houses are like fortresses in the wilderness, but Franklin and Bob are not worried about the apocalypse. They're hiding from the mind-boggling scrutiny that all of us are subjected to. I didn't realize that we're just bugs under a microscope."

"Science is advancing faster than our minds and hearts can handle," Greg said. "We're creating things that invade our privacy to the point that there's no place outside our homes where we're not being observed and it's only going to get worse. Robots are already stronger and faster and can beat the greatest chess players—what's going to happen when they can outsmart us about everything else?"

"I'm getting a headache just thinking about what a mess my life and the world is in." Ali moved aside a drape enough to check out the window and threw up her hands. "Bars. I hope this isn't a sign of things to come in my life."

# 55

Leon parked the van around the corner and went on foot to the house as he'd been told to do. He wore his utility company uniform and carried the high-tech-appearing device that conveyed the impression it was testing equipment. Hanging from his shoulder was a tool bag.

He would have preferred to have used a gun in carrying out his assignments but the Voice forbade it. Besides the noise and evidence a gun created, there was too much chance for Leon to go wild and crazy with a gun as he had when he'd got his hands on a foster father's gun when he was a young teen.

He walked slowly, in no hurry. Along the way he saw people through picture windows, families eating dinner, people watching TV. He felt no curiosity, no envy, no loneliness, when he saw the people dining and relaxing together. What he felt was irritation at the thought of trying to be sociable. If he had been at a dinner table with other people he would have been angry and rattled. Almost anything he didn't flow with could cause him to go into a frenzy until medication and the soothing Voice calmed him.

He felt isolated and alienated from all people—and angry at them for his powerlessness. When he fantasized about people it was not being part of a warm family group but having people fear him. Punishing them for the way they treated him and getting their rapt attention by frightening them gave him power.

He didn't understand the concept of respect for others and didn't give it to anyone. What he thought of as respect from others to him was their fear and trepidation of him.

Several times he had briefly experienced living in a house with a family during attempts at getting him foster care, but he preferred being by himself. As usual, last night he stayed at a motel—a different one than he stayed in the night before. He didn't choose the place, pay for it or sign the register. He found the address to the motel and a key on his passenger seat when he returned from relieving himself at a gas station restroom. The room was always booked for him and he never stayed in the same room for more than two nights.

He always ate in his room or the van because he didn't do well in restaurants—too often he heard someone speaking that reminded him of his nonexistent father. And sometimes he just stared at people. Not really out of curiosity, not wondering about their lives—mostly because sometimes he just kept looking at the same person for no apparent reason, making the target nervous as hell.

Soon after he arrived at the motel a pizza was delivered. It was almost always pizza because he liked it better than most other foods, but occasionally he told the Voice he wanted Chinese food. He never ordered the food but was told by the Voice how much to give the deliveryperson, including a tip. He didn't like the idea of giving a tip but was punished when he disobeyed because failing to tip would make him more memorable to the deliveryman.

He brought his tablet into his room. He never watched television or listened to the radio. Instead, he used the tablet this night for virtual gambling.

The instructions from the Voice tonight were more complicated and dangerous than for most other assignments. As he walked up the sidewalk toward the front door of the house he decided he would ask for more than the usual amount of virtual money to play the shots. A bonus, he thought. He would ask for a bonus for this kill.

# 56

As soon as Bob had his guests tucked away, he loaded up food and personal items in the house except for his portable TV and beer and took the stuff out to the truck. Having company told him it was time to move on, to keep on truckin' to somewhere he knew no one.

The two people he'd agreed to hide out for the night were using one of his sleeping bags so after he loaded up, he went back inside to wait until morning to move on.

Another small town? he wondered. It was easier to find people in small towns than big cities, but there were more cameras in big cities and he got tired of counting them. He decided he'd head east on the freeway and look for a town that was so poor it had few cameras. Once he got on the freeway, there were a thousand miles of desert and plenty of dusty, thirsty towns along the way. *Sounds like a plan,* he told himself.

He had a beer in his hand and a basketball game on the portable TV when he heard knocking on his front door. He didn't get visitors but a neighbor once dropped by to borrow jumper cables to start his car and another time a Jehovah's Witness tried to save his soul. Neither did their calling at night but he didn't think of that as he got off the couch and went to the door.

He opened the door to find a man in a utility company uniform holding a gadget that looked like testing equipment.

"Checking for gas leaks," Leon said.

"Gas leak?" Bob sniffed and glanced behind him, toward the kitchen. "I don't have any leaks."

"You soon will." Leon pulled the hidden trigger on the weapon.

Bob was hit with a beam from the device that sent him stumbling backward. He dropped to his knees, disoriented. Leon kicked him in the face, sending Bob over, flat on his back.

Leon looked down at him for a moment and then took his foot and stomped Bob in the solar plexus.

Leaving Bob on the floor with the man gasping for breath and his legs twitching, Leon closed the front door. He went across the living room to the kitchen. He quickly checked the gas stove, turning on a burner to see if the gas was working. It was—the burner ignited.

He left the kitchen and looked down the hallway. The bathroom door at the end of the hall was open; the two bedroom doors, one on each side of the hallway, were closed. He needed to know which one held the prey.

Leon went back to Bob, who had struggled into a sitting position on the floor. Bob was still dazed and his arms and limbs weren't cooperating. He stood in front of him and took his foot and shoved Bob back down, onto the floor. Then he knelt down, putting his knee on Bob's chest, pinning him to the floor.

He pulled out a knife from a sheath and put the point on Bob's Adam's apple, applying enough pressure to penetrate the skin.

"Tell me what room your guests are holed up in."

# 57

Greg lay on the bed with his head elevated, supported by his coat, which he'd laid over the foot rail. Ali was opposite to him, back against the headboard.

So close, but so far away. It reminded him of a story he'd read in an English class in school an eon ago about a knight and his lady love who were doomed to sleep with a sword between them for some offense they had committed. Only in his case, the issues between Ali and him were as explosive as the IED Franklin claimed he had his road mined with.

It was hard for him to imagine being on a bed with an attractive woman and not making love. Despite the strange, grinding tension of what they were up against, he still felt attracted to Ali. More than that, she ignited another feeling in him. Being around her brought home how lonely and emotionally isolated he felt because his lifestyle dominated his existence.

His relationships with women had always been strained by his total commitment to his show, a dedication bordering sometimes on an obsession as he got more caught up in both the intrigue and excitement of unraveling what he saw as a threat from the unknown. Probing the unknown, giving others the opportunity to tell the world about their experiences, were more than a job to him. They were a full-time commitment to uncover the truth.

He wondered what was going on in her head. Women and men had different paths toward sexual arousal. Did she want to make love with him? Or at least cuddle close for comfort as they faced danger together?

He shut his eyes and tried to think but questions roiled in his head on bumpy waves. *Is the NRO doing the killing? Some governmental black ops agency? The controllers? Someone else who is affected? How does Mond fit into the scenario? Bad guy? Or just a bureaucrat doing his job? Should we try to contact Mond? Try to convince him that we don't have, and have never had, Ethan's file?*

His instinct said that Mond wouldn't believe him. More than that—from everything he'd been told about Mond and the interagency, it was most likely that Mond didn't want to believe him. Greg's instincts about people were usually pretty good and Mond struck him as having a brain and nervous system wrapped in bureaucratic red tape at best. At worst, the man was working for an agency that was deliberately keeping the "alien invasion" a secret from the world.

The bottom line was that he didn't trust Mond. Period.

He turned his thoughts back to Ethan, trying to get into Ethan's mind, the guy's way of thinking. Like Ali, Mond and the Aarons, he was now convinced that Ethan had intended to give him the secret file. That was bizarre, but there was no reason to believe Ethan was thinking rationally and it fit too nicely to rebut. It wasn't just that Ethan told people he gave the file to Greg. Greg sensed that he was still alive because they—whoever they were—wanted to give him enough rope to get to the file so they could retrieve it before dealing with him.

Ethan could have lied and told people he gave the file to Greg, but what purpose would that have served? He also could have intended to give Greg the file but never got around to it before demon drugs and a killer found him.

The notion Ali threw onto the table earlier, that Greg had the file but just didn't know it, was sounding more reasonable to him. Also that Ethan might have sent the file to him via e-mail so deeply encrypted that it would take another hacker to break in and read it. He was reasonably sure that Ethan, like so many high-tech mentalities, didn't always understand that the average person's technical skill on computers was limited to clicking on icons and getting hopelessly lost when the link went nowhere.

From the call-ins to the show before he was barred because of his tone and language, it was obvious that Ethan was wound up tight with idealism and that he saw Greg's talk show, which reached millions of people, as an outlet to expose the wrongs he believed the government was doing.

If Ethan sent the file to Greg's personal or show e-mail, it was a certainty Mond had it. Not only did the government have full access to his e-mails even before they physically seized his computers at home and at the office, once they had the computers in their possession, they had another shot at anything they'd missed.

Ali was convinced that Ethan would have gotten the file to him in a way that made it difficult for even government computer experts to find. Great. If Ethan was so clever that people who knew what they were doing couldn't find the file, how would Greg have found it?

"Could Ethan have sent me the file other than by e-mail?" he asked Ali.

"If you're thinking he sent you the actual file, I would say that was unlikely. He most likely would have sent you a link that took you to it because the file itself may be enormous. He could get a link to you in any number of ways."

"Attach it to my Facebook page? As a text message or tweet?"

"Those and many other ways. It could be an express link or he could have gotten clever and provided only a clue to a link or hid the link in a message that's on an entirely different subject."

"Hidden in a Viagra spam, a message from an online retailer offering me a discount on the next best-seller, written on a sign in the background of a selfie of Ethan on the beach?"

She groaned. "I think Ethan was cleverer than that, but I do like the link printed on a beach sign. Obviously, he needed to get it to you so you'd recognize it yet it would fool an expert."

"Good luck on that. You have any idea as to how Ethan would pull that off?" he asked.

She sighed. "Not the foggiest. Ethan didn't think like ordinary people and he didn't hack like ordinary hackers. How he could get it to you without immediately tipping off government experts is beyond me."

Greg didn't know enough about the strange world of hacking to even start imagining ways Ethan might have done it.

"How does hacking work?" he asked Ali.

"How does it work?"

"I'm trying to get into Ethan's head, at least the technical part of his brain that enabled him to hack into my bank account and send me a file that I don't know I have."

"It's all about vulnerabilities in the system you want to enter and take control of, exploiting a weakness, an opening. You've seen *Star Wars*, the original movie?"

"Who hasn't?"

"Remember how the rebels fought the empire's planet-killing space thing? It was the largest man-made thing in the universe, but there was a tiny opening someone neglected to seal. Something like an air vent but it's outer space. That's how a hacker goes after the system of a corporation or the government. They're looking for that door that someone forgot to nail shut. Ethan was capable of taking it farther than most hackers."

"Because he had access to the big NSA computer?"

"That helped but so did the Aarons, and they needed to team up with Ethan. You have to appreciate that there are few people on the entire planet, even with help from the Aarons, who could have used the NSA's super-quantum code-breaking machine to hack into a system as secure as the NRO's. That alone took a special talent that Ethan had, something I mentioned before.

"Ethan wasn't just a hacker, he wrote programs. Once he got a foot in, he would rewrite the program to make it do what he wanted. So he wasn't just capable of getting into the program and using it, he could manipulate it. As I said, hacking is done by taking advantage of flaws in software or flaws in the humans who put the pieces all together. Once Ethan learned how the software was made, there would be no stopping him from entering and plundering, if that's what his objective was."

"I imagine that it would have been a piece of cake for a pro like Ethan to crack my bank account," Greg said.

"For a world-class hacker like Ethan it would have been easy, especially when you consider that he had the resources of the NSA's super-encryption-breaking computer to do it with, not to mention he had NRO assets, too. With computers from the world's two most important spy agencies, he probably could have broken into any system on the planet."

"Or broken into a system that originated in a galaxy far, far—"

"Please. We have enough problems with our earthly menaces. We don't need to import any from Planet X."

He leaned up to meet her eye. "We don't have to worry about alien invasions. The bugs will take care of that."

"Come again?"

"H. G. Wells, *War of the Worlds*; the Martians kicked our butts, but microscopic bacteria killed them. So there's hope. But getting back to Ethan, he sat at home and used his computer to access the site he stole the files from?"

"Yes. I know he did a lot of his work from home and he had a much more powerful processor than this tablet to do it with. I don't know what type of access the Aarons had arranged to the NSA program. But to really understand Ethan you need to realize that hacking, cracking, whatever you want to call it, isn't just science or mechanics, which most people think it is, but an art form."

"An art form," Greg told the ceiling. "So Ethan wasn't just a hopped-up guy with a computer, he was the Michelangelo of geeks."

"Exactly, sans the sarcasm. As his mother said, he was a self-taught prodigy when it came to hacking. Like a child sitting down at a piano and suddenly putting out brilliant Chopin, when Ethan's fingers went onto a computer keyboard they took him to places with locked doors and he started unlocking them. It's like plotting your way through a maze, a labyrinth with intricate combinations of paths that make it difficult to find one's way or to reach the exit because some roads lead to dead ends and others keep taking you back to where you started.

"I also don't know anyone who could do what Ethan did for the NRO. I'm talking about the legitimate work he did. He was able to quickly learn the language that created an NRO file, no matter which one was used. I had a Spanish teacher who escaped from a

North Korean gulag and came to America. He never had a lesson in English or Spanish. He learned Spanish, English and other languages well enough to teach them without having formal instruction himself. He said the key was his ability to mimic languages. He was a savant when it came to spoken languages, just like Ethan was one with computers. Ethan had a reputation of being able to crack the esoteric computer languages other programmers created for fun to stump other geeks.

"But as you know, Ethan was really immature in his thinking, not just with drugs and society in general, but his attitude toward the world of computing. He was like a kid who couldn't stand to see a puzzle that went unsolved. He had to know what the secret was, what was worth hiding."

Greg said, "Unfortunately for him, Rohan and us, he hacked into a secret someone is willing to kill for."

"Greg, don't just think about Ethan's abilities to hack into a system; he also was a master at secret encoding. It goes with the territory. Ethan's mother probably created disappearing ink with lemon juice to write secret messages when she was a kid. Ethan most likely e-mailed a picture of his dog with a message weaved in the hair. They say bin Laden hid secret messages in porn flicks."

"Steganography."

"Yes, the art of concealing a message in plain sight or within a message. My favorite is a trick used in ancient times. The king would have a slave's head shaved, have a message tattooed on it and send the slave to deliver the message after his hair had grown back. Things moved a bit slower back then."

"Sounds like a death sentence for the slave after he delivered the message and had his head shaved to read it. They couldn't have let him wander around loose with an important message on his head. Besides the world moving slower, life was cheaper."

Greg's favorite secret messages were the ones where American POWs in Vietnam blinked out *T-O-R-T-U-R-E* to let the world know prisoners were being tortured, and the POWs who gave the finger to their unsuspecting North Korean captors while being televised.

"Anyway," she said, "like all other hackers on the planet, Ethan would be fascinated by the art of secret messages. Unfortunately, he would also be better at it than most of us. He could easily hide a message in just the color spectrum of a picture."

"But I'd never find it and from what you've said, he could do one that only a few people in the world could decode. So we always go back to the same premise—it's likely Ethan did send a message that I could decipher myself or with little help. Which means the government or whoever would have read it."

They were silent for a while, each alone with their thoughts before Ali spoke again. "Was there ever a time in the world when there wasn't a great threat to humanity? My father served in the military during the Cold War, when people dug holes in their backyards to protect them from the nuclear fallout they expected; my grandparents fought the Nazis' insane lust to conquer the world and reshape it into their twisted image. Now something—your aliens or government run amuck—is strangling the world with electronics."

"The troubles all began with the forbidden fruit of the Tree of Knowledge," Greg said. "It's back again. The computers, the Internet, the Web, satellites circling around us day and night, cameras photographing our every move—they're hanging over us like a twenty-first-century Tree of Knowledge, wrapping around and strangling us like a giant boa."

# 58

Leon went quietly down the hallway. He paused by the door that Bob told him the guests were staying in and listened. He could hear the hum of the occupants speaking, but couldn't make out the words. He slipped across the hallway and listened at the door that he was told was unoccupied. Not hearing any sounds he quietly opened the door. The room had neither people nor furniture.

He shut the door and went back to the door to the bedroom that Greg and Ali were in. He removed his shoulder bag, opened it and took out a thin cable and quietly tied the end of it to the door handle. He strung the cable across the hallway to the opposite door and tied it to the handle, pulling it tight.

He put a screwdriver through a loop on the cable halfway between the two doors and began twisting the wire with the screwdriver.

Greg and Ali were lying back, their eyes closed, when Greg suddenly shot up.

"What's the matter?" Ali asked.

"I heard something. From the hallway." He got off the bed.

"Maybe it's just Bob."

Greg went to the door and turned the handle to open the door and take a peek out. The door handle turned but he couldn't open the door. He gave it a jerk and pulled hard. It opened just an inch before flying shut, just enough to give him a glimpse of Leon in the hallway twisting the screwdriver in the cable loop, making the line more taut. When he tried to jerk the door open again, it wouldn't budge.

Ali asked, "What's the matter?"

"Someone's out there! We're locked in!"

He tried the door again and she grabbed his arm with both hands and tried to help pull.

He said, "It's no use. He's got us trapped."

"Bob?"

"No. Some guy in a uniform."

"Your van driver." Ali banged on the door. "Open the door. We'll pay you."

"With what?" Greg muttered.

He went to the only window in the room to check it out. Iron bars. The backyard had tall yellow grass that would act like kindling when sparks hit it. The house next door had appeared empty when they drove by and half of the fence between the properties had fallen down, confirming his suspicion that there was no one nearby to whom to shout for help.

Ali said, "We need to convince him we have the file. If he lets us out, we'd have a chance to escape."

"I don't know. He'll know we're lying about the file." Greg pounded on the door. "Hey! Open up. Let us out and we'll talk about the file."

"What do you think he's going to do?"

He shook his head. They both knew the answer to that one. It didn't matter if Greg had the file and gave it to the man. They would get the same treatment Ethan and Rohan got.

# 59

Leon kept twisting the long screwdriver until the cable was too tight to twist anymore. He aligned the tool with the cable and wrapped strong tape around them so the screwdriver wouldn't release the tension when he let go.

Testing the cable, satisfied it was taut enough to keep the occupants from opening the door, he grinned and patted the cable with his hand as if it were a work of art. He had followed the instructions given to him precisely and felt proud of his accomplishment.

The people inside the room banged on the door and yelled to get his attention.

"You want the file, let's talk about it," the man inside the room yelled.

Leon knew nothing about a file. It puzzled him that the man thought he wanted a file. He knew better than to deviate from the exact instructions given to him. He had once accepted money from someone he had been sent to terminate. He took the money and still killed the man, but the pain inflicted on him for disobeying orders was horrible.

But they kept shouting about the file and he wondered if he had missed something in his instructions. Had he been told to get a file from the people before he killed them? He didn't think so, but he couldn't remember.

Leon stepped over to the door and knocked on it.

"Let us out," he heard Ali say from the other side of the door.

"Where's the file?" Leon shouted at the door.

"Let us out and we'll talk about it."

Leon repeated in his head what the man had said. That they

would talk about the file. And he still couldn't remember being told about a file. Confusion and uncertainty made him angry and caused his rage to grow. He didn't know about a file and he sensed the people in the room were lying to him. But he wasn't sure.

Leon said, "Give me the file." He looked down at the crack at the bottom of the door. "Put it under the door, slip the file under."

Greg replied, "We don't have it but we know how to get it. Let us out and we'll tell you."

Leon heard desperation in the man's voice. He shouted at the door, "You're lying to me!"

He left the hallway and went back into the living room, passing Bob's body. The floor beside the body was wet from Saint Leon's work with the blade. He went into the kitchen.

He turned on all four burners on the stove and the oven, blowing out the flames, leaving the gas escaping.

He took a position just around the corner from the hallway. From the work bag he carried he took out an incendiary grenade, pulled the pin and threw it around the corner and down the corridor. The grenade bounced on the wood floor, not exploding with shrapnel but spewing fire and smoke.

Leon left the house walking, not running, proud of himself. Turning on the gas had been his idea. He didn't know how long it would take before the house blew, whether the fire would get them first, but he marveled at his own ingenuity.

# 60

The house shook from the explosion. They stared at the door. And smelled smoke.

"He's blowing up the place," Ali said.

"Starting a fire." Greg heard the flames, saw the smoke coming in under the door. It was unbelievable. Bizarre. Impossible. They would be burned alive.

As Ali struggled with trying to open the door, Greg quietly walked back to the barred window, staring at it stupidly. He knew the bars were there before he went to the window, knew they wouldn't be able to open it, had heard many times about the dangers of installing window bars without a release latch inside, but few people bothered with the release because they figured they could leave by the door—or that there would never be a fire.

He realized it wasn't the window that had drawn him away from the door. His mind was telling him something, but what it was didn't come through.

Ali was suddenly at his side. With the heel of her shoe, she broke the window and started yelling for help.

He didn't think the house next door was occupied. It was dark and looked abandoned when they drove by it. The next house was across the street from the abandoned one. It occurred to him the broken window would let in air that could feed the fire.

"What's the matter with you?" she shouted at him. "You're just standing there frozen."

"I—I got it." He finally grasped the notion he had been wrestling with. "The house has a pitched roof."

"Meaning what?"

"There's an attic."

"What does—"

"I saw a gabled attic window. There'd be one at both ends of the house."

"What are you talking about?"

He headed for the closet with her behind him. "When I was a kid, we lived in a house like this." He pointed up to the closet ceiling. To a trapdoor that opened into the attic. "We can break out through an attic window. They have wood slats but we can kick the slats out."

"Are you sure?"

"I need a chair," he said.

The room was filling with smoke, which made them go into choking spasms. Greg got a wooden chair and put it under the trapdoor, closing the closet door behind them to hold out some of the smoke. "You ever been in an attic?"

"I don't know. No—never."

"Boards run across the attic every few feet—there's nothing solid in between. Stay on the beams, the wood joists for support. If you step off, the ceiling can't hold you; you'll fall through into the fire."

She stood on the chair and he wrapped his arms around her legs and lifted her up, off the chair. He got her up high enough so she could push her way through the trapdoor and get a purchase on the frame. With him pushing her up and her pulling, she wiggled through the opening.

As she disappeared into the attic, he got on the chair and reached up to get a grip on the two-by-fours framing the trapdoor. He hadn't done pull-ups in an eon but a fire below helped motivate him. He pulled himself halfway up but fell back down again. He took a deep breath and choked on smoke, going into a coughing spasm.

Choking on the smoke, he once again got a grip on the wood frame of the trapdoor and pulled until he could get a purchase with the side of one arm and then the other arm. Lifting himself even more with his left arm, he got his right hand on the frame and pushed himself up until he had both hands on it. Pushing up he got his butt on the frame and then fell forward onto his hands and then his knees so he could crawl on the attic supports.

The space was dark and thick with smoke, sending them both gasping for air and into coughing spasms. *Smoke not fire is the real killer* rang in his head, something he'd read or heard.

Ali was gagging badly; he quickly caught up with her and urged her on. "Keep moving. We'll die if we stop."

She went forward on her knees but missed a cross board and broke through, letting out a scream. He grabbed her by her clothes and pulled her back, putting his arms around her to get her steady on a cross beam.

Unable to see well in the smoke and darkness, they moved forward by touch, crawling along on their knees, keeping on the beams, coughing as smoke from the fire burned their lungs.

When they reached the attic window he'd seen earlier, strength fueled by the fire raging behind them enabled him to yank out a slat and then another until he had all four slats off and the window opening was wide enough for Ali to slip through headfirst.

She went through the window, landing on the single-story roof to the garage, which was lower than the main house.

He pushed in the opening, sure he wasn't going to make it and he was right, he was too wide for it. He backed out and took off his coat. He threw the coat through the opening and went at it again, turning himself almost completely sideways because the window frame was taller than it was wide.

# 61

They slid off the garden shed to the ground on the backyard side because Greg could hear people out on the street. The house was being completely engulfed in flames as they went over the collapsed wood fence, around to the other side of the neighboring house and out through the gate to the street.

There was no sign of the man who had trapped and nearly burned them to death. He might be long gone from the scene, Greg thought, but he wasn't sure. Didn't fire starters love to stay and watch their work? But Greg doubted the arsonist would stay around to marvel over his fiery work. He was most probably an assassin who got in, killed and left before the police arrived.

There was no sign of Bob.

"He would have killed him," Ali said. She was asking for confirmation that the poor man wasn't burning to death.

"Before the fire." He didn't say that to comfort her but as confirmation to himself. It was a sure thing Bob never left the house—his truck was still in the driveway. The only way the killer could have gotten into the house and roamed around to find them was to get past Bob.

The people who had gathered on the street in front were mostly staying back out of fear of an explosion. They would be wondering if someone was still in the house, but Greg doubted anyone in the neighborhood actually knew the man well enough to know Bob's name.

A car pulled up near Greg and Ali, a Ford Taurus, and stopped in the middle of the street. A man got out, leaving the driver's door open and the car running as he ran to join the crowd near the house.

As men were coasting the camper down the driveway to keep its gas tank from going up, the fire flared and the big front picture window exploded. The men abandoned the camper and got away from the front of the house.

Ali started in the direction of where they had parked their car and Greg grabbed her arm to divert her.

"The guy might be out there," he said. "Let's take this to our car."

They were on the driver's side of the Ford Taurus idling in the street. He got behind the wheel and she got into the rear passenger seat behind him to avoid having to run to the other side of the car and get in. He put the car into gear and started backing up when the guy who had gotten out of it yelled and ran toward them. Greg hit the gas still going in reverse and the Ford careened down the street backward, sideswiping a parked car before he got the vehicle turned around and headed front end first away from the guy who was yelling for them to stop.

They had parked two blocks away. They quickly got out of the stolen car as they came up and stopped behind the Honda. The angry car owner was not far back, running for them.

"Must be a damn track star," Greg said.

He tossed the man's car keys into the bushes to make sure the guy couldn't pile into his car and give chase. They got into Franklin's loaner with Greg behind the wheel and Ali next to him. As Greg fumbled getting the key into the ignition, Ali screamed as Greg's door was jerked open by the owner of the car they'd stolen.

"Bastard!" the man shouted.

Greg put the car into gear as the man grabbed at his neck. As the car jerked forward, the guy got his fingers on Greg's shirt collar but his grip broke as Greg hit the gas and the car picked up speed faster than the man's legs could pedal, and he let go and stumbled and fell.

Ali said, "God—I hope he doesn't have a spare key under his seat. He's madder than hell. Greg, do you think we can—is there anything—"

"Bob's gone. And I'm sure before the fire. Anyone who opens

NIGHT TALK | 267

a door to that killer is doomed. Bob got what he's been running and hiding from most of his life. A visit from Big Brother."

"I—I just don't . . . I can't—"

"You and Agent Scully. But she was getting paid by the network to be a diehard skeptic." He glanced back in the rearview mirror as they put road between them and the man whose car they had borrowed. "He's gotten back into his car but I don't see headlights so there's still hope. For sure, he's not a happy camper."

"Let's hope he doesn't find his keys until morning. He's mad enough to hunt us down and ram us."

A white van with a utility company emblem on it appeared on the main road just ahead of them.

"He'd have to get in line," Greg said.

# 62

The white van was waiting for them with its headlights off where the residential street met the highway back into town. Greg hit the brakes, not sure which way to go, but the decision had been made for them. They couldn't go back into the residential area without running into a lynch mob and they couldn't turn right and head into town because the van was waiting there.

The only place to go was to make a left turn and head in the opposite direction, up the foothills and into the mountains.

"Where's this road go?" Ali asked. "Is there a town?"

"I'm not even sure there are any houses. It's a national forest."

He had no idea as to where the road went or even how far it went but knew that the area got more and more deserted and desolate the farther they went in. Many of the roads in the mountains ended up as dead ends.

The moment they made the turn toward the foothills the van followed them and its headlights came on.

"He's going to kill us," Ali said.

That appeared to be self-evident.

"He's a patient bastard," Greg told her. The killer had been waiting in case they didn't burn up with the house. "Now he's forcing us away from town."

Staring out through the back window, Ali said, "He's not catching up; maybe it's just a coincidence, another van."

"No, he's pushing us up the mountain where the road's narrower and bordered by steep cliffs. The van's bigger than this car. He's planning on pushing us over a cliff."

"What are we going to do?"

"We can't turn off. I've been in the San Gabriels before, the side roads are mostly dead ends. I'm not sure any roads go all the way over the mountains. This one may peter out, too."

"Getting out and running is better than being pushed off a cliff."

"Not if he has a gun."

Greg didn't say it, but he couldn't imagine the killer without a gun. He looked up at the rearview mirror, at the headlights behind them. There was no turning back. No way to go except heading up the mountain and hope for a break.

"Can we outrun him?" Ali asked.

There was fear in her voice, but not panic. He felt surprisingly calm. Escaping the burning house had used up all the fear he had.

"No way. Franklin chose the car because it wouldn't pop out, not for speed. He's going to ram us. The faster we go, the more likely we'll be unable to keep the car under control when he hits us."

He tried to imagine what he should do when the killer in the van made his move. The van would come up behind them and . . . then what? Hit their car in the rear? Not likely, at least not square-on bumper to bumper because it would just push the small car forward and potentially disable the van by getting its front grill pushed into the engine fan.

A cop on Greg's show once described how bumping a car in the rear off center during a high speed chase, hitting the left or right rear corner near where the taillights are, caused the car to spin out of control. It wouldn't take much for the larger vehicle to knock the Civic out of control by hitting it in a rear corner. Would the killer try that? Maybe not. Police cars commonly had strong bumpers or push bars that kept the engine from being disabled. More likely he would push them off the road by hitting the Honda on the side with the side of the van. That way the van wouldn't be immobilized.

The van kept its distance. The killer was in no hurry. As they went up the desolate road that wound up the mountain the van stayed back a hundred feet.

"He's still hanging back," Ali said. "What's he up to?"

"Waiting for the right spot. I think he'll come up beside us when there are cliffs on the right."

"And send us over. Let's stop and run for it on foot."

"If that's what you want, we'll do it, but if he has a gun . . ." Greg shook his head. The terrain was too steep and rocky for them to outrun bullets. "I'd rather take my chances in the car."

"He can pull up beside us and shoot. We'd be sitting ducks in the car. Or just push us over the side. How can we stop him?"

"I have an idea." He described how a bump to the rear corner of a car could throw it out of control. "The same goes for the front corner. At some point when we have nothing but cliffs on our side he's going to gun it to come up beside us and push us off. As he comes up, I'll swerve and hit the van in the right front corner and send it out of control."

The plan made him breathless. It assumed everything would go perfectly—including keeping the smaller car under control after it was rammed by the bigger one.

She stared at him as if she was amazed at his audacity and shook her head slowly, in wonderment. "I hope to God all that information you learn working radio's graveyard shift isn't going to get us killed."

They waited, with Ali turned in her seat to watch the headlights, and Greg keeping an eye on the rearview mirror.

He realized there were flaws in his thinking but couldn't get his head around what the problem was. The road was only two lanes, one in each direction, with almost no shoulder on either side. It had been carved out of the mountain, leaving a wall on the left side. On the right side there would be short spurts where the terrain was extremely steep just a couple of feet off the pavement with nothing but a short metal guardrail between the asphalt road and the cliff.

The guardrails weren't much protection. They were only a couple feet high, the sort that would wake you up if you started sideswiping them, but they wouldn't keep a car receiving a direct hit from going over.

The van's high beams went on.

Greg said, "He's looking ahead, waiting for a section where there are cliffs running long enough to—"

"He's coming!" Ali screamed.

The van sped up, riding the center line of the road. It seemed to cover the distance between them in a flash.

Greg jerked the wheel, sending the car into the oncoming lane, and jerked it again to keep the car from going all the way across the lane and hitting the rocky wall that paralleled the road, missing the van.

A frantic glance behind him only showed blinding headlights and he jerked the wheel again, careening to the left and then again to the right. As the car swerved it rocked on its tires and for a moment appeared ready to go over, then settled back on four wheels.

The van was suddenly beside them and Greg slammed on the brakes, sending the Honda into a skid as the van hit it, the van's passenger door striking the left front quarter panel of the car, sending it into a spin around and around and into the side railing with a clash of metals.

Suddenly the noise of screeching tires and bending metal stopped. For a frozen moment Greg couldn't move, couldn't think. Ali cried out beside him and his nervous system kicked back on.

"Cliff!" she said.

The Honda was still in the northbound lane but was now facing the opposite direction, the driver's door pressed up against the railing. The cliff was on his side and started a couple of feet after the railing. As he looked out all he saw was a dark emptiness.

He jerked around in the seat. The van was behind them. It had spun out also and was now sideways against the rocky mountain wall across the road. The van driver's door was against the wall. The passenger door was open, indicating the killer had climbed out that way. The man was out of the van and running toward them.

The Honda's engine died.

Greg stared at the steering wheel, stupefied.

"He's coming!" Ali screamed.

Greg turned the key again and the engine came on and started to fade and came on again, rocking the whole car for a second.

He put the car in reverse and turned in the seat to look out the rearview mirror as he hit the gas.

"What are you doing?" Ali shouted.

The Honda hesitated for a moment and then kicked into gear, lurching back and suddenly accelerating. Greg couldn't keep the car going straight back. The Honda screeched as metal ground against metal, as the driver's side scraped the guardrail.

The man running full speed up behind them darted to the left to get out of the path of the car, throwing one foot over the rail and then the other foot, straddling the narrow space before the cliff.

Greg hit the brakes and shoved the car into "drive." The trans rumbled and the car skidded backward for a second, then leaped forward. Behind them the man came back over the railing and ran for his van.

# 63

They went back down the road with Greg keeping a heavy foot on the gas and no idea as to whether the killer and the van were on their tail.

There were no headlights behind them and they saw nothing coming up from behind them.

"I didn't see what happened to the van," Ali said.

"It was on the shoulder with the lights on. Maybe it blew a tire when it skidded, got stuck or whatever. Something made him get out of that van and come at us on foot."

"Maybe he thought that was the best way to kill us rather than trying to shove the car over the cliff."

That hit home. "You're right. He wouldn't want to risk banging up the van until it didn't run, leaving him stranded out here in the middle of nowhere. He had something in his hand. I'm not sure what it was; it didn't look like a gun but it must have been a weapon."

Greg suddenly turned to the right onto a road that was even narrower than the mountain highway. He turned off the car lights and leaned forward in the seat to get closer to the windshield and navigate with moonlight. The road had thick vegetation on both sides.

"What are you doing?"

"Hiding."

The pavement quickly ended and he continued on the dirt road.

"You shouldn't have turned off. If he comes behind us we'll be trapped," she said. "This dirt road isn't going to go anywhere and we won't be able to get around him."

She was right. He questioned his impulse to get them off the main road and hide. He did it because he was certain that the killer was coming down the mountain without his lights on. There was enough moonlight to do it.

"He would catch up with us on the main road because he's crazy. He's the guy who went nuts and tried to kill me on a public street. Even if we made it to the bottom I don't want to end up on city streets in a wild car chase that would attract cops."

"If he catches up with us, we'll need cops."

"He knows we're ahead of him. When he reaches the streets below he'll keep going onto the freeway."

She shook her head. "I just hope this guy is as logical as you are. Who the hell is this nut? A killer someone hired to get the file?"

"No, not to get the file. He didn't seem to know anything about a file back at the house. He just wanted to kill us, make it look like a gas explosion. Not caring that arson investigators would find evidence that it was set."

"If they don't want the file, what do they want?" she asked.

They both knew the answer. "They want to kill us. They are eliminating everyone who had anything to do with the file. I think whoever is behind this at some point decided I really don't have the file but might get my hands on it."

"So they kill us before we can find it."

He took his eyes off the dark road just long enough to glance at her. "If you know anything about the contents of the file you better share it now. This isn't a time to have any cards under the table."

"I don't have anything under the table but my shaking knees. It's called the God Project and Ethan said they were trying to play God. Who they are and how you play God is beyond me."

He drove slow, keeping his foot off the brake to keep the brake lights off. He used the hand brake when he had to slow the car down.

They went deeper in, not knowing where the road went or how long it was, but unable to turn around because it was too narrow.

Something suddenly shot in front of them and Greg jerked the wheel, swerving to the right. Ali shouted, "Deer!" and they hit a tree head-on. Neither had a seatbelt on and the impact threw them both forward.

Greg bounced back from the wheel. He was strangely disoriented but he didn't think he had hit his head. It was quiet, eerily calm, with everything frozen in place as if the very earth had paused in its rotation.

Light—bright light—erupted in front of them.

At first he thought it was the headlights of the van but the lights were too intensely bright, not just blinding but penetrating, like X-rays piercing him, stabbing his eyes and exploding in his brain.

# 64

The stabbing light vanished as quickly as it had erupted. Greg no longer felt his core being penetrated by the rays. But now he couldn't move. He was a prisoner of whoever or whatever had sent the light.

It was dark, pitch black, a void as empty and endless as outer space, where there is a complete absence of light beyond the pinpoint shine and sparkle of heavenly bodies. But he knew the light was still there; it was his mind that had been shut off, not the piercing rays.

He had consciousness, an awareness of who he was, but he could not feel anything or move any part of his body. He was numb, all of his nerves deadened. He didn't sense his heart pumping, his lungs working. He didn't feel paralyzed even though he could not move a muscle. Instead he sensed that the light had encased him, wrapped around him like a tight membrane that kept him from moving and deadened his sensations to a state of morbidity. He was in a cocoon, a wrapping in which all his bodily needs and homeostasis—body temperature, fluids, blood oxygen, kidney filtering—were maintained.

Sensations of life were gone but he still had an awareness of self, of being—he knew that he existed because a small spark was still lit in a deep recess of his mind. He had no sense of feel or smell or taste, heard nothing, had no ability to move and no thoughts except for that quiet awareness of still existing, of knowing that he was Greg Nowell.

His awareness of self also told him that there was something out there beyond the paralyzing light, living things but not like him;

they were entities not of Earth. He was their prisoner, held by the light.

Then there was movement, not initiated by him, but as if whatever he was encapsulated in was being drawn up, pulling him out of the car, his body floating with no effort on his part, as if his spirit was rising, being drawn, sucked out without effort on his part, leaving his corporal body behind as if his essence was lighter than air, like the helium used in party balloons.

Was this how dying worked? Giving up the ghost? His soul rising? But where was the light at the end of the tunnel?

He moved deeper into the darkness, as if the utter black wasn't empty space but a fluid, an ocean he floated in, his essence not carried by someone or something but as if he flowed in a source of energy, a dense gaseous plasma thicker than water and lighter than air, being carried on a river of the substance to a large silver object he realized had generated the lights. The smooth sleek metallic lines told him that it was a spacecraft as he flowed toward it and entered through a dark opening on the craft's side and into another black void.

He still didn't breathe. Couldn't breathe, but didn't feel the need to take a breath or let one out. His heart remained still. He stayed in suspended animation. No blood was circulating, no oxygen feeding his brain. He was clinically dead. But he still had that spark that told him he existed.

He saw nothing inside. Felt nothing. Heard nothing. He had an utter loss of his five senses and of the senses beyond those ordinary five—pain, balance, internal functions.

What he did sense was a presence. Not creatures, beings or entities. Just movement in the utter bottomless void as if parts of the darkness had substance. Midnight shadows, he thought of them, movements in the void that told him he wasn't alone yet nothing took shape.

He sensed minds. Not like his, not human or machine, not animal, vegetable or mineral. Something different. Alien. Energy without a form visible to the naked eye. Masses of neutrons similar to those humans carried in their brains and nervous systems but free-floating rather than in a brain encased by protective bone. He sensed small, individual clouds of them in the darkness, swarms of neutrons. Or were they just screwing with his mind, giving him images and memories that were false and misleading?

There was communication, not to him, but between the alien minds to each other. Thoughts that he understood but could not describe because they were not human thinking. Even though he couldn't have told others precisely what was said, he understood the essence. He realized that there was no malice toward him. No emotion at all. Rather the thoughts revealed curiosity being satisfied by a systematic evaluation of him. Measurements and testing of both his mental qualities and physical quantities was being done without any strong feeling toward him. What he would expect from a human scientist examining a lab rat. One they had examined before—he felt as if he was there for a follow-up medical visit.

He sensed that they believed they were superior to him. He understood why. He was a modern human being, Homo sapiens, whose closest living relatives were gorillas and chimpanzees; he shared 98.8 percent of his DNA with tree-swinging, knuckle-walking chimps.

The entities examining him knew about the creatures on planet Earth, knew about man and ape. Biologically, he was a naked ape who had a larger brain capacity but was physically weaker than his hairier cousins. Pound for pound man was weaker and frailer than most of the other animals and insects on the planet, with just a fraction of the strength of an ape or an ant.

The entity examining him knew that humans were incapable of surviving without proper food, shelter and temperature, making them a primitive biological specimen that could only function in a narrow range of environments. Compared to creatures that had fur, fat or other biological features that allowed them to function in extremes, the naked ape had a body temperature range so restrictive that the species could not survive most environments without clothing and shelter.

Also unlike its hairy cousins, many Homo sapiens were morally weak and easily tempted to harm their own kind and other creatures not just for food and survival, but for their own gratification. He sensed that the entity didn't find as much fault with killing as it did with the base motives that most often underlined it.

He realized that the comparison of people to animals was wrong because all the physical, brain capacity, artistic and technological comparisons left out the most important human trait of all—the soul-searching introspection mankind does, pondering his being, his fate, the meaning of life and his purpose on the planet and in the universe.

No other creature thought about, talked about and wrote about where it had come from and where it was going, or what the meaning, the purpose, of human existence and its spirit was.

He knew that he was far inferior biologically and in terms of brain capacity to the midnight shadows that were examining him. But then he realized that he sensed their thoughts—and they didn't know it.

He had a sense beyond the five-plus counted by science. He didn't know what it was called or how it worked. A sixth sense? A form of psi—the extrasensory perception of telepathy? He was not a mind reader, had never experienced sensing the thoughts of another human being, but he understood if not the actual thoughts at least the reasoning of the entities that were examining him.

They had controlled his life forces, his breathing and heart rate, paralyzed his muscles and put his body and brain into temporary hibernation, but they didn't realize that in some deep place, hidden among the billions of the electrical- and chemical-charged signals in his brain, a tiny spark glowed that gave him an awareness of their thoughts without them knowing it.

And he understood that despite their superiority in technology, despite their ability to travel light-years across empty space, feats far beyond human accomplishments achieved perhaps for no other reason than that they had been on a planet that developed long before Earth, his mind was superior to theirs.

It just had some catching up to do.

# 65

Greg was awake. He was in the car, on the driver's seat, his hands on the steering wheel. He felt the pain in his chest from hitting the steering wheel. The pain was good. It told him he was alive.

His eyes told him he was looking at a tree. The front bumper of the car was against it. There was no bright light, no light at all except the soft glow from the moon. No enormous UFO squatting in the forest.

"What happened?" Ali rubbed her head. "I hit my head on the windshield. We hit a tree."

"The light blinded me."

"Light? What light?"

"Ali . . . you saw the light. You must have."

"What light? What are you talking about?"

"The bright light. It blinded me—us."

"I didn't see a light, but that's definitely a tree we're up against. Does the car still run? Did we damage the engine?"

"I—I don't know." He turned the key and the engine kicked on. "Did you—do you remember?"

"What?"

"There was a UFO, its lights blinded us, that's why we hit the tree. Then it took us aboard."

"Aboard? Are you crazy? What are you talking about?"

"I—" He pointed at the car key in the ignition. "The key was in the off position a minute ago. The motor was turned off."

"You must have turned it off."

"I didn't turn it off. You didn't see me turn it off." He was getting frustrated. And he knew it was useless.

"I hit my head—" Ali began.

"I never turned the engine off. How did it get turned off?"

"Oh my God. Are you telling me that aliens turned off the engine? Is that what you're saying?"

"I'm telling you that there was a passage of time between when I saw the light that was so blinding it caused me to hit the tree and the time we both were aware again of being in the car. During that time I experienced being aboard an extraterrestrial craft."

"You were aboard a spacecraft for the couple of seconds I was stunned by hitting my head? Is that what you're telling me?"

"I don't know how long we were out. A couple seconds to us could be hours if an entity is able to control our sense of time. Remember what I told you about the Hills? They experienced an altered state of consciousness in which they lost track of the passage of time."

"I don't have any lost time," Ali said. "I was stunned but probably not more than a second or two. It doesn't add up to the time it would take to be abducted and examined, whatever it is that you said you experienced."

"You don't remember having an experience in which time passed. I do. It happened to me before. Years ago. I experienced an abduction. It's haunted me my entire life. I was awake during it, Ali. Awake when I was taken aboard an alien craft and examined. I was awake again tonight. They didn't know that I could tell what they were thinking, that I knew they had examined me before."

She leaned toward him, staring at him intently, concerned. "Greg, listen to me. I don't know if you hit your head or what, but nothing happened here except we hit a tree in the dark and we both went flying forward. Anything else is something you've imagined because you've been immersed in the UFO thing for so long. I don't blame you, we've been hit by crazy things in spades today."

"You don't understand. For some reason they didn't want you."

"I can handle that kind of rejection any day. Let me drive. You need some rest."

He put the car into "reverse" and it backed up without any horrible noises that would indicate there was damage.

"Are you sure you're all right to drive?" she asked.

"The key was in the off position. I didn't turn the ignition off, you didn't see me turn it off. They turned it off."

"Greg—"

"Drop it. We have to get out of here with no headlights and my foot off the brake."

# 66

Greg turned the car around and got it moving back down the bumpy dirt road. He was acting out of pure instinct because his mind wasn't on driving or escaping a killer. Disgust over what had happened to him when he was abducted and examined like a bug had taken the place of fear and caution.

They had not only handled him like a lab rat, but left him unable to prove it and subject to ridicule if he even tried. Had he and Ali both experienced it, he would have had proof and support, but only his experiencing the abduction left him doubting even himself.

Was she right? Was he so deep into believing aliens were taking control of the planet that he imagined it? Dreamed the abduction and examination?

No. It was real. The memory wasn't something vague in his mind, not hazy, ethereal images of a dream world but of being physically handled. He remembered not only seeing things but being touched.

They came to the main road and he turned onto it almost absent-mindedly. Deep in thought, he had to be reminded by her to turn on the headlights.

"You have that expression," she said, "the one where you look angry and disgusted at the same time. Are you mad at me because I didn't have the experience you had?"

"I've been thinking about Ming the Clam."

"Who?"

"It's a sea clam that was found a while back in the ocean somewhere around Iceland, I think. It was old, really old. They figured it was about four hundred years old so they opened the clam to get a better estimate of its age and found out it was even older—it had been down on the ocean floor for over five hundred years."

"Okay . . . is there going to be a point to this story? Is it going to be something that makes me feel guilty for eating clams?"

"Turns out that Ming was the world's oldest living creature. But opening it up to see how old it was killed it. Apparently finding Ming's age could have been done another way without killing it but the scientists doing it didn't realize it was the oldest living thing."

"Are you saying you felt like Ming the Clam tonight when, uh . . . ?"

He shrugged. "I think the way we treated the oldest living creature even accidentally says a lot about us, about humans. We killed a living creature to satisfy our curiosity about it. People treat other people infinitely worse than the way Ming got treated. I can see why aliens would believe they have the right to dissect us to find out what makes us tick. Not just that, but looking at what we've done to each other and this beautiful green planet, aliens would be justified to send in exterminators to bait traps with sex and money to rid the world of us pests before they took over."

She nodded and bit her lip. "Greg, do you want to pull over so I can drive while you get some rest?" Ali asked again.

"It's all a matter of the food chain."

She just looked at him.

"The one highest on the chain gets to slice and dice everyone else," he said.

# 67

They went back down the hill on the main mountain road, with Ali keeping up a conversation about their route. Greg was sure she was talking to keep him focused because she worried about where his mind was and where it was going. He went along with the conversation. He was worried about where his mind was, too.

"He saw us head down," she said, "so this would be the way he went with his van. He might be waiting for us at the bottom."

" 'Half a league, half a league, half a league onward . . . into the jaws of Death, into the mouth of hell, rode the six hundred.' "

"What?"

" 'Charge of the Light Brigade.' I had to memorize a poem in grammar school and chose it. Like those British soldiers who made a suicidal charge, we don't have a choice. There may be a way to make it over the mountain from this road but it's just as likely we would end up on a dirt path fit only for goats and all-terrain vehicles or dead-ended. He thinks we're ahead of him so it would be a natural assumption that we're long gone. His only decision would be whether we went east or west on the freeway."

"I know you don't want to stop the car long enough for me to drive, but please do me a favor. If you start daydreaming again about nineteenth-century poetry or the food chain, just slow down enough so I can leap out before you accidentally drive over a cliff."

Greg thought over his conclusion that the van driver would assume they had continued down the mountain and got on the freeway. Would he believe they were heading back to L.A. or east toward San Bernardino and the desert?

"My take is that he'll think we went east, away from L.A., connecting to the 10 a few miles down the road. That's what anyone with good sense would do because the highway goes all the way to Florida. So right now he's on the freeway looking for us."

"I don't know what to think."

He didn't, either. Steering the car down the mountain and foothills toward the freeway was more autopilot than concentration.

He went from quietly introspective to a sense of anguish and horror about Bob and what must have happened to him, when from the foothills they had an aerial view of the housing area where Bob's house had gone up in flames. No fire was visible but emergency lights of fire trucks and police were still flashing.

As soon as they came to a major intersection, Greg turned off the road that led between the mountain and the freeway to make his way through city streets they hadn't been on before.

Ali asked, "Do you think we should call Franklin and let him know about Bob?"

"I think we should call him mostly to let him know so he can get away somewhere safer than his isolated place."

She used the car phone but didn't get an answer. They looked at each other, both with dread.

"Throw the phone out," he said, "rip it out and throw it out the window."

"You think—"

"I've stopped thinking. I don't want to think about the mess we're in or what's happened to people who tried to help us. I just want to concentrate on finding the file and making sure the bastards behind the violence burn in hell."

He put them on the freeway going back toward Pasadena and the San Fernando Valley, watching other cars, half expecting a van to pull up beside them and the killer to open fire. He was angry enough to be ready to ram the van at the driver's door if it showed up.

He wondered again why the killer hadn't opened fire when they were driving away from him on the mountain. It implied he didn't have a gun, but that didn't work for Greg. Guns were too easy to get.

"Any ideas?" she asked.

He knew what she meant. Where were they going now? What were they to do next? Time was running out; so was the money to finance places to hide. They also had no more clues about where the file was than when they started.

"We can go to newspapers, television or radio news," he said.

"And tell them what? We have nothing to offer them except a bizarre tale in which all the incriminating evidence points toward you because of what Ethan told people. And me, too, now that someone who gave us a hand is probably dead. What do they call that kind of death? Suspicious circumstances? With us the persons of interest?"

Greg said, "There's no one I would ask for help because it would put them in danger."

"I agree, I won't do that, either. I don't know about you, but I'm going to contact Inez Kaufman and ask her to put me into contact with the Aarons. She at least is in it voluntarily."

"If you don't have the file, what are they going to do for you?"

"I don't know. What other options are there?"

None. He knew it. Maybe she was right. Maybe the Aarons could figure out a way of extracting the file from him. A file he didn't have, at least knowingly. And didn't know what it even contained. But he resisted the idea because he didn't trust them to help him out once they had what they wanted.

He was angry enough not to want help but to strike back, but they were still boxing against shadows. Most of all at the moment he needed rest. He could see that she did, too. They were both a little rummy from being on the run and one step ahead of a killer. Nerves stretched to the point where they were ready to snap. Anger mounting until he would do something stupid—like ramming the first white van that got in his way.

He needed to get off the road and think. Sleep on it without being disturbed by a cold-blooded killer. He could usually think while driving, but half expecting to be pulled over by the police or rammed by a van at any moment wasn't conducive toward puzzle solving.

He said, "I need to think about the file. With your help leading me through the ways Ethan could have hidden that file while expecting me to be able to find and open it, even though the NRO and everyone else on"—he glanced at her—"and off the planet aren't able to find it. There are cheap motels in the Valley, places with hourly rates because they do a booming lunch-hour business. I'm sure they get a lot of John and Jane Does registering. Let's get a room and think it out."

"You're right, we need to get into Ethan's brain, figure out what he was thinking. He must have known you have zero ability to access an encrypted file. That means he must have expected you to get help. Maybe that's why he told me about you, to get me to help you decode it."

That made sense to him. "You're still positive he sent it to me?"

"Absolutely. That's what he said. There's another reason, too. When Ethan spoke of you it was with admiration. He was an antiestablishment guy, you know, the kind who didn't have much respect for anyone who he didn't think was aware of all the invasions of privacy and Big Brother stuff that was going on. He admired you for standing up and saying what you believed was the truth. You were the obvious choice for receipt of the file."

"Start thinking about the ways he could have sent it to me so we can discuss it at the motel."

The world was truly cockeyed when he went to a motel with an attractive woman to use his mind.

# 68

The motel room they checked into had hourly rates and the musties. Musties was how Ali described the smell of the place. It was a little dank, a little armpit, topped off with stale cigarette smoke that had become part of the paint. He figured nicotine was the yellowish tint on the walls.

"There must be people who still have a cigarette after sex," he said.

Besides the bed, the room had two end tables, one lamp that worked, a cheap TV on a dresser, a desk and chair. The low-wattage bulb in the working lamp was intended to hide the ambience, not create it.

Someone, perhaps a nooner who had enjoyed a brief but no doubt passionate stay in the room, had carved a heart with $TR+LC$ on the top of the desk. Ali set her wasp spray can on the initials.

They assumed that the only thing that ever got changed in the room was the sheets, so they stripped the bed down to the sheets, whose stains appeared old enough to have survived wash cycles.

Ali laid out her coat to sit on when she got on the bed and leaned back against two thin pillows.

Focusing on how Ethan would have sent him the file in a way that avoided the clutches of the world's most sophisticated spy agencies had frustrated both of them for a good reason.

"There is no way it can be done," Ali said. "Anything Ethan sent you could be intercepted and opened by the encryption crackers the NRO would put to use. Even if you were teamed up with a world-class hacker-cracker, like Ethan. If nothing else, that NSA encryption-breaking system the Aarons helped Ethan get access to could break anything Ethan came up with."

That was just common sense to Greg. If he could open it or have someone help him open the file, experts like Ethan that the government kept in its employ would be able to open it.

"So," she went on, "let's assume that Ethan couldn't encrypt the file in a way that permitted only you to open it because no matter what form he sent it in decoders could crack it. The question then becomes not what form the file was sent in but how he sent it for your eyes only."

Greg sat at the chair next to the desk and leaned his head back to stretch the tight muscles of his neck. "How he sent it for my eyes only. Sounds like something from James Bond."

"It's been more like *The Rocky Horror Picture Show.* If they can open anything Ethan sent, and if Ethan's telling the truth that he sent it—"

"They must already have it."

She shook her head. "They don't have it. I have a friend in the NRO, attached to the director's office. The one who helped me get into Mond's investigation results. He told me they definitely didn't have it. At least not twenty-four hours ago."

"So if Ethan was thinking straight when he sent the file, he would know that it would be intercepted if he sent it in a traditional way. Since they haven't found the file, he sent it in a way that only I would recognize."

"Making it invisible to everyone else."

"How can I see it but no one else can?" Greg asked.

"Greg, if I knew the answer to that . . ."

She got off the bed and paced, frustrated and angry.

He sat in a chair at the desk and kept his mouth shut. Watching her steaming and pacing, he decided that if she'd had a hammer, she would have demolished the place, starting with him.

She said, "Three people are dead that we know of, God knows how many others. We're hiding like trapped rats in a sewer. Something pretty weird is going on at the NRO that's making them cover their asses any way they can."

"Tell me something I don't know."

"Whatever is going on has nothing to do with aliens invading and taking over the world. We don't need aliens to mess up our lives, we're already pretty good at that ourselves. It's a given that whatever the God Project is, it's going to blow the roof off the NRO just as Snowden's revelations did with the NSA."

"So who's behind the killings, the attempt to retrieve Ethan's file? The NRO? A bureaucratic monster out of control?"

"I don't know who, but I have a pretty good idea of why. A big part of the Snowden effect was the loss of billions of dollars by U.S. firms in security products and services around the world because countries and big companies realized that we were spying on them. The financial fallout from the NRO will be infinitely greater because it's not a big agency with beaucoup employees like the CIA and NSA. The NRO only has a couple thousand administrative employees and most of those are on loan from the CIA and Department of Defense. Everything else is contracted out to corporations. And you can bet there's a short list of who has made the right political contributions to get themselves on the short list."

"You think that a corporation that's going to lose a big NRO contract is behind the killings."

"We're not talking about pocket change. Over seventy-five percent of the NRO's budget goes to the companies contracting with it. That's over ten billion dollars a year. I don't know how much goes to the contractor for the God Project, but we could be talking about a billion dollars or more."

"People have killed for less," he said.

She stopped pacing and faced him. "You're pacifying me. You don't believe a word I've said."

"Actually, I believe everything you've said, even about a corporation hiring a killer to make sure its dirty work isn't exposed. Not only has it been done for money plenty of times, but murder has been committed by governments for what they call patriotic reasons and the employees of businesses to protect their company. But where we part ways is who is ultimately behind it."

"You think it's your visitors."

"I guess at this stage I'd use Inez Kaufman's 'invaders' label since they've hung around now for decades." He held up his hand to ward off another attack. "Let me finish. I've had two strange encounters in my life. In your eyes they never happened. So it comes back to me, personally. Am I lying? Maybe going around telling people I'd been abducted to get some attention. Am I crazy? Hallucinating during moments of extreme stress? It has to be one of those things. So tell me, am I lying or crazy?"

She went into the bathroom and slammed the door.

# 69

Inside the bathroom Ali leaned back against the door and took deep breaths to get her emotions and breathing in order. Her heart was pumping wildly, her eyes tearing. She'd almost completely lost her composure in front of Greg. She lost it now because she knew what she had to do and hated it. The worst possible thing had happened—she had bonded with Greg. More than bonded—had they met at the gym or at a party, there would have been chemistry between them.

She had lied to him from the beginning and it was getting harder and harder for her to keep up a front. Had even lied about the name she took, along with a car from another woman. She was no longer able to handle it. She felt horrible for lying to him and now betraying him, but the world was spinning out of control and she was being tossed in a vortex with it.

Ali still believed that in some mysterious way, Ethan had managed to send the stolen file to Greg, but she no longer believed that they would be able to find it. Time was running out. She was certain that the motel was their last stop, that she and Greg no longer had any options.

Torn but determined she undid the front of her pants and reached down, pulling out a tiny transmitter taped to the inside of her thigh.

Closing her eyes, fighting back tears, she pressed the transmission button.

# 70

Greg stared at the closed bathroom door, sorry that he was adding to Ali's hell, sorry that they were so close emotionally and so far apart intellectually in how they saw the world and the dangers surrounding them. He knew she was struggling and he wanted to comfort her. To protect her. Hold her in his arms.

He had never completely trusted her and he still didn't, but trust was no longer an issue. She appeared ready to bolt. He just wondered what direction she would run—and what it would mean to him.

He shifted his weight in the chair and felt a bulge in his coat pocket that rubbed up against the side of the chair. It was the junk mail he had taken and shoved into his pocket at the front desk of his apartment building when he was still there. He took the envelopes and fliers out, merely glanced at them and tossed them in the trash can next to the desk.

His eye caught scribbled writing on a piece of mail and he reached back into the can and took the item out. It was the take-out menu from a Chinese restaurant. His name and address were handwritten in the otherwise blank address block with awkward block letters by someone who hadn't spent too much time in school learning penmanship but whose fingers probably would fly across a keyboard.

Most important, the restaurant was the one below the apartment of Ethan's girlfriend in Culver City.

Greg's hands trembled as he tore open the folded advertisement, pulling the ends apart from the staple.

His name was not inside, nor was Ethan's. There was no ordinary message, at least not one that he was capable of reading, but there was a set of numbers and letters and an Internet address, all scribbled in that awkward hand that had put his name in the address slot.

And he understood what Ethan was telling him—it was a link to a Web site and the key that would open a file. He recognized that the Web site was to a government agency.

He tried to hold back but couldn't help himself—he started laughing, holding his hand over his mouth to keep from howling at the utter cleverness of it. Ethan had not lied. He had in fact given the file to Greg. Or more precisely, he had told Greg where to find the file and how to open it.

Incredible. Ethan, the computer whiz, geek, cracker, hacker, high-tech savant who played with computers when other boys were kicking balls or working on their car had fooled everyone. He had hidden the message in plain sight. On an advertising flier with a postage stamp.

Snail mail. No one on the planet—even those who had recently arrived—would suspect Ethan of using the slow and notoriously inept United States Postal Service to deliver something he could have sent to Greg in a flash, at the speed of bits and bytes. Instead the flier had been carried by small and big mail trucks, to and through processing centers, and back out onto the roads by another gas-burning, pollution-causing truck before ending up with a pizza parlor menu and store coupons, junk mail he and every other resident in the building received daily.

On top of that Ethan had hidden the actual electronics file at an Internet-accessible location of the government.

It was so simple, so deceptive, so unexpected from Ethan, beyond clever; it was a master stroke of genius. Yet sad. Ethan was dead. So were Rohan and Bob. Maybe others.

He hoped that revelation of what was in the file was worth the lives of innocent people.

Now he had to decide what to do next.

# 71

Ali stepped out of the bathroom after replacing the transmitter and repairing the damage to her makeup that tears had caused.

She knew from Greg's face that something had happened.

"What is it?"

He held up an advertising leaflet. "This. Ethan did send me the file, at least the link to it. By snail mail, not e-mail. Ali, he wrote the information on a flier he'd probably received himself, put a stamp on it and sent it to me."

She stood unmoving, stunned. "I don't believe it." She rushed to him and grabbed the leaflet and skimmed it, shaking her head. "Oh my God, he hid the file at the FCC. The Federal Communications Commission! What a joke; they regulate radio."

"My show and everyone else's."

"He must have been laughing like crazy when he stuck it there." She yelped. "I still can't believe it. He really did send the file to you. No wonder no one could find it. Who would have ever thought he'd be so clever?"

"It was inspired on Ethan's part," Greg said. "We—they—all of us, had a mind-set that a guy like Ethan who teethed on a computer would use the tools he knew. The government has behind it thousands of analysts and a trillion dollars' worth of incredibly complex computers at the NSA, NRO, FBI, CIA and those other capital-letter entities capable of tracking every move everyone on the planet makes. They know the number of times a terrorist in Afghanistan takes a piss, but Ethan put it over everyone by simply snail-mailing the information on a piece of common advertising."

He threw up his hands. "You know what? I almost tossed it away. Hell, I did toss it and had to dig it out of the trash."

"This is—it has to go to the Aarons. They'll help for sure now."

"I'm not giving it to the Aarons. I don't trust them. They're insiders working to keep the government from taking away our freedom. They came at me with threats, threatened to turn me into the people they're supposed to oppose."

"You didn't give them what they wanted."

"I didn't have what they wanted, you know that. And who are these people? Wannabe whistleblowers? I think they're hacking into the systems because that's their obsession. And they'll release secret information even if it hurts the country because they're more interested in breaking open secret files and letting the world know they managed it than they are in our national security. Besides, we don't know what's in the file, whether there's stuff in it that can hurt the country. They haven't given me any reason to trust them. I'll go to them if I think it's the best route after we find out what we're dealing with."

"It can't be done in five minutes. Ethan was too clever for that. He'll make it harder to access than you think."

"I don't think so. It looks like he's given me a link and a password. Even I can manage that. Besides, we have all night. And so far you've proven to be pretty clever when it comes to hacking into programs." He got up and headed for the bathroom. "Give me a minute and then let's open the file and check it out."

He went into the bathroom, shutting the door behind him.

She stood still, staring at the bathroom door and then at the flier in her hands, her heart pounding, emotion welling up in her as she hesitated, not knowing which way to turn.

When he came out of the bathroom, she was gone.

So was the flier he gave her.

# 72

Greg had expected it, knew before he left the bathroom that she would be gone, but it was still a blow. She had seemed more and more torn between two forces, between a growing attachment to him and loyalty to something else. The something else won out in the end.

He went out the door and stepped to the railing and looked down to the parking lot. She waited with her back to him as a car pulled up and stopped.

The front passenger door of the car opened and a big man whose flabby body was swollen by too much fast food and sugar drinks stepped out. Aaron 11—whatever—looked up at Greg. Ali showed the advertising flier to the Aaron and the man gave Greg a smirk.

Ali turned and looked up at him, too. He kept his features blank, but he felt a hot flush of anger, not at her but at the insane situation that had driven a wedge between them.

She held his gaze for only a second, her features frozen to control guilt and regret, before quickly getting into the car and shutting the door. The Aaron slipped into the passenger seat and the car pulled away.

Greg watched until the car had left the parking lot and disappeared down the street.

He stayed at the railing for another moment, not wanting to go back inside, hating that his gut feeling from the very beginning had come true—he couldn't trust her. Like the other Aarons, she was a hacker on a mission to crack open the government's secrets. He wished she had trusted him, had accepted the fact that he would not back away from exposing wrongdoing but wouldn't operate blindly.

He went into the room with the musties and shut and locked the door behind him before pulling out the Chinese restaurant menu.

He had given Ali a mailer from a pizza parlor. And wrote different but similar information on it. Ethan hadn't hidden the file at the Federal Communications Commission, which supervised radio and television, but at the Department of Agriculture unit that dealt with brain-melting mad cow disease.

Ethan's contemptuous poke at the world was telling. Sometimes the world was spinning so fast it did make a person's brain feel like it was melting down.

Greg had newfound respect for the guy. He may have been wasted on drugs, but there was more depth about him than being just a hacker. Ethan lacked everyday common sense but had a deep understanding not about life in general, but about the esoteric world of electronics. He knew how dangerous the world had become as people were pushed aside and "intelligent" machines that worked faster and more efficiently than the human mind took over—at the same time people became so accustomed to the ease of technology that they stopped using their brains.

Machines could be made smarter than humans about most things, they could add and subtract quicker, beat masters at chess and even do surgery on people and other machines more efficiently, but Ethan understood that they didn't have hearts or souls or comprehend pain or the joys of love.

Alone in the room, Greg wished Ali were there. He should have come clean with her and got her to stay and help him out. But he knew that was a daydream. She was one of them, whatever they were. And he knew he had deliberately driven her away out of fear for her, fear that the powers out to stop them would succeed.

Being with her on the run, facing real danger rather than the threats he only envisioned, made him realize that his problem with relationships wasn't just being a workaholic with a job that kept him out all night, but fear that whoever he drew close to might fall victim to the hounds of hell that had dogged him.

That was how he thought of the entities that had taken him as a youth and again as a man. They were diabolical, relentless bastards. Yes, they were technologically advanced but the fact they kept hidden and pulled strings told him that their intentions were not honorable. They kidnapped people to examine them as if humans were lab rats. They didn't accept the people of earth as equals.

So what was their game? He was certain that's what Ethan had discovered. And why the young hacker was killed and why other deaths had followed.

No doubt Ethan didn't just tell people that he was working with Greg, he actually thought he was. Despite his great insights into the world of electronics, Ethan didn't seem to always have his feet firmly planted, even when reality to him wasn't twisted by drugs. He may have wished he was teamed with Greg, a person who could broadcast his findings to the world. And that wishful thinking became an actuality to him, literally a virtual reality.

Greg had cut him off from the show—was that what Ethan meant when he said Greg killed him? That Greg had cut him off from the protection he thought he'd get from Greg after cracking open the God Project?

The money was transferred from his account right after that. Ethan may have deluded himself into thinking it was okay because he needed proof to the Aarons that he was legit and working with Greg in order to have a source to put it out to the world. And he would need money to get out of Dodge.

Working his way through Ethan's mind, he was sure Ethan was naive enough to believe that all would be forgiven in the end because he was giving Greg something sensational.

Was it sensational? Ethan's mind was often polluted with drugs but he had enough sense to cleverly hide the file and even more shrewdly get the information to Greg. If Ethan had that much of a grip on reality, Greg was sure the hacker wouldn't have sent him something benign or even stupid.

But how was he going to open the file? He needed a computer

with access to the Internet. He could buy a computer and take the risk of being captured soon after his credit card was scanned. It was too late anyway—malls and electronics stores were closed.

Internet cafés were still in existence even though most people now used their cell phones for access. He went to the scarred desk in the room and found a phone book in the top drawer.

He sat back down on the bed to leaf through the book and glanced back at the desk as he thought about driving to an Internet café.

The car keys weren't there.

He made a quick search of the room and bathroom. *Nada*. She had taken the keys. Why? To strand him. So he could be caught? No, he didn't think she would do that. Didn't want to think that she would do that. More likely she took the keys so he wouldn't be able to pursue them to get the flier back. That had to be it. He could understand her taking access to the file out of her own sense of justice in terms of what information to release, but he refused to believe that she had deliberately stranded him to make it easier for the killer or the government to find him.

He also needed to make a decision about which newsperson to contact. He needed someone with guts and enough pull to get the entire news organization behind him. He knew several news media people from rubbing shoulders with them at events but not on a personal basis.

He heard a noise at the room door and looked over. Someone was trying the door handle. He got to his feet as the door crashed open.

# 73

The man in a utility company uniform stood in the doorway with his "meter reader" in hand. God's warrior had arrived, with fire, brimstone and a sardonic grin.

"Gas leak?" Leon asked.

As Greg froze in surprise the self-appointed avenging angel pushed the trigger on the weapon.

A green laser beam traveling at the speed of light flashed across the room and exploded in Greg's eyes, sending a shockwave through his brain. He staggered back, blinded and disoriented. It felt like acid had just been thrown into his eyes.

He dropped to his knees, his hands clawing at his eyes as if he was trying to pull the pain from them.

The weapon Leon used was not a stun gun, though it also had the effect of stunning the person—it was a dazzler, a laser weapon developed for the military to temporarily disable a person with a blow to the eyes.

The handheld one he carried walloped and disoriented a person with a blast of directed radiated energy that temporarily caused blindness.

In Iraq and other war zones, dazzlers larger than Leon's handheld weapon were mounted on rifles used to disorient drivers who didn't heed warnings to reduce their speed as they approached military checkpoints. Larger versions of dazzlers were mounted on warships and battle tanks.

The stunning, blinding effect lasted only a few minutes. Greg's vision was blurred by a changing array of movement and colors melting into each other in kaleidoscopic patterns.

Leon entered the room and closed the door behind him.

Greg knew the man was coming for him but he only saw a hazy dark figure. He struggled to his feet to meet an attack.

Leon sidestepped Greg and whacked him on the side of the head with the weapon, sending Greg back down to his knees.

"You caused me a lot of trouble," Leon said. "God wasn't happy that you got off that mountain."

He kicked Greg in the ribs, knocking him sideways to the floor.

"Before that you got my balls kicked because you made me try to run you down on the street."

He walked around Greg and kicked him in the face.

"You destroyed my perfect record. That caused me a lot of pain."

He reached down and grabbed a handful of Greg's hair and jerked his head back. "You took something from my master and he wants it back." He let go of Greg's hair and slipped the laser gun into a leather holster strapped to his hip.

He checked the two outside pockets to Greg's coat. Not finding what he was looking for, he jerked the coat open and checked an inside breast pocket and pulled Greg's wallet out. He went through the wallet, took out the money and tossed the billfold aside. He knew he shouldn't take the money, but this time he wouldn't let the Voice know he had it.

Greg's eyes poured tears but he had enough vision to see the man's form. He reared back and threw a punch but he was still disoriented and clumsy. Leon easily blocked the blow and punched him in the face.

"I'm not supposed to cut your throat but if you do that again I'll take the pain for disobeying an order just for the pleasure of seeing you bleed out like a pig in a slaughterhouse."

Greg knew not getting his throat cut wasn't an act of mercy—his death would be a clean kill, another suicide.

Leon straightened up and started pacing, his anger rising from his frustration. He pulled out a knife hidden inside his shirt. "Where is it?" As he was losing his control from rising rage, he suddenly felt a jolt of medication. He quivered for a moment and then stood very still, feeling warmth and a calm as his violent impulse faded.

Erasing rage didn't make him a nicer person—it simply kept him on the straight-and-narrow murderous track he had been put on.

Leon put away the knife and began to move around the room, muttering to himself, "Computer stuff, that's what it would be. On a computer, a tablet or one of those little gadgets no bigger than a finger."

Greg concentrated, trying to get control of his own body. His vision was no longer kaleidoscopic but it was still too blurred to see detail. He tried to form in his mind's eye what his eyes couldn't make out. The man was not much bigger than him. Heavier, but some of that was blubber. They were about the same height. The man had stunned him with a blast of light, probably a laser that hit him in the eyes. He had felt the weapon on the man's hip when they brushed against each other, but wouldn't know how to operate it even if he got his hands on it.

The killer also had a knife. Greg thought the man had put away the knife but didn't see where.

"No, I can't find any computer thing," Leon said. "If I can't find it, he doesn't have it on him, that's what I was told. So to the next step."

Greg heard his name called and he turned to the sound, his eyes half open. As he came around he saw the dazzler in the man's hand and he shut his eyes, blocking some of the force of the laser but still getting enough of a dose to increase his blindness. He cried out and covered his face with his hands, staying on his knees as he rubbed his eyes.

Leon holstered the weapon. He raised Greg's right arm with one hand and reached under Greg's shoulder with the other, pulling Greg to his feet. "Let's go, dude, there's one more thing you have to do so you can close your eyes for good." He laughed at his own humor.

Greg was wobbly; his knees started to fold and the killer jerked him upright and supported him as they moved toward the door.

"Good thing about this light gizmo," Leon said, talking to himself, "it makes them real submissive but doesn't leave any marks. 'Course, they get banged up all to hell anyway."

Greg was oriented enough to see that they were heading for the door. Beyond the door was the exterior corridor. Over the railing headfirst was a long enough drop to splatter his brains on the concrete below.

Leon leaned him against the wall by the door and held him steady with one hand and used the other hand to open the door.

Greg felt the weapon on the man's hip brush against him again. How had the man triggered the blast? He didn't think the weapon was fired like a pistol because he didn't see a trigger. The killer had held the weapon with his whole hand wrapped around it, more like holding a flashlight than a gun. There was probably a button that he had pressed but Greg didn't know if it was activated by squeezing the cylinder or pressed with thumb or finger.

Greg knew the man wasn't opening the door to take him down to the van. The killer staged suicides. The man would push him over the railing headfirst. He wasn't going without a fight. The bastard had attacked his eyes and he went for the killer's eyes, blindly clawing at the man's face.

Leon knocked the hands away from his face and punched him. Greg banged his forehead into the killer's face. He missed the man's nose but Greg lurched forward, hitting him with his shoulder with all the strength his anger-driven adrenaline could muster.

The killer stumbled backward and Greg went off balance and staggered, slamming into the desk and falling to the floor. As he hit the floor on his back he felt something underneath him, a round cylinder. Ali's wasp spray.

Greg twisted onto his stomach and reached out, groping blindly for the canister. He felt it against the tips of his fingers but didn't have a grip on it as the killer bent down and jerked Greg's head back by his hair, then got an arm around his neck in a chokehold.

As Greg pulled at the arm to keep it from choking the life out of him he felt something else that had been knocked off the desk—the hotel pen he had used to write the fake information on the pizza menu he gave Ali. He got a grip on it and stabbed the killer's arm around his neck. He kept stabbing until the man released his grip and began to wildly punch at Greg in a rage.

Greg dropped forward onto his stomach and reached out, getting a handhold on the wasp spray. As Greg twisted around, Leon turned his head and held up his arm to block the spray.

Some of the mist got to Leon because he let out a shriek of pain and rage. Greg fired the spray again but Leon went under the spray, knocking into Greg and driving him back. The killer struck Greg's wrist, sending the canister flying.

Leon punched him on the head and face. "You son of a bitch, you're dead—dead! I'll rip out your heart and eat it."

He got Greg to his feet and used both hands to get a firm grip to propel Greg out the door. Greg knew he was finished if he got close enough to the railing to be pushed over. He clutched at the door frame, trying to hold himself back, and the man broke the hold by hitting his arms.

Leon pushed him and Greg let his knees fold, dropping down to the floor. No longer able to push Greg, Leon moved around him, cursing as he did so, and bent down to use both hands to pull Greg up.

Greg went along, half rising, as Leon pulled him until the killer had his own back to the rail.

Greg dropped lower again, his face almost touching the laser weapon, but his vision wasn't good enough to make out any detail except the fact that it had a tubular shape.

Cursing him, Leon bent down and grabbed him by the collar with both hands to pull him up. As the killer pulled, Greg's right arm went behind the killer's knees. Greg reared up, lifting the man off his feet and pushing him back against the rail.

Leon hit the railing with his butt. He let go of Greg's collar with one hand to grab for his weapon. The move created a sudden release of the tension holding Greg back. Greg gave him a shove with his shoulder and grabbed onto the rail as the man slipped backward.

The killer shouted and clutched desperately at Greg as he went over, falling backward, wildly flailing his arms and legs as he dropped headfirst to the concrete below.

Greg leaned over the rail and stared down, out of breath and with too much adrenaline to feel all the pain he would soon be feeling from the beating he had taken. With blurred vision he saw a body on the concrete. Lying still.

Greg staggered back inside, not bothering to close the door behind him.

# 74

He stumbled into the bathroom and splashed water on his face. Water wouldn't wash away the effect of the dazzler but the cool wetness made him feel better and his eyes cleared enough so he could see his blurred reflection in the mirror. His eyes were still watering. He didn't get much of the wasp spray in his eyes but could taste it in his throat.

In the bedroom he grabbed the flier and shoved it into his coat pocket. He started to leave without his wallet and looked around until he spotted it on the floor. He bent down and picked the wallet up and pocketed it.

He left the room, stepping out into the exterior corridor. He heard voices from below and didn't bother focusing enough to understand what was being said, though he caught the drift that someone thought the man on the ground had been a drunk who fell off the railing.

He went to the end of the corridor farthest from where the killer had gone off. It was too dark and his eyes too blurred for him to see the steps and he stumbled on them, shuffling down the stairs and using the handrail for support. When he reached the bottom, he moved off in the opposite direction from where the people had gathered around the body.

Greg got to a wide boulevard, eight or ten lanes with traffic flowing in both directions. It was a major artery out into the San Fernando Valley from the hills that Ventura Boulevard shouldered.

He was in a hurry but couldn't move fast. His head hurt, his face was raw and bruised, he had weak knees and blurred vision and he was on foot in a city that sprawled for miles in every direction, one of the most pedestrian-unfriendly cities in the world. Taxis had to be called, not waved down on the street. A few subways existed somewhere in the city but at the moment he had no idea where they were located and had no money for the fare. He couldn't even get on a bus. Where would he go even if he could beg money and find public transportation?

He needed to hole up somewhere so he could think. If Ali hadn't taken the damn car keys he could have parked somewhere and rested until his eyes and mind were working right again.

He kept walking, on the sidewalk, away from the motel. Where he was going, he didn't know, or how to get anywhere farther than his feet could carry him, but he knew he had to get out of the area because it would soon be swarming with police.

*Keep moving keep moving keep moving,* he told his feet.

He heard sirens and they sounded like the same ones he had heard when he walked away from Rohan's apartment after looking down and seeing a body sprawled on the street.

Greg hadn't gone more than a block when he saw a white van parked along the curb.

He stumbled as his feet lost coordination because his mind took up all his energy. It couldn't be a coincidence. It had to be the same van. He should have gone down to where the killer was lying and rifled through the man's pockets to find the van keys.

He stopped beside the van and peered through the closed passenger-side window. It was dark and his sight was still too blurred to see the interior except to notice there was no one in the van.

He tried the passenger door and it opened. He leaned in and there it was—a key in the ignition. That was all, just a plain key, not even with a ring or a remote door opener. But it was the most beautiful key he had ever seen.

He slipped onto the passenger seat and shut the door behind him. It would have been easier to have walked around to the other side of the car and gotten onto the driver's seat the usual way, but he was driven almost by paranoia that if he didn't climb in and take possession he would lose the van.

His ribs screamed in pain as he worked his way laboriously over the seat and got settled on the driver's side, now more exhausted than ever. He tried the key and the engine started and he muttered a little thanks.

He pulled away from the curb. With his watery eyes it looked like Christmas as he slowly headed down the boulevard, the white, red, yellow and green lights glowing like bright bulbs.

He still didn't know where he was going. He just drove straight. After he'd driven a few minutes he pulled over in a business section, a light industrial area filled with small shops and warehouses that were closed for the night, and parked the van.

A red glow to the rear reminded him to take his foot off the brake.

He scooted lower in the seat and closed his eyes. Images of a body free-falling and spinning like a top popped into his head.

# 75

For the moment he was safe. But surviving the killer hadn't increased his life expectancy by much. He wondered if the van was rigged with a tracking device so whoever sent the killer would know his location. He didn't see anything obvious but it was dark in the van and a tracking device could be anywhere, even underneath or in the engine compartment. A camera the size of a pinhead could be recording him. But what were the chances there was another killer waiting to go into action?

Fumbling around the interior, he found a bottle of water and poured it on his face and onto his eyes. Wedged in between the center divider and the passenger seat was a slender computer tablet. He weighed it in his hands for a moment, wondering if he dared use it to access Ethan's hidden file. No, that would be stupid not only because it would make it easier to track him, but it would also let them know where the file was so it could be destroyed.

He rolled down the passenger window and threw the tablet out. As far as he was concerned, anything electronic could be used to track him.

In the center divider he found eleven twenties—$220. Not much but enough for an untraceable stay in another cheap motel, although that trick wouldn't fool anyone. It hadn't even worked the first time.

Finding the money made him feel better. Having no money or plastic in a big city felt like being lost in a forest without food or shelter.

He shut his eyes again, leaned back and concentrated. *What's the plan, man?* Get on the freeway and drive as far as $220's worth of gas would take him? Then what? Broke and stranded, lie down on the freeway and become roadkill? Go downtown and camp on the door of a newspaper or TV station in the hopes of running into someone who could help?

Getting the media involved seemed to be the only way to survive the morass that was swallowing him. He wouldn't have had a killer after him if Ethan hadn't penetrated something super-big, evidence that would expose a conspiracy he and so many others felt was strangling government of and for the people. From what Ethan had told others, that had to be what the God Project entailed. Getting the evidence publicized would make the secret forces back off, even if it was written off by the authorities as a hoax.

But he didn't give himself a respectable chance of surviving alone until morning—not camped where he was or downtown. Not much chance of hiding out in the van without being discovered in short order, period. He had to get out of the van. Going to a motel would only delay the inevitable—the door would come crashing in sometime in the night and he would be finished.

"Finished." The word stuck with him. Ethan had started something big. He'd broken into a secret government program and discovered something that launched a black operation to find and destroy the evidence and kill anyone who knew about it.

Ethan had started it and passed it on to him to finish.

Greg shook his head to clear his thoughts. Ethan hadn't passed the file to him to find someone else to expose the truth—he sent it to him because he was a media personality known to millions.

He didn't need to camp downtown and beg someone to listen before he was dragged out of the van and murdered during the night. He'd publicize the dirty secrets himself. What he needed was a way to access the file and then broadcast the information to the world.

That boiled down to getting on the Internet to get to the file and find a way to spread the information out to the world once he had it. Dropping in at his broadcasting studio and going on the air nationally wasn't in the cards. Besides never getting past the front door at the studio, he was certain he would be cut off even if he managed to get on the air.

He thought about how clever Ethan had been to fool everyone by getting the information to him in a way no one would have suspected. Every aspect of his own life must be under a microscope—phones, Internet, e-mails, tweets, texting, blogs, Facebook and every other social media and electronic communication. And there was no way for him to send out a message to thousands by snail mail.

They had him electronically hog-tied, but what if he worked through someone else?

If he got on another person's computer, he could get on the Internet and access the file. He'd only be able to send it out to whatever social networking was on that computer because anything with greater access, like his radio program's database of his fans, would be intercepted. He might end up being able to access only a couple dozen people. And he wasn't about to endanger family or friends by using their computers even if Mond didn't have them blocked.

Even more on point, when they had put him under the microscope he was certain they would've included everyone in his personal circle of friends and family because they would be the ones whom he was most likely to contact.

While shielding himself and anyone he contacted, he still needed to get the information out to tens of thousands, millions of people, if possible, and the only database available to him with that kind of access was the one his radio show maintained.

A door suddenly opened in his mind and he realized how he could pull it off. It was an audacious path that he hoped, like Ethan's snail mail, the authorities or black ops would never have thought of and intercept.

Once he got on the Internet, he knew how to get the information out to the world.

# 76

Using a stranger's computer seemed like a reasonable plan. Whoever was trying to keep the information secret couldn't be tracking every computer in the world, and where Ethan hid the file didn't sound like a location that the NRO would be monitoring. It also wouldn't put a stranger in danger because there would be no connection to Greg, other than his briefly borrowing the computer.

The most likely place to find a computer was at a coffeehouse, coffee bar or whatever the "in" name was now for places where people sat around and drank lattes while they played with their phones and computers.

He drove back toward the hills, to Ventura Boulevard, to a coffeehouse he had been to before. The place was half a block off the boulevard, down an alley too narrow for a vehicle.

He thought about parking the van a couple of blocks away but decided that if they were tracking the van, by now they would know where it was. He had to get in and get the job done before he got dragged out of the coffeehouse or ended up getting killed "resisting arrest."

He left the van half a block from the alley, at the first available space he saw, and headed for the coffeehouse.

Greg took a look at himself in the reflection of a store window before he reached the alley. His eyes had been stung and he'd been kicked and beaten up and fought a killer to the death. He appeared to have lost the fight and some of life's other battles along the way.

There was a streetlight at the corner where the alley and boulevard met, but none down the alley itself to the coffee place. It felt good on his eyes to walk in the darkness.

Before stepping into the coffee bar he straightened his clothes and blinked his eyes several times, wiping tears away.

He paused just inside and got some stares he ignored. He needed a computer with a webcam and went for the first person he saw who had one. He took the eleven twenties out of his pocket and stuffed one back in so he had money for a cup of coffee.

The guy with the computer webcam looked up as Greg approached. Slender, in his late twenties, with glasses and a goatee, he had *IT* written all over him. Just the kind of guy who would be comfortable accessing data. But he didn't look receptive to being interrupted. His body language said he was a person who was only barely comfortable being alone and yet couldn't handle anyone intruding on his space. The kind of guy no one would like at the office but who was efficient, knew it and let everyone else know it. A twerp.

Greg stopped in front of him, feeling a little breathless. "Hi, this is crazy, but I need to make a quick webcast. I'll give you two hundred dollars if I can use your—"

"Fuck off."

"I know it's weird—"

"Beat it or I'll call the cops."

Greg scoffed at that one. "Sorry, private joke." He looked around the room and said out loud, "Anyone, I need to make an urgent webcast. I've got two hundred dollars for a few minutes on a computer."

"I'm calling 911," the twerp said.

A barista approached Greg. "Excuse me, sir, but you can't come in here and disturb—"

"Hey!" The interruption came from a young woman with a wheat-colored ponytail three tables away. "You're Greg Nowell."

"Who's Greg Nowell?" the twerp asked.

"You've been in here before," the barista said. "You're the radio guy."

"Why do you need to do a webcast?" ponytail asked. "My computer will do it and you don't have to pay me."

Greg sat down beside her. "You don't want to know. I'm serious."

"Really? Hey, I listen to your show. 'Night Talk with the Nighthawk.' This have anything to do with conspiracies and aliens and Bigfoot stuff?"

"All of them."

"Epic!"

"I need to first access a file and then send it by linking it to a database that has about a million e-mail addresses on it. Take this anyway." He set the ten twenties on the seat beside her.

"Whose database is it?"

"It's a charity I'm one of the founders of. I make periodic webcasts to raise money for them. This time I'm using it to send out important information."

"Why don't you just go to your station and—"

"I know I look like crap but I got hit with some crazy laser thing. They're trying to kill me. I need to get out the webcast before they manage it."

"Who tried to kill you?" the twerp asked.

A crowd had gathered. "It's a publicity stunt," someone said.

"It's prank time!" the twerp yelled.

Greg said to ponytail, "Look at my face. Do I look like I have makeup on?"

She nodded. "You look like someone didn't like your face and decided to use it as a punching bag. Your eyes have that look Dracula gets when he's thirsty."

He waved off questions from the group. "Let's get this done," he told the young woman. "We need to start by opening a file." He unfolded the Chinese take-out menu and set it on the table, pointing out the scribbled link. "This is the Web site we first need to access."

She shook her head as she read Ethan's scribbles. "Department of Agriculture? Mad cow division? On a Chinese menu. Hey, dude, this really is a joke."

Greg stood up and pulled up his shirt, exposing a raw, black and bloody wound. He took her hand and put it against the hot, raw bruise on his face. "Is this a joke? Look at my eyes again. I got hit by a laser that almost blinded me and then a guy tried to finish me off." He tapped the flier. "To get that information."

She looked around the room for support or for someone to tell her to walk away from it. The wounds had shut up the crowd.

The girl with the ponytail took a big breath. "Okay, okay, it's crazy, I'm nuts, but I'm with you. Let's do it."

# 77

I'll read off the Web site to you," Greg told the young woman.
Getting into the Department of Agriculture and the mad cow site was easy. Nothing stopped them. The woman entered the path as Greg read aloud Ethan's scribbled information. A file called "For Greg" popped up.

Once again Greg had to admire Ethan's ingenuity, his cunning. Ethan had made it easy for a computer klutz like him to access the site without a hitch.

"Pretty clever, isn't it," he told the young woman. "He hid it in plain sight where they'd never find it."

She nodded. "If you say so. Uh, Mr. Nowell, am I going to get in trouble, go to jail?"

"No. Once this stuff is broadcast, there's nothing they can do."

She leaned forward and whispered, "Who are . . . they?"

He whispered back, "You don't want to know. The guy who gave me these bruises wanted to kill me."

"You're right, I don't want to know. Do I tap into this file that has your name?"

Greg hesitated. He didn't know how much time he had. He would have to send Ethan's "For Greg" file blind if Mond or other ops suddenly burst in. He decided he needed to get the file and the database linked and ready to send at the press of a button before he even read Ethan's file.

"We need to get into the charity Web site first."

"What exactly are we going to do?"

"Link the file with the database and send the file to the people on the database after I check the file. The charity site has a list of hundreds of thousands of my listeners coast to coast and internationally. People who have signed up to receive the webcasts. The database is used to solicit donations but tonight we'll use it for saving the world."

"We're saving the world?"

"Absolutely."

"Epic."

It came from the twerp who was going to call the cops.

Greg couldn't imagine that Mond or other ops would have included the charity site in places connected to him, but he was in a state of dread until the girl accessed it without a problem.

"I feel like I'm a real hacker. Oh my God, we are hackers." She thought about that for a moment and then rolled her eyes at the group gathered around. "You are all witnesses to the fact that I was coerced into this."

The barista who was going to throw Greg out earlier worked her way through the crowd. She handed him a small towel and a plastic bag with ice in it. "For your face. I remembered how you take your coffee." She sat a cup down.

He smiled his thanks. They were into the database and had the file linked. It was now time to open the "For Greg" file and see what evidence Ethan had compiled.

The hands of the young woman with a wheat-colored ponytail flew on her computer. An "access failure" message appeared and she started to say something but he interrupted her. "You missed a digit."

She redid it and opened the file. "It's a message for you," she said. "Recorded."

"Also there's a file attached within the 'For Greg' file."

The file within the file had to be the top-secret one, he thought.

Ethan's voice came over her computer speaker.

*"I'm glad you're still alive, Greg. I'm pretty sure it's you because the information I gave you was used to get here. I wasn't taking any chances on you having a problem getting in, so I gave you a simple password. If*

*anyone tried to hack into the site I had it set up to self-destruct. You got this far and you're ready to get out the most important information to the world since the words God wrote on that tablet of stone for Moses.*

*"I know you think I'm crazy and hell, yeah, I had a few chemical cocktails in my system before I went on your show. You think all hacking is bad shit but, hey, the stuff that the government is up to is evil. I found out about the God Project when this good-lookin' woman approached me one night in a bar and laid it onto me about cracking a super-secret project that this hacking organization she belonged to had heard about."*

So much for Ali's story about learning of the project during an after-work drink with a guy putting the make on her. She was an Aaron who roped in Ethan to do the hacking.

*"This God Project thing is being built and operated through the NRO because the NRO gets the most money and the least oversight from the government. What they are building is a system that's not only going to link other systems together like a super Internet, but a system that will link all people together."*

"What's he talking about?" the twerp asked.

"I think we're about to find out," Greg said.

*"Everyone knows how interconnected the world has become with computers and phones and everything else. I spend more time texting people than talking to them and everyone I know does the same thing. I don't know how people like my mother dealt with the world without using a smartphone. But here's the thing. They know we are interconnected, especially the younger you are. And that's what the God Project is all about. They want to play God, dude.*

*"Now you ask, who are 'they'? They've been around probably as long as we humans have, but they're not from here. I've heard them called aliens, extraterrestrials and visitors. 'Aliens' sound like something with big teeth that chased Sigourney Weaver, 'E.T.s' sound like teddy bears, and 'visitors' sound like they dropped by your crib to smoke a joint, so I'll call them what a smart woman described them as—invaders."*

Greg was sure the woman was Inez Kaufman.

*"The invaders have been around forever, watching us for thousands*

*of years, but then suddenly in no time we went from horse and buggies to nuclear bombs that could destroy whole nations and poison the whole world and space probes that have gone to the moon and Mars and beyond.*

*"You gotta understand, Greg, the invaders have always planned to take control of us and have kept themselves secret so we wouldn't be prepared. Now they realize that we're advancing so fast that they had to make a move. Why? What do these dudes from somewhere out there want with us? They're an advanced race who see us as higher on the food chain than zoo animals but lower than them, with violent tendencies and weapons to boot. They not only want to study us, but experiment with modifying our behavior so we're less aggressive and easier to manage. They now see a way to do it.*

*"Think the world has become tech crazy? These invaders sound to me like they have gotten so advanced with technology they don't even have real bodies anymore but engineer whatever ones they want. That's why you get so many different sightings, they're shape-shifters who don't have solid bodies."*

Greg took a quick scan of the crowd that had gathered to listen to Ethan's message. He saw blank faces, cautious interest and smirks. Few people would readily accept the concept of alien invaders, at least publicly.

Greg knew from his own abduction experience that the invaders had inexhaustible curiosity, that the world was a giant Skinner box of lab rats for them to play with. They did what he thought of as pure science, science for the purpose of doing science rather than seeking a cure for a disease or solving a human problem. They weren't unlike human researchers who cut off the legs of frogs to see how well they'd swim without legs or put a snake in a box of rats just to satisfy their curiosity.

*"They know humans can be stubborn and violent, that they will be difficult to manage and are armed with everything from handguns to nuclear weapons. There are more assault rifles in the hands of civilians in the good old USA than any foreign army. Because humans would react violently to the invaders running the world, the invaders feel they*

*have to take control in secret or they would end up with endless warfare that would devastate the planet when nukes start getting dropped."*

"They're watching our movies!" a guy in the crowd yelled and got a laugh.

Greg hit the "pause" button. "They don't have to watch movies, the whole planet's a reality show of violence and man's inhumanity to man. You can't blame the invaders for thinking of humans as a lower species. Besides the savage atrocities people do to each other, during the time that the invaders have been observing earth's civilizations, tens of millions of people have died violently from wars, from battles between this religion or that one or simply by the crazed hand of their fellow man. There has been no time in recorded history when people weren't dying violently at the hands of other people or when wars weren't raging somewhere in the world—and often many places at the same time."

He hit the "play" button.

*"Here's what they're up to, Greg. The invaders are building an electronic network that will eventually be everywhere and control everything and everybody. They've studied humans and know that they are molded by conditioning that begins in the womb and continues most of their lives. Hell, they know that from our behavioral scientists who proved it with dogs and rats and then people. The mind is most open to conditioning from a person's conception up to the late twenties. They want to shape the minds of humans to make them manageable and the easiest way to do it is by starting with the young. After thirty years old people can be conditioned but not as quickly and effectively as when they were younger.*

*"The invaders realize that during the past couple of decades advances in technology have created electronic devices that capture young people's attention for most of their waking hours. Dude, I can testify that I spend more time on my phone and computer than I do sleeping and all my friends are the same way.*

*"Since the brain is nothing but a computer it shouldn't come as a surprise that the invaders know that the minds of people raised in the Electronic Age are different than past generations', that young minds today don't work like their parents' minds do. The invaders believe that this is*

*the first radical difference between the way human brains work from one generation to the next."*

Ponytail hit the pause button. "He's right—they're—the invaders are right."

# 78

The young woman went on. "We—people my age—don't relate and interact much face-to-face anymore. My mother says she has more imagination that me because she had to imagine more when she was young because there was no Internet and social media stuff, no mind-blowing visual effects on TV and movies. She says I don't even talk to her anymore unless it's through my phone and I don't listen to her unless she says it in a text message."

Greg realized that the difference between his generation and that of his parents had been things like the choice of music, movies and what to smoke. But there wasn't a difference in the way people thought or how they related to each other.

She hit "play" and Ethan came back on.

*"A common trait of people my age is that we're often not comfortable dealing on a personal level with others. If you're like me, you've been relating to your best friend with text messages instead of face-to-face even as you sit together in a school cafeteria during lunchtime. That makes me a whiz with electronics but I have a hard time dealing with people face-to-face because I don't know how to read their body language. I am so used to dealing with people through an LCD screen that I've been out on dates where me and my girlfriend spent most of our time texting."*

Ponytail hit the "pause" button again. "Even texting the person right across the table. I'm guilty of it. It's more comfortable than staring into each other's eyes and trying to think of things to say."

The changes in young people had been obvious but Greg hadn't really thought it through until tonight. How did you get empathy for another person, walk in their shoes, feel their pain, with the other person recognizing your concern if you'd never related enough with people on a one-to-one basis to have developed that social skill? He knew from experience that young people had more difficulty recognizing the emotional nuances and social cues being transmitted by others because those nontech skills had never been taught to them. Getting confronted with situations in which traditional social skills were needed could create anger and frustration for people conditioned by their electronics.

*"The invaders realized that people born during the electronic age are not evolving the same as past generations because their brains are wired differently. And they know how to use it to their advantage. Much of the ability for social skills comes from conditioning that is stored in the frontal lobe which allows a person to choose between good and bad options and suppress socially unacceptable actions. And catch this, dude—the frontal lobe is not fully developed until a person is nearly thirty years old. So those of us who have been dealing with people through an LCD screen most of our lives won't ever develop the skills necessary to interact with people face-to-face socially or at work.*

*"These invaders from wherever the hell they flew in from know that people who have been electronically conditioned rather than through intimate contact with family and friends can be left socially isolated without the training that makes them comfortable as coworkers, friends and lovers."*

Even worse than feeling isolated was for the person to strike back, Greg thought. Too many young people reacted to a world they saw as vindictive toward them with a rage that sent them to a school or shopping mall with a gun. Not that the young had a monopoly on being crazy with a gun.

Along with social isolation, an overdose of movies and TV and computer games featuring never-ending violence desensitized the young to the effects of actual violence. That could result in a lack of sympathy and understanding for victims—and worse, it could cause young people to act aggressively because they didn't have empathy and a true sense of consequences.

*"The invaders have started making their move now because we have advanced so much electronically that we have made it easy for them to shape our minds. They are doing the shaping by subliminal messages*

*generated through the Internet. You know, advertisers have been put-
ting subliminal messages in what we see and hear for decades but the
invaders have electronic capabilities far exceeding what we've developed.*

"*They're not just shaping young minds by putting the messages in
what people see and hear on the Internet, on computer games and on their
cell phones, they're doing it in every type of social media, from Facebook
to sexting. They know that the addiction to social media gives them the
easiest way to shape young brains.*"

It occurred to Greg that the invaders could use memes. Memes
were an idea, behavior or style that spread from person to person
within a culture. Slender Man was one example of a meme that affected the minds of young people, but there had been thousands
of others.

By attaching messages to Internet memes that went viral the
invaders would be able to reach people around the world. They
knew that people raised in the electronic age were coalescing into
a mass society in which fads raced around the world and were
embraced at the speed of wi-fi. That "Gangnam Style" Korean rap
video with unusual dancing alone got two billion plays. An idea,
joke, prank or any number of other things could pop up and in
short order thousands of people picked up on it and then it soon
went viral and connected to millions.

With young people molding together more and more as a unit,
creating a homogenous unit that had the same values, the invaders
could take advantage of the human "herding" instinct by manipulating fads and ideas. Facebook manipulated the emotions of nearly
a million of its subscribers by sending some positive news feeds and
others negative feeds. Greg had even heard of an Internet experiment that caused hundreds of thousands of people to turn out and
vote who otherwise wouldn't have.

The problem with people being led around in a herd was that
sometimes they were driven like lemmings to disaster.

How long would it take for the invaders to pollute the minds of
young people? Another generation? Two? Had there already been
enough manipulation that they could take control by swaying elec-
tions?

Ethan went on to say that the subliminal message would be that people would benefit from their control. *"The invaders realize that people must accept them and believe they will benefit from their control. The thing is they need some good PR to get rid of that image of aliens as flesh-ripping monsters."*

Ethan's tone suddenly became graver. *"Listen, Greg, the secret files are attached but even though I've cracked the encryption, it will take people light-years ahead of you in terms of computer knowledge to open them. But that's okay, there are some people out there who can do it, you just need to get it out to enough of them so the invaders can't silence them all. Safety in numbers, you know. Get it out and it'll go viral and there'll be no stopping it."*

Ethan was silent for a moment. *"That's it, dude. Attach my stuff to a mailing to everyone you know and then run like hell."*

Someone entered and Greg looked to the door. It was Murad, the professor who Rohan called a procurer for the invaders.

Murad pulled out his phone and made a call.

## YOUNG PEOPLE ARE LOSING THE ABILITY TO READ EMOTIONS

People send many vital nonverbal cues about their emotions, motives and actions. From face-to-face contact we learn what body language like eye contact, foot and finger tapping, fidgeting, etc., are signaling.

A UCLA 2014 study noted that for thousands of years most of social communication and social learning took place face-to-face, but that young people under eighteen today spend an average of nearly eight hours a day using mobile media and the Internet.

Text messaging alone occupies more of teenagers' time than does face-to-face communications.

The study found that as little as five days away from social media screens significantly improved the ability of the group studied to read nonverbal emotional cues such as facial expressions.

UCLA NEWS ROOM, August 21, 2014;
article by Stuart Wolpert

# 79

"What now, Mr. Nowell?" ponytail asked.

"We have to attach Ethan's message with its link to the secret files to the charity database and send it to the people on it. I'll also do a webcast and tell the world what's coming down."

"Everyone gets the file?" ponytail asked.

"I hope so even if just a few will be able to open it," he said. He kept an eye on Murad as he spoke. Murad had turned his back and was still on the phone. "But enough of them will. Let's do this. I don't have much time."

She attached the files to the database and hit "send."

"This is going to take a while," she said. "Those files may be really big. I tried to check the size but it wouldn't tell me."

"Let's get the webcast going."

When the webcast online light came on, Greg faced the computer's webcam and talked fast. He half expected Murad to turn around and yell, "Grab him! He's a murderer!"

"What's coming through," Greg said on the webcast, "is the solution to the mystery of how there could be so many UFO sightings by so many credible people and have it all covered up. The proof is in the file I'm transmitting. Few of you will be able to open the encrypted file, but get it to every computer-smart person you know.

"The file reveals that they're here, alien invaders, and they are all around us, trying to take control. I can't tell you if they control the whole government or just key areas of it, but for sure they have most of our spy and intelligence agencies in their grasp."

Murad turned and looked at him. It suddenly struck Greg that they might be still able to block his transmission because of the time it would take an ordinary computer to send the information.

Greg said, "They're trying to play God, to shape us in an image they want so that they can control us. They're creating a mass mentality."

"Oh no," ponytail said. "We got knocked off."

"How much of it got sent?"

She shrugged and threw up her hands. "Some. I don't know how much. We don't even know the size of the file."

"More than you think probably went through," the twerp said. "It's not being sent by her computer, but by the computer at the charity, which has to have more power if it handles a big database."

He hoped the guy was right.

He looked up and realized that the crowd had doubled and everyone in the place was looking at him. He stood up and spotted Murad leaving.

A guy asked, "Hey, dude, is any of that weird stuff true?"

Greg nodded. He was exhausted, wasted. He had forgotten how much he hurt, but he felt more like striking back if anyone got in his way than crawling into a corner and dying.

"Must be. You heard it on talk radio."

# 80

Greg stepped out of the coffeehouse, the cool night air brushing his warm face. He didn't realize he'd been sweating. He suddenly felt drained. Being on the run and nearly being murdered more than once in the same day had left him stupefied. Almost catatonic. He wouldn't have run for his life even if an alien spacecraft suddenly descended on him. But he also felt relief. And triumph. He had no fear. He was tired but ready for a fight.

He didn't see Murad. The alley was dark and he turned left, for Ventura Boulevard. The van was on the boulevard but he had no intention of getting into it and risking being arrested for driving a dead man's wheels. He had twenty dollars. Not enough for a taxi to get to his place in Malibu but once he got there he had some emergency cash stashed. But where the hell do you find a taxi around here? Or a phone booth with a phone book to call one? He laughed without humor. Not having a cell phone made him feel a little naked and helpless.

He heard his name called and he turned to Murad, who came up behind him, out of the darkness.

Murad said, "You think it's over, that you've accomplished a great deal tonight, but you're wrong."

"Am I?"

"Oh, it'll cause excitement among the conspiracy theory crowd, who'll take your accusations and add on so many ridiculous other ramifications to what you said it will make no sense to anyone with a reasonable mind."

"There's the file."

"The file? Prepared by aliens?" Murad scoffed. "A clever fraud put together by a young hacker with a criminal record and a history of acting erratic, so much that even the Nighthawk would not permit him on his radio show. It will get the same sort of treatment as the pictures of Frisbees got when people photographed them and claimed they were flying saucers."

"Ridicule. Your favorite weapon."

"Of course. Denials with an amused edge by the powers that be will be issued within hours. By morning you will be considered just another conspiracy kook who thinks the government is hiding aliens. Even if your bizarre tale got some news agency to request information from the NRO under the Freedom of Information Act they would never find infiltration by these aliens you claim are invaders."

"Only because it'll be erased."

"You can be assured that it already has been erased so well that it was never there. The moment they realized Ethan had accessed it." He gave Greg a sour look. "You seem to be taking your defeat calmly."

Greg shook his head. "Defeat? No, you don't understand because you really don't know people. Having a college degree that says you do doesn't count. Ethan started something, set a wave of information into motion that will keep moving, slowly, just a little at a time, but will someday be a tsunami that will rip apart all the facades that creatures and traitors like you have been hiding under. You're a traitor, a quisling, and you'll end up like all turncoats do."

"You're going to be watched. You know that, don't you?"

"You don't get it, Murad; I don't matter. I could have an accident, plane crash, maybe get hit by a drunk driver, whatever your friends come up with, but if I'm not around to fight you, someone else will be. You're not going to win."

Greg turned his back on Murad and walked toward the boulevard and the streetlight at the corner. A car pulled up on the boulevard. Ali was in the backseat, Aaron 11-whatever was in the passenger front.

Greg met her eye for a moment and wavered with regret for all the things that could have been. He turned from her and walked into the light.